Salem's Daughters

Stephen Tremp

Karen,
Have a safe and prosperous
Holiday season and thanks
for your interest in
Salem's Daughters.
Enjoy! Stephen Tremp
11-21-2015

ASIN: B012JN6PKE
ISBN: 978-1515311195

Edited by Marvin Wilson
Cover Art by Jeremy Tremp

Other Books by Stephen Tremp

- Breakthrough: The Adventures of Chase Manhattan
- Opening: The Adventures of Chase Manhattan
- Escalation: The Adventures of Chase Manhattan

Please visit me at my blog on http://www.stephentremp.com for more information. To contact the author, please email me at stephen.trempy@yahoo.com

Dedicated to my beautiful wife, Deena, and my family, who supported me while I wrote the Breakthrough series. For many days and nights all you saw of me was the back of my head as I researched and typed this manuscript. Thank you for bearing with me.

Chapter 1   Boston 1705

This was a hell of a way to hold a monthly meeting and welcome newcomers to the coven. Emily Livingston ran faster and harder than she thought possible. Her body's defenses kicked into rapid, automatic responses as the cacophony of her pursuers' shrieking blasted through the late autumn night.

Her heart slammed against her rib cage. Her bare bloodied feet pounded against the ground as she fled. The sounds of torches blazing, brandished pitchforks whistling and stabbing in the air, flintlock pistols cocking, and hollering curses from the stampeding mob slammed into her eardrums.

She stared straight ahead, her gaze fixated on a tall thick oak tree where the trail turned to the right. The stress caused her muscles to tighten and her heart pound ever faster. Emily pumped her legs high and hard. She thrust her arms back and forth in perfect rhythm. Her chest heaved as she fought the urge to vomit.

She had witnessed what her pursuers' fathers did to her mother twelve years earlier. Emily would not go peacefully like her beloved mother. She would run for her life, then fight another day; for herself, her family name, and against those chasing her.

But it wasn't only her safety Emily was concerned with; her younger sister needed protection. She swore to her mama she would safeguard Sarah for the rest of their lives.

Behind her, the mob from surrounding villages and towns had flushed out their coven at the midnight hour. They'd been compromised by one of her closest followers. Olivia Shepherd. *I should have known,* Emily thought between exasperated breaths. *She's so weak and frail of mind and heart. It probably took those bastards less than an hour to force her to surrender our secret place. Then kill her.*

Though Emily's senses were heightened and her awareness of the surroundings at peak levels, she could not find Sarah in the mass panic of dozens of young women running to save their lives; all daughters of those hung at the Salem Witch Trials and other untold witch hunts in the following years.

The space between the hunters and the hunted lessened with each breath. Emily and her coven sisters did have gifts, powers above the natural abilities of normal people. Some were unique to the individual, while others shared more than one. Emily possessed them all, and that fact plus her director type personality, had made her the natural leader of the group.

But it was difficult to use their powers while running for their lives. It took concentration and a steady heartbeat—a luxury far from available at the moment.

Fear gripped Emily's heart in a vise and tried to strangle her courage. She needed to be strong, not only for her own safety, but for that of her younger sister. Emily tried to communicate telepathically as she ducked a hatchet thrown her way.

Sarah, where are you?

"Thou art a witch for sure," one of the villagers yelled. "How else could you know my hatchet was coming from behind?"

The drunken mass of people was closing fast. She had to force herself to vomit the night's dinner in stride, helping her to run faster.

But it was the pounding of approaching horse hooves that caused her legs to carry her faster. She cast a glance over her shoulder to see the beasts break through the running horde—their noses snorting streams of hot white vapor in the cool of the night.

The two-wheel path through the woods curved to the right, giving sight to a large red barn that was their refuge. The ground was soaked from recent torrential rains. A treacherous mixture of wet grass and mud threatened to fall them on their panicked way to their haven of safety.

A few of her followers slipped while rounding the bend and fell, spinning and sprawling in the muck and mire. Emily didn't bother to look back. They were as good as dead. Their screams were drowned as the villagers descended on them.

Sarah. Where are you? You have to keep close to me.

The horsemen were upon her. To her left and right she saw her friends cut down under the ax-wielding and pistol-holding riders. Emily's lungs racked with excruciating pain as she burst out air faster than she could gulp it in. The daughter of a local businessman, she was not raised to quit anything. She would not give in to these local drunken thugs chasing her and her friends, more for sport than religious reasons.

As a six year old living in Salem, Massachusetts in 1693, her beautiful and loving mother explained the meaning of their last name was intended to inspire people to a higher cause. Emily remembered the elation she felt at her mama's words. She had a calling on her life and could help people. Young Emily daydreamed of the possibilities when a loud snap of her mother's fingers jolted her to attention. Mama had a stern look as she'd ordered her to be caretaker of her four year old sister Sarah.

Those were the last moments they spent together. Moments later, her mother was dragged by her ankles to the town square and hanged by an angry gang. Much, Emily knew, like the group chasing her wanted to do.

Straight ahead was the two-story red barn, standing alone in a clearing and illuminated by the full moon. Her salvation. She was almost there.

Sarah, my beloved sister, are you okay?

Horses' hooves thundered and shook the ground under her feet, threatening to break her stride. But Emily maintained her breakneck pace. She needed to survive for Sarah's sake.

To her left a horseman bumped her. She quickly regained her pace. Another to the right nudged her into the horse to her left. Back and forth she bounced as the riders focused on pummeling her followers on either side. Emily kept her balance as the riders were so close they served to help keep her upright as she ran.

The riders surged ahead. Emily looked back to see another friend trip and fall. Lydia Tanner. Her friend was swallowed into the riotous horde.

Emily's heart rate increased—how was that possible?

Sarah, look for me and stay close.

A third horseman was behind her, rearing a hatchet over his head. She glanced back. That face. She knew him. Impossible to speak, she planted her voice in his head.

Thomas Fitzgerald. You do not have to follow in your father's footsteps.

He was the sheriff's son. His father had helped kill her mother. And the junior had taken it upon himself to torment her publicly since she was a child. Emily closed her eyes. She knew she would die.

But a pair of hands on her back thrust her forward. She stumbled and looked over her shoulder. Her sister Sarah had pushed her away from the oncoming hatchet.

Sarah's eyes froze wide open. Her pale freckled face, framed within her matted auburn hair, stared silent. People had told Emily the two sisters could easily be mistaken as twins, even though two years separated them. Sarah was dead before she hit face first in the muck. She slid to a stop on her belly, the hatchet's blade buried in her back.

Emily couldn't scream. Her gasping lungs would not allow it. But she swore inwardly she'd live to fight another day. Up ahead the two barn doors opened as if they had a will of their own.

Chloe Livingston. Her cousin could lift things and move objects. Like doors. She must still be alive.

The three horsemen were the first to enter. Emily, and what remained of her sisterhood, followed. They collapsed on the cold dirt ground as the doors abruptly swung shut. A long plank slammed down on steel braces, locking the wooden sliding panels from the inside. The villagers arrived seconds later, ramming the doors and trying to force them open.

There was silence as Emily and her following fought to catch their breath. Each horseman held a torch that produced deep flickering shadows of the young women that streamed across the barn floor and onto the walls. They walked their steeds through the assemblage as if they had vanquished an enemy of invincible powers.

"No need to worry," one shouted to the villagers outside. "We've got the bloody devils trapped."

9

Thomas Fitzgerald.

Emily stood and clutched her knees, staring up at the sheriff's son. She wiped mud from her face and chuckled between deep breaths. The ability to read their minds wasn't necessary. Thomas's smug, arrogant face revealed he thought he had the women trapped.

"Now we got you filthy witches," Fitzgerald slurred through a drunken stupor. "My father, he will surely honor me in front of the entire town for this."

The other two laughed as Fitzgerald raised his torch, like a mighty warrior ready to be immortalized as a folk legend hero.

Emily expected only half the women would make it to the barn. Out of the thirty-nine the mob flushed out, many were shot while others bludgeoned to death. The remaining female mystics, still catching their breath, were now standing. Twenty-three had miraculously made it inside. Twenty-six, counting the pursuers who foolishly entered with them. Emily knew the riders well. All were prominent young men in the town and bastards of the worst kind, as were their fathers.

The women formed an arch behind Emily and slowly closed in, forcing the riders to back their horses. Emily looked who remained from her coven. They were a mess, their dresses and cloaks wet and covered in mud. But this, Emily knew, made them look more menacing. The horsemen stopped at the barn doors, shuddering against the stress of the mob trying to force them open.

But the crossbar held fast. Her cousin Chloe, still on her knees, squinted hard to focus. She had used her powers to open the barn doors while on in a full run, then closed and locked them, expending much of her energy and leaving her exhausted.

The doors shuddered with each push from the villagers. Not much time left. They had to escape. But first, Emily implanted an image in the men's minds. A simple message; they were all as good as dead.

The mental communication was of three rotting vermin hanging by a noose, their eyes bulging and tongues hanging out. Their facial tones drooped as they realized they were not only cornered, but outnumbered. Emily now saw only terror on their faces. She smiled wickedly.

The witches remained silent and stared at their hunters. Adam Jefferson, the town cobbler, tried to reload his flintlock pistol, but shook violently and dropped the gunpowder to the ground.

Emily finally caught her breath. So did the rest. Chloe was able to stand with the others. They could now use their abilities much more effectively. Her biggest challenge was deciding who would take down the three villagers who unwisely trapped themselves with an opponent they had no chance of defeating.

The doors continued to quake with each thrust of the mob. Emily had to act.

"Rebecca. Let's make this fast. You know what to do."

Rebecca Smyth, a raven haired girl of seventeen and Emily's best friend, grinned as she stepped forward. "Thank you. I'm honored."

Emily knew what would happen next. Rebecca gave a quick backhand wave of her arm, and Adam Jefferson's blood began to boil. He screamed and cursed as he grabbed his head, his eyes rolling back. Within moments he fell off his horse, dead.

"Sweet mother of Mary," a paled Thomas Fitzgerald said. "You had her kill Adam, you did. You're a murderer for sure. Both of you."

Emily locked her eyes on Fitzgerald. "I'm a defender. And that slime is the least of your worries."

The third horseman, Richard Dibble, son of the town banker, began pleading for his life. "My good ladies. Please, I beg of you. Let me go. I did not want to do this." He pointed toward Thomas. "He made me come along. I swear it."

Emily would hear no more. "Your father, he is a master thief. He financed then foreclosed any business my father tried to start. He sent my papa to the poor house, as if this were a sick sporting game for him. And my mother—"

Dibble raised his hands in the air. "Spare me. I have family. Children. I've ... we've known each other since we were children."

"Your father helped kill her, he did," Emily said, aiming and waving her hands up and down in quick motions, as if she were shooting pistols. Richard Dibble and Thomas Fitzgerald tried to hide their faces in their hands.

"And," Emily continued as she stepped toward them. "Her blood is on your family's hands."

"We don't have much time," Scarlett Hanson interrupted.

The blonde-haired maiden pointed to the corner of the barn. Next to the horse stalls, behind stacks of hay, were four wooden crates. Inside were more than enough cats to accommodate the women for their escape.

"What are we waiting for? Let's take our leave." The barn doors seemed ready to explode wide open. "We have to go now if we want to live."

Emily grabbed Scarlett by the shoulders. "Take Angel and Esther. Prepare the cats. Rebecca, Annie, and I will take care of these scums."

Emily looked at the rest of the women, scared and needing to be led. "Everyone else, follow Scarlett and ready yourselves to escape. We've practiced this enough to get it right the first time."

Emily turned her attention to Annie Smyth, Rebecca's younger sister. "Make haste and take out Dibble. Thomas Fitzgerald, he's all mine."

Annie stomped toward the men and spit on the banker's son. She raised her arms and spun her hands in a tight circle, faster and faster. Adam Jefferson clutched at his chest.

"I pray you, cease and desist! What ... what the devil are you doing?"

"Exactly what you think," Annie shouted. "I'm speeding up your heart."

Annie sped her hands even faster. Adam was shaking, clawing and digging at the side of his face. "In the name of God, I beg you. Stop. I—"

Annie laughed as he screamed, his eyes bulging out of their sockets as he fell off his mount. The hideous cry caused the mob outside to pause. Silence replaced their mad shouting. The doors were still.

Emily looked back at the other women. They crowded around Scarlett, who was pulling a tarp off four wooden crates.

"How's it going back there? Are we ready to go?"

Scarlett shouted back. "Um, I don't know what to say. But the first crate is empty."

Emily couldn't believe it. "Impossible. We fed the critters this morning."

"Well, I guess I didn't put the top on tight."

"What about the other three crates?"

"I can hear meowing. We'll be okay. We have more than enough cats to go around."

Emily stared down Thomas Fitzgerald, a sadistic son-of-a-bitch if there ever was one. He'd pull her hair when they were kids to get a laugh out of anyone watching.

Emily stepped into him as he tried to shield his face.

"Mercy. Please. Emily, I ... I beg of you. Have mercy on me."

"You showed me no mercy. Your father helped kill my mother. And you took great pleasure in shaming me from a youth even until this past week."

"I'm ... I'm sorry."

"What a pathetic display of cowardice." Emily sniffed the air. "Oh my, it seems you have relieved yourself in your pants. But yes, I will show you a measure of mercy and not end your pitiable life."

Thomas Kennedy removed his hands from his face. Tears streamed down his cheeks. "Thank you. Oh, thank you," he groveled in his saddle, bending forward with folded hands.

"But I assure you, you would much rather be dead than what I have in store for you. From this day forward, you shall live the rest of your life as a madman. Bugs in the dirt you will forever eat. Never again will you speak anything coherent. Running through the streets naked will you do, while the rest of the townsfolk laugh and mock you. Much as you made them laugh at me."

Thomas Fitzgerald was a broken man, slumped in his saddle and crying aloud. Emily raised a palm in the air.

"Wait. I'm not finished. Not by the length of an arrow shot. Your wife and children, they will forever be ashamed to bear your last name."

Emily threw both her arms up then whisked them down. Thomas Fitzgerald fell off his horse. He stumbled to his feet and tore off his clothes, then began babbling to his horse as if they were close friends who hadn't seen each other in years.

Emily turned her attention back to Scarlett. A small panic ensued as the girls began fighting over the second crate. Someone toppled the box.

Another tore off the top. The rest screamed and shouted. It was all so loud and confusing.

The young cats scurried out in different directions. Some ran up an incline that led to the loft. The rest disappeared, seeking safety in other areas of the barn.

"Scarlett," Emily shouted through cupped hands. "You need to get control over there. Only two crates of cats are left."

"Look," Rebecca said, pointing up.

Lit torches soared through the open upper windows. Four in all. They missed the hay stacks and landed harmlessly on the floor.

Emily had to laugh. "If they want a fire, then a fire they shall surely see."

Rebecca ran in a circle, ever-tightening the radius, and a small flame appeared in the middle. She stopped and raised her hands. Four plumes of fire rose together, then spread out to the corners of the barn.

The villagers were again ramming the doors. The sense of urgency returned. Many of her followers died a violent and gruesome death tonight. The others were frantic for a cat. A mass panic would doom them all. Time for Emily to regain control.

"Rebecca, Annie," Emily beckoned. "To the cats. Make haste."

Emily took a deep breath and accepted the inevitable. This had been their emergency exit plan, a last ditch effort when all else failed. To escape certain death, they would forever leave their physical human bodies. Their souls would live on in a new body, inhabiting the young cats in their first of their nine lives.

There would be no magic that would allow them to undo what happened next.

Scarlett pulled the blanket off the remaining boxes. "We still have two crates."

The rest of the women closed in, fighting for position. They elbowed each other. Some pushed and shoved. A few punches were thrown. More yelling erupted. Angel and Esther tried to keep them back so Scarlett could bring the cats out.

"Quiet," Emily said as she plowed her way to the front and stood next to Scarlett. "We can't have these last cats run off."

Scarlett took the lids off and gently tipped the boxes over. Emily helped her coax the terrified six-month old felines out. A huddled group of young cats sat looking up, meowing.

Rebecca nudged her way between Emily and Annie and counted the women, then the cats. "There are twenty-three of us and only seventeen cats," she said stoically. "There's not enough to go around."

Emily knew would happen next. There was a brief moment of silence as her group assessed their situation, then they turned on each other. The competition to inhabit a cat would be fierce.

The barn was ablaze. The horses and cows were panicked. The villagers continued shouting and cursing. The doors burst open and the mob poured in, stumbling over and piling on top of each other.

Emily had prepared for this feat. It was tricky, and deadly if one got it wrong. She closed her eyes, exhaled the air in her lungs, and left her body. Her five foot three inch mass of flesh and bones thumped to the floor. She was half way into a cat when two icy grips pulled her back.

"I'm wise to you, deceiver. I'm not easily distracted like the rest," said one of her followers who had also left her body.

Mary Davenport. The only thing she had in common with this rival, outside of their extraordinary abilities, was they abhorred each other.

Emily despised the woman who continually undermined and tried to usurp her authority as leader.

A brief fight ensued. Emily was prepared for an eventual attack from Mary, and cast a jinx that covered her eyes with scales. Then she spun loose as her attacker tried to tear off the crusty covering.

Emily took advantage of the confusion in the barn and entered the first kitten's body she saw. The cat hacked out a fur ball in which its own soul was forced out. Emily shoved her head into the feline's skull and thrust her arms and legs into the furry limbs. She inhaled and, with a four limbed yank and mighty exhalation, thrust her torso in. She was now fully in charge of the cat's body. The transition, aside from the altercation with Mary, was smooth and took less than fifteen seconds.

Emily wiggled her four paws to make sure her arms and legs were properly fitted and squeezed her eyelids shut a few times, then peered out through the cat's eyes as her focus became clear.

There was a mad scramble as the witches left their physical bodies and competed for a feline host. Their bodies dropped to the floor one after the other, mouths wide open, the only openings for their soul to leave. Standing at the barn doors the villagers stood silent, staring at the macabre sight.

Fire and smoke climbed from the four corners of the barn upward to the loft and roof. The women, seeing the peril spread, fought against each other to enter a host. Rebecca Smyth battled Samantha Coleman, an arrogant witch who, like Mary Davenport, challenged Emily's leadership. Emily was overjoyed to see her best friend triumph and find a cat to call her new home.

Trapped between the blazing fires from behind and the townspeople blocking the doors, she saw three of her closest friends still standing. They

17

had failed to separate from their bodies. Emily cried out with a mental warning to try again, but her voice was drowned in the mob's shouts. She was powerless to help. The townspeople cut them down within seconds.

Emily looked back and forth across the barn. In front of her, so many things were happening at the same time. Panic erupted among her sisters as they adjusted to their new feline bodies. Many stumbled over each other as they tried their new legs. Villagers were shouting. Up above, the four smaller fires Rebecca started had spread across the rafters and united into one major inferno.

Three women who did perform the arduous separation were not able to possess a cat. The seventeen feline hosts were quickly filled. Emily could only watch as the lost souls, including Mary and Samantha, floated aimlessly into the dark cold of the Netherworld. They screamed and cursed all those who had made the successful transition. But their main focus was aimed at her.

"Emily Livingston, I declare you will never find peace," Mary Davenport shouted. "I witnessed your sister Sarah cut down like a mangy dog as she saved your worthless life. May her death haunt your sleep for eternity."

The cats huddled, scared and confused.

"We can't escape," Scarlett shouted. "The village idiots are blocking the door."

Another cried out. "We're going to die in this horrible fire. Thanks, Rebecca. And yes, I'm mocking you."

Emily needed to lead her surviving flock to safety. Time to create a distraction. She had to move the rabble from blocking their only exit. Behind her the horses and cows trapped in their stalls were desperate to escape.

That's it.

The livestock could forge a path through the riotous mob.

"Everyone, be ready to make a run for it. Wait for my command."

Emily focused on the stall doors. With a simple wave of her paw the gates swung open, and the beasts of burden rushed out. They cleared a swath through the bewildered and frightened horde, now scattering. Some of the villagers were too slow and were trampled in the frenzied rush. Thomas Fitzgerald followed naked and still rambling indiscernible nonsense.

Emily gave the order. "Get out now. Be quick. Let your flight of feet carry you."

Emily and sixteen cats with their human hosts, along with rats and other vermin of the barn, followed the stampeding livestock.

One of the townsfolk shouted out. "The witches, they are not dead. This is truly a trick. They must be in the cats. Kill them."

Her sisters sprinted forward, dodging pitchforks, clubs, and stomping feet. Emily's duty was to make sure the rest of her followers had a chance of escape. Frustrated and terrified, she could only watch while four cats were cut down before she had a chance to do anything more to help. Her sisters' souls were forced out and joined Mary and Samantha, screaming and floating off into the Netherworld wasteland.

Emily was the last to leave the barn. Once again, she pumped her legs hard, her lungs pushing out the cold night air faster than she could suck it in. She was amazed to see the trees straight ahead, thinking it was a miracle she escaped. Less than twenty yards ahead, twelve cats disappeared into the bushes forming the border of the surrounding forest.

Emily felt a great sense of relief as the trees added welcomed protection from the incoming hatchets and full-caliber balls fired from muskets. The

19

villagers were in pursuit, but fell back as the cats maneuvered through the thick timberland and climbed the sloping hillside. They ran through the underbrush and moved forward with ease, while their pursuers lagged behind, failing to make efficient progress through the dense forest and foliage.

Once in the safety of the woods, Emily stopped halfway up the ridge. In front of her lay a tangled mass of fallen trees and branches. This would give cover and protection until they could find better, more permanent shelter.

Behind her, Emily could hear the faint cries of the villagers. She looked through the barren, autumn trees onto the valley below. The barn, now fully ablaze, lit up the eastern horizon. She estimated they were a half mile from the madness below.

Emily spied a gathering place in the middle of the clustered fallen timbers and branches—a small clearing not observable from down the slope. She called out, "Everyone," and motioned with her head. "Over here. Let's come together and take an assessment of who's who and what to do next."

Emily gasped for air as she looked at what remained of her sisters. Twelve cats sat together; wide eyed, catching their breath, and terrified. Her following studied themselves and each other, exploring their new bodies.

Emily didn't know who had escaped from the barn and who died. There was such a confused frenzy to find a host she wasn't sure who ended up in which feline body. Time to find out who sat in front of her and the gifting they possessed.

The one ability the witches shared was they could communicate by a mental clairvoyance; but only with each other. This is how Emily identified and recruited those to her secret close-knit group. If any were found out by the villagers and townspeople, they were persecuted and hung or burned. Just like their mothers at the Salem Witch Trials and untold clandestine trials throughout the countryside villages.

Emily stood in front of her frightened sisters. The felines, all six months old of differing colors and patterns, huddled together. They were shaking, not only from the bitter cold, but from the trauma of what just happened. All their hopes and dreams were left behind. They were now outcasts, alone in new bodies, with nowhere to go and no one to help them.

"Everyone, it's me. Emily Livingston. Don't be scared. I'm here to lead the lot of you. But to be sure, let's see who's still alive. New bodies we all possess, and honestly, I do not recognize any of you. Call out your names and the gifting you have."

Emily was sure she recognized the first to step forward. She was a black, brown, and white colored cat, and one whom the rest gravitated toward. The feline was a natural leader and her best friend.

She raised a paw and saluted. "Hello Emily. If you please, I shall go first. 'Tis me, Rebecca Smyth." She looked to the cats. "For those new to our gathering, I start fires and make liquids boil."

Rebecca returned her look to Emily. "And I loved watching you beat down Mary Davenport and sent her screaming off to the Netherworld. Ha! I never did like that witch bitch."

Emily took a brief bow. "I never liked her, either. Okay, who's next?"

A brown and white cat took her place beside Rebecca. "My name is Annie Smyth. I'm Rebecca's younger sister. I speed things up and slow them down."

Emily knew Annie well and welcomed the talented sisters. She studied the next cat, solid ginger in color. She thought of taking a wild guess, having no idea who it was.

"Hello cousin. Do you not know your own flesh and blood?"

Emily recognized the tone immediately.

"My name is Chloe Livingston," she said, presenting herself to the clan. "I can levitate and hurl things through the air better than any archer."

Emily was elated Chloe was alive. This helped ease a little of the sting from losing her sister Sarah. She still had family. "I'm glad to see you, cousin. You opened the barn doors while in full stride. That was amazing. You saved our lives."

"Think nothing of it," Chloe said. "Let's move on. I'm freezing out here."

A pitch black cat with green eyes introduced herself to the clan. "I'm Amy Worth. I can disappear from one place, then reappear somewhere else. I just hope I can do it living inside a cat's body. I have to say, this is all so very strange."

Emily nodded. "I'm sure we're all wondering the same thing. Go on. Give it a try."

Amy sat in the middle of the cats. She squeezed her eyes shut and disappeared. An instant later, she reappeared behind Emily.

Emily jerked her neck and spotted Amy behind her. "Well done. Thank you for the demonstration."

She looked at the next cat and studied the grey and white striped feline. "Okay, I give up. You are ..."

"It's me. Helen Dornan."

Emily was relieved to see her extroverted neighbor and very good friend. "Helen, I'm so glad you're here. I'm quite amazed at your gifting."

Emily looked at the cats. "Her abilities to reverse things and lock and unlock doors will be most helpful. I promise you that."

"I'm Angel Warren," the next cat said to the group. "I cause people to not only dream, but influence their dreams and prophecy about their future. You can be sure this gifting will come in handy."

"I'm next," a cat with a mixture of brown and black stripes and spots said. "Scarlett Hansen is my name. I'm new to your group. This was my first meeting." She looked at Emily. "And I can also cause madness to descend; much like you did to that two-bit louse Adam Fitzgerald in the barn."

Emily again nodded. "Since you're new, you might not be aware that I have a unique gift. I assimilate and possess a certain amount of the abilities of other witches I am near. I simply used your gifting that I'm able to tap into. The more witches who join my tribe makes me more powerful as a leader."

Emily looked at the clan. "I will begin to mimic a measure of all of yours, as well, as long as you are alive, of course." She looked back to Scarlett. "We'll get along just fine, I'm sure. Next."

"Hi. Isabella Mills here." She gave a wave of her paw. "My specialty is sending thoughts to a human or animal without using any physical interaction."

"Don't be modest," Emily said. "You possess two abilities. An expert in illusion casting you surely are."

Emily walked up to the next cat, thick furred, brown and white, with gray eyes. She stood nose to nose and looked deep into the cat's eyes. "Try as I might, I cannot perceive your identity."

"It's me. Rachel Kinsbury. I can separate my soul from my body and spy on people."

Emily's eyebrows lifted. "Aha—I observed you being the fastest to make the transition out of your body. Now I know why. Okay, who's next?"

"Jacqueline Chambers here. My family, like many of yours, left Salem for Boston only to find the same lot of drunken crumbs here. Bastards, they all are. Like Scarlett, I'm new, too. And I can freeze things."

Rebecca blurted out. "Like we have need of that with winter coming."

The comment brought a small round of laughs. Emily was quick to diffuse anything that would cause dissension. "That's quite enough. We should all be thankful we're not still in that burning barn. Welcome, Jacqueline. I know you will fit in with our lot just fine."

Emily looked at the rest of the shivering cats. "Who else do we have?"

"Esther Lawson. And I'm right heartedly glad to be here than in that barn."

"For those new to us," Emily said to the clan. "Esther can cause small explosions. I do greatly admire her for that."

"That's quite impressive," Scarlett said. "I feel much safer now. I pity any beetle-headed dog that tries to attack us."

Emily stepped up to the last cat. A patchwork of large brown, black, and white spots stood trembling. "Hi. My name is Madelyn Sumner."

"You're also new," Emily said. "Sorry for such a batty first night. Pray tell, what is your gifting?"

"I'm ..." she paused as she looked at the other cats.

Rebecca craned her neck. "Yes?"

"Well, I ..."

"Come on, spit it out. It's not getting any safer out here in the woods."

"I'm great at research," she blurted out. "I love to read. And I'm really very smart."

"Great," Rebecca said. "Just what we need. Someone who can organize our clan alphabetically."

The round of laughter was louder this time. Madelyn shrank back. Emily was quick to brush up against her for support.

Madelyn looked up and down the circle of cats. "I can contribute. Your abilities, they're all so amazing. Mine, well, they are harder to see and appreciate. My gifts work internally while you all do yours externally, so it's hard to see what I can do. But I'm very smart. I remember everything I see and read. And I process information faster and better than anyone and solve incredibly complex problems. You'll see."

The others stared. Emily could almost read their thoughts. *That's it? That's all you can do?*

"Madelyn, how old are you?"

"I'm thirteen. Almost fourteen."

Emily hugged her with her long, slender tail. "Well, Madelyn, you are the youngest. But I'm sure we can make good use of your brains. Welcome to our clan."

Emily strutted back and forth in front of the twelve cats. Her sister, Sarah, was missing. Sarah, the bravest of all, who sacrificed her life so Emily could live. But there was no time to mourn. The fear in her followers' eyes demanded she take charge. Rally her people. Instill hope and courage. She would cry for Sarah later.

"Ladies, here we are. Thirteen out of thirty-nine of us survived. Make no mistake, we are lucky to be alive. But our troubles, they are not over not by a long shot. They've actually just begun."

"Look at us, in the middle of the forest with nowhere to go," Rebecca said. "Winter is coming fast. And wild beasts abound in every direction. But, I know we can count on your leadership."

Rebecca looked at the rest of the cats. "Right, everyone?"

The unison of nodding of heads was convincing and gave Emily much needed confidence.

"Thank you, Rebecca. I certainly need your support. I won't let you down. First things first. We need shelter. Like an isolated farmhouse far away from this wretched place, where people won't know the better of what happened. This will be easier if we form in four groups of three while we find our way out of this terrible place. We can better defend ourselves if attacked. Tonight, we rest here and leave at daybreak."

"What about food," Helen asked.

"Mice and rabbits we shall eat, or whatever we can kill."

"Ewww," Scarlett said. "No way am I eating a mouse. Even though we're cats, I still crave human food."

An owl's hoot caused the cats to close their circle tighter.

"This is really bad," Isabella said. "I spy an owl perched in that tree over yonder. And it's not just an ordinary owl. It's a great horned owl. He looks really hungry."

"Time to check my powers," Esther said. "Fear not. Go ahead, plant a thought in that stupid bird's head to come after us. I'll take care of this threat."

Madelyn cocked her head to the side and scrunched her eyebrows. "I don't think that's a good idea."

Isabella stepped forward. "Too late. The deed is done."

The owl left its perch and glided down. The flight was graceful and silent, almost hypnotic. The cats clustered closer. The night predator's feet came forward. Talons separated. He was almost on top of them when the raptor exploded into a hundred pieces of red gore and feathers.

"That was amazing," Isabella said as a shower of blasted feathers descended, slow, like a torn apart down pillow. "How do you do that?"

"To be truthful, I'm not sure. It's a gift I was born with. Gave my family fits when I was a child."

The howl of a nearby wolf followed.

"Now I'm really scared," Chloe said. "Forget about owls. Foxes and wolves and all kinds of predators prowl these woods."

"Fear not," Rebecca said. "I'll roast alive any wild animal we come across."

"Speaking of fire," Annie said. "Can you start a small one to keep us warm?"

Annie pushed dry branches, twigs, and leaves in a pile. Rebecca circled the kindling and timber and a small fire started. The cats closed in.

Emily liked Rebecca's courage and the way the others respected her. If something untoward were to happen to me, she thought, Rebecca is the obvious choice for a successor.

"Rebecca, my second in command you surely are. And a leader of three. Your sister Annie and Jacqueline shall be in your group."

Emily looked at her best friend, Rebecca. They had grown up together. She knew Rebecca could be wild and unpredictable, but she was popular and the others looked up to her. This was an easy choice.

Rebecca bowed. "Thank you. I humbly accept."

The rest of the cats nodded in agreement.

Emily continued. "Let's see. Chloe, you're also a leader with Amy and Helen."

The three cats merged to help keep each other warm.

"Next is Scarlett. You are young and new to our clan. But I sense you are mature beyond your years. You, Angel, and Esther will band together under your leadership."

Emily moved on to the last three cats. "And finally, Isabella. You will be looking over Rachel and Madelyn."

Emily presented herself to the twelve huddling close to the fire. "I am at my wits end as to how to do this. This is bizarre, being in a cat's body. But together, we shall fight and survive. I promise you that."

"And we have eight more lives ahead of us," Rebecca said. "I think I shall truly like this."

Emily smiled. "As do I. This as an opportunity. Just look at us. We're cats with nine lives, possessing incredible powers. For the life of me I cannot fathom what adventures await. But be sure we are far better off like this than to have villages of drunken fools chasing us with torches and pitchforks."

Chapter 2   Caledonia Springs

Debbie Stevens stared out her kitchen bay windows as she finished cleaning the cast iron skillets. On the table, scrambled eggs and bacon gave off a soft vapor she was sure gave testament of the loving kindness used to make Bob's breakfast. She didn't need to wake him. The smell of her husband's favorite morning meal combined with the aroma of coffee was his daily alarm clock.

Debbie was happy to perform menial tasks like making Bob his predictable and, in her opinion, mundane breakfast. Day after day. Month after month. For the first three years of their blissful marriage. Robert Jeremy Stevens was a great husband, protector, and provider.

But he was also a calculable creature of habit. This had its good points. Planning meals was a cinch. But the drawback was getting Bob to change—like making the decision to have children.

Debbie sighed as she turned off the water and again directed her attention at the panoramic view. Less than fifty yards behind her two-story, three bedroom brick house with white wooden trim was the neighborhood playground, the centerpiece to their planned community in Caledonia, Michigan. Caledonia Springs was developed to attract young well-to-do families, and life in this residential housing tract revolved around the park.

It was the first weekend of June and barely eight-thirty in the morning, yet dozens of neighborhood kids filled the park's playgrounds. Winter had been one of the worst in fifty years; spring, among the grayest and wettest in recent memory.

The young children, all of whom Debbie knew as the offspring of her tightly knit community, had been anxious for the past seven months to play outdoors. Kids and adults were finally able to enjoy the seventy-five degree weather and clear blue skies that had not been seen together since last October.

Debbie loved Caledonia Springs and the promise it held for young couples. This was a place where new money lived. People could leave college and forthright claim careers that allowed them to buy a nice new house with a big yard next to a golf course. She was living her American dream.

They only drawback was the new money could be a bit, well … snobby. She was raised in an environment of old money, among humble families whose grandparents grew up during the Great Depression and World War II. Decent, hard-working people who knew the value of money and that, at any time, they could lose it all. This is where their meekness came from, a concept many of her young neighbors had yet to develop.

Debbie dried the cast iron skillets and set them on the stove, returning her gaze on the kids playing outside her back door. She stepped out the double slider onto the patio and stared out across the ninth fairway to the playground. The landscape was now a lush green as opposed to sweeping snowdrifts that had melted into large pools of muddy slushy water.

On the west end of the park, junior high aged boys and girls started a game of baseball. Straight ahead, a soccer game made up of kids from various ages played out. To the east end, the smaller children played on monkey bars and swings. Young women, all of whom she knew, talked to each other or chatted on their cell phones while their kids frolicked about with every ounce of energy stored up over the winter.

The scene was bittersweet. The sound of laughter tugged on her heart. She let out a combined laugh and a cry as she wiped a single tear from her right eye.

Debbie Elaine Stevens desperately wanted children. Who stood in her way? Her husband Bob and his obsession with numbers. Bob wanted kids. They both agreed on four. The more the merrier. But the financials needed to make sense.

Debbie was twenty-six. Bob was twenty-seven. Thirty was right around the corner. She needed to do something drastic yet calculated to accelerate the process. Bob would understand the calculated part. Debbie, a free spirited risk taker, would handle the drastic part.

"Debbie, sweetie, where are you?"

Debbie broke her gaze and shook her head, clearing the thoughts of another barren living room at the year-end holidays. Back to reality. Bob. She had to take care of her hubby.

But she also knew she needed to take matters in her own hands if they were to have kids soon, and today was the big day. Debbie was ready to implement what she called 'The Fantastic Plan Gone Drastic'.

"Your eggs and toast are on the table, honey," she said as she entered the kitchen and closed the sliders.

Bob sat at the table and she watched his predictable early day routine. He held a fork and ate with one hand while going over the budget, bills, and savings with the other. And, as usual, he systematically ate a bite of eggs, then a bite of bacon, followed by a chew of toast, then a sip of coffee. This process repeated in that same order until it came down to the last spoonful, his calculated system rationing the portions so that the eggs were the final mouthful.

"Bob, dear," she said as he looked up from reading their most recent bank statement. "Don't talk. Just eat and listen to me."

Debbie undid the top button of her blouse, sat at the table, and leaned in showing plenty of cleavage and flirted with her blinking eyes in an exaggerated manner. Bob rolled his eyes. He knows what's coming, she knew.

"Darling, we can do this. We can budget the house, student loans, and bills. And have kids."

Bob set a bank statement on a neat stack of previous statements. "Baby dolls, I love you," he said, returning his eyes to the pile of monthly bills and punching numbers into a calculator. "But the numbers, they simply don't make sense."

Debbie spread her arms wide. "As usual, you're right," she said with overdone glee. "They don't. That's why we need financial independence."

"I still can't fathom you're quitting your job."

Debbie stood and rounded the table. She rubbed Bob's shoulders and pressed her breasts against his back. "The timing is perfect. With your new promotion, I can start my business venture with my friends. This will bring in so much money. The bank has the loan ready for us. You can clearly see this is a great opportunity for me. For us."

Debbie paused for a moment, waiting for Bob to say something. But he took another sip of coffee and continued keying numbers into the calculator.

"Okay. I also hate working as a supervisor at The Apple Dumpling Company. And I despise my boss, Bernie Butthead."

Bob gave Debbie a wary look.

"He's so mean to everyone. And he's such a manipulative control freak. I swear, if he says anything cross to me—one more time—I'll drop kick the little ass—"

Bob stood, loosening Debbie's massaging yet manipulative grip on his shoulders. "Okay. Just stop. Your company is American Credit Services.

And your manager's last name is Mortensen. That's Mr. Mortensen to you. He's still your boss and you should treat him with respect."

Debbie fought the urge to vomit.

"Anyway," Bob said, now massaging Debbie's shoulders, "you have to look at this through my eyes. Even with your job we're barely covering the mortgage and the bills. Now you're giving your two week notice. Without the additional income, we'll have to make serious adjustments until you start to see a profit."

"Bob, dear. Listen to me. You're twenty-seven. I'm twenty-six. How much longer do you want to wait? When is anyone ever ready to have a baby? All of our friends have kids. The McDowells already have two and one in the oven. I want our children to grow up and go to school with our friends' kids. I have to do this. And you need to support me."

Bob stepped back, took a last sip of coffee, and arranged the bills in a nice neat pile, then placed them into the credenza. "Last chance. Are you sure you want to do this?"

Debbie poured her husband a thermos container of coffee for his drive to work. "I have to, sweetie. I really think it's time to start this new business."

Bob gave Debbie a look. "Old Country Tuscany Olive Oil? Here? In Grand Rapids, Michigan?"

Debbie placed her hands on her hips. "You're mocking me, right?"

"No. Not at all. It's just that the timing isn't right."

Debbie needed to melt the layer of icy resistance Bob could be so adept at constructing. She took a moment to look into a small oval mirror on the wall. Time to let off a little steam.

Leaning her weight to one side of her hips, she ran her fingers through her shoulder length blond hair, puckered her lips and put on a quick layer

33

of lipstick. Debbie knew she had hubby's attention. She looked at Bob in the reflection and caught him stealing a glance.

So busted.

Debbie moved into Bob and gave him a snuggle, then manicured his hair with her fingers. "Actually, my new Vice President of Sales," she said with much pride for her husband. "The timing couldn't be better. With the merger of Thorbough and Tomlinson with Nippon International, you have nowhere to go but up."

"Well, I'm sure you're right. You always are. I really need to work on my Japanese. I'll download an app and practice while driving to work this week."

"And with the promotion you've been promised, we'll be fine. I'll meet the girls at the bank later this week and sign the loan documents. Hey, I'm splitting the investment and risk with three people. Besides, there's nothing else like this for hundreds of miles. It'll be a real winner. Trust me. I have everything under control."

"I've heard that before." Bob started for the front door, looked in the same mirror Debbie tried and almost succeeded to entice him a few minutes earlier, and straightened his tie with confidence. Business before pleasure. Not that the latter would be neglected. His lean six feet two inch frame, brown hair slightly receding, and conservative dark blue business suit reflection stared back. Bob gave himself a thumbs up.

"Well, maybe you're right. We'll see. Day's not over yet. This morning, I'll officially double my salary and can triple it with year-end bonuses. And, to add to my most excellent day, I'll finally beat out Ronnie Taylor for the position."

Debbie scrunched her face in disgust. "Ugh. I can't stand that guy. Rotten Ronnie. He's so arrogant and condescending. What a jackass. Just thinking of him makes me nauseous."

"And he insulted you at the Christmas party." Debbie observed Bob's face reddening. "He said you—"

Debbie waved him off. "Stop. You don't need to repeat it. Let's just say he said I wore the pants in our house. And you were jus—"

Bob's turn to flag a stop. "No need to finish the sentence. Believe me, I haven't forgotten about that. One of the first things I do this morning will be to fire that jerk."

Bob gave Debbie a kiss. "We'll discuss this more tonight over a celebratory dinner. You pick the restaurant. Can't be late for my promotion."

Debbie handed Bob his coffee in a traveler mug and snatched her car keys off the kitchen counter. "I'm right behind you. Today, the new Debbie Stevens breaks free. By the time we eat dinner tonight, we'll both have new lives. I promise."

Chapter 3   Bernie Mortensen

Debbie braced her cell phone between her neck and shoulder as she pulled into the parking lot at American Credit Services. She looked at the time. Thirteen minutes past nine. No worries about being late. Today she was giving her two weeks' notice.

"Are you sure you want to do this," her best friend and soon to be partner Linda Ryan asked. "This is your last chance to back out. Once you quit, you know that runt of a man will never hire you back."

"I have to admit, I'm a bit nervous." Debbie shrugged off the doubt. "But I need to do something. I hate my job. I hate my boss. And I know Old Country Tuscany Olive Oil will be a huge success. I can make more money than Bob, even with his new promotion. Then he'll have to agree we can start having kids."

Debbie, expecting she'd have to drive to the far end of the lot since she was late, saw the Employee Of The month spot empty. Resistance was futile. She chuckled as she pulled into it.

"What's so funny?"

"I'm taking Bernie's spot. That contemptible runt refuses to award this coveted prize so he doesn't have to move those short pork sausage legs of his and walk across the parking lot like the rest of us."

Debbie imagined his pale rotund face turn beat red with fury when he sees another car in his spot.

"Okay. Thought I'd give you one final gut check. This week we'll sign the loan docs and then sign the tenant lease, officially opening Old Country Tuscany Olive Oil. The local news channels will do a grand opening piece next month, so that's going to be huge for our launch."

"Sounds great. Hey, I have to go. Butthead will be here any minute and I need to be inside before he arrives."

Debbie could hear Linda laughing as she ended the call. She entered the twenty-two story office building in downtown Grand Rapids. Ecstatic could not begin to explain how she felt. After her two weeks' notice was up, she swore she'd never again enter the building.

She opened the double doors on the sixteenth floor that gave way to a thirty thousand square foot room. Debbie shuddered at what lay ahead. Her workplace resembled a non-descript warehouse filled with two thousand cubicles laid out in a perfect grid. The customer service center answered calls from dozens of retailers and wholesalers across the country.

The cubicles were lined perfectly in a north-south and east-west layout. For the majority of employees, the place was so quiet the only sound came from their own hushed voices and their fingers clacking away on keyboards. The place was sterile. Boring. Lifeless. Just as if Bernie Butthead designed it to mimic his soul.

She walked down the aisle that led to her cubicle on the far side of the building. For as large as the place was, and for the amount of people working, it was eerie how quiet the place was. She looked back and forth at

37

the near bare walls of each employee cubicle. Bernie would allow only one family picture per cubicle. He said anything more was a distraction from work.

Debbie was barely a quarter-way across the floor when she heard the shrill of her boss's voice echo through the vast office.

"Who the hell parked in my parking spot?"

Debbie could see her manager sweating profusely as he had to walk the extra hundred yards across the parking lot to the building. His cheeks were flush. For someone in his early forties, he was really out of shape.

Debbie suddenly didn't think taking the spot was a good idea. He would find out the car was hers. What to do?

Always the quick thinker, she would tell him she sprained her knee. Yeah. That'll work. And she'd say she wanted to work rather than get a doctor's order to stay off her feet.

Debbie started to limp toward her boss. Better to get this over with and move the car.

Bernie Mortensen, all five feet four inches and two hundred thirty pounds including his usually bad comb over, zig-zagged east and west though the aisles of cubicles, shouting out at whoever took his parking spot. Debbie watched down the main aisle as he disappeared to her left, only to reappear three rows closer to her, then disappearing to the right.

His voice faded, then came back. She estimated he would re-appear a few aisles closer and fake hobbled toward the spot. That's when an intern bringing him his usual morning coffee appeared in the center aisle, looking back and forth for Bernie. What was her name? Beatrice maybe? Regardless, she was a sweet young thing everyone liked.

Everything happened in a flash. Bernie crashed into Beatrice. She fell on her back. Bernie's white shirt was soaked with hot coffee. Beatrice rose and tried to do something to calm him, but he was on the tips of his tip toes screaming at the intern. The young woman started to cry.

Debbie scowled and balled her fists. That's it. No more.

In a flash she was between the two and bore down on Bernard Herman Mortensen. She jammed her finger in his chest and pushed him back. "Okay, now you listen to me, you obese little turd. You've been pushing people around from the first day I came here. And I think I speak for everyone here that you are a despicable excuse for a human being. How dare you yell at a young girl like that?"

Bernie, never one to back down from anyone, slapped her finger away. "You can't talk to me like that."

"I can and I will." Debbie shoved her finger again into his chest, forcing him to take a step back. "Look around. Everyone knows you suffer from the banty rooster syndrome. That's why you're such a bully. Well, not anymore. Those days are over."

Debbie didn't think Bernie could get any meaner. But she swore steam was about to shoot out his ears and his head explode. She wondered if she should fear for her safety.

On his tip toes again, he waved a chubby finger in her face. "Mrs. Stevens, you are officially—"

Debbie knew what was next, but wasn't giving him the satisfaction. "I quit. You can give this job to someone else, you arrogant excuse for a human being."

Debbie looked around the department. A sea of heads stared over their cubicle walls at her. She did a quick salute to her former employees, turned on her heels, and walked out the door. She knew this was one burned bridge she could never cross again.

Chapter 4   Treachery

Bob Stevens couldn't stop adjusting his full Windsor tie knot. This was a nervous habit he'd developed when he donned his first clip-on as a child going to church. Even posing for his high school prom, senior picture, or standing with his groomsmen at his wedding were a challenge to keep his arms at his side and leave his tie alone.

Finally satisfied, no wait—a little more to the left, there, that's it—he strode with pluck and resolve toward the boardroom on the posh thirty-second floor of the Plaza Towers. He passed numerous offices and break rooms, looking in at fellow executives and expecting them to interrupt their work and congratulation him.

Instead, an eerie silence greeted Bob. No one left their chair to shake his hand. There were no smiles or encouraging words. Uneasiness tried to muscle in and shove aside his anticipation as he walked down the hall. The quiet was ominous, almost a warning, Bob thought.

Debbie had bought him a new pair of Prada leather wingtips for this occasion. She said the shoes made him look more professional. But the hard leather soles, attached with dozens of tiny nails, made a sharp clacking noise against the laminated hardwood floor. The sound echoed off the walls with each step. What he wouldn't give to be wearing his more comfortable fifty dollar rubber soled dress shoes from Kohls.

Bob fought off of dread as his coworkers, many who were friends he had known for years, turned their backs as he passed their office doors. His gait slowed and he adjusted his Windsor knot.

Probably nothing, Bob thought. He assumed they were jealous of his promotion, or scared of the inevitable corporate culture change with the merger. He picked up his pace. Not to worry. He'd be a good boss to them. The very best.

All except for this one. His head turned to his nemesis's office.

He stopped at Ron Taylor's door. Or Rotten Ronnie as he and Debbie called him. He would fire his insolent rival as soon as his promotion was official. *Insult my wife at the Christmas party in front of everyone? I have a long memory, pal. Let's make this quick and painless. You're fired!*

Ronnie's door was open but the lights were off. Strange. He clicked on the light. The office was empty. The lone remaining items were a desk, a chair, and an empty plastic waste basket.

Bob kept walking. He was a bit disappointed. Rotten Ronnie must have been fired. He wanted the satisfaction of canning him. But as long as his contemptible rival was gone, then the day was only getting better.

Bob picked up his pace, ignoring the irritating clacking of his shoes, and worked his tie knot again. He made a left turn down the next corridor, and approached the boardroom. His pace slowed as he looked through the glass walls, revealing a long oval table with twenty-four empty high back leather chairs. His manager Phil McKenzie, known as Big Phil around the office, met him at the door. Phil gave Bob an empty smile.

"Good morning," Bob said, looking again through the glass wall at the barren room. "Where is everybody?"

Phil placed his arm around Bob's shoulders. "Our meeting is in the HR office."

Bob was rendered almost senseless. But he didn't have time to make conclusions as Phil turned him around and led him back through same halls where everyone again ignored him. He could feel his manager's grip on his shoulder tighten into a hug as he patted Bob's back.

"Why Human Resources? Are there forms I need to fill out for the promotion?" was all Bob could manage.

"Yeah. Something like that," Phil said with a deep, gravelly voice.

Phil opened the door with an indiscrete white sign and block letters that simply said HUMAN RESOURCESS and entered. The small impersonal office was barely large enough to accommodate the HR manager and a few Japanese executives he had never seen. And against the far wall, leaning back in his chair, was a smiling, almost mocking, Ronnie Taylor.

"What the ..." was all Bob could mutter, as he realized what was unfolding.

Phil again placed his hand on his shoulder. "Bob, this is never easy."

Bob took a step back. "Wait a minute. Phil, you promised. You ... my father worked here."

"And God rest his soul. Damn good man, he was."

Bob again looked around the office. The Japanese executives stared at him without expression. Rotten Ronnie covered his mouth, trying to suppress his laughter.

"Phil. You knew my father. You go way back. You both came out of college together and helped build this company from the ground up. You'd be honoring him."

Ron stood and interrupted. "Let's face it, Bob. You got into this firm because of your old man."

Bob turned to his rival and snapped, "Don't you ever speak of Dad as my old man."

Ron placed his hands up in feigned fear and smiled wide, his big toothy grin looking much like a worthy bullseye for a knuckle sandwich.

Phil stepped between them. "Bob. Please. Let's not make this any more difficult than it needs to be."

Bob realized he was sweating and breathing deep. He wiped his brow and looked at the Japanese executives. They stood along the wall. Their arms were folded, saying nothing, staring back without expression.

"Phil. Wait. You're on the board. Talk to them. Ask them ..."

"Listen to me. I did talk to the board members. The best I could do is getting you a very generous severance package. And you can retain your medical and dental benefits for a full year."

This was all happening way too fast. Bob felt sucker punched. He searched for something to say and took a few measured steps in front of the HR manager's desk. His wingtips clacked loud in the small office.

"Nice shoes, "Ronnie said with a smirk, resting an ankle over his knee and showing off his rubber soles.

"But the merger. I can help."

Phil reached over to the Human Resource Director's desk and picked up a manila envelope. He handed it to Bob. "You'll be fine. Listen to me. You're young and bright. And I've taken the liberty to write you an amazing letter of recommendation. It's in the envelope."

Bob shook his head. He couldn't think of anything else to say in his defense. "Clean and easy. Just like that, Phil?"

"Quick and painless is more like it," Rotten Ronnie jeered. "Oh, you can't understand just how much I'm enjoying this."

Bob once more glanced at the Japanese executives, who stood looking like a row of blank-faced statues.

"No." Bob tried to give Phil the manila folder back. "I can't accept this."

Phil sucked in a deep breath and pushed out his barrel chest. "Bob, let me level with you. What your father did was invaluable to Thorbough and Tomlinson. But you have to understand there is no such thing as a merger. There are only acquisitions. And Nippon International has acquired us. They now call the shots."

Bob again looked along the row of Nippon executives. They remained silent, but nodded toward Phil in support.

"Please try to see this from my perspective. Your father, as great as he was, represents the old way we did things." Phil sighed deep and shook his head. "And Bob, so do you. That's the problem."

"But Ron here," Phil eye-nodded toward Ronnie Taylor, who was still wearing the wide cheesy grin. "He represents everything we need for the position of Vice President of Sales for the Midwest."

Bob opened his mouth to speak, but Rotten Ronnie stood and interrupted. "Please Bob. Just stop. You're embarrassing yourself. Do the right thing. Turn around and leave with grace and dignity."

Phil reached out his hand toward Bob, who reluctantly went to shake it.

"Um ... no, Bob. I need your employee badge. And your parking pass. I've called ahead. Security will escort you out of the building and let you out of the parking lot."

Chapter 5   Burned Bridges

The past fifteen minutes had been a blur. Fifteen minutes. That's all the time it took for Nippon International to sever ties with Bob and literally kick him off their premises. Fifteen minutes compared to a lifetime of employment and security wherein he could build the rest of his life and plan his retirement.

Ever since he was fast tracked four months ago to be the new Midwest Executive Vice President of Sales, Bob had run the personal financials over and over to the point where Debbie asked him to stop quoting the numbers. Of course, the next two decades would experience good years and downswings in the economy. Surely there would be more promotions. He factored everything into the countless equations and algorithms he developed using paper and pencil, Excel, and statistical software programs. Regardless of the scenario, after twenty-eight years, he would retire at the age of fifty-five with a cushy upper middle class lifestyle.

Now, instead, that manipulative back stabbing Ronnie Taylor was sitting in the corner office he was promised. Bob sighed. He tossed the unopened manila envelope in his back seat in disgust as he drove. Still stunned, he just wanted to go home and gather his thoughts. Talk to Debbie. She was always a source of inspiration.

Even though many of her ideas were less than practical, her enthusiasm would make them work. Oh, he'd have to call a certain percentage of what her ideas were as plain wacky. So far out you couldn't even see the box. Debbie often went against the grain, but she somehow found a way to make them work.

And now he needed Debbie and her gumption, wisdom, and perseverance. Debbie. His love and soul mate. She was more than just a wife and eventual mother to his offspring. She was his best friend and the smartest person he had ever known, having bailed him out of countless foolish situations. Yet she never tried to take credit or force him to acknowledge her brilliance that rescued him from the consequences of his male oriented decision making process.

Debbie.

Oh, crap!

Bob grabbed his android from his inside jacket pocket. He looked at the time on his dashboard. Nine thirty. Good Lord Almighty. Bob hoped it wasn't too late. He called his wife.

Before he could say a word, Debbie answered and said with much excitement, "So how is my new junior executive? Bob honey, I'm so proud of you. I knew you could do this."

Bob didn't know what to say. There was a long pause he could not fill.

"Bob? Are you there?"

"Honey, please tell me you didn't give your notice."

"I did better than that. I quit. And I'm so happy. I feel so ... I'm not sure. But I feel great. I told that jackass of a manager off right in front of everyone. You should have been there."

Bob slammed on his brakes. He lost focus and almost ran a red light.

"How's your new promotion, Mr. Vice President of Sales for the Midwest. That sounds so dignified. It rolls off my tongue like honey off a hot buttered biscuit. I'm going to call my mom and dad and tell them it's official."

Bob took a deep breath. He just had to say it. "I ... I got fired."

Silence thundered.

Several seconds later Debbie cleared her throat. "Um, fired? Did I hear you say ..."

"Yes, dear. Fired."

"But Bob, honey ... I-I ... I don't understand."

"Neither do I. But I was just sacked."

"What happened? Phil. He promised. He and your dad helped build the company when it was little more than chicken shit."

"Don't know what happened. Well, I do know now, but basically Phil took me into Human Resources where Ronnie Taylor was." Bob forced back the urge to vomit at the thought of Rotten Ronnie and his smug arrogant smile, his mouth and gums lined with large polished monkey teeth.

"Rotten Ronnie? Are you kidding? Bob, please say you're pulling a joke on me."

The light turned green. Bob eased forward. He didn't have the energy to step on the accelerator and ignored the beeping of the angry driver behind him.

"Debbie. Sweetheart. I wish I could. But it's true. The Japanese executives, and Phil, thought I was too much like my father. Old school, they said. Can you believe it? They told me Ronnie was more progressive."

"No. No, no, no. We can't accept this. Bob, you need to go back and get your job back. Forget about the promotion. Just get your old position back."

Bob almost rear ended the car in front of him.

"Listen to me. There's nothing I can do. My place with Thorbough and Tomlinson is over. What can *you* do to get *your* job back?"

The reply took longer than Bob wanted. "Nothing. I burned that bridge down to way below sea level."

"I thought you were giving a two weeks' notice."

"I'm sorry. But Bernie is such a jerk. He went into one of his tirades. He belittled a sweet innocent little intern. I couldn't take it. So I told him off and quit on the spot."

Bob didn't know what to do. But he understood they were both unemployed. He needed to take charge, not argue and instigate a yelling match. He spoke in a gentle tone. "Don't worry about it. Where are you now?"

"I'm on my way to Linda Ryan's house. I have an idea. I'll try to arrange a meeting at the bank today to sign the papers for Old Country Tuscany Olive Oil."

Bob's 'Numbers Rule the World' mind kicked into high gear. He couldn't allow hope to stand in the way of reality.

"Honey, listen to me. You no longer have a job. Neither do I. Translation, we're both unemployed. The bank giving you a loan, as part of their due diligence, will look for one of us to be gainfully employed."

Bob could hear the despondency in his beloved's tone. "This is really bad timing. I'm not sure what to do."

"Since we no longer have a paycheck, neither do I." He entered the 131 South toward Caledonia. "Meet me at home. We need to figure out what the heck we're going to do."

Chapter 6   Despair

Debbie refilled Bob's coffee cup and sat with him at the kitchen table. A month earlier she'd be pouring his second cup into a travel mug and they'd be walking out the door; him on his way to work, she to her new business.

But this early July morning Bob still sat, mulling over the bills and budget. Instead of the papers being stacked in nice neat piles, they were spread out in a big mess. Debbie was concerned for her husband's well-being. He looked disconnected, still in his morning robe, with four days of dark stubble on his face.

"Bob, honey, are you okay? I think we need to get out of the house. It's the Fourth of July weekend. We can take a walk. Or go see a movie." She sniffed the air. "After you shower and shave."

Bob didn't look up. He keyed more numbers into his calculator while shuffling through the bills. "This is not good. I don't know how we'll make it. We have about four, maybe five months' worth of savings and investments—including my *oh-so-generous* severance package—of money to live on. Six if we really cut back. And that's it."

Debbie had to inject enthusiasm into this conversation. It was bad enough Bob was descending into a twenty-four hour grump. Now she was feeling his anxiety.

"We'll both find new jobs, sweetie," she said with a mixed tone of authority and encouragement. "It's only been a month since we lost our jobs. We just have to be patient. The right doors will open up. Trust me. You'll see."

Bob held up two statements and acted as if he didn't hear a word Debbie said. "Look at our student loans. Together they total over a hundred thousand dollars."

He set them down and shuffled through the mess of other various documents. "And somewhere in here are bills for two cars payments and five credit cards. Not to mention our home equity line of credit."

He looked around the well-furnished house. "Look at all this furniture we bought. Unbelievable. What were we thinking? We might have to sell everything. We'll have to eat and sleep on the floor."

Bob looked directly at Debbie. For the first time since she had met him, she was genuinely startled. Dark circles formed around his eyes. He had lost ten pounds off an already lean frame and he was in dire need of a haircut.

Bob continued his unblinking gaze. "We're in deep trouble."

Debbie refused to quit. She felt her heart jump. A problem? A challenge? She was up to it. And she would pull Bob up from his dark pit of despair.

"Something will break. If today is problematic, then tomorrow is a brand new day full of opportunities." She reached across the table and held his hand. "Don't worry, Papa Bear. Something amazing will open up. For the both of us. I promise."

Bob pulled back and scrolled through his tablet. "I called everyone I know—family, friends, Pastor Thompson. People from high school and college. I thought for sure I could get another job. But nothing. Nada. Zip. Zilch. That jerk Rotten Ronnie blacklisted me. I don't think I can get a job anywhere. At least not here in Grand Rapids."

"What about Detroit?"

"Tried. Nothing."

"Chicago? Cleveland, maybe?"

"Too far of a commute. We'd have to sell the house and move there. After I find employment first."

He tossed the bills on the table. "How about you? How's your job search going?"

Debbie fidgeted, then sipped her coffee. "Nada for me as well. Seems like Bernie Butthead blacklisted me, too."

Bob gave her a stern look. "You should show respect for those who signed your paycheck, regardless of how difficult of a personality they are."

Debbie cupped her chin in her hands. "He's still a royal butthead."

"What about Linda and Old Country Tuscany Olive Oil?"

Debbie knew Bob was getting desperate. He had not asked about her business venture during the past thirty days.

"The bank won't include me on the loan docs. Linda, Janette, and Monica waited two weeks for us to get new jobs." Debbie sighed. "But they had to move forward without me."

Bob stood to stretch and yawned. "You're right. We need to get out of the house."

Debbie wasn't about to let an opportunity pass. She stood and met her husband before he could change his mind. "Great idea. And, as your wife, I submit to your authority. Let's see a movie."

Bob shook his head and scratched his facial stubble. "No can do. Movies cost money. But, we can take that walk."

Debbie knew when to concede and find the middle ground. "Okay, a walk it is, hubby of mine. But only after you take a shower. And please, a shave? And after that, I'm giving you a haircut."

Chapter 7   Now or Never

Bob plopped the stack of bills on the kitchen table. He didn't bother to open the new ones that came in the morning's mail. The pile was larger than last month's.

Adding to their financial dilemma were new expenses. Four new tires for Debbie's car. Fixing a slab leak under the living room. Carpet cleaning and water damage bills. A risky investment in a stock that went south. These unforeseen costs added to his stress and eroded away two months' worth of savings.

He looked up at the clock on the kitchen wall: 11:08 a.m. He and Debbie were still in their bathrobes. Debbie's inherent enthusiasm and encouragement waned as they accepted summer was coming to a close, as were opportunities for finding a decent job. Hiring for good positions in Michigan was largely seasonal, and once summer ended, so did the probability of going back to work.

Bob rubbed the stubble on his chin and looked up at Debbie as she sipped her first cup of coffee. His always positive and forward moving wife was beginning to look a bit haggard. But of course he would never tell her that. Bob couldn't think of anything else to say. Better to let her start the conversation.

"It's Labor Day weekend, sweetie. Come on. Let's do something fun," Debbie muttered. "Anything. I have to admit, I'm frustrated. This summer has been a roller coaster of emotions."

"Welcome to my world. No money, honey. I'm looking at the numbers. Our savings is dwindling faster than expected. At this rate, we'll last another month. Maybe two. And that's all."

Debbie rubbed her head and massaged her fingers deep into her scalp, making even more a mess of her hair.

"And then what?"

"Then," Bob said in a reserved manner, having accepted what he thought was inevitable. "We'll have to put our house up for sale."

Debbie pushed her chair back and stood. "No. That's unacceptable. Something will break. Trust me. Tomorrow's a new day. No way are we selling our house."

Bob noticed Debbie had far less conviction in her words. But his honey was trying. He admired her eternal optimism and desire to push forward. That's one of the allures that caused him to fall in love with the ravishing, blonde haired, hazel eyed beauty. He stood and walked around the table and held Debbie in a Tango pose, his six foot two frame rising almost a foot above her.

"Listen to me. We have to be realistic about our situation. We can't risk going into foreclosure and losing what little equity we have. The bank, they'll short sell our house and recoup what's owed and that's all. The greedy bastards won't care about our assets. They'll look out for their best interests, not ours. And without jobs, we can't pull any money out of the house. You have to understand, this is the way the world works."

55

Debbie forced Bob to lead her into a horizontal dip. "I say we hold out. So what if we get behind on payments. If the bank short sells our house, we can legally live here for months."

Bob pulled her up and gave her a quick spin. "No. We can't have bad credit or bankruptcy. Not an option."

"So where does this leave us?"

Bob reached with one arm and picked up the pile of bills, held them level to Debbie, then tipped his hand and dropped them in a cascading free fall. "We have enough cash left for one last mortgage. And utilities. Car payments. Credit cards. Student loans. That's it. You need to be realistic and face the facts. This is our reality. Right here. Right now."

Debbie, still in Bob's other arm, snapped her fingers. "Job prospects. What do we have?"

Bob snapped his fingers back in a mocking fashion. "Not a damn thing. What do you have?"

Debbie had to laugh. "Nothing."

Bob returned to his normal self. "Same as me. Nothing."

Debbie, submissive but not quite ready to relent, peered through sleepy and sultry Marilyn Monroe bedroom eyes. "So, Mr. Numbers Man with all the answers, what do we do now?"

Bob had to take charge and fight off his urge to spend another day with Debbie cooped up inside the house. Not that he was complaining, but he did need to balance pleasure with business. He released Debbie from their tango pose.

"You need to follow my lead. We did things your way over the summer. And you did your best. I love you dearly for that. But these are the facts and I need to take action."

Debbie sat back down and sipped her coffee. "Okay, you win. I'm on board. What do you think we need to do? I'll follow your lead. You know I trust you."

Bob flipped the wall calendar one month forward and wrote a large X with a red pen. "I'm setting a goal of thirty days from today. If we both don't have good jobs, then we'll run out of cash. We will miss November's mortgage payment."

Debbie folded her arms on the kitchen table and buried her head.

"For now, save everything." Bob sighed. "We'll have to go to food banks at local churches."

Debbie looked up and scowled. "No. I'm not going to show my face at our church pantry. Or any local pantry. They all know us. I'll be humiliated."

Bob placed his hands up to slow her down. "I know. We'll go to Battle Creek and visit the Catholic churches."

Debbie wagged her head, then clutched Bob's hand. "That's it. No more. I can't deal with this. We need an escape. This is Labor Day Weekend. Go take a shower and get dressed. Right now."

"Where are we going?"

"For a drive."

"Where?"

"I'm not sure. But I'm packing a picnic basket with leftovers from the fridge. And a couple bottles of wine. Now get moving. One hour. Then we hit the road."

Chapter 8   The Vision

Bob drove his Ford Escape. It was more fuel efficient than Debbie's Explorer. For no particular reason, he took US Route 131 South. They had no destination in mind for their outdoor excursion. He assumed Debbie would know it when she saw it. His job was to drive.

"Anything you need, babe?"

Debbie shook her head without turning her gaze from the rural scenery. "No. I'm enjoying the drive. The countryside is so relaxing."

Debbie was happy soaking in the scenery and Bob wasn't complaining. He didn't feel like talking. There were times, they had agreed, when saying nothing was preferable to speaking. This was Debbie's way of silently venting and releasing the bad emotions and frustrations she had been channeling since the loss of their jobs.

Ahead, a large green sign loomed over the freeway and signaled the I-96 Interchange, along with the major exits for downtown Kalamazoo. He switched highways and drove east. The time was spent in a peacefulness that can only come from an absence of conversation. Thirty minutes later they were just outside Battle Creek.

"Let's get off here," Debbie said as she sat up straight. "I've always liked the country roads and rolling hills along the Kalamazoo River. We'll find a really nice place to have our picnic."

Bob exited onto a two-lane road as it cut across Southern Michigan in an east-west direction toward Marshall. "Where to now?"

"Oh, I don't know. Let's just keep driving. Maybe we'll stop in Marshall. I've always liked the town fountain. They light it up at night and play music. It's a lot of fun. Maybe that will help cheer us up."

Bob had to admit Debbi had the right idea. This was a perfect way on a perfect day to help forget the stress of running out of money. Lush verdant grass and trees still in full green bloom were framed by a deep blue early afternoon sky, accentuated by a few silver feathery cirrus clouds.

"I'm really enjoying this ride in the country. The weather is pleasant, unseasonably cool and lower humidity than normal for this time of year." He turned off the air conditioning and lowered the front windows.

Debbie stared out on the picturesque landscape and sighed. "This stretch of countryside is untouched by development, strip malls, and planned communities. I hope it stays this way forever."

Debbie was starting to perk up. The eternal optimist couldn't stay down for long. She always saw opportunity when most people only saw gloom and doom. The area was magical, Bob thought, like an island protected from encroaching civilization and all the horrors it brought. Out here, there were no corporations with a Rotten Ronnie or Phil—the trusted family 'friend'—to stab you in the back.

Together, they admired and appreciated the farm houses and barns. There were new fixtures mixed with the old. Names of the families who owned the properties, painted on the roofs of barns, shouted with pride to those driving by.

Debbie took a few pictures with her iPhone. "Bob, look how nice that house is. And check out the size of the front yard. It's bigger than the block we live on."

"We'll be saying *used* to live next month."

Debbie punched his shoulder. "Stop it. You have to think positive. Just follow my lead."

Bob smirked at Debbie and relented. "Yeah, it's big. And I know what you're thinking. However, I don't want to live in the country."

"And I know what you're thinking. Bob, it's not like we'd be isolated. These are small farms, maybe a hundred acres or less. They've probably been in their family for generations. Look, I can see more houses in front and in back of us. It's not like there aren't other people around. And there are towns close by. We just left Battle Creek. Marshall is about fifteen minutes forward. I bet we could find a place for a lot less money than what our house cost. What do you think?"

Bob squirmed in his seat. "Mmm, I don't know. What if the local kinfolk kidnap and sacrifice us to their corn gods?"

Debbie delivered a more forceful punch to Bob's shoulder as he burst out laughing. "Work with me. Just look at all the wild flowers. Honey, it's so beautiful out here."

Bob was still laughing at his joke when they came upon an old abandoned burned down house and barn. He dropped his speed to take a better look.

"Wow. Would you take a look at that place? What a dump."

Debbie craned her neck to look over Bob and through the driver's side window. "Looks like it burned down, except for a small section of the barn and parts of the house."

"I wonder what's holding up the remaining section. It looks like it'll collapse any minute."

"I think that was the kitchen. Pull over."

"Why?"

"I'm not sure. I feel lured to this place for some reason. And I'm hungry. We'll spread our blanket on the front lawn. Besides, we can look at this old burned down home and be thankful that we're not this bad off."

His better judgment telling him to keep going, Bob felt his stomach growl and surrendered to Debbie's idea. He pulled in the gravel driveway overgrown with tall grass, took out the blanket, and laid it in the front yard. Debbie placed the picnic basket in the center.

Bob looked at the rubble again. "Yep. It's a real dump. But you're right. I do feel better. And not because we don't live here. I'm actually enjoying our time in the country."

Debbie finished setting out the plates, homemade chicken, and various leftovers sealed in Tupperware. Bob felt a second grumble in his stomach, held Debbie's hand, and said a rushed prayer.

"Thank you Lord for this food and bless it to our use. Thank you for taking care of us during this difficult time." He lifted an eye to the wreckage of a house and said with a grin, "And thank you we don't live in a dump like this. Amen."

Debbie took a chicken breast and giggled. "This place does look pretty bad. Compared to it, we have it pretty good. I think."

Debbie started to bite into a chicken breast, then took another look at the place. She set her food down and walked toward the foundation.

"Um ... what are you doing?"

"I'm not sure. I feel a pull, like I want to investigate this place." She stepped up and onto the concrete slab and looked around. "I hope no one died in the fire."

"I'm sure who ever lived here got out okay," Bob said through a mouthful of chicken.

"You know, I think I can see beyond the charred piles of wood and broken furniture. This place was pretty big." Debbie started pacing back and forth from end to end. "This was two stories. I bet it was around five thousand square feet. At least."

"Be careful," Bob said. "Stay away from the structure still standing. It looks like it's going to collapse any minute."

He joined her and tossed his chicken bone in the rubble. Debbie gave him a look.

"What?" Bob shrugged. "This place is a dump."

Debbie continued her self-guided tour. "I wonder if the family had children. They must have. I mean, just look at how big this must have been. There could have been as many as ten bedrooms."

"Yeah. Maybe. After all, there's a big barn and lots of land. Maybe they were farmers. Families had lots of kids a hundred years ago to help work the fields. My grandfather was raised on a farm. He had eleven siblings. There were two sets of twins. Granddad was one."

Debbie balanced a smile and a shudder. "As bad as I want kids, I couldn't imagine a family that size. I'd never leave the kitchen."

"Except to get back to the bedroom," Bob said with a devilish wink and a playful squeeze of her rump.

"*Bob.*" She rolled her eyes and looked skyward, shaking her head. "Men."

Bob chuckled. It felt good to laugh. "Well now honey, a little levity didn't hurt did it? You know we'll cap ours at four kids. That's it. Then I get the ol' snip-snip."

Debbie went back to being mesmerized by the place. Bob thought she was almost in a trance. Then it hit him. "What are you thinking? No ... wait. Whatever it is, the answer is no."

Debbie twirled, snapping out of her hypnotic state. "You know me all too well, lover."

Bob took Debbie's hand and tried to walk back toward his car. "Let's go. We'll find another place to finish our picnic."

Debbie jerked back and then broke free. He was surprised at her—she had never displayed such strength.

Debbie placed her hands over her face like a camera and began to pan the rubble. "Just think about it. We can totally rebuild. I'm sure we can buy it real cheap."

Bob looked around. "Not cheap enough. It'd have to be practically free. Rebuilding a house from this base of a condition is much more expensive than building a new house."

"I bet it's been like this for years. Decades. I mean, just look at this place. Obviously no one has made an offer to buy the property since it burned down, which must have been before we were born. We could come in with a really low offer and see what happens."

Bob placed his hands on his hips and spread his feet wide as if he was blocking a charging rhinoceros. "No. Absolutely not. I strictly forbid—"

Debbie was almost gliding between the piles of rubble. "Where do you want to put the kitchen?"

"Um, this is the kitchen. At least it was. The rusted sink and stove attest to that." Bob stepped around a pile of wooden planks with large rusty nails sticking out at all angles.

Debbie didn't miss a beat, floating dangerously but smoothly around the debris and painting a picture for Bob with her words, motions, and passion much like a renowned artist describing a concept yet to be painted.

She swept her right arm in a slow long arcing motion. "The grand entrance and living room are over there. Can you imagine it? I can."

"Stop. Just please, stop, okay?"

She did not. Bob thought Debbie might be going back into a trance like state. "We could have a study or library off to the left. Then some kind of man cave for you and our future sons to the left. We'll get the biggest wall mounted big screen you've ever seen."

She gave Bob a seductive wink. Bob knew his wife was casting her web and luring him in, speaking to him in a language he could understand.

"You could watch football and basketball games here with your friends."

Bob shook his head. "In case you haven't noticed, we're in the boonies. No one would know we exist. And if they did, they'd think we were crazy and never visit."

Bob reached again for Debbie's hand. "Let's go."

Debbie continued to move in one fluid movement, as if presenting a work of priceless art to a captive audience. What a brat, Bob thought. But I love her anyway.

"Over here is the staircase to the upstairs. Do you see it?"

Bob rolled his eyes and tried to suppress a laugh as he didn't want to humor his wife. But he couldn't contain a hearty chuckle.

"Yeah. Okay, I see it. Just don't ask me to walk up it."

"We'll have a master bedroom and Jack-and-Jill bedrooms with bathrooms for our kids. Don't forget, we're having four. Boy, girl, boy girl. And close together."

Now Bob had to burst forth with laughter, while reaching for her hand. "Sure. And just where do you think we'll get the money to support four kids, purchase this land, and build a house large enough that we won't kill each other? Come on, let's go. I'm starving."

"Wait. You don't understand. Surprise, surprise." Debbie panned her arms wide in dramatic flair. "This is our solution."

"What are you talking about? Our solution? We have a mountain of financial problems. And you think a dilapidated burned down house in the sticks is our saving grace? I don't have to crunch the numbers to know they don't add up. Did you chug down a whole bottle of wine when I wasn't looking?"

Debbie spun round and grabbed Bob by the head, pulling him in close. Ouch! He could feel her breath and smell the spearmint from her gum.

"That's right. This *is* our solution to all our problems."

"Now I know I have to get you out of here. There's a spirit of stupid upon this place. And I think it landed on you."

"Hear me out." Debbie started counting off on her fingers. "One, we need a house. Two, we need it cheap. Three, we need it big. Four, we need an income stream."

"So far all I see are a lot of expenses and no revenues."

Debbie nestled in close. "You still don't see it, do you?" She again spread her arms wide. "We open a bed and breakfast. We'll have the best of both worlds. A large house to raise a family. And revenue from tourists and the locals."

Bob paused and raised his right forefinger, ready to rebuttal yet another of his wife's farfetched ideas. But this time he couldn't deny her. Her plan made sense.

He looked around. As if the image was telepathically implanted in his mind, he saw the decrepit, stinky, rat infested place miraculously rebuilt into a grand place.

But Bob didn't just visualize a good idea. He saw in great detail a sprawling Royal Victorian Manor, complete with spindles and spires. The outside colors were yellow with white trim and a rust colored shingled roof.

The place was teeming with life. People were coming and leaving. Success. Money. And a place to call home. Home Sweet Home.

Bob pulled back. This had never happened. His conservative mind would never allow such an event. But he could not deny that he experienced a vision, one that told him what the future held: for him, Debbie, and their four future children. The image left such a positive imprint in his heart and mind, he felt a momentary state of bliss.

He grabbed Debbie by the shoulders. "Okay. I'll at least consider this. I think this might actually work."

"You do?"

Bob could see the doubtful look in Debbie's eyes. She had not expected this response.

"Yes. I think this is a much better idea than the Tuscony Oil ... umm, Oily Tuscon, I mean ...."

"That would be the Old Country Tuscany Olive Oil. Anyway, with a bed and breakfast, it's just you and me. No partners to share the wealth. No back stabbing bosses. We can finally be financially free."

Bob paused for a moment to take it all in. Although the vision was brief, the scene was seared in his memory, down to minute details such as travertine tile and a large open arched entry connecting the living room to the kitchen.

Bob gave Debbie a quick kiss and hug, then turned back to the burned down rubble. "Debbie, you've done it agai—"

"Again?" she interrupted. "You mean, as usual, dear, hm?"

"Let's find who owns this property and make an offer."

"Why the sudden change of heart. I mean, that was fast."

Bob gripped his forehead and squeezed his eyes closed. "I … I'm not sure. I …"

Debbie waited patiently. "Yes?"

"I saw this vision."

Debbie laughed. "A vision? You? You don't believe in anything outside of your five senses. Are you trying to tell me you saw a vision?"

"I'm not sure. But yes. I'm pretty sure I did."

Bob started to traipse across the rubble hewn concrete slab. "I saw a two-story bed and breakfast. It was magnificent. And it was full of people. We were happy." He held Debbie by the shoulders. "And we were making lots of money."

Debbie closed in. "Happy? And lots of money? Honey, happy wife means a happy life for you."

"Let's be serious. I just had an actual vision for the first time in my life."

Debbie paused. "You. Bob. My husband, Mr. Conservative. A vision?'

"Yes, I had a vision. I can't explain it. But it was vivid." Bob started to pace. "It's just like you said. I mean the layout and all. But I saw more. I saw the actual colors. And the rooms, each had an individual theme."

Debbie stepped back. "I don't know if I should be happy or scared. Bob, you always mocked things like visions."

"I know. But this was *real*. It's as if the images were downloaded into my brain."

Debbie pulled out her cell phone. "That's all I need to hear. I'm not waiting for you to change your mind."

"Who are you calling?"

"The nearest realtor."

Chapter 9   Cursed Property

Bob debated with himself. Visions were for old men in the Old Testament of the Bible, people who lived in the desert and ran around naked and ate wild honey and locusts. They were social outcasts proclaiming the end of the world. Supernatural revelations were not for civilized, educated, and conservative people. Everything he was taught to believe was true, first through his family, then his church, school, and college, was now challenged in an abrupt yet elegant manner.

But he was excited with his precognition, even if it lasted only a few moments. He could still see the large manor in his mind. Ten bedrooms. The largest residential kitchen he had ever seen and a place where Debbie was in her natural element. Forget about Oily Tuscany or whatever it was called. People were packing the rooms and his bank account was full. He envisioned adding an addition with more rooms in the near future.

"Okay Bob. I've Googled local realtors and I'm calling the first one. I want to find out if this place is for sale."

Bob picked up a large chicken breast from the picnic basket and opened a can of Coke. He thought it better to stay fully sober and leave the wine alone. He paced while taking large bites, finally realizing he was excitedly rambling out loud about what he saw.

Bob stopped mid-sentence.

Debbie ended her call. "What is it, hon?"

"I hear meowing."

"Meowing?"

"Like lots of cute baby kittens."

Debbie placed her cell phone in her pocket. "I don't hear anything. And you don't like cats."

Bob looked around but couldn't tell which direction the crying sounds came. He started to tell Debbie again of his revelatory experience, then stopped. "There. Do you hear it now?"

Debbie craned her neck, intent on listening. "No. I don't hear anything. Maybe it's the rats in the rubble."

"Shush—I do." Bob had a forefinger to his lips, his eyes enlarged. "There are baby kittens close by."

He held his arm up in a gesture to remain quiet. Eerie silence prevailed for a minute—not so much as a bird's chirp sounded in the windless hush.

Debbie shrugged her shoulders. "No. Nothing. Must be the stress of everything. Now you're not only seeing things you're hearing them, too. One more reason to move forward with this."

Bob tried to quiet Debbie again with a shush finger to his mouth, a hand cupping his ear, and a look that said 'don't talk, listen'.

"But don't you worry," she said anyway. "I'll handle everything from here. The realtor is on his way now. His name is Clark Hodgkins from Battle Creek. He'll be here in twenty minutes."

Bob couldn't contain himself. He continued telling Debbie about his experience. She was in her own world, laying out the house. Both vied for each other's attention. Twenty minutes later, a Ford Escalade pulled in with a large magnetic sign on the driver's door. The words 'Hodgkins Realty' and a picture of a young handsome man smiled wide at Bob and Debbie.

Out stepped a much older version than the image on the door magnet. A short rotund man with suspenders walked toward them. Even before the man spoke, Bob thought he had a nervous energy. He could sense he sweated more than most people.

Hodgkins had his cell phone to one ear as he shook Bob and Debbie's hand. He ended the call and smiled nervously. "Hello Mr. and Mrs. Stevenson. Thank you for calling. I'm delighted to help you."

"Of course," Debbie said.

Hodgkins spread his arms in a sweep. "Well, what you see is what you get. This is the old Turner place. You're basically paying for the land. Twenty-five acres to be exact."

He pointed to a row of trees to the west, swaying in the mild, late summer wind. "The property line is that row of elm trees. The Bradys live on the other side. Been there for five generations. Nice people. You'll like them."

He swept his arm to his right. "Just follow the wooden fence around the field straight ahead, then come back this way across the eastern boundary. This is what you're looking at. Twenty-five acres."

"Were you talking to the property owners when you drove up," Debbie asked.

"Yes, ma'am. I can tell you, they're anxious to sell."

"How anxious."

"I hear they prefer to unload it. They've had no serious offers going back decades."

"So, what are twenty-five acres of farmland in this area of Michigan worth these days," Bob asked.

"About a quarter mil—you're lookin' at ten K per—is the norm around these parts. But for this particular property?" Hodgkins winked, "A lot less than you'd think."

Bob placed his hands on his hips and panned the acreage. "I guess I should've done my homework while we were waiting for you to drive here. What do you think should be our opening bid?"

Hodgkins clapped Bob on the back. "Well, don't you worry about a thing." He pulled out his cell phone. "I'll call them back and come in at a ridiculously low offer. We'll start from there."

Hodgkins turned his back and strolled to his car, again wiping his brow. Bob held Debbie's hand. "Can you believe it? What a day. I really think our luck is turning around."

Hodgkins whistled and motioned Bob and Debbie to follow. "Let's go back to my office."

"What did they say?" Bob and Debbie blurted out together.

Hodgkins grinned. "I came in at eighty G's. They countered at one fifty. But I know they want to get rid of this place. It's actually the grandkids of the original owners. They just want the money—any money at all. I think I can get this for you at about one hundred thousand. And that is a steal, my friends. Now let's go back to my office where we can talk business."

Bob opened the passenger door for Debbie when he heard the distinct sound of baby cats.

"Wait. There it is again."

Hodgkins cocked an eyebrow. "There's what again?"

"Cats. Baby kittens. Meowing."

Debbie rolled her eyes.

"Mr. Stevens, I don't hear anything but the wind rustling through the elm trees."

"Come on," Debbie said as she got in their car and Bob closed her door. He listened one more time and could hear the kittens as if they were beside him.

Debbie honked the horn. He could see her mouth the words through the windshield, "Bob. Hurry up. Let's go."

Bob followed Hodgkins into Battle Creek. The office was small. The walls were paneled and a well-worn path directed traffic down the center of the parquet floor. A row of real estate plaques in chronological order dating back to 1982 lined the walls. Bob thought he must have kept the same decor as the first day he opened for business.

Bob and Debbie took a seat opposite Hodgkins at his desk. He was again on his cell phone. Negotiations were short and sweet.

Hodgkins laughed as he ended the call. "What'd I tell you?" He pulled out his red hankie and wiped his brow and neck. "One hundred thousand even. The Turner property is yours for the taking."

"That's great. Thank you so much," Debbie said. "What do you think, honey? A hundred thousand? We have to do this."

Although Bob was happy and Debbie was elated, the obvious question loomed. He leaned into the desk. "Why so cheap?"

"Well, truth be told Mr. Stevens," Hodgkins said deadpanned. "The old Turner place burned under mysterious conditions in the nineteen sixty-seven. Matter of fact, so did the one before that in nineteen-seventeen. There was an Amish family that died there under similar circumstances."

Debbie clucked her tongue. "Well, the place is in the country, far away from any help. And they didn't have smoke alarms back then. Or building codes. Old knob and tube wiring run helter skelter ... not so surprising."

Hodgkins was navigating through documents on his computer and printing them. "Makes sense to me, Mrs. Stevens. I'll tell you what I know. The Turners were husband and wife, right about both your ages. They, along with ten others, all perished in the nineteen sixty-seven fire. So did everyone in the first fire. Seven people if memory serves me right. Both house and barn for both families burned to the ground. No one knows how they started."

"Okay," Bob said. "Like Debbie mentioned, houses burn down every day. At least they used to a lot more frequently."

Hodgkins looked up from his computer enough so the top half of his deadpan could look straight at Bob. "True. But I have to admit, the stories surrounding the Turner place, well, they are very strange."

Debbie kicked Bob under the table and gave him a look he'd better dig deeper and not blow this off as silly superstition for country folk.

"Stories?" Bob said, feigning interest on Hodgkins' tall tale. "What kind of stories?"

"There were rumors the place was haunted. Of course, I don't believe in such things. But other folks around here, well, they do. Many of the locals think the land was cursed. Two houses with barns on the same property burning down and everyone dying? I can understand why some people believe the way they do. Not me though. I'm not superstitious."

Debbie shivered and rubbed her arms. "Whew. That is a bit creepy. I got goose bumps just listening to you."

Bob noticed she looked a bit panicked. But Debbie was always quick to recover and think of a way to move forward.

"Hey, we can just build the house and skip building the barn. That should break any chance of having anything we build burn down or from having ghosts haunt the place. No barn, no fire." She hunched her shoulders, looked at Bob, then Hodgkins. "Right?"

"You don't believe in ghosts, do you Mrs. Stevens," Hodgkins asked as he retrieved the documents from the printer tray.

Debbie shrugged. "Maybe. I'm not sure. I did when I as a kid. But for a hundred thousand, I think we have to move forward with this."

Hodgkins' gaze passed to Bob. "What about you, Mr. Stevens. Believe in ghosts, do you?"

"Of course not. Unless hearing kittens when no one else does qualifies me."

Hodgkins looked Bob and Debbie over, staring deep into their eyes, challenging them. Bob refused to move. But he thought Hodgkins, for being such a funny stout looking man, had one of the best poker faces he had ever seen.

Hodgkins cracked a grin. "Of course you don't. You both look like educated and intelligent people."

He opened a yellow highlighter and colored a place here and a place there on the papers. "These are a few forms you need to sign and initial. The first is that you will use me exclusively for ninety days when it comes to the Turner property. I don't work for free."

"Fair enough," Bob said, taking the first forms, signing them, and passing them on to Debbie.

"Congratulations." Hodgkins offered his hand to Bob and Debbie. "I'm officially your real estate agent. I will be the best friend you ever have when it comes to the Turner place. Now sign this. This form is for my fee. Three percent from you. That's three thousand dollars upon the close of the sale. I'll collect the same from the Turner family."

Bob started to sign, then stopped. His better judgment clouded his enthusiasm for the potential of a better life for him and Debbie. "How do you know so much about the place?"

Hodgkins folded his hands on his desk and displayed his poker face with a smile scribbled on it. He chortled. "It's all part of disclosure we have to tell as real estate agents. Believe me. Every agent in the area knows about the Turner place. The difference today is they have all failed to understand the property, let alone sell it."

"And you?"

"Me? I feed off the locals' superstitions, then find a solution around them." Hodgkins reached across his desk, gathered the signed and initialed documents, and placed them in a drawer at his side.

"This is the number one trick in sales. Find a need, and then offer a solution. Now don't get me wrong. I'm an ethical man with an ethical solution to a superstitious problem. The upside here is the superstitions of the locals have driven down and kept the selling price of the Turner property low. The downside is, people are afraid to buy the property because of the rumors it's cursed."

Hodgkins finally smiled and spread his arms wide. "And I'm here to help you take advantage of both. Now you look like rational people. We exploited everyone's irrational beliefs. And you made a bid that was higher than any previous offer. Check and mate. One hundred thousand dollars." He shook his head and snickered. "What a steal."

Hodgkins rose from his chair and led Bob and Debbie to his front door. "All you have to do is find the financing to purchase the property."

Debbie thought for a moment. "Let's bring my mom and dad tomorrow to look at the place. I'll give them the grand tour and paint a vision for them."

Bob laughed. "The grand tour. Sure. No matter how big the vision, the place is still a dump. This'll take a lot of convincing."

Debbie elbowed Bob in the ribs. "Just leave everything to me. I'm calling Mom now."

"You think they'll come on such short notice."

"I'll bribe them with buying dinner at Cornwell's Turkeyville."

"A turkey dinner? Really?"

"The place has sentimental value to them. It's where they met and Daddy later proposed to her. Trust me Bob. I got this."

Chapter 10   Meddling Erma

Twenty-four hours. That's all the time it took for Bob and Debbie's lives to be transformed from the edge of despair to one of hope and promise. Only yesterday, Bob saw himself at the kitchen table, looking over their bills with only a month's worth of savings left and no job prospects. His always ambitious and virtuous wife had finally succumbed to the strain, and was joining him in a steadying spiral of despondency.

Since then, they found a property in the country, met with a local realtor, and made a ridiculous offer that was accepted. Now Debbie was going to pitch her parents, Jack and Elisa Collins, to cosign a loan to purchase the property and build their bed and breakfast.

Debbie's grandparents, Ross and Erma Dempsey, were also along for the ride. They sat in the back and remained silent. At least for now. Bob knew Erma could change that in an instant.

Ross, seventy-two years young, was a large silver haired man with a barrel chest who dressed with a vest and jacket. Subtle plaids of various colors were his favorites. Erma was petite, at least sitting next to Ross. She always wore a dress and hat of some sort. Bob had never seen her wear anything but solid color ensembles.

They were fashionable in their own sort of old-fashioned way. Bob thought the traditional couple to be a bit adorable—even with Erma's dark wit and sharp tongue.

Three generations all with different surname; Dempsey, Collins, and Stevens out for a leisurely drive in the country on a warm September Labor Day weekend. They filled Debbie's Ford Explorer to a cozy but comfortable capacity.

It was mid-afternoon, the sun heading west. Bob felt great as he looked out on the small family farms they passed. It was a serene sight of lush green grass and trees under a dazzling cobalt sky, laced with long, thin, lazy wispy clouds.

Bob was able to relax. The load of the world pressing down on him for the past three months had been miraculously lifted. He was a new man with a vision and renewed vigor.

"This is such a lovely drive," Erma said. "Thank you Bob, for inviting us. This is so much fun."

Bob snickered inwardly. You can thank yourself for inviting yourself.

"Debbie dear," Erma continued. Bob knew she would carry the conversation. "As you well know, your grandfather and I were born and raised in this very area. Oh Bob, make a right on this road." Erma's voice always tightened when she addressed Bob, then softened when she spoke to Debbie.

I ... hear ... and ... obey. Bob cracked a smirk at his internal snarky remark.

Bob looked in his rear view mirror to see Debbie's grandparents beaming as they stared out their windows and reminisced about their youth. They were such a happy couple. Bob had never seen them in a bad mood.

As much as Erma would chide him for being too soft, he did like the woman. She was always there to help anyone in the family who needed it. With gentle kindness to blood relatives and tough love to those related by law not of Irish descent. He was the only one in Debbie's extended family that fit in the latter category.

Erma lowered her window. "You can turn the air conditioning off now, Bob," she snapped. Her tone then softened. "You know Debbie, this area has escaped all the surrounding development. It's really not changed much since we were raised here."

"The only difference," Ross said, "are Interstates Ninety-Four and Sixty-Nine now intersecting through it. Fortunately, there are only a few off-ramps between Battle Creek and Marshall, so the landscape is pretty much the same as when we were kids. There are no sprawling sub divisions, box stores, or modern strip malls for miles."

Bob could easily picture their era since, like Erma said, not much had changed. He listened as the elderly couple described a magical, enchanted world from an era lost to time. A place he now deeply desired. He wondered why he had been so opposed to living in the country. Like Debbie said, there were neighbors within view of each other. Just not so close they could see into your windows like in his planned community.

"Things were sure different then," Ross said. "We walked over a mile to school, then back. Even if there was two feet of snow and blistering winds. We'd gather around the wood stove in a one room schoolhouse for our lessons. Kindergarten through fifth grade. All in one class with only one teacher. Mrs. Kipp was her name. I can still see her. A mean old lady with a wart on the end of her tongue. She'd whoop you senseless if you got out of line. I kid you not. This was back when a teacher wouldn't take guff from anyone."

Ross started to chuckle. "I confess, she whooped me a few times."

Bob laughed. "Sounds like a terrible way to grow up."

Erma snorted. "You wouldn't have survived. No offense. You're a good man, Bob. But back then you had to tough it out. That's how we coped. Understand? And it paid off. Life was hard. During World War Two, everything was rationed. There wasn't a surplus of anything. If we wanted something, we were brought up to fight and take it."

Bob could see Erma sitting up tall and glaring at him in the rear view mirror.

"But there was some work," Ross said. "Marshall was where the lumber barons lived. Kellogg's Cereal was in Battle Creek."

"But here in the rural area where your grandfather and I were raised," Erma said, "many of the parents worked in the onion fields. They weren't good paying jobs. But they kept food on the table and wood in the stoves."

Ross's stomach jerked with a snigger. "I remember most kids would bring a flapjack to school for their lunch. That's what most ate every day. I tell you, we had to rely on our wits to get ahead."

"What did you do to make money, Grandpa," Debbie asked.

"My friends and I, we'd work for the farmers baling hay after school and on weekends. Hard work it was. I'll tell you that. It was sweltering hot in those barns. But we saved our money and bought bicycles so we could get around. Some of us lived miles away from each other and our bikes were the only way we could meet up."

"Remember the dentist, Mr. Peabody?" Erma cringed at the name when she said it.

"Do I. Tall. Skinny. Biggest darn teeth I'd ever seen. As ugly as they came. He refused to use Novocain. But he was the only dentist around. I remember mother refused to drive our jalopy on the highways and would only commute no more than ten miles from home. So if you had a toothache, it was Doctor Peabody or suffer."

Erma leaned forward and touched Debbie's shoulder. "Not to mention we were both born in the houses we grew up in. The doctor, he made house calls back then, you see. He was usually drunk. But he was good and reliable. And back then, that was good as gold. He delivered your mother right in our bedroom."

"I couldn't imagine," Bob said, glancing back. "That's mind boggling. How did you manage childbirth without an epidural?"

"Whiskey, Bob. We were both drunk. Both the doctor and me. Epidurals? Pfhhht." Erma leaned back in her seat. "Good old fashioned Irish whiskey is what got me through four child births."

Although Bob wasn't much of a drinker outside the occasional glass or two of wine, he thought he might need a bottle of good old fashioned Irish whiskey to survive much more of Erma. For a petite woman, she sure packed a lot of spunk, Bob thought. Not being Irish, the little spitfire placed him in a prejudicial disadvantage. Losing his job and not finding a new one hadn't helped. Bob knew the only reason she accepted him—at all—was because he's so good to Debbie.

"Get this," Ross said, laughing loud. "We had two outhouses. His and hers. Running water and electricity came to our houses only after World War Two was over."

Bob caught himself before he could respond with another *that's amazing* reply. Outhouses could open the door to even snarkier snap backs from Erma than drunken childbirths.

"After the war, lots of things that were rationed or non-existent were sold and delivered door to door by truck. Meat. Bread. Cheese. Even tools.

You name it. They'd drive down the street, and if we needed anything, we'd flag them down and buy it on the spot with cash."

"Back then," Erma said, "we didn't have grocery stores or Seven-Elevens. Milk was delivered to our front door in the early morning in glass bottles. We'd leave the empties on the porch in the evening. Oh Bob, make a left here. Now. Don't miss the turn. Bob? Are you paying attention?"

I ... hear ... and ... obey.

Bob passed more farmhouses, some with pristine manicured lawns and postcard red barns and others with rusted farm equipment in the yard.

"Over there. That was where the house I was raised in stood." Erma pointed down a long overgrown two-tire lane path. "It's gone now. A tornado destroyed it a few years after my siblings and I left home and my parents moved to Lansing. I remember there were mean dogs that roamed the area. Daddy would have to walk all the way to the road with a club to get the mail in case that pack of wild mongrels attacked him."

"That's quite a story, Grandma," Debbie said. "Wild dogs roaming the roads? Things were sure different then."

Erma sighed deep. "That's not all. It was those dogs that kept your grandfather and I separated as kids. You see, he lived on the other side of that row of trees over there against the horizon. We rarely left our property on foot for fear of those damned varmints."

Erma grabbed Ross's hand and kissed him. "I only met your grandfather in high school, because my parents home schooled us in the morning, and then we worked our small farm in the afternoon and evening. And to think as young kids we lived a few short miles apart. All those wasted years because of those confounded mutts."

Erma looked at Debbie. "When we graduated we were married and moved to Lyon Lake just outside Marshall. Your Grandfather was hired by a lumber baron. Ross, he was already an artisan. This man, I can tell you he could build anything out of wood. It wasn't long before he opened up a furniture building business. Dempsey Furniture was born and has been around for over fifty years and still going strong."

Bob passed a row of one hundred foot tall elm trees that formed the eastern border of the Turner place. Up ahead, the dilapidated hulk came into view. He slowed to a stop.

"Bob. What are we stopping here for?" Erma snapped.

"We're ah … we're here," Bob nearly stammered the words out.

There was silence for almost a minute as the Dempseys and the Collins stared, stunned at the burned down rubble. Bob tried to think of something, anything, to say.

Debbie broke the silence. "Okay, put your jaws back into your mouths. Let's go."

Bob opened the side back doors and helped Ross and Erma out.

"Well," Debbie said, flashing a smile and with a pose similar to a model on a daytime television game show. "This is it. What do you think? Wait. Don't say anything. Let me give you the grand tour."

"And don't forget to bring your imaginations," Bob said.

He laughed out loud, observing, for the first time since he'd met her, Erma, dumbfounded into silence, bereft of any snide comebacks to throw at him.

Chapter 11   Cornwell's Turkeyville

The sun was passing toward the western horizon. It was almost four o'clock. Bob pulled into the parking lot of Cornwell's Turkeyville, just north of Marshall.

He knew how much Debbie and her family loved the restaurant. All the countless times they took him there when dating Debbie, from high school and college, and his career with Thorbough and Tomlinson, he feigned interest to get in their good graces because he loved Debbie and wanted to fit into her family.

But now he was appreciative of the journey back in time. The place was built on four hundred acres and boasted an ice cream parlor, gift shop, general store, dinner theatre, Civil War re-enactments, summer kids' camps, to a heated pool for RV parking. The place was huge, and situated at the intersection of two interstate highways, he understood why the lines to get in were always so long.

Today was no exception. Since this was the last holiday weekend of the summer, Cornwell's was even more packed. By the time they found a parking spot and entered the line, Bob surmised it would be at least a thirty minute wait to order their food. Finding an open booth or table would present a whole new challenge.

As the line slowly progressed there was small talk with Debbie, her parents, and Ross and Erma. But he was surprised to see the Dempseys and the Collins texting for most of the wait.

For their age, Ross and Erma were tech savvy. Being retired, they had time to spend on social media using cell phones and tablets with their kids and grandchildren. Both were up to date on most of the latest technologies.

After more than a half hour in line and with Bob's feet starting to ache, they had their homemade turkey dinners and were sitting at one of the few recently emptied and re-cleaned booths.

Once seated, Debbie's dad, Thomas Collins spoke. "So let's get right down to business. Bob, Debbie, we have some good news and some bad news regarding cosigning for your loan."

Bob almost choked on his mouthful of hot turkey sandwich, set atop a pile of mashed potatoes and smothered in gravy. "Here it comes," he mumbled under his breath. "I should have known this was too good to be true."

"Your mother and I have decided that this whole idea is, well, crazy."

Bob could see Debbie's face wilt. Her mom smiled and patted her knee.

But good ol' Erma took it from there. She took Debbie's hands in hers and smiled wide, a grin that told his wife her world just became a much better place. But a smile that communicated to Bob he'd best be on guard. Things could get out of his control real fast.

"Debbie dear, don't you fret one bit. The good news is your grandfather and I have decided we'll co-sign the loan docs." Erma smiled warm and wide. "That's right, honey. We're retired now and getting up in years, you see. And we want to do something to help you. So we've decided to co-sign the loan. You know, since Bob's not able to get a job."

Bob fought off the urge to lob a heaping spoonful of gravy smothered mashed potatoes at the snarky matriarch. But they needed help, even if it came from Erma. For the moment, silence seemed to be the best recourse.

"Now, before you can say no, I understand there is risk involved in building and opening a bed and breakfast. But your grandfather and I did some research last night."

Again with Erma's online expertise, Bob thought. That caustic old woman does have her amazing attributes. And much of her better characteristics I can see in Debbie. Ross and Erma came from humble beginnings and were hardworking, successful people who raised four children and so far have seven grandchildren. It seems whatever they've touched has turned to gold.

"Did you know, Bob," Ross said in a jovial sense, dropping his fork and leaning into the table. "There are eighty million people who live around the Great Lakes. And Michigan is at the center. This area is centrally located between a dozen major metropolitan cities in Michigan, Ohio, Indiana, Illinois, Wisconsin, and Canada. What do you think of that?"

"I didn't know that," Bob said around another mouthful of mashed potatoes.

"Not only that, my boy, but there are only a handful of bed and breakfasts within an hour radius of here."

"What can I say? I didn't have time to research any of this."

Ross grinned. "But Erma and I have. And it only gets better."

"Thank you," Bob said. "Both of you. I mean it."

"Oh, think nothing of it. We're all family here," Erma said, and she *smiled* at Bob.

Huh? Did she just smile at me, Bob wondered. Wow—first time for everything. Or was it a smirk?

"I've also taken the liberty to crunch some numbers," Ross said. "I know events have happened so fast it's hard to get your arms around everything."

Erma's scowl returned. "Now Bob, do you have any idea how much a bed and breakfast will cost?"

"Well, not really."

"I didn't think you did. Take a wild guess."

"Well," Bob scratched his chin, "we have a three bedroom house. So a ten room bed and breakfast would cost at least three times as much."

Erma rolled her eyes and tossed her napkin in the air.

Ross, roaring with laughter, slowed his guffaws enough to say, "Three and a half million dollars. Let's get right down to brass tacks."

"That's furniture jargon, in case you didn't realize it," Erma said. "Brass. Tacks. That's what's used to secure the fabric to the wooden frame."

"Well, I, I mean—"

"That's okay Bob. Just let me talk. A three and a half million dollar loan, amortized over thirty years, at today's interest rates, comes out to six million four hundred thousand dollars."

Debbie gasped. "How much? Oh, no. That's way over our heads."

Bob was quick to calculate the numbers. "That's a seventeen thousand eight hundred dollars a month mortgage payment we would have. Or over two hundred thousand dollars a year."

Debbie looked as if she were about to faint.

Ross maintained eye contact with Bob and smiled, drawing Bob in. Anything next to Erma was charming. "But if you have full occupancy during the summer at two hundred and fifty dollars a night for ten rooms, then average thirty percent through the remaining nine months, you can cover the mortgage, interest, and expenses and still clear aroun—"

Bob interrupted. "We'd bring in four hundred fifty thousand dollars a year in revenues. After utilities and maintenance, we'd still clear a hundred thousand dollars."

"And we'd live there," Debbie said. "We could write off utilities, repairs, and food as expenses."

"That's great." Bob looked at Debbie. "And the guests would be paying the mortgage and building our equity. We can make a killing with a bed and breakfast."

"We sure can," Ross said, slapping the table. "We sure can."

We?

"Just think if we could raise occupancy to forty percent during non-summer months. Or fifty percent. We can do this. Remember, eighty million people are living around the Great Lakes. And we're at the center of it all."

"Umm... wait? Did you just say we?"

Ross formed an exaggerated sly grin. Erma clutched Debbie's hand on the table and glared at Bob.

Bob's mind raced through the unfolding scenario. He thought he and Debbie would have to pitch this deal with little chance of success. But Ross and Erma were now pitching him. They want a slice of the pie.

Retirement my ass, Bob thought. Wait. Did Erma just take a long swig from a flask she had in her purse? She took a second swallow and smiled wide at Bob.

Ross, no longer his jovial self, displayed a side Bob had never seen. He's now a shrewd business man seeing an opportunity and going for the jugular. His.

"Bob, my furniture company has been very good to us over the past fifty years. We have a lot of money to work with. Trust me on this."

Erma tucked her flask away in her purse. "And with your knowledge of numbers, and Debbie with your gumption, which you got from me I'm sure, I really believe you can do this. You're so young and full of energy and amazing ideas. And we want to help."

"Your grandmother and grandfather had told us their intents this morning," Debbie's dad said. "We've been texting them while waiting in line trying to talk them out of it. But they insisted."

Ross rose from his chair. "I'll be right back. I'm going to the car for something."

Bob leaned into Debbie. But she wasn't there. She was hugging Erma.

"Thank you." She kissed her grandmother on the cheeks repeatedly. "Thank you. Thank you. Thank you."

Ross returned, both arms wielding a large object wrapped in a blanket. He offered it to Debbie, who scooted her chair back to make room to place it across her lap.

"What is it," Debbie asked as she opened the mysterious package with a fascination that scared Bob. She gently unfolded the blanket and held up a carved and painted wooden ornament.

It was a Celtic cross. Debbie gasped and stood, holding up the green and white relic from the past. The stanchion stood three feet tall. The intersection was encircled by a ring. Three branches spread out to the top and both sides.

There was a stunned silence at the table. Even the patrons in surrounding tables looked in awe at its magnificence.

Bob recognized the piece was from the top of Ross and Erma's two story house on the west side of Lansing. He never paid much heed to the piece, since it was so high off the ground. When visiting, he usually walked straight from the car into the house. But what he noticed now was how intricate and colorful the hand crafted piece was. It was truly a treasure.

"This," Erma proudly declared while wiping a tear from her eye. "This is the priceless family heirloom my grandfather, Brendan Murcat, made after arriving from Ireland at Ellis Island in eighteen ninety-five. After ten years struggling in the boroughs of New York, he moved to eastern Pennsylvania and bought a small farm. There he built a house and raised a family. He made this and placed it at the apex of his house over the front door. It was designed to bless all those entering and exiting."

Erma wiped another tear. "The three arms and the base stretch toward the north, south, east, and west. They will protect your mind, body, soul, and heart. The ring symbolizes eternal life and God's infinite love for you, child. But most importantly, inside the ring is the Murcat family heirloom. Now, our names may be different because of the wonderful men we have married." Erma glanced past Bob at Ross and Debbie's dad and smiled.

Bob looked at the image on the coat of arms. Two lions on their hind legs faced each other. He thought there should be a bottle of Irish whiskey instead. He suppressed a laugh—an outburst might mean certain death at the claws of Erma.

"My grandfather then passed this on to my father, who moved to this very area between Battle Creek and Marshall. He also built a house, raised a wonderful family, and placed this at the top of his home."

91

Erma fought to hold back more tears. Ross held her hand and took over the conversation. "And this most beautiful piece that has weathered three generations of hot summer sun, ice cold blizzards, and rain, was passed on to us. It has blessed and protected everyone who enters and exits our house. And we now pass this on to you."

Debbie was crying and laughing as she tucked her head into Bob's chest.

"Now don't you worry about a thing, dearie. I'll take care of everything regarding the loan." Erma looked at Bob. "You'll have to sell your house, of course. Put it on the market tomorrow. Don't try to hold out for as much money as you can get. You'll need to get out from underneath the debt as soon as possible."

I ... hear ... and ... obey.

"Then we'll go to our bank and sign the loan documents. Oh, Debbie, I'm so proud of you. You are going to be a huge success. I just know it. And you have my grandfather's heirloom. You are truly blessed, child."

"But where are we going to live while the house is built," Debbie asked.

Erma gave her a wink. "We've thought that through. You can live in our RV on the property. This way you can oversee the construction."

Ross clapped his hands once to get everyone's attention. "We all have a lot of work to do. You'll need an architect and a general contractor. Winter's right around the corner and the builders will need to repair and bring the foundation up to code, rough frame in the house, install all the windows and entry doors, put siding on the walls, and get the roof on before it freezes."

"Eat up," Erma said. "Food's getting cold."

"I'm going to make this same turkey dinner one of my signature meals every Sunday at the Bed and Breakfast," Debbie said.

"What are we going to name the place?" Bob said, trying to find some way to get into the conversation.

Debbie proudly held up the family heirloom above her head with much gusto. "How about Murcat Manor?"

Bob had to refrain from rolling his eyes as he observed Erma's face melting into teary eyed gratitude. She looks like she might swoon, wilt, and pass out from all the schmaltzy melodramatic emotion, he figured.

Erma laid a hand on Debbie's shoulder and said, "Bless you my child. I'm sure my grandfather is looking down from heaven and smiling on you."

Chapter 12   Thirteen Kittens

Bob pulled Ross and Erma's Winnebago into the driveway of their new property on Oak Hill Road, cutting a swath through gigantic renegade weeds, gravel crunching under the weight of the RV. On the lawn close to the street was a large white sign with blue letters: DeShawn Hill Construction.

Debbie pointed at two men on the other side of the concrete slab. "The architect and general contractor are already here. They're not wasting any time."

A dozen pickup trucks of various makes and sizes were parked close to the existing foundation. The usual serene quietness of the peaceful countryside was broken by sounds of men hard at work. A crew of a dozen people with bulldozers, wheel barrels, and shovels were filling ten green, thirty yard contractor's containers with debris and rubble from the previous house.

Michael Fronteria waved and smiled as he walked toward them, blueprints for the bed and breakfast rolled up in his hands.

"This is incredible," Bob said as he helped Debbie step out of the RV. "We're actually breaking ground on Murcat Manor. I have to admit, I was leery of becoming business partners with your grandparents. But they got the loan docs to go through and helped sell our house in just thirty days."

Debbie beamed at him. "They're great. Now, I know Grandma can be cranky toward you. But she has accepted you into her clan."

"You could've fooled me by the way she talks to me."

Fronteria stopped in front of them, smiled, and smacked his blueprint roll with one hand into the palm of the other. "Mr. and Mrs. Stevens, welcome to your new property. Let's go around back," he said, using his plans roll as a pointer. The three walked a ways and he pointed again.

"As you can see, DeShawn Hill has begun the demo work, clearing out all the debris from the previous house and barn. They're also clearing out all the dead trees and shrubs. He's one of the finest general contractors around. I've worked with him several times. You're in the best of hands with him."

Hill stopped giving orders to his crew and shook Bob and Debbie's hands. He looked every bit the general contractor. Early forties. Big guy with a growing belly. Blue jeans, Keen Tacoma steel toed leather boots, and a collared blue shirt with his name stitched in white on his left pocket and the company logo on the back. His crew all wore the same color and style, company logo'd T-shirts with their names stitched on them, but his had the distinction of being a collared polo shirt with a pocket—which held two pens and a pencil clipped in it.

Fronteria unrolled the blueprints and flipped to the foundation plan. "We'll have this place cleared by the end of the afternoon. Tomorrow, we'll demo the foundation. Then we'll dig the basement. The full basement area won't be the entire footprint of the house—just under the kitchen."

DeShawn Hill swung his forefinger in a circular motion around the large kitchen floor plan. "The rest of the house will be supported on a

95

forty-eight inch deep, sixteen inch wide, steel rod reinforced concrete footing with a full thirty-six inch tall crawl space. But trust me, the basement will be plenty big to store all the things you need and provide shelter in the event of a tornado."

"I'm impressed," Bob said. "You don't see any problems with winter a couple months away?"

Hill shook his head. "No sir. While we're building the basement we'll have the water main put in. The old structure was balloon framed which is not up to code. So we'll be using platform construction which means we can frame entire sections on the ground. Once the basement is finished and the cement has cured, we'll begin fitting the prefabricated components of the house together. We'll use a crane for the decked joists and the roof trusses."

"And the barn?"

Hill swatted at a fly. "More like a very large storage shed. The biggest you've probably ever seen. The older barns—well most barns, really—don't have concrete floors, just packed dirt, so that chore isn't one we have to deal with, far as demo. Your new large shed, though, will have a concrete pad for a floor."

He took another vicious swat at a fly. "And again, the shed will be smaller than a barn, but still plenty big to store two riding lawnmowers, snowplows and snowmobiles, lots of work benches, tools, and abundant space to move around. Two large sliding wooden doors will be in the north and south ends so you can easily access whatever you need."

Debbie pulled out her iPad and looked at something that brought a smile across her face. She tilted the screen so Bob could see a computer generated image of a yellow with white trim grand Victorian Manor, complete with a wraparound porch, turrets and spires. She sighed and held it close to her chest.

"This is our dream come true. Thank you both. This is not just a bed and breakfast. It's our home and I love everything about it."

"You're welcome," Hill said. "Next spring I'll build a white latticed gazebo in the front yard. And we haven't forgotten about your husband. Although the outside is fashioned in Grand Victorian just like you want, the interior will be modern in every sense of the word, per Mr. Stevens' instructions."

DeShawn Hill directed Bob's attention to what remained of the barn. "And on the east side of the storage shed will be a cement patio with basket hoops on each end. It'll be smaller than an NBA court. But the hoops will be adjustable. You can raise them to be regulation ten feet tall. Or, you can lower them so you can dunk and pretend you're a super star."

"That's great," Bob said. "I'm sure I'll be spending a lot of time out here."

"And we'll add two soccer goal posts. When families bring their kids with them here, they'll have a place to play outside."

"You really did think of everything." Bob smiled wide, imagining a small crowd of reckless freckled rascals playing outside, rather than destroying the inside of Murcat Manor.

"Let's take one quick walk around," Hill said, leading Bob, Debbie, and Fronteria. "Remember, everything's set in stone. If you make any changes, it's going to cost a lot of money and probably hold back construction. And we all want Murcat Manor finished by next Memorial Day."

"I understand," Debbie said. "It's perfect as is."

Hill had to yell over the sound of three bulldozers attacking and breaking down barren oak trees that looked like they'd been standing there dead since the fall of Rome. They crashed to the ground with an awful sound.

"The framing and roof will be up by Halloween," Hill said. "We'll have the walls up and wrapped with Tyvek, entry doors and windows installed before the first snow falls. That'll allow us to complete the interior by spring, then finish the exterior before Memorial Day weekend. You'll be open for business just in time for summer." He jutted his chin and winked at Debbie. "And you can take my words to the bank."

Bob stopped as he again heard the cries of small cats. He wondered if he was losing his mind, what with all the deafening sounds of bulldozers and rowdy men noises—yelling and carrying and dumping debris in large metal bins.

Debbie was ten steps ahead with Hill and Fronteria when she looked back. "Bob," she shouted. "Are you okay? Stay with us."

"Shhhh. I hear the kittens again."

Debbie cupped her hand to her ear. "What?"

Bob ran to Debbie and lowered his mouth to her ear, "I said I hear those kittens crying out again."

Debbie's eyes rolled a one-eighty. "Bob, there are no cats here."

"Maybe feral cats," Hill yelled.

The meowing grew more intense. They tugged on his heart to help them. He could discern individual meows among the cacophony of crying kittens. He thought he counted thirteen.

"Yes, there are cats." Bob said forcefully. "I can hear their unmistakable mews."

Hill pulled a whistle from his pocket and blew. His crew and the loud noise they made stopped. He held up his arm and motioned. "Everyone, take five. I need you to be quiet for a minute."

"What's going on," a crew member asked.

"I want you all to listen for the sound of kittens."

A strange silence fell as the crew looked bewildered at the boss, then around at each other.

DeShawn Hill's eyes widened and he made a little huff sound. "I hear it too. The sound of little kittens meowing."

"So do I," Debbie said. "Honey, you're not losing your mind, like Grandma said."

Bob knew Debbie let that slip out. "I can assure you, I'm in a perfectly sound state of mind."

One of the workers with a shovel and wheel barrel bent over a pile of burned timber on the main foundation and said, "Hey boss, there are some little kittens here in the rubble."

Within seconds, everyone crowded around the mound of weather rotted, mismatched planks and boards and began pulling out tiny pussycats.

"Thirteen," a hired hand said. "There's thirteen of 'em." He held one up, cradled in his upright palm. "These's sure some cute li'l rascals."

DeShawn Hill's big burley crew cuddled the tiny multi-colored cats. They ooh'd and ah'd over them. The kittens looked like helpless wee puffs of fur in their large hands. Bob and Debbie joined the crowd along with Hill and Fronteria.

One of the workers went to his truck and returned with a cardboard box and clean rags lining the bottom. "Put the li'l fuzz balls in here."

Hill turned to Bob. "Well, what do you wanna do with them? Don't mean to be abrupt, but … as cute as these little buggers are, we do need to get back to work." He nodded toward the tarped stacks of new lumber. "This house ain't building itself. And winter's only a couple months away."

Debbie stepped in. "I don't think that is a matter of question. We're keeping the cats."

Bob's jaw gaped open. "What?"

"You heard me." She looked directly at DeShawn Hill. "I don't want to know what alternative plans you had for these itty bitty bundles of joy. But we're keeping these kittens."

"No. No way."

Debbie was already walking toward the RV. "Yes way, Bob. Our first day here, and we already have a family. Come on."

Bob tried to protest. But the sound of their helpless mews resonated in his heart as if they'd found a crack they could crawl into, clutching tight with their teeny claws and not letting go. For a moment, Bob thought they were trying to manipulate him. He shook that thought off.

Impossible. I don't like cats.

Once inside, Debbie set the box on the kitchen table. She smiled and laughed, her hands held together over her heart. The helpless mass of fur crawled back and forth across the bottom of the box, their eyes barely open. The stared up at Bob and Debbie and meowed, soft and innocent, yet demanding.

"Oh Bob, just look at them. They're so adorable. What breed do you think they are?"

Bob peered in the box. "I don't know. They're a mix of colors with differing patterns and patches. I think they're a bunch of mutts."

"Admit it. You love them."

"Umm, in case you don't remember, I don't particularly care for cats."

Debbie lifted one, pitch black with three white spots on its back. It looked at Debbie and spread its paws wide as if to say hello.

"Aww, so cute. Let's see. What am I going to call you? You seem to be the leader. Hmm, how about Emily? You look like an Emily."

"Emily? That's a weird name for a cat."

"Well, it just popped in my head. So Emily it is."

Debbie set Emily back in the box and pulled out a second cat. "I think I'll call you Rebecca."

"Debbie, these are human names. You need to call them Tabby. Or Patches. Or Mittens."

"I don't know. I admit, it's strange. Their names, they just come to me as soon as I hold them up."

Bob walked over to the refrigerator and pulled out ham, cheese, and bread to make a sandwich. "How are you possibly going to remember all their names five minutes from now?"

"Good question." Debbie took out her cell phone and took a picture of Rebecca, then recorded her voice to the image. "Rebecca."

She picked up the third cat and spoke baby talk to it. She snapped a picture and recorded the name. "Annie."

She repeated the process as she called off their names one at a time, took a picture, and captured their names.

"Angel."

"Scarlett."

"Esther."

"Chloe."

"Helen."

"Jacqueline."

"Isabella."

"Rachel."

"Madelyn."

Debbie held up the last kitten. It stared at her as if in anticipation of what Debbie would name it. Debbie tapped her finger to her chin. "Hmmm. I'm thinking Amy."

"Amy? The cat's pitch black. You should call it Midnight."

The cat looked at Bob and gave off a small hiss.

"Oh Bob, isn't that so cute. She hissed at you. I don't think she likes the name Midnight."

The kitten looked at Debbie and hissed again. Bob finished making his sandwich and cut it in half. "Whatever. Anyway, I get to name at least one cat. And I say this one is Midnight."

"Congratulations, honey. You're officially a daddy."

Again, the kitten looked to Bob and gave a disapproving sharp sibilant sound.

"Okay. Midnight it is," Debbie said as she placed it back in the box. With a yelp she yanked her hand out.

"What's the matter," Bob said as he took a large bite of his snack.

"Midnight scratched me as I put her back in the box." Debbie, scowling, held up her forefinger. A small red line ran down it. "For a little kitten she sure packs quite a scratch. I guess she really doesn't like the name Midnight."

Bob peered inside the box. Thirteen kittens. Twelve had different colors and patterns and were crawling over each other and mewing. And one pitch black with green eyes looking up and hissing at him.

The fur balls didn't appear cute at all. Rather, they looked like malevolent burdens. Debbie thought of them, as crazy as it sounded, as part of their extended family. Bob dipped his chin, knowing that was part his fault for delaying the decision to having children.

But these cats, they weren't the answer. They were animals, not people. Bob saw his mistake. It was his pride in rebutting Debbie and her wish to have a family. She adopted the helpless kittens to fill a void he'd created. Totally my fault, he thought, and wanted to kick himself.

Bob knew he needed to step up. Once Murcat Manor was completed, together he and Debbie would have their first child. Until then, he would have to tolerate these furry little rug rats while allowing his soul mate to fulfill her need to mother a family.

Chapter 13 Christmas Eve at Erma's

Christmas Eve at the Dempseys. My least favorite holiday, Bob thought. He dreaded visiting Ross and Erma here in their home. This was their territory—where Erma ruled supreme.

During past holidays, the more Irish whiskey Debbie's extended family drank, the more he became the butt of Erma's jokes. She was quick with the whiskey. Quicker with the wit. Ross would laugh harder as the evening progressed and the whiskey flowed. So would Debbie's siblings and their spouses. And tonight was no different.

All in good fun, Debbie assured him. Bob knew he had to take it. He was family, although related by law and not blood to Erma. Still, there was not much he could do to defend himself. Challenging Erma in her house would be most unwise. So he took Debbie's advice, laughed, and went with the tide.

Having lived in an RV for the past three months, he welcomed the comforts of the Ross's sprawling estate, built next to the Grand River on the west side of Lansing. Bob never ceased to be amazed at how large their living room was. It boasted three fire places, two gigantic aquariums built into the walls, and enough furniture to accommodate all the adults and children of their extended family. The view of the river through two sets of glass sliding doors and the bay windows, even during winter, was spectacular.

There were three Christmas trees, with scores of perfectly wrapped gifts extended out from their bases. The room was dim and the setting peaceful, almost choreographed. It was illuminated only by lights from the holiday trees and the aquariums. Christmas carols by crooners from an era gone by softly serenaded the family.

"So, Bob," Ross said, toning down his laugh. "All kidding aside, how's the progress of Murcat Manor?"

Bob took another slow sip of his whiskey. Not much of a drinker, he lagged behind everyone else in the room. But he understood he had to look like he was at least trying to keep up with the Dempsey clan.

"The contractor is a couple weeks ahead of schedule. They completed the walls and roof before the first snow, and they're now working on the inside. The plumbing and electrical is finished. So are the heating and air conditioning ducts. Once the crew returns after the holidays, they'll insulate the drywall—first the large common rooms, and then they'll start on the individual bedrooms."

"When will you be able to stay inside," Brendan Collins asked. He was Debbie's older brother who Bob got along well with. His wife, Christie, the sun bed queen with a dark orange tan and an enormous set of bio-rubber breasts, not so much.

"The good news is," Debbie said. "Our master bedroom and bathroom will be finished in late March. We gave specific instructions for the completion of our bedroom and the kitchen to be top priority. I can't wait to sleep and eat inside our house."

"Debbie dear," Erma said, after yet another good pull of whiskey. "What about the themes for the ten bedrooms?"

"They're diverse to say the least. We can appeal to just about any crowd."

"Well, don't keep us in suspense, child." Erma smiled with pride at Debbie. "What creative ideas did you come up with?"

Debbie started counting off on her fingers. "I'll go down the upstairs hallway starting from the top of the stairs. The Roadhouse Blues, which will feature a wild honky-tonk theme, is the first room. Then we have the Disco Room, modeled after a seventies disco club. Next up is The Love Machine. It's pink and red with a heart shaped bed and mirrors on the ceiling."

"Ooooh, that sounds like fun," Christie said in her annoying coquettish squeal, as she downed her drink in one gulp, and then squeezed her titanic melons together with her upper arms followed by a coy wink toward Brendan.

Bob could feel Debbie trying to suppress a laugh. He couldn't help but wonder if Christine's twins felt as stiff as they looked. And … what would it be like, to—he shook his head free of that train of thought as Debbie continued.

"We'll also have The Frontiersman. That'll be a lodge or cabin theme with a large fireplace and moose head on the wall. The Victorian will have a romantic canopy bed as its main feature. The Summer of Love will be a late sixties theme. The Neptune Room will be under the sea. Rounding out the ten rooms are the Safari Room, the Egyptian Room, and the Steampunk Room."

"But until then," Bob said with a bit of a sigh, "we'll be staying on the property in the Winnebago."

"I can't imagine spending the winter in an RV," Christie said, then placed her forefinger in her mouth and mimicked throwing up. "I'd go bonkers. Brendan and I would kill each other. And with all those smelly cats? Ugh. Totally major gross."

Christie's remarks brought yet another inebriated round of laughs at Bob's expense.

Ross stepped across the living room and poured Bob another glass of Bushmills twenty-one year old single malt whiskey, the usual grin on his face. Erma simply stared Bob down, as she'd done the entire evening.

Bob, wanting anything but yet another drink, took a long pull. Better not to incite Erma and her sharp tongue. Truth was, the liquid courage was helping—he needed a shot of confidence. He followed up with an even longer drink and emptied his glass, trying to hold a straight face.

"That's my boy," Ross chuckled, pouring him another.

"Debbie and I are getting along just fine," Bob continued. "Actually, it's the cats that are driving me nuts."

"There are thirteen, right? Thirteen cats in the RV with you?" Christie said, scrunching her face. She poured herself another drink and downed it, throwing her head back and, Bob was sure, *intentionally* lifting and showing off her twenty thousand dollar pair of Neimen Marcus specials. Bob imagined her awesome eye-candy—yet synthetic—looks thirty years from now and shuddered.

"That's right, Christie," Bob said, careful to keep his eyes up on her face, "Thirteen of them."

"How do you tell the little rag balls apart?"

Rag balls. Bob cracked a grin and considered Christie in a slightly higher regard. Anyone who can't stand cats can't be all bad.

"I named them," Debbie said. "And I gave them each a collar with a little tag with their names engraved and a gemstone to tell them apart. I gave one cat, Emily, who seems to be the leader, all twelve gemstones on her collar—plus her own, of course."

"What are their names?"

Debbie rattled them off with ease. "Emily, Rebecca, Chloe, Annie, Helen, Madelyn, Jacqueline, Angel, Scarlett, Esther, Isabella, Rachel, and Midnight."

"Do you have a favorite," Toy Chest asked.

"Emily. She's the leader. The other cats follow her. And Emily follows me around."

"Does Bob have a favorite cat?"

"No," came Bob's quick reply.

"One cat, Rachel, loves Bob. She follows him everywhere. She even sleeps next to his head."

"Wait a minute," Erma said. "Did you say one cat was named Midnight? The other twelve names are human names. Why Midnight?"

"Well," Debbie looked at Bob and smiled, as if to say 'no offense, hubby'. "Bob named that one."

"Phffft. Way to go, Bob. Always have to deviate from the norm."

Bob had to keep things moving to avoid more laughter directed his way. Say something. Anything.

"They're getting bigger by the day," he somehow produced the words.

"How do you do it?" Christie crinkled her nose in disgust. "Isn't it crowded in there?"

Bob forced a chuckle. "They're mischievous. That's for sure. We can't leave things of value on counters or tables. They'll knock anything we leave out onto the floor."

"They swat them with their tails," Debbie said with a laugh. "Or nudge them with their shoulders. It's like a game to them. I think they're bored. But it's too cold to let them outside."

"But most of the time," Bob added in a disdainful droll. "They just eat and sleep."

"Bob doesn't particularly care for the cats," Debbie said.

"*Noooo* ... you don't say?" Erma chided.

Bob shrugged. "What's to like about them. They're lazy. They don't do anything. And you can't tell them what to do."

"That's because they're cats," Erma said with *duh* intonation. "That's what cats do, Bob. Eat. Sleep. Break things. Shed hair all over the place."

A chorus of schnockered laughter filled the living room, replacing any advantage Bob had gained. Just smile, Bob told himself. Tomorrow I'll be with my side of the family. Hopefully, without a massive hangover.

"I have to admit, there's something spooky about them."

"Spooky?" Ross said, leaning in and topping off Bob's drink. "Good thing the lights are dimmed. Now this is interesting. Just the right setting for a spooky story."

Silence fell on the room. Everyone leaned in, expecting a fascinating tale to be told.

"The cats, they're always watching me."

"Well, yer all confined t' the RV. Not much else t' look at," a flush in the face Christie said, emptying another glass of Irish whiskey. Erma looked at her and smiled, stepping in and giving her a refill.

"It's hard to explain. But it's like, they're studying me. Getting to know everything they can about me."

"I'm na—" Christie hiccupped, "Oops," she giggled, "Sorry, 'm jus' not followin'?"

109

Bob pulled out his cell phone and stood. The whiskey was getting to him, too. It was providing much needed courage, but also making him dizzy. But he couldn't show weakness. Not with Erma in the room. A man has to be able to hold his liquor, even if he didn't drink it other than during Christmas holidays at the Dempseys. He kept his composure and held out the image on his phone.

"Look at this picture I took of them the other night."

Christie blinked her eyes back to wide open and peered at it. "Ooooh, yeah, now tha's szhur spooky, alright."

"It was about three o'clock in the morning. I was sure I heard Debbie calling out my name. I woke up, yet she was fast asleep. But the cats, all thirteen of them, were lined up side to side on the top of our dresser. The moonlight coming in the windows shed some light in our bedroom. They were just staring at me, their tails swaying up in the air in unison."

Bob handed Brendan his cell phone and he looked at it with interest, then passed it around the room. "Wow, that is creepy," Brendan said. "They're all looking directly at you, and ... just ... like they're locked in on you."

"An' thur eyez," Christine said, swerving in her chair. "Th're all red. Like layzshur beams. Freaky."

Erma huffed and dismissed Bob with a flail of her hand. "Okay. So the cats stare at you. Big deal. They're nocturnal. What else are they going to do at night cramped up in the RV? Surf the Internet?"

"The cats also eat people food. They've refused cat food since day one."

Bob wasn't sure if he should've said that, but everyone was so liquored up they probably wouldn't remember much of the conversation the following day.

"And another thing. One of the cats, if I leave my laptop open and walk away, I'll come back and there she'll be, gazing at the monitor. It looks like she's reading the news."

Erma threw her arms up in the air and rolled her eyes. I *must* be drunk, Bob thought, if I brought that up.

"I'll back Bob up on that one," Debbie said. "And it's Madelyn. We have Yahoo and CNN news in our favorites. Our desktops and tablets are touch screens. Madelyn uses her paw to open those sites. The science and technology pages seem to be her favorites. She has two black rings around her eyes that look like thick glasses, giving her a nerdy look. It's kind of cute, I think."

"It's weird," Bob said. "These cats are strange. They don't act like normal cats. It seems like they're always plotting something. Even while we're sleeping."

"Plotting?" Erma said. "Cats? I can see if Debbie's plotting something against you while you sleep. But ... *cats?*"

Another peal of laughter bordered on a noisy ruckus, most in the room almost falling out of their seats.

Bob shrugged off her comment. "It's hard to explain. I don't trust them. But we'll be living inside Murcat Manor soon enough."

Bob could see Erma begin to smirk. He knew another grenade was about to be tossed his way.

"Until then Bob, you'll just have to battle those cats. Don't let them push you around. You're the man of the RV."

The living room was again full of drunken laughter, with Bob the brunt of it. At the rate the evening was progressing, he couldn't wait to leave and get back into the RV. Even sharing a confined space with those blasted infernal fuzz rats would be better than this.

111

Stephen Tremp

Chapter 14   First Blood

Debbie carried a bin of fresh vegetables to one of the island sinks to wash and cut them for the evening's dinner. The kitchen, her personal domain where she ruled supreme, was a commercial quality high-end equipped room. It was as large as the entire downstairs of their house they sold in Caledonia Springs.

The architect had thought of everything: a giant walk-in cooler, two of the largest stainless steel refrigerators she had ever seen, and four pantries. There were more cupboards than you could shake a soup ladle at. Two large islands, each with a sink, refrigerated drawers, grill and hot plate equipped with a full cutlery set of blue-and-white-steel forged Japanese Chubo kitchen knives.

Along one entire wall was a thirty foot long stainless steel counter, with three sinks in the middle—the center sink cavernous in depth, flanked by two wider but shallow basins. Numerous cast iron skillets, stainless steel with copper bottom cookware, hard anodized pots and pans, carbon steel woks, sauce pans and griddles of every size and purpose imaginable hung from the ceiling. Three industrial sized dish washers stood ready to handle the gigantic task of dishware and cookware cleanups.

The centerpiece of the twelve hundred square foot kitchen was a custom elongated table made from solid oak that stretched twenty-four feet by six feet. Twenty high-back oak chairs surrounded the table. DeShawn Hill, a building contractor by profession, but also with a passion for woodworking, had personally made the table from the many oak trees on the property.

Hill had pull with a local kiln-drying and millwork company, having given them a great deal of business over the years. He had gotten his fresh cut, still wet timbers rough sawn, kiln-dried to furniture grade quality, then milled into workable dimension boards. What would usually take six months or more, he had done for him in just two months.

He had worked weekends in his woodworking shop, and gifted the fine piece to Bob and Debbie, saying his pleasure in crafting it was payment enough for him. All they had to purchase was the chairs, and Hill was tight with a major Grand Rapids furniture maker, who sold them chairs perfectly matched to the table in color and grain, at a deep discount.

The dining area could accommodate two shifts of patrons for the meals. With ten rooms in Murcat Manor, one couple per room, and factoring in a handful or two of children, Debbie estimated—with full bookings—there could be up to thirty people per day. Two shifts meant the table had to seat fifteen people plus Bob and Debbie along with additional guests, such as Ross and Erma.

Debbie was in her element, preparing to host and entertain over sixty meals a day for breakfast and dinner. The guests would be responsible for lunch.

Bob sat at the table looking over bills. "I think we're going to be okay. As long as the construction crew stays ahead of schedule, we'll be open for business well on time. And if we don't ask for any change orders or alterations to the plans, we won't run out of money."

"That's great, honey. How are the advanced reservations?"

"So far, so good. But not great."

Debbie reached for a drawer and pulled out a perfectly wrapped box with a blue ribbon and handed it to Bob.

"For me?"

"Yes, you. This is to help you blend in better with our guests. Go on. Open it."

Bob was usually the one to surprise Debbie with gifts, predictable presents she correctly guessed before opening. But when Bob received one from Debbie, he never had an inkling of what it would be.

He took off the lid and pulled out a blue and red flannel shirt by the collar. "You shouldn't have. Really. I mean it. You really shouldn't have."

Debbie was holding her belly laughing. "I know you hate flannel shirts. But I think you need to make more of an effort to make friends around here. This will help. Trust me on this one."

"Sure," Bob said, more of a grumble. "Just like the winged tip shoes that clicked and clacked down the hallway right before I got canned."

Debbie gave him a look, but allowed Bob his little grouse fit.

Bob leaned back in his chair and stretched his arms over his head. Debbie watched as, no sooner had he sat back to relax, he jerked and spread his legs. Skittering around his ankles, the rambunctious American Shorthairs of various colors and patterns invaded the kitchen and spread out, as if Debbie's proprietary province rather belonged to them.

Within seconds, half the felines competed with each other for lap time with Bob. Rebecca and Annie, grey and white striped cats who were always together, jumped up on the table and walked over his file folders and bills. Rachel, brown and white with gray eyes, spread herself belly down on his open laptop.

Debbie laughed as the other felines walked back and forth across the table, their varying appearances too confusing for Bob to remember their individual names. "Honey, you just have to look at their name tags. You'll remember who they are in no time."

Bob had, she appreciated, been learning to at least like the cats. Sort of. More so to please me, she knew. But his motto was always business before pleasure. At least when it came to the cats. He tried shooing them off the table, his lap, and from between his feet. The cats simply traded places with each other. Nerdy Madelyn, a patchwork of brown, black, and white hair, now sat on Bob's lap and looked up at him with her studious, dark-ringed eyes. The old joke, 'about as easy as herding cats,' came to Debbie's mind.

Bob removed Rachel from off his keyboard and set her on the floor. "We have all ten rooms booked for Labor Day Weekend. That'll be a welcomed influx of cash. But after that, we have lots of openings from June all the way up to Memorial Day weekend."

"Please don't stress, sweetie. Once the local papers and travel blogs run their stories on Murcat Manor in a couple weeks, this place will fill up fast. Trust me, okay? I've got this."

"Well, it better. The mortgage payment will be close to eighteen thousand dollars a month. With ten rooms at two hundred fifty dollars a night, we need to pack the place over the summer. From fall through spring, business will be slower."

Bob looked around the kitchen. "The food alone will be over five thousand dollars a month if we have full capacity. And that's with bulk discounts the local grocers and bakeries have agreed to give us."

Scarlett swatted at the neatly stacked piles of bills. They skidded across the table, half falling to the floor.

Bob clenched his jaw. "Debbie, honey. Can you do something with all these critters?"

Debbie scooped up Emily, her favorite, and stroked the back of her head. "Oh Bob, just go with it. Do what I do and pretend they're our kids. It'll be good practice for you."

Bob picked up Madelyn from his lap and placed her on the floor with Rachel. They ran back out into the living room, the other cats following.

"Um, no. They're cats. Not kids."

"Well then, at least use them as a de-stressor. They only want to love you. Isn't that right, Emily? Yes, it is. Oh, yes it is, you cute cuddly little kitty."

Bob slumped in his chair and heaved a sigh. "Not going to promise anything. I tell you, those cats always seem like they're up to no good. I think they're plotting something."

Debbie couldn't contain her laughter as she muttered, "Cats—planning an insidious scheme of some sort."

She stopped laughing and donned a sober expression. "I do know what you mean, though. The way they huddle together, it sometimes looks like they're having a board meeting. And Emily's here is their leader. Isn't that right, Emily? Are you and the others really nefarious villains, conspiring to take over the world?"

117

"Well, it's a good thing they don't have opposable digits. Who knows what kind of evil they could do." Bob got up from his chair and stretched. "I wonder how DeShawn's coming along with the family heirloom."

Debbie snapped her fingers. "I'll go check."

"On second thought, maybe you should wait for him to finish. He doesn't like to be interrupted."

"No worries." Debbie set Emily down and picked up a pair of scissors. "I'll pretend I'm stepping out to prune the plants in the front yard."

Bob laughed. "*Lame-oh.* Men aren't that dumb. He'll know you're being nosy."

"I'll be subtle."

Bob's eyes rolled up into his head. "Subtle. Sure."

Debbie opened the front door. A ladder was planted in the ground twenty feet in front of the porch and leaned forward. It went upward out of sight. Debbie stepped out on the front lawn and looked up.

The landscape had long been bare of snow. The grass, which started peeking and pushing up green out from under the last remnants of the winter's snow weeks ago, was now growing thick and lush under near seventy degree sunny weather. The trees were beginning to leaf out, small brown buds unfolding into verdant foliage. In a few weeks, they would enclose Murcat Manor from her neighbors' views on both sides.

At the top of the ladder, a full three stories up and leaning into the pinnacle of the attic, was DeShawn Hill. Debbie's heart jumped with joy, seeing him fastening the crown jewel of Murcat Manor, her great-great grandfather's Celtic cross, to a metal frame to hold it in place.

"How's it going, Mr. Hill?"

Hill didn't bother to look, he only signaled thumbs up. "Almost finished. I'll secure this to the pinnacle, then call it a day."

"Well, don't mind me. I'm just coming out to prune a few flowers and shrubs."

She could hear Hill chuckle. "Sure. Prune the plants. You can watch. Just don't touch the ladder."

"Debbie, get back inside." Bob was standing on the porch. "Let the man work."

"Okay. Alright. Men. Sheeesh. You're so sensitive."

She joined Bob inside the door. Bob had one hand on his hip and waving his other in the air while giving her a lecture about letting the workers do their job. Debbie playfully mocked her husband, one hand on hip, other hand opening and closing, mimicking him talking, and saying, "Blah blah blah blah blah."

An explosive noise like the loud crack of a whip and a shriek of terror rocked their banter to a dead stop.

Debbie whirled around toward the sound and looked through the still open front door. She gasped in horror. DeShawn Hill, clutching madly at the top of the ladder, came into view in a dreadful fall backward away from the house. He slammed down on his back on the peaked roof of the gazebo in the front yard. The combined thud, splat, and crunching of bones was horrifying.

Debbie grabbed her head with both hands, her mouth wide open but so aghast she was breathless to scream. It seemed to her the scene was in shuddersome slow motion. The ladder bounced a few feet off Hill, dangled in the air like a sword wielded by an invisible assailant, and then smashed back onto his chest.

Debbie's breath came back to her in a violent scream. She cut her hand with the scissors while whipping them away in a mad dash to the door. Bob had already run out, streaking across the lawn to the gazebo. Debbie

119

was right behind him. In less than a minute, three crew members working upstairs had joined them.

One of the carpenters, a local handyman—quite the redneck, but all in all a likeable guy—named Phil Hampton, scaled the gazebo with ease and tossed the ladder off his boss. He cupped Deshawn's head in his hands. But the look on Phil's face made it evident right away.

DeShawn Hill was dead.

He'd been impaled through the back by the sharp point of the spire atop the gazebo, now protruding like a blood-soaked sword out of his chest. From the ground Debbie could see the bottom half of his torso and his legs, still twitching with residual nerve endings sending out futile warnings to a dead brain.

She moved to her right several steps and observed the upper torso, arms and head on the other side of the bludgeoning cast iron steeple, facing the street. The two crew members on the ground, brothers in their mid-thirties from Battle Creed named Jerry and Jack Hansen, cried, crossed themselves, and said prayers.

Jack pulled out his cell phone. "I'll call nine-one-one. Jerry, go find a towel for Mrs. Stevens. Her hand's bleeding pretty bad."

Debbie stuffed her head into Bob's shoulder and cried hysterically.

"What the ..."

"What is it, Bob?"

"The cats."

"Cats? What about them?"

"There are three of them. On the roof. Right where DeShawn was working."

Debbie looked up and rubbed her eyes dry. "I don't see any cats."

"They ran off just before you looked. But they were there. Plain as day. Right where he was securing your family's heirloom."

Bob looked back at the family heirloom, then directed Debbie's attention to it. "Look, honey, at the cross."

She did. It was dangling upside down, swaying slightly, barely held in place to the metal frame DeShawn Hill was securing it to. It seemed to be broken. The arms were tilted at weird angles. And the family crest was missing.

"Bob, Where's the crest?"

"Not sure. I was wondering that too. Oh wait," he pointed nearby. "Look, there it is, lying in the grass."

A moment later, Debbie heard a crackling, tearing apart sound from above. She looked up to see the heirloom fall. It hit the porch roof and bounced onto the cement steps in an unceremonious splat. The pride of five generations was now destroyed, lying shattered in dozens of splintered pieces.

Chapter 15 Detective Darrowby

Bob didn't move. He held Debbie close while looking back and forth at the broken Celtic cross and demolished family crest. Phil stayed on the roof of the gazebo with his boss. Jack ended his call. "Police and emergency are on their way now," he said through a broken voice.

Bob gazed at the top of the three story peak where he was sure three cats sat, their tails wagging in unison. They stared at him for a several long seconds. Then they were gone—taking an auspicious exit just before anyone but he noticed their presence. He tried to make sense of what in the hell just happened.

Jerry Hansen's yelling yanked Bob's mind out of his mysterious musing. He was running back across the lawn with a clean towel from his truck.

"Let me see your hand, Mrs. Stevens. You're bleeding something awful."

Debbie pulled her hand out from Bob's chest and held it up. Blood ran down her palm and past her wrist, soaking her sleeve in warm, dark, crimson goo. The front of his shirt had a large red spot where it soaked up her blood.

The older Hansen took Debbie's arm. "Here, let me wrap your hand. That cut looks pretty deep. It'll hold back the blood loss until you can get inside and clean the wound, which you should do right away."

Bob had been a bit leery of the crew Hill brought to work with him. They were kind of scruffy. And he was sure they were sneaking beer in while on the job.

But the guys were great at what they did. And now he saw a side of them that was caring. They had acted faster than he had as he tried to recover from the shock of DeShawn Hill dead in his front yard.

"Debbie, honey that must hurt."

Debbie snapped out of her own shock. "Well, yes. Now that you mention it, there's a massive throbbing pain unlike anything I've ever felt."

The Hansen brothers tossed Phil Hampton a large drop cloth who respectfully laid it over Hill. Silence reverberated throughout the area for several minutes, mitigated only by the occasional whimpers and whispered prayers. A few minutes later, faint sirens grew louder, coming closer.

Two black and white Battle Creek Police SUVs sped up to the house and skidded to a halt in the gravel driveway. They killed their sirens but left the blue and red lights on. From the lead car two men with suits emerged. Two Battle Creek police officers from the second vehicle flanked them.

The lead man, Bob recognized by his suit and the way he led, was a detective. Tall. Six foot two. Lean. Early forties. Wore his suit well. Dark thick black hair and mustache. A gait telling the world he was not afraid of anyone or anything.

"Good afternoon," the man said as shook Bob's hand. His voice was soothing, almost like a counselor giving comfort. Bob started to feel at ease.

"My name is Captain Detective Thomas Darrowby. This is my partner, Sergeant Detective David Kowalski."

The sergeant looked like a tank. He had a large flat head that looked like a turret, swivel-mounted directly on a pair of wide shoulders—any semblance of a neck was missing. His long, pointy nose was the war machine's gun. He only nodded, rotating his line of sight past Bob, Debbie, and the Hansen brothers toward the gazebo.

"I'm Robert Stevens. But people call me Bob. This is my wife Debbie. And these two are Jack and Jerry Hansen. Hampton, erm, Phil's his first name, is the one on top of the gazebo. They're carpenters working on the house."

More sirens approached. An ambulance arrived along with two more patrol cars. Bob could see his neighbors starting to make their way toward his house. Some cruised by slow, gawking. Others were on foot and stood along the gravel between the two-lane Oak Hill Road and his property. Most were taking pictures and filming the event with their cell phones.

"The five of you look shook up," Darrowby said. "I understand a man working on your house fell off his ladder and died. Is that right?"

"Yes. That's right," Bob said. "It all happened so fast."

Darrowby placed his hand on Debbie's shoulder. "Are you okay, ma'am? That towel around your hand is soaked with blood."

"I'm fine. I ... I saw it happen from the living room window. I had a pair of scissors in my hand. It was terrible. In my shock, I ... I," she frowned, looking at her wrapped wound, "somehow cut myself."

Darrowby's warm smile and pacifying bass voice calmed Debbie. Her sobbing slowed and her grip on Bob loosened. "Well, don't you worry. The paramedics will stitch you up good as new. I promise you that."

Darrowby turned to Bob. "Mr. Stevens, I know this can be traumatic. This looks to be a terrible accident. And right in front of your wife, no less."

This was the first time Bob ever had an encounter with the police. Darrowby was a real professional. He liked the detective. He seemed to care.

"I saw the sign in the front yard," Darrowby continued, and Bob detected something about the man that told him he could look much more menacing than his initial Mr. Nice Guy approach. Darrowby looked over at the Hansen brothers.

"DeShawn Hill Construction. I know the man well. He's a great friend of mine. We played football together for Battle Creek Central High School. I take it it's one of his crew who fell off the ladder?" Darrowby looked around. "Is he here? DeShawn?"

Oh God, how terribly awkward, Bob thought, but pointed to the Gazebo roof. "Um ... there ... that's Mr. Hill."

Darrowby's body locked up. He and Kowalski exchanged a long glance at each other. Without saying anything, they walked over to the extension ladder and picked it off the ground. It was twisted and mangled along its full forty foot length. Too awkward to use, they dropped it and scaled the gazebo posts.

Darrowby yanked the drop cloth off. It caught in a snag on the steeple spire, so he yanked it again, breaking it loose with a ripping tear and loud snap, and tossed it to the ground. After an ominous silence, Bob heard the detective wail.

Bob tried to climb up to the gazebo roof. He wasn't nearly as athletic as the detectives. He stood on the hand rail and grabbed the edge of the roof. Struggling to pull himself up, Bob tried to swing is left leg over the edge but felt his grip loosen. A strong meaty hand grabbed him and he was pulled up with great force.

In an instant, he was safely lying belly down on the 5/12 pitched roof. He felt his weight pulling him down the incline, but before he could react, Kowalski pulled him to his feet.

Bob felt uneasy on the incline of the roof. He bent his knees deep to keep his balance, then mimicked the more experienced detectives and put one foot higher up the incline, and adjusted his weight to bear on the upper foot, belayed by the stop force of his lower foot.

Still feeling queasy and precarious, he turned his head to the roof peak. In front of him lay a broken and crushed body. It was as if Hill had no bones. His corpse simply wilted across the top of the gazebo, sprawled out, the iron point jutting out of chest, seeming to pin him tight against the shingles and refusing to let him go.

He had to turn his eyes. He looked at Darrowby, who tried to hold back his sobs, and held his right hand against his heart. Phil Hampton stood and placed his hand on Darrowby's shoulder, sharing grief for a fallen friend.

The lead detective acknowledged the gesture with a look and a nod at Phil. "DeShawn Hill was a damn good man. A family man. And a great friend. God rest his soul."

The men went quiet for a while. Bob didn't know what to say. He waited for someone to break the silence.

Darrowby wiped his eyes with a handkerchief and composed himself. "Do you know what, or how, this happened?"

Bob watched as the detective traced his finger from where Hill lay in an arching motion to follow the trajectory of his fall back to the top of the three story pinnacle.

"I'm not sure. My wife and I, we were in the living room when we heard Hill scream. We watched through the open front door as the ladder fell backwards."

Darrowby snapped his head back at Bob. "Fell backwards? What exactly do you mean?"

"Well, the ladder ... it simply fell backward. Hill was clutching the top rungs when he fell and landed on the gazebo." Bob shuddered at the thought and the grotesque sound of the impact echoing in his mind.

Darrowby stood, hands on hips, staring at Bob. "Uh huhn."

The detective stroked his chin and looked in every direction except directly at Bob. Bob could read his face. And he was finally making the connection the detective was struggling with. Ladders leaning into the roof with a large man at the top do not fall backward without a force pushing against them.

Darrowby glanced at Bob. His tone now was not so caring. "That doesn't make sense. I've known DeShawn Hill since high school. He's a very competent and capable building contractor."

He looked again at Hill, then at the top of the roof. "What do you think, Mr. Hampton? Does that make any sense, his ladder suddenly falling backward, to you?"

"No," Hampton said with an emphatic shake of the head. "It sure doesn't. I've known Mr. Hill and worked for him for more than twenty years now. No way could he have fallen backwards. Not like this here. Not DeShawn. Ain't no way, sir. He's a professional. There's been no high winds today at all. If they'd been, he would've secured the top of the ladder to something solid up there with bungee cords."

Darrowby, still looking at the roof, peeked at Bob through the corner of his eyes. Bob noticed the change in the detective's facial expressions. He looked angry. Threatening. The man's hand moved toward the side of his waist, opening up his blazer enough that Bob could see a holstered gun and a set of handcuffs. Then his arm relaxed. For a moment, Bob thought the detective was going to arrest him.

Chapter 16   No More Mr. Nice Guy

Bob's attention was drawn to his throbbing ankles. He could hardly stand. And the glares from Darrowby, Kowalski, and Hampton told him he was now an outsider looking in.

"I'm going down. It's hard to stand on this pitch."

Bob thought of asking for a ladder, but Hill's ladder lay twisted on the grass. It didn't seem like the right question to ask of Jack and Jerry Hansen, if they could get one from their trucks, considering the circumstances. They were staring at him with suspicion, too.

Bob got on all fours, scooted himself down to the bottom, and gripped the roof's eave. It was only ten feet to the ground, and only a two foot or so drop if he could hang off the edge. Before he could act, Darrowby, Kowalski, and Phil had performed the same maneuver with ease.

He started to swing his legs over the side and the next thing he knew he was on the ground seeing stars. Debbie helped him up.

"Bob, dear. Are you okay?"

"I'm fine. Thanks." Bob noticed neighbors gathering from nearby farms numbered close to a hundred. "Where the heck did they all come from? For a rural community, news sure does travel fast around here."

As Bob brushed grass and dirt off his shirt, Darrowby stepped between him and Debbie. "Mr. Stevens, tell me again, in precise detail; what exactly happened here?"

Bob didn't appreciate the invasion and took a step back, giving himself personal space. "I was in the living room with my wife. Inside the house. We saw Mr. Hill fall backwards while clinging to the top of the ladder. That's really about it."

Darrowby turned to Debbie. "That so, Mrs. Stevens?"

Debbie took her place again at Bob's side. "Yes. DeShawn Hill was finishing the day by placing a family heirloom at the pinnacle of the house. I was anxious to see how that project was coming along. So I stepped outside, and, pretending to be trimming the flowers, I asked him how it was going. He gave me a thumbs up. Bob pulled me back inside and it wasn't more than a minute later when we saw the ladder falling away from the house, with Mr. Hill clinging and screaming to it."

Debbie cringed and gulped air. Bob could see where this was heading. He wasn't going to allow his wife to be grilled, and eased himself between her and Darrowby.

"Detective, it's like we told you," he said with more force. "We were inside the house when this happened."

Darrowby stepped into Bob, again devouring his personal space. "And what again did you see—exactly?"

"Actually, I first heard Hill scream. Debbie heard it, too. I turned to see him as he fell on top of the gazebo."

Darrowby pointed. "Over there?"

What a jerk, Bob thought. Obviously over there, he knows damn well by now where.

Bob kept his calm. "That's right. I saw the ladder falling. It was all so surreal feeling. It seemed to take forever for him to fall. But he did. Then he hit the pavilion."

"Anything else?" Darrowby apparently had forgotten how to blink.

"No. That's about it."

"Are you sure?"

"Well, there is one thing, but ... nah, I mean it couldn't hav—"

"Don't hold back anything. I'll decide what is of importance or not."

Crap, Bob thought. Why did I even start to mention this? He cleared his throat, and said, "Well, when I came outside, after witnessing the fall onto the gazebo, I turned, looked back up at where Hill had been, and ... well, I saw three of our cats at the top of the house."

"Cats?"

The straight-faced response was expected. Bob shuffled his feet. He knew whatever followed would sound stupid. "Yeah. We have thirteen cats."

Darrowby and Kowalski gave Bob a strange look. Darrowby finally blinked. Once. Then said, deadpan, "Cats."

"Yeah. Cats. They're my wife's. Anyway, three cats were sitting where Hill was fastening the Celtic cross." Bob pointed. "At the peak of the house."

Darrowby made a funny face. "Cats? Really? Are you suggesting cats had anything to do with this horrible event? I have to be the one to break the news to his wife and children. Am I supposed to say three cats are our prime suspects?"

"Well I—I mean, no. Of course not. I only ... wait, did you just say prime suspects?"

Darrowby looked around. "And where are the cats now?"

"I'm not sure. Why?"

"Maybe we should question them," Kowalski smirked.

Darrowby looked back at the gazebo, again tracing the trajectory of the fall with his forefinger. "The ladder went back, away from this house, like this. As if it was pushed. Hard. Hard enough to rise upward, reach the fulcrum point, and then topple over to the ground. DeShawn Hill was a big man. He looks to be a solid two hundred and fifty pounds. It would take a considerable amount of force to push the ladder, with him on it, into an arc like ..."

He looked down as his voice trailed off and shook his head, then looked back at Bob. "I'll be sure to have forensics calculate the force needed to push that amount of mass backward. And I honestly don't think *cats* could do that."

Bob felt Debbie nudge past him. "Pushed? What exactly are you saying?"

"I'll take care of this, honey."

Darrowby bore down on Bob. Kowalski put away his pad and pencil and stood close to his side.

"What I'm saying is DeShawn Hill was a very competent man. He was smart. Strong. He didn't just fall. If that were the case, he would have landed on the porch roof directly below. Instead, the ladder was forced away from the house. Either he shoved off in an effort to commit suicide, or the ladder was pushed by another source."

"I don't like what you're insinuating," Bob said as he held Debbie close.

"Where were you again?"

Bob sighed in frustration. "For the third time. In the living room. Inside our house."

"Any witnesses?" Kowalski said, looking down and again taking notes.

"My wife. Debbie."

Darrowby spread his arms wide in an exaggerated gesture. "Oh, right. Debbie. With a large cut on her hand and a towel wrapped around it. Oh, and there's blood all over her sleeve and on your shirt. We'll come back to your wife and her wound. Don't go away."

Darrowby turned to the three workers. "Did you witness where either Mr. or Mrs. Stevens were, or what they were doing at the time the ladder with your boss fell backwards?"

"No sir." Phil said. "We was all upstairs, installin' ceiling fans in the bedrooms."

Darrowby bore back down on Bob. Bob stood his ground. "We were inside the house when he fell. Now I don't know what happened. But I can assure you, my wife and I were in the living room at the time. For God's sake, man, we liked Mr. Hill. We'd gotten close during the project. He even made a beautiful oak table for our guests and gave it to us as a gift. There's no way my wife or I would think of causing the man any harm."

"Mmhmm." Darrowby chewed on his lower lip. "Right. Sure. And the cats. Maybe they pushed him."

Now he's flat out mocking me. "That's ridiculous, and we both know it."

Darrowby cracked a wry smile and whispered, "So is this whole event. And I'm not buying it."

Bob noticed three news vans positioning themselves on the street. Although surprised, he was glad Darrowby's attention was now toward the news crews.

Darrowby pulled out a comb and ran it through his thick dark wavy hair, then gave his mustache a once over. He straightened his tie as he looked back at Bob. "Saved by the bell. But I'll be back. You can count on that. DeShawn Hill was a very good friend of mine. And this was no accident."

"Great," Bob said to Debbie as the detectives turned and walked away. "That's all we need. Our general contractor is dead in our front yard and Darrowby thinks we had something to do with it. Now the news crews are here. And right before Memorial Day Weekend."

Chapter 17   Emergency Meeting

Emily Livingston called an emergency meeting for the cats in the basement of Murcat Manor. DeShawn Hill was kind enough to place animal doors throughout the bed and breakfast, including Bob and Debbie's bedroom and the basement. The cats had free reign, except for the guest rooms on the second floor.

Emily jumped up on a storage shelf five feet off the basement floor. She focused on a dozen large cans of fruit cocktail and, with a swift wave of her paw, easily tipped them over. They rolled off the edge and clanked onto the floor, making space for her to assume her position as leader of the twelve cats, her multi-gemmed collar displaying her authority over the extraordinarily gifted felines.

The twelve followers sat on a long workbench in groups of three. Rebecca, Chloe, Scarlett, and Isabella clustered with the two cats in their charges. That was the pecking order. Emily was the leader. Rebecca, her best friend, was second in command. Rebecca, along with Chloe, Scarlett, and Isabella, were responsible to keep the other cats in line.

Emily was seething. She looked down on her gathering, angry for the deed one of the four groups had so flagrantly performed without her permission. Some of the felines stared off in the distance. Others licked their paws. Not one looked Emily directly in the eyes. Discipline and respect were not their long suits.

"Alright, which one of you did it?"

She glared back and forth at the silent cats who continued to look in every direction but hers.

Emily's eyes narrowed. "I mean it. This is serious. We agreed not to kill anyone during this, our sixth life. And now, there is a dead man in the front yard. All it took was a couple minutes as Debbie held me in the kitchen while you all ran off. For the sixth life of me, it is incomprehensible why one of you did this."

More silence.

Emily knew this was really defiance. She leapt across the shelf onto the workbench and paced back and forth, stepping over scattered power tools. "Hmm ... who could have done it? Let's see now."

She stopped in front of her second in command and looked deep into the eyes of Rebecca. "Well?"

"Well, what?" Rebecca sighed, as she playfully patted a live mouse between her paws.

"Who killed him," Emily hissed.

"Certainly not us. And by us, I mean Annie, Jacqueline, and myself. Isn't that right, ladies?"

Jacqueline and Annie nodded in agreement, still refusing to look at Emily. They moved close to Rebecca and watched as she played with the mouse.

Emily would not be detoured by their insolence. "Rebecca, you have the ability to start fires, heat things up, and make blood boil. Jacqueline can freeze things. And Annie can speed or slow down just about anything, including a person's heart rate. So tell me. Where were you?"

Rebecca rolled her eyes in an overt display of boredom. "We were in their bedroom, messing with a few loads of clean laundry Debbie had stacked nice and neat on their bed. You'd be proud of us. We scattered clothes everywhere."

Rebecca stared down on Emily. "Which brings to question, where were you?"

There was a united chorus of hmmms among the twelve as they nodded in agreement.

"Stop it. You know I'm the one trying to keep us from making the same mistakes we committed in our past five lives."

"Can we go now?" Rebecca said, sounding insulted at being cross-examined.

"No." Emily continued to pace, then stopped at Isabella. "Your group's turn. Telepathy and illusion casting is your strong suit. Rachel has the gift of astral projection. And Madelyn has one of the smartest brains on the planet."

Isabella and the other two giggled.

"Oh, you think this is a big joke, do you? Tell me, where were you three?"

Isabella casually licked herself on her shoulders. "Who us?"

"Don't get smart with me."

"Hey, take it easy, will you? We were with the workers painting the bedrooms upstairs."

"They're always petting us," Rachel said.

"And they bring us treats," Madelyn added.

Emily strutted to Chloe, the only ginger colored cat of the group. "Of course. My cousin and blood relative. I should have asked you first. You can move or levitate objects short distances. Midnight can teleport herself anywhere in the house, including the roof top of Murcat Manor. And Helen, she's quite adept at reversing or cross connecting things. This is too easy. Give me the what, how and why."

Chloe stared at Emily, expressionless. "Oh, just stop it? You always think you're so smart. Yet, once again, you have to go through three of our groups before you find the real culprit."

"That's because you're all too good at this."

"I'll take that as a compliment."

Emily walked over to Scarlett. "I should have known." Scarlett backed up, Angel and Esther trying to hide behind her.

"Okay. Why'd you do it? And how? Wait. Let me guess."

Emily strutted back and forth before them, her tail in a curved arc swaying back and forth.

"I presume I have this. And don't even think of running off. Angel, your specialty influencing people's dreams."

Angel shrugged, as if she didn't care she was found out. "I was simply looking out for his best interests."

"His? Or yours."

"Please allow be to elaborate. DeShawn Hill had just taken a short nap in his truck. I thought he should know how dangerous it was to work three stories up and not to have someone holding the ladder at the bottom. Especially with three witches from four centuries ago who have an itch to kill. But, he had a deadline to meet and foolishly ignored his dream."

"And that's all you needed, right?"

Angel laughed. "What more do I need than an opportunity? That, and the stupid things stupid people do."

Emily walked around Scarlett, rubbing up against her and brushing her tail in her face. "Then you threw a bout of madness, causing Hill to freak out for a few moments. He lost all touch with reality."

"Only for a few moments," she said as if this interrogation was an extreme bother.

"Ah, and finally we have Esther. You, who has the power to release energy from inanimate objects, causing sudden bursts of energy."

Esther licked her front paws. "Only on a very small scale. You know that."

"But enough to push the ladder backward."

"I used the metal on the family crest from the cross Hill was fastening to the roof. I converted a small portion to energy, just enough to thrust the ladder away from the house and cause him to fall to a horrifying death."

Esther's eyes twinkled with sinister glee. "But here's the real kicker. I could have caused him to drop to his death. But I forced the ladder straight backwards."

Emily shook her head. "I'm not following. So what."

Esther rolled her eyes. "So, this means it looks like the ladder was pushed with great force."

"I'm still not following."

"Stay with me. It's as if someone, like, oh, let's just say Bob, did the pushing. A fact I'm sure Darrowby and his Neanderthal sidekick won't miss."

The other cats gave their support and congratulations to Esther.

"Stop it, all of you. Esther, are you proud of yourself?"

"Well, yeah. I mean, duh? Need you even ask?"

"That's it? That's all you can say?"

"What else do you want us to say?"

Emily jumped back to her shelf and took her place as head of the cats. "Look, I know it's tempting to use your powers and work together and kill people."

"Oh, it's so easy," Midnight said. "Even though we lack opposable digits." She held up her paws. "Look mom, no thumbs."

"That's why we need to work together," Annie said as she sashayed across the work bench. "And we're bored. I mean, come on. Has there been anyone more boring than Bob, ever, in all of our lifetimes?"

"Stop it, all of you. You know we can't do this again. This always turns out badly."

"Yeah. For the humans."

"And for us. We're already on our sixth lives. Only three more after this, ladies. Then it's all over. Then we'll be stuck in the cold, dark Netherworld forever with countless screaming lost souls."

Emily now had their attention. The twelve cats hung their heads in shame.

"Now promise me. No more killing people. No matter how hard you're tempted."

Emily watched as her dozen followers one by one raised a paw and reluctantly agreed.

"Oh, one more thing. Try to warm up to Bob, regardless of how boring he is."

"We are," Rebecca said. "Just last night I fell asleep on his face while he was sleeping. Debbie thought it was adorable and took a picture with her cell phone, then sent it to Erma."

"But you're faking it. All of you are mocking Bob."

"And he doesn't even know it. Neither does Debbie."

Chloe spoke. "And I left him a special um ... *care package* in his shoe last week."

Everyone was laughing hard. Except Emily.

"Is this meeting dismissed? I'm bored," Rebecca said as the mouse she was playing with almost got away. She trapped it again between her paws.

"Hey sis, aren't you going to kill and eat that thing," Annie asked.

"No. You eat it."

"Disgusting. Give me a steak any day to gnaw on."

"As long as we've been cats," Rebecca said, "and we've certainly taken on some of their characteristics, I've never developed a taste for dead mice or birds."

"Good thing Debbie feeds us normal people food," Scarlett said.

The mouse started to rise. Rebecca held its tail to the table with her paws to keep it from floating away.

"Chloe, stop fooling around," Emily said. "I know you're levitating that mouse."

"That is so cool how you do that," Annie said. "How much can you lift?"

Chloe puffed her breast with pride. "I can raise fifteen pounds and should be up to twenty by the end of the summer. But it takes all my strength. I need a few minutes to recover after raising something that large. It's exhausting."

Rebecca let go of the mouse's tail and stared at the rodent as it rotated in the air in front of her face. She tapped it with her paw. The mouse moved forward about a foot, then Chloe guided it back in front of Rebecca's nose and made it to again rotate.

Rebecca was captivated by the slow gyrating rodent when it exploded into a ball of fur and shredded red flesh. She jumped high with a screech, her back arched and hair standing on end. The rest of the cats erupted in laughter. She landed in the same spot and frantically wiped the rodent gore off her face with her paws.

Rebecca stared down Esther. "Real mature. Look at the mess you made. So gross."

Esther tried to stop laughing. She took a deep breath, held it, then let out a long roll of laughter.

"Stop it. All of you," Emily cried out. "Esther, I demand you cease causing things to explode. You helped kill DeShawn Hill. Now the mouse. I mean it. No more."

Emily could feel the meeting slipping away from her.

"Can we go?" Jacqueline said.

"One more thing. Madelyn, since you're the only one of us that can read past a fourth grade level, I need you to keep studying anything you can. Bob's laptop. Books. Magazines. The world has changed so much since our last lives. And technology has made this information readily available. Anything you can learn, especially about science, can only help us better understand our abilities, and thus use them more effectively."

She had their undivided attention now.

"But let me make it clear. We will not use them to kill people."

Undivided attention gone.

Helen yawned deep. "I want to take a nap."

"Me too," Madelyn said.

They had their taste of first blood in this life. Emily had more to say, but she knew no one would stay and listen.

"Okay, ladies. Let's get out of here. But I mean it. No more killings," Emily said as she watched the twelve cats already dispersing in various directions.

Chapter 18   Open for Business

Bob gazed at the farm themed calendar on the kitchen wall. Roosters and hens were the country motif of the month. It was Memorial Day weekend. Saturday morning. The summer season had officially begun. Murcat Manor was now open for business.

He and Debbie had put DeShawn Hill's death behind them as best they could. All their hard work was about to pay off. And not a day too soon, since the first payment of eighteen thousand dollars to the bank would be due in thirty days. Insurance, food, and utility bills would follow.

The sound of a car pulling onto the gravel driveway told Bob the first guests had arrived.

Debbie jumped up from her kitchen chair, a printed list of the ten families in her hand. "Bob, they're here. I wonder which family it is. I bet it's the O'Dells from Toledo. Or maybe it's the Parkers from Fort Wayne. Oh, I'm just so excited."

Bob opened the front door as an older Ford pickup truck pulled up to one of the round wooden posts designating a parking spot. Debbie gasped and muttered, "Oh my."

Bob looked at the rust around all four wheels. One of the doors was a different color than the rest of the car. The hood was held down with a bungee cord. Red duct tape covered one of the broken rear parking lights.

He placed his hand on the small of Debbie's back and led her out onto the front porch. "Um, well now dear, they had the money to pay for their stay, okay? Let's be nice, and welcome our first guests."

Bob watched as three children piled out. Triplets. Red haired, freckled faced, pasty-skinned boys all under the age of ten. Their energy demonstrated they'd been cooped up in the truck for a long time.

They ran past him before Debbie could say 'hi' and into Murcat Manor. Within seconds the sound of screaming cats filled the air. Something glass broke.

"Looks like the cats have met their match," Bob said through a wide grin.

"Hello," came a loud boisterous voice. Bob turned to see the parents approaching. He was large with a barrel chest and beer belly. Bob wondered if the buttons on his dreaded flannel shirt would pop at any moment.

She was dressed in tight loud clothes and bright cheap jewelry. Poorly red-dyed bushy hair flopped down across her shoulders.

Debbie whispered in his ear, "I'm amazed she can walk across gravel with those cheap high heels."

The beer bellied man stumbled up the porch steps. "We're the Barnetts. Eugene's my name. And this here's my beautiful and bodacious wife, Beatrice."

"Looks like we're the first ones to break in the place," Beatrice said, avoiding eye contact and chomping on a wad of gum.

Bob thought he smelled alcohol on their breath. He looked at his watch. It was barely eleven o'clock in the morning.

"Well, won't you come this way," Debbie said. "I'll show you to your room. Bob will bring your luggage."

Bob looked at the pickup bed. There must be a dozen pieces of mismatched luggage, all held together with duct tape.

He sighed. This was one detail he hadn't thought through, hauling luggage for ten families across a gravel parking lot and upstairs, then taking it back to their cars when they left. It was already hot and humid. As he entered the front door balancing five of the suit cases, he heard something else break. Three cats scampered between his legs and out the front door.

Once in the foyer and at the bottom of the stairs, Bob dropped the luggage at the sight in front of him. He should be mad as hell with three uncontrolled kids terrorizing the American Shorthair felines. But he was enjoying the scene. Two more cats scampered to safety outside.

Debbie stepped next to Bob. "Do something," she whispered. "There's a soccer field in our backyard."

Bob tried to stifle a chuckle. "Are you kidding? This will humble those cats. Maybe they'll stop messing with my laptops and the stack of utility and mortgage statements."

She elbowed him. "Take the luggage up to the Roadhouse Blues Room, dear."

Bob looked at Beatrice Barnett standing in her way-too-tight jeans and high heels, hands on hips, chomping her gum, staring off into the ceiling. Eugene somehow managed to have an opened beer in his hand and grabbed her tush. Beatrice snapped out of her daydream as he chased her around the living room, both laughing loud and obnoxious.

"I'm glad they're not staying in The Love Machine."

Debbie couldn't refrain from snickering. "No way would I launder those sheets. I'd have to burn them in the back yard."

Chapter 19   Help is on the Way

Within a few hours all ten rooms were filled. A total of thirteen kids were running around Murcat Manor and terrorizing the cats. One cat for each kid, Bob thought, and then considered stuffing a feline in each of their suitcases while carrying their luggage out to their cars when they left—the guests wouldn't know it until they arrived home.

Bob stepped into the vastness of their kitchen, which doubled as their work space where he and Debbie spent most of their time. As a youth, Bob envisioned having a home office complete with a fireplace and mahogany walls lined with bookshelves.

But within one generation, times had changed. Now, laptops and a flat surface to place their electronic workstations replaced the need for what he now considered a ridiculous and pompous vision.

Bob sat his laptop on the kitchen table and plugged the AC adaptor into the wall. He looked with amazement at his wife. He wondered if she knew he'd entered the kitchen.

Debbie was in a world unto herself, hard at work, preparing the very first dinner for a full house of guests. Bob could smell the unmistakable aroma of pot roast and roasted vegetables as it filled the kitchen. He pictured pulling the meat apart with his fork and savoring the taste of the first fruits of Murcat Manor's opening weekend.

"Finally. A few minutes alone." He wiped his brow as he looked at food cooking on all three stoves and ovens. "I'm beat. That was a lot of work, hauling their luggage from the parking lot up to their rooms. There must have been close to a hundred pieces. And yesterday, I spent the entire day mowing the lawn. I still have a list of twenty things I need to do. This is more work than I thought it would be."

Debbie was chopping vegetables on a cutting board. She struggled as her hand was still not healed where she sliced her palm the day DeShawn Hill died.

"I've been thinking about that. We need to hire full time help. I'm thinking two people, at least for the summer."

Bob rose and slipped his hands around Debbie's waist. "You need help in the kitchen. I need a helper with the luggage and for maintenance. It's only the first day and those unruly triplets have broken just about everything they've touched. Let's face it. I'm not the best at fixing things."

Debbie turned and wrapped her arms around Bob's neck. "At least the place is packed. I thought for sure the death of Mr. Hill would ruin us before we had a chance to start. The local news channels were all over that."

Bob reached around her and snatched a freshly baked chocolate chip cookie. "It was a slow summer," he said, tossing it in his mouth. "I guess we were the only thing happening. They kept coming out for follow up stories. I was scared too. But the extra coverage helped us book out rooms well into the fall and much of December."

Debbie slapped away Bob's hand as he reached in for a second treat. "The positive reviews and write ups in the Battle Creek and Kalamazoo newspapers and a few online sites and blogs helped too. They focused on the themes of the ten rooms rather than Hill's death."

Bob moved on to one of the refrigerators. "I think we'll be okay, as long as Detectives Darrowby and his goon sidekick Kowalski stay away."

"Darrowby scares me. Why hasn't he closed this case? It should be a simple but freak accident. Although he's not calling this a homicide, he sure seems to be treating it like one."

Bob sniffed the air. "Something's burning."

Debbie rushed back and forth from stove to stove, juggling pots and pans of food, then zeroing in on a sauce pan she had neglected.

"No worries. I can make another batch," she said as she scraped the ingredients into the garbage disposal and ran the pan under the water faucet. "It'll just take a few minutes."

"You're amazing. You know that?"

Debbie used her apron to wipe her brow. "What? You're only now noticing? I'm telling Grandma."

Bob laughed harder than he had in days. "Thanks. I needed that. Still, you do need help running this place and so do I."

"So you concede? We'll hire a handy man slash bell boy slash cook slash cleaning person?"

Bob didn't need to consider. "Yeah. We can afford one. Actually two. One for you and one for me. I'm not up for trying to be a handyman. Not in my genes."

Debbie ran over to the next stove and looked over her shoulder at Bob. "Like that toilet Eugene Barnett clogged in the Roadhouse Blues?"

"Ugh. Don't remind me." Bob sat at the table and opened his laptop. "That's motivation enough to put an ad on Craigslist right away."

"Well, for now, let's enjoy the success of a full house."

"You got that right." Bob discretely reached over the table and snatched a blueberry muffin from a tin cooling under a kitchen towel.

"Maybe we can plan on an addition for next summer? Add a few more quest rooms. We could add two additional rooms downstairs for the full-time help so they can be here around the clock. What do you think?"

"With the money we're making, I don't see why not."

"When you're finished with the muffin, "Debbie said with a grin Bob did not expect, "please set the table. The first shift of five families will eat in thirty minutes. That's ten adults and seven children."

"Are the Barnetts and their triplets part of the first group?"

"Afraid so. Let's hope Eugene doesn't eat his worth in weight. Or you'll be plunging the toilet in The Roadhouse Blues again tomorrow."

"Oh yeah, we definitely need help." Bob finished writing his ad for two full time summer helpers on Craigslist. He hit the Enter key with gusto. "With any luck, we'll hire someone before good ol' Eugene leaves."

Chapter 20   One Less Cat

It was Monday morning, the last day of Memorial Weekend. Bob's alarm on his cell phone played a recording of a rooster crowing. Without opening his eyes, he reached over to the night stand and turned it off.

He plopped his head back on his pillow, still exhausted, then opened his eyes and stared at the out the bedroom window. The morning sun would break over the eastern horizon in less than an hour.

Every muscle in his body ached. To his left, Debbie breathed in a soft cadence. She had failed to heed the belligerent barnyard fowl.

Bob knew Debbie worked harder than he had, and wanted nothing more than to let her sleep. Five o'clock in the morning. He shook his head. They had gotten less than four hours rest.

Their work was far from over. Debbie's focus was on keeping the kitchen clean and organized. Her injured hand prevented her from doing half of what she was capable of accomplishing.

There would be a turnover of guests today. That meant changing the sheets and towels from all ten guest rooms, then washing the dirty laundry, drying, folding, and putting them away in the upstairs pantry. Luggage to carry out to the departing cars. More luggage to bring in from the new arrivals. A breakfast and a dinner to cook and the cleanup that followed.

Bob shook Debbie. She muffled a snort as she woke. "What ... what time is it?"

"Five in the morning."

"So much to do," she mumbled as she pulled off the covers, a half dozen sleeping cats jumping to the floor then making their way to the cat beds lining the wall. "Ugh. I haven't even stood up and I need a day off."

Bob never imagined how hard and strenuous it would be to run a bed and breakfast. They both got out of bed, backs sore, shoulders hunched. "All I want to do is watch the last of our guests leave, then take a long nap."

Debbie looked in the mirror and stuck out her tongue. "Blech. I look awful," she said as she tried to fix her shoulder length blonde bob with her fingers. Bob wrapped his arms around her slender waist. He grinned at Debbie in the mirror. "You look pretty darn good from where I stand."

Debbie turned. "Thanks, lover boy. Tempting. But I have work to do. The afternoon will bring new guests. All ten rooms will be filled again. And I'll have to cook what the newspapers, websites, and blogs promised will be my biggest and grandest meal; a turkey dinner that will rival Cornwell's Turkeyville."

Debbie let out a flap of air through her lips. Bob tried not to cringe at her morning breath. He smiled weakly, but didn't think he was convincing.

"What in the heck was I thinking, letting them write that? I sorely regret that now. How's the ad in Craigslist coming?"

"I've gotten a few responses and set up interviews beginning this afternoon. The first is Raymond Hettinger. He's twenty-seven years old and a local handyman. Claims he can fix anything. Second is Maria

153

Gonzalez who would help you. She's twenty-two and a medical student at Western Michigan University looking for a summer job. At this rate, I'll probably hire them out of necessity before the day is over."

"At least the Barnetts will be gone. Hopefully their toilet isn't blown apart."

Bob helped Debbie make breakfast for both shifts. But time flew by too fast and the guests needed their luggage brought down to their cars. The dishes, piled high and dirty in the sinks, would have to wait.

Bob and Debbie donned their best smiles and hoped they didn't look as bad as they felt. One by one the guests left. He did feel good there were no complaints. The weekend, as demanding as it was, had been a tremendous success.

Bob shook the hands of a couple leaving for home in nearby Battle Creek. "Thank you again for visiting Murcat Manor."

"I hope to see you back again soon," Debbie said with a genuine smile. "Check our website for available listings. We're open all year."

"Thank you," the wife beamed. "I can't tell you how much this weekend away from the kids has helped us. We really needed this three day weekend alone."

Debbie nudged Bob and grinned.

Bob wasn't merely happy with the money coming in. He was thankful he and Debbie were able to make people happy. Couples getting away from a stressful life were taking a weekend to reconnect. He saw this venture in a new light. It wasn't just himself benefiting. He was helping make a difference in other people's lives.

Another couple stepped off the porch and into the driveway. Patrick and Marian Allen was it? A young man and woman on their honeymoon. They stayed in their room the entire three days, emerging only to eat.

"The Love Machine was amazing," Patrick said, his wife hugging his waist tight and smiling brightly. "We'll have to book this room again soon."

"We'd love to have you back," Debbie said. "Check our website for available days."

Bob noticed a handful of cats emerge, now that the Barnetts and their red headed triplets of terror had finally left. He'd wondered if the cats might have run off the property, never to return. Instead, the felines huddled and purred around his legs.

"Oh, isn't that just darling," Marian said. "These cats love you so much."

Bob's eyes revolved in a three-sixty.

She bent over and picked one up, uncurling it off Bob's lower leg. "Oh, this one is just such a cutie. I'm instantly in love." She looked to her husband. "Can we keep it?"

Patrick Allen saw the pleasure in his wife's face as she hugged the cat and wasted no time. "Say Bob, just how many cats do you have?"

"Too many, trust me."

Marian held Rebecca tight as the cat tried in vain to escape. "Wow. This one sure is warm to the touch. It's almost like she's on fire on the inside. I guess that means extra loving. Oh, she's so adorable."

She looked at Bob with a pouty face, her lower lip sticking out. "Can we have him? Please?"

Before Debbie could say no, Bob blurted out, "Yes. Of course you can. And it's a her. Take her home with you. Please."

"Oh, thank you very much. We don't have kids yet, although we sure put in the effort this weekend to get a running start."

She looked at the collar charm. "Rebecca. I like that. I have a niece named Rebecca. I think she'll work out just fine."

"Don't forget to have her spayed," Bob said. "You don't want thirteen cats like we have."

As Bob said this, his head started to feel hot. He thought the cat glared at him. There were brief thoughts of revenge. For the first time in his life, Bob thought of seeking retribution for any and all frustrations on someone else. But the quick thinker he was, Bob realized this wasn't his revenge. It was someone else's. Rebecca locked eyes with Bob and hissed loud.

But that of course, was nonsense. Rebecca was just a cat. Bob shook his head clear and waved to the Allens as they got in their car.

"Thank you. Hope to see you again. Without the cat."

Chapter 21   Burning Down The House

Emily lay on the one of the two couches in the living room, soaking up the sun's rays beaming through the bay windows. Annie and Jacqueline took up the other cushions. Through her droopy eyes she saw the other cats lying together in their usual groups on various pieces of furniture. Scarlett, Angel, and Esther each took a cushion on the second sofa facing the fireplace. Isabella, Rachel, and Madelyn commandeered three of the oversized sitting chairs. Chloe, Midnight, and Helen found a place on the ottomans.

Emily dozed off into what she hoped would be a peaceful slumber. Minutes into her morning nap she faded back four hundred years into the dark forests on the outskirts of Boston. It was midnight. She was gasping for air. Her legs ached as she ran faster than she ever could imagine.

Sarah, where are you?

"Emily, wake up."

The ground rumbled as three raging demons rode dragon-like beasts and descended upon her. There was nowhere to hide. To her left and to her right, her friends were cut down by the terrifying monsters.

Sarah, please run harder.

"Emily, open your eyes. Now."

Up ahead was their city of refuge. She had to make it. But she sensed her impending death. A hatchet hurling through the air end over end. Her beloved sister pushing her out of the way. Sarah's eyes frozen wide open as she joined her fallen kindred in the muddied trail.

"Emily."

The voice echoed in her head. Emily awoke with a snap.

"You were having another nightmare," Midnight said.

The other cats, minus her best friend Rebecca, lifted their sleepy heads and glared at her.

"I'm sorry," her cousin Chloe said as she jumped up on the sofa and joined her. "I know you miss your sister, and my cousin, Sarah. But you need to understand it wasn't your fault. You did the best you could to save her. It's been four hundred years. Time to move on from that evening. The rest of us have."

Emily took a long, strenuous stretch. "I know. I'm trying. And thanks for waking me up. I just don't know what else to do. That night haunts my sleep."

"Nothing a little mischief won't cure," Midnight said. "Come on, let's go and find some trouble to get into. Remember the last time we burned this place to the ground? Rebecca was standing right about here when she started the first fire. She blocked the front door with a tremendous blaze so no one could escape. Helen locked all the windows and the back door. We can do it again."

Midnight stood in the center of the living room floor and started walking in a circle. She mimicked Rebecca and gradually picked up her speed until she was in a steady trot.

"This is how Rebecca did her thing. Just like in the barn in Boston. And the Turner house. And the Amish property before that. She'd run around in a circle until a fire started in the center, then she'd project the flames up and out to start multiple fires and blocking the exits."

"No," Emily fired back. "Absolutely not. Stop right now. We need to keep a low profile here. Good ol' boring Bob and this bed and breakfast is the perfect setting for us."

"How about the neighbors," Scarlett countered. "We can perform our craft at night."

"Hey, that's a great idea," Isabella said. "They'll never know what happened."

The other cats nodded in agreement.

"Rebecca's not here," Emily said. "We can't start any fires."

"I can cause inanimate objects with dormant energy to explode," Esther said. "Bet I can start a fire. I'll focus on a car's gas tank."

"What about the new hired help," Midnight said. "Raymond and Maria. Bob just hired them. It's their first day. Those two have no idea what they just walked into. I say let's kill them."

"No. Just stop it, okay? No more trouble. No more mischief. No more fires. And no more murders."

The silence from the cats gave way to laughter from the kitchen. Debbie was serving the second shift breakfast. Five families. Ten adults. Three children.

"I really hate kids now," Jacqueline said as she walked to the large arch that led to the kitchen and peered in.

"The Barnett triplets were the worse," Chloe said. "The ones here aren't so bad. But that freckled faced girl at the end of the table pulled my tail again last night. I almost lost it and wanted to levitate her right out her second story bedroom window."

"I considered speeding up the synaptic transmissions in her brain receptors to the point she'd take in every piece of information her five senses detected." Annie said. "Give the little brat a case of sensory overload that would drive her and her parents crazy."

"Wow. Look at you," Helen said. "You sound like a college professor."

"We can thank Madelyn for that," Annie said. "She's the one researching and teaching us the latest and greatest in the scientific and medical fields. We're learning how to better understand our powers and use them far more efficiently."

"She's helped explain what I can do," Rachel said. "I've never understood how I can leave my body and travel around."

"Now we know," Madelyn said. "The term is astral projection. Some call it an out of body experience. As long as you leave your physical body in a safe place where people won't find it and think you're dead, you'll always have a place to come back to. Remember during our fourth life when you separated and the Amish family found your body and buried it in the backyard?"

Rachel shuddered at the thought. "Sure do. With no way to get back, I floated off to the Netherworld. I had to wait for you all to join me until we could come back in our fifth lives at the Turner place."

"Too bad Rebecca's not here," Scarlett said. "She could catch that kid's pony tails on fire."

"I can short circuit the thoughts of that brother and sister," Helen said. "Make them think they're each other. And if we see those Barnett triplets here again, I'll rewire their brains so every month they'll think they're one of the other brothers. Their parents will never be able to tell which one is which ever again."

"We all know we can't do things like that," Emily said. "And thanks to all of you for showing constraint. We'll just have to do our best to stay out of the way of children."

Chloe started to nod off. "Okay, *Mom*."

"Maybe we need lookouts while the rest of us sleep," Annie said. "Like a sentry."

"Great idea," Chloe said through a yawn. "I second that motion."

"And since you mentioned it," Esther said, laying her sleepy head on her folded paws, "you get the first shift. All in favor ..."

The remaining cats all said, "Aye," in unison.

"Fine," Annie said as she stood and stretched. She walked over to the large arched door leading into the kitchen. "Those kids are such brats. Isabella, maybe you could implant a thought in the parents' minds to smack some sense into them."

"Better yet," Scarlett said. "Plant the thought into one of the adults to slap another person's kid. That'll start a fight between families at the table."

"Great idea. I can do that."

"*Isabella?*" Emily glared at her, "Don't you *dare*."

"But it's so boring here. There's no excitement, unless you count the kids chasing us and pulling our tails."

Emily knew she needed a diversion. "Madelyn, the Battle Creek newspaper is on the coffee table. Anything interesting on the front page?"

Madelyn jumped up on the low table in front of the couch. Emily saw her gasp.

"What is it?"

The cat used her paw to read back and forth and down the column of the lead story. "You won't believe this. Remember the couple who took Rebecca home with them?"

Emily knew this could not be good. She joined Madelyn, who pointed at a large picture of the remnants of a house, still smoldering from a fire.

"Damn it. Rebecca's at it again."

The other cats jumped up on the table and gathered around the newspaper. Front and center was a picture of Patrick and Marian Allen.

"Madelyn, what's the story say? You're the only one that can read worth a darn."

"A young couple from Battle Creek died yesterday while they slept when their house caught on fire. By the time fire trucks arrived, the entire structure was engulfed in flames. The cause of the fire is under investigation."

Emily shook her head. "I shouldn't be surprised. Out of all the cats the Allens could have chosen, they had to take Rebecca. She has the shortest temper. And of course, she can start a fire in dozens of ways."

"What did you expect?" Midnight said.

"I expect everyone to follow my orders."

"Well, maybe you should broaden your horizons. The rest of us are getting real tired restraining what comes natural to us. Of course, living inside a cat's body helps take on their personality traits as well. And there's nothing we can do about that. We're trapped inside cats, Emily. Do you understand? You need to. Otherwise, you may soon have a mutiny on your hands."

Chapter 22   Unity or Mutiny

The word mutiny stayed in Emily's mind. To appease her followers' boredom, she allowed a little mischief when the guests at Murcat Manor went to sleep. The cats split up into their usual groups of three. Scarlett, along with Angel and Esther, hid the left shoes of all the families at the bed and breakfast in the kitchen pantry.

Chloe, Midnight, and Helen switched credit card charges with the wild biker couple in Roadhouse Blues and the Amish couple the Victorian Room. The latter's wife would erroneously see her husband frequented strip bars on their next statement.

Isabella, and Rachel, and Madelyn caused the wife in the Frontiersman Room to believe the moose head and other animal heads on the wall would talk to her just as she dozed off. She screamed every time, waking everyone in Murcat Manor.

It had been a busy night for all, guests and cats. Emily waited for her following to fall asleep across the assorted pieces of living room furniture before allowing herself to doze off.

The sun broke through the darkness and a new day had begun. Bob and Debbie, along with the two new summer employees, Raymond Hettinger and Maria Rodriguez, were in the kitchen. Emily went to her favorite spot on the living room sofa. Bob had left the front door open, letting a cool morning breeze in.

Slumber overtook her. Her eyelids sagged. A yawn escaped as she stretched her arms and legs. Drifting between consciousness and sleep, she envisioned a tired and ragged dark gray cat with a blend of white stripes across its back and belly arriving at the front door. She didn't need to confirm if this was a dream or reality. Rebecca had found her way home.

Emily shook the sleep from her head and jumped onto the floor, then sauntered to the screen door. On the other side sat Rebecca, licking her paws, as if this were just another boring morning with the Stevens.

Emily stared at her second in command. She would hold the glare for as long as it took. After a few minutes, she could see in Rebecca's eyes she was ready to submit to her authority as leader. Emily surmised Rebecca was starving, and thus her willingness to relent.

"Well, aren't you going to open the door for me?"

Emily summoned Chloe and Helen. "Wake up. I need you to open the screen door and let our prodigal sister in."

Rebecca stopped cleaning her dirty, matted fur. "Why don't you open the door," she asked calmly. "You assume all the individual powers we possess."

"Because I'm mad as hell at you for starting a fire and killing that young couple. I told you, no more killing. Remember?"

"Oh, so you heard."

"It was on the front page of the papers, news channels, and local websites. And Madelyn can read."

"So what. Just let me in. We're a sisterhood. Remember?"

"That's not going to work on me. I want to refuse you to come back. But I know if I turn you away, the others will rebel against me."

"Such a drama queen. Look, I'm your best friend, remember? Four hundred years in the making? You won't leave me out. Oh, here are Helen and Chloe. Never mind."

It was an insignificant effort for Helen to reverse the latch. Chloe, with a lazy wave of her paw, caused the screen door to swing open.

Rebecca strolled in with her tail high in the air, an aura of entitlement emanating from her. She walked in front of Emily and allowed her tail to rub against her face as she passed, her nose lifted up.

Emily swatted the intrusive tail away. "That is so disrespectful."

"What do you expect? I'm a cat."

Emily smoldered with anger. She sent out the communication to the sisterhood. "Get up. Everyone. Rebecca's back and we need an emergency meeting in the basement. Now."

Emily led Rebecca, Chloe, and Helen into the kitchen where Bob was going over bills. Rebecca jumped up on the table and leisurely walked across his work. She stepped onto the keyboard of his laptop, shuffled documents with her paws, then jumped back on the floor.

Bob did a double take. "What the …"

The rest of the cats ran into the kitchen and mimicked Rebecca, jumping onto the table and trotting across Bob's laptop and papers, then followed Emily as she ran toward the basement.

"What's wrong," Debbie asked, looking over her shoulder as she unloaded three dishwashers from last night's dinner.

"It's those frickin' crazy cats again. Not sure what they're all up to. But they're all running through the kitchen and into the basement like they're being herded. And hey—isn't that Rebecca?"

Debbie poured two cups of coffee. "It is. Awww. It looks like she missed her family and found her way back."

Bob scratched his head. "Incredible. But how?"

Debbie laughed. "Just remember what Grandma Erma said. They're cats. They do what they want, when they want."

"Well, maybe that'll explain why we found all those left shoes in the pantry this morning." Bob looked at the small mountain of shoes, slippers, and sandals he'd piled in the center of the table, waiting for the guest to come down for breakfast and claim the footwear.

"Or how those large cans of fruit cocktail end up on the floor every time I go down in the basement," Debbie said. "Maybe we should do ourselves a favor, and try not to make sense of their actions."

Emily snickered at Debbie's comment and passed through the animal door and down the stairs. She took her usual position on the shelf of canned foods overlooking the new handyman's workbench. Once again, with a wave of her paw, the large cans of fruit cocktail pocked with dents from dozens of falls fell over and rolled off onto the cement floor in a clanking cacophony.

She watched as the other eleven cats welcomed Rebecca back with squeals and hugs, as best they could inside cat bodies. She looked a mess, but the others helped groom and lick dirt off her.

"Okay, listen up. Quiet everybody."

Rebecca emerged from the group hug. "No, Emily, You listen. I want to tell the sisterhood what happened. And I think they want to hear what I have to say."

"Rebecca. You're my best friend. I love you. But you need to understand we can't do this again. We'll all die a horrible death. Just like our previous five lives. Then we'll have to wait in the dark cold Netherworld for the right time to emerge into the next life. It's near impossible to find a litter of thirteen healthy female cats. That can take years or decades. And after this life is over, we only have three more. Don't screw it up for the rest of us."

Rebecca stood her ground. "This is what we do. It's who we are. Try as you might, Emily, you can't deny it."

"Stop it, Rebecca."

"No. You need to stop and reflect on our past. You can't change who we are. Or what we do. We're witches. And we're trapped in the bodies of cats. That's a double threat. We've taken on both personas. This doesn't leave much room to do anything else, now does it?"

Emily looked for support, but found none. The other cats remained on the workbench with Rebecca.

"Look, I understand how you feel. How all of you feel."

"But do you understand your own feelings?"

"Rebecca's right," Annie said. "Emily, you're having nightmares of that night in Boston. Your sister. Our sister. Sarah. She was our friend, too."

Emily's shoulders drooped. "My mother trusted in me for Sarah's care and protection. And I failed."

"But that's just it," Rebecca said. "We've all moved on. Except you. Now either you move on with us, or we'll have to elect another leader."

"Listen to me," Chloe said. "I'm your cousin. You can trust me when I say we're not trying to usurp your authority. We respect your leadership. You saved us all that night back in Boston. You are the strongest, most gifted of us all. And we want to follow you. But we all have to be in agreement. Lead us as a democracy, where we get a vote; not a dictatorship where you make all the rules."

Emily paused to consider. What they were saying was not at all unreasonable. She sighed, shook her head. "I'm trying. But it's so hard to get Sarah out of my head. Even after four hundred years. I'm not sure if I can do this."

Chloe jumped up on the shelf next to Emily. "Then change your strategy. Instead of guilt, funnel your energies through revenge."

"But that's always been your tactics. Not mine."

"And it's worked. That's how we keep our sanity. We don't have nightmares like you."

"Remember, Sarah," Rebecca said. "Your blood sister, she gave her life so that you could live. I beg of you. Don't let her die in vain. I'm your best friend. You can trust me. Avenge her death. The only way we can do this is by doing what comes natural. That's why we had to kill DeShawn Hill and I torched that couple from Battle Creek. And that's why more people need to die."

"We're witches—evil witches," Chloe said. "Sure, we didn't start out this way. We just wanted to be left alone. It's not our fault we were born with these abilities and people want to kill us for it. But six lives over four centuries, and living inside the body of cats, this is what we've evolved into —and you can't fight fate."

The other cats formed an arc behind Rebecca, their long tails swaying back and forth in synchronized rhythm to show support. Emily, now enraged with the thoughts of their harrowing escape centuries ago and her younger sister's death, capitulated.

She saw no other way to keep her sanity, or to prevent an open rebellion from the other cats. This will certainly come to an ugly conclusion, Emily knew, and will eventually cost another of their precious few remaining lives. But damn it, her sisters were right.

Emily sat up straight, jutted her chin, and struck the shelf with a slap of her tail. She puffed her chest like a general about to deliver the attack orders to his troops, and set the inevitable in motion.

Her gathering nodded in approval.

"Rachel, hide behind those boxes of cleaning supplies and prepare to teleport yourself," Emily ordered. "Your body will be safe there. I want you to follow the guests. Gather any intelligence you can find. Ten rooms. Thirty three people including adults and children. There must be someone we can kill this weekend."

Chapter 23   Choking or Heart Attack

One thing about being a cat, Emily thought, is that cats are patient. They can wait, stay cool until just the right moment to pounce. Strategizing, observing, and discerning the prey's movements, habits, strengths and weaknesses. It's all there to observe and use to their advantage if they have the patience of a true predator—and that's what cats are. This was definitely one inherited feline attribute Emily appreciated.

The cats lounged around the living room basking in the sunbeams. They studied each couple and family, looking for strengths and weaknesses to exploit. A full week had gone by as guests came and went. They had to wait for the perfect victim. And now, Rachel had finally found their target.

"Paul Knudson," the astral projectionist said. "Fifty-two years old. He's large, intimidating, and a total jackass. His wife is Kathleen. Not sure why she married him. She's beautiful and could have done a lot better."

"What else?"

"He has high blood pressure and hardened arteries. A smoker and heavy drinker. Overweight. He's one blow up from a heart attack. Oh, this is too easy."

"I can hear him shouting at the breakfast table," Emily said. "He's insulting everybody."

"Last night he completely humiliated his wife while eating dinner. I hid my body in the basement for protection, then followed him to the Roadhouse Blues."

"What is it with that room," Emily asked. "Sure seems to attract the undesirables."

"Maybe it's the theme," Rachel said. "Anyway, he was drunk as a funky skunk. He roughed up his wife a bit. She's wearing makeup to cover the bruises."

"Thank you, Rachel. You did great. We can do this right now in front of everyone."

Emily led the cats in a slow and confident stride closer to the kitchen.

"Look at him eating like that," Annie said. "What a pig. Talking with his mouth all full. Spittle-laden food spraying in every direction." She shook all over. "Disgusting."

"This is one time I feel sorry for Bob," Scarlett said. "He's trying to keep the guy in check. But Knudson outweighs him by a hundred pounds and is as belligerent as an angry bull elephant. He looks extremely hung over, too."

"Hey Susan, can't you do anything right," Knudson bellowed to his wife.

"Why don't you take it easy," Debbie said. "This is my house. And you never speak to a woman like that. Especially your wife."

Knudson finished wiping his hands with his cloth napkin and spread his hands wide. "And just what'n the hell're you gonna to do about it? Wait, I know. Feed me more of your slop? I'd prob'ly choke on it. Or it'll give me a damn heart attack."

171

"Hey—that's a great idea," Emily said, trying to snap her fingers, then realizing she didn't have any. She looked to Helen. "He must have three breakfasts in his big fat belly. Do your thing."

Helen pranced into the kitchen, head held high. "Choking? Or heart attack?"

"You choose," Emily said.

"With pleasure."

Helen, who caused solids, fluids, and energy to flow in reverse or stop altogether, pulled up short of the table and glared at the mountain of a man, just as Bob rose from his chair and growled at him.

"That's it. You don't speak to my wife like that."

Scarlett nudged Emily with a wink. "Got to give it to Boring Bob. He does have guts."

Emily peeked through the archway. The other eleven jostled for a position alongside her to witness Helen and her craft.

Knudson stood, sending his chair back across the kitchen floor. Six feet four inches and two hundred seventy pounds of mass and grizzle loomed over Bob, scrambled eggs still in his mouth, jabbering away. Knudson's chair came flying back and hit him behind his knees, almost causing him to fall over backward.

"Nice *touch*, Chloe."

"Why, thank you," she said with a pleased purr.

The other guests, gasped and shrieked at the sight of the chair slamming into Knudson as if it had a will of its own, darted from their chairs and dashed into the living room like a stampede of frightened rodents. Emily moved just in time from being trampled under a dozen feet. The exodus was filled with cats screeching as many had their tails stepped on.

Convinced now only Bob, Debbie, Raymond, Maria, Paul Knudson and his wife were left inside the kitchen, Emily peeked back in, as did the other cats. Bob's shirt was a ball of cloth in Knudson's oversized fists, which held Bob's feet dangling a foot off the ground. Debbie was on Knudson's back, her legs wrapped around his chest, clawing and punching the hulk trying to break his grip off Bob.

"Oh, this is just too rich," Knudson said, his head in an appreciative sway, "I'm thoroughly enjoying this. What a great way to start the day. Now I'm going to ..."

Kundson's eyes bulged. They looked like they were about to explode out of his head. His face turned crimson. He dropped Bob, grabbed for his throat, and motioned with his hands something was terribly wrong.

Debbie jumped off his back and Raymond and Maria pulled her and Bob out of harm's way. Knudson flailed about in a panic, tossing dishes and water glasses around the kitchen, breaking them in a bizarre display of macabre, random futility.

Bob and Debbie continued to back-step. Knudson dropped to his knees and grasped his hands like he was praying. He pointed to his neck, then stood and clutched his chest. Eyes enlarged to beyond the breaking point, with blood oozing out and down from their sockets. Face flushed beet red, he froze for a moment, then dropped onto the kitchen table, face first into a large bowl of oatmeal. He slid, inching backward, until he fell on his back, his head smacking against the wooden floor with a hideous thump.

Emily laughed inside as Helen entered the living room.

"Well, which one was it?" she said, "Choking? Or heart attack?"

Helen purred as she turned and strutted for the best sitting spot in the sunlight streaming in through the windows. She hunched a shoulder, brought a paw to her mouth and blew on it like a gunslinger cooling off his six-shooter.

"Both."

Chapter 24   Vacating Guests

Bob could not think of a worse position to be in. All their guests were vacating Murcat Manor and demanding a refund—which he would have to give them. It was mid-June and news of a second death at the bed and breakfast could ruin reservations for the rest of the summer. The first of many bills, including the mortgage totaling twenty-five thousand dollars, would be due in less than two weeks.

He sat next to Debbie at the kitchen table. She looked numb, staring out the kitchen bay window as she sipped a glass of ice water. He was worried for her. The violent death of DeShawn Hill still loomed over them. They'd been so busy preparing to open Murcat Manor and hosting the first wave of guests, they had not had time to properly mourn Hill's passing. After talking with him almost every day for nine months, the general contractor had become like family.

But this second death happened in her kitchen—Debbie's domain. This was her *home* and the one place where she thrived. Everything she did originated from here. He could see her soul was damaged from the fight and death of Paul Knudson.

But these weren't the worse of their problems.

Bob looked at the yellow police tape wrapped throughout the kitchen. A corpse lay on its back a few feet from him. The Battle Creek coroner was lifting the red and white checkered tablecloth Bob had tossed over the dead body to examine the head. Police officers took pictures of the kitchen. Broken plates and glasses littered the floor. Chairs were tipped over and strewn about.

And things only got worse.

Across the large oak table sat Detectives Darrowby and Kowalski. Staring. Waiting for Bob to say something. He looked to Debbie, who tried to formulate her thoughts, but could only manage a shrug.

Darrowby, tapping his pen on the table, finally broke the ice. "Two deaths in Murcat Manor. One in May. One in June. You're averaging one a month."

Bob squeezed his eyes shut and took a long deep breath to calm himself. Debbie rubbed between his shoulders for support. "Look. I know DeShawn Hill was a close friend of yours. And I'm sorry he's gone."

"Are you?"

Bob opened his eyes. All he could see was a pompous, misguided, arrogant twit whose mission was to make his and Debbie's life miserable. Blood rushed to his head, making him dizzy. Darrowby had only been inside a few minutes, and Bob was allowing the detective to get the upper hand.

Time to take a few slow breaths. Calm down. The man's a professional. A professional asshole, that is. Can't let him to get the better of us.

"Tell us once again. What exactly happened here?" Darrowby looked around. "There are shattered dishes and glasses everywhere. Looks like one helluva fight occurred."

Bob sighed. "It was self-defense. Knudson had serious anger management problems. I'm sure you can dig something up on him."

"Wrong," Kowalski said, scrolling through his iPad. "Matter of fact, he had no police record. Looks like he paid his taxes on time. Awww ... look here. He adopted a rescue puppy a few years ago."

"Now isn't that special," Darrowby said. "Looks like Paul Knudson was just a large misunderstood teddy bear. You ask me, I'd say he was an upstanding citizen."

Blood pressure rising. Shortness of breath. The urge to throw Darrowby out of his house. Bob needed to control his rage. He took another slow breath and stood.

"Listen to me." He pointed at Knudson, pausing to keep his emotions in check. "This guy was the most belligerent, obnoxious numbskull I've ever met."

Darrowby stood to meet him. "Last time I checked, being obnoxious isn't against the law."

"You have to admit," Kowalski added, his big, thick, flat head pivoting this way and that on his shoulders. "Things do look suspicious. That's why we're not closing the DeShawn Hill case."

Bob threw his arms in the air. "Oh, that's just great. I suppose you're not going to close this case, too."

"Not until we resolve what happened to Hill. As far as we're concerned, we see a pattern forming."

Bob couldn't believe what he was hearing. "Pattern? What pattern?"

"A pattern of dead people on your property. And not just dead. These two men have died violently."

Bob pointed at Knudson. "And I suppose calling the coroner out here rather than paramedics and transporting the body to their office only makes your visit more dramatic."

Darrowby smirked. "No, Mr. Stevens. You're being paranoid. The coroner only comes out directly if the death is unexpected."

Bob was really starting to hate Darrowby and the way he twisted his words.

"You can translate that as suspicious," Kowalski said.

Bob looked back and forth at the Numbskull Duo. There's no good cop bad cop routine with these two guys. They're both assholes.

Darrowby looked over to the coroner. "How's it going, Jimmy?"

"Almost finished. We've examined and documented the scene and the body of the deceased."

"Looks like you're finishing recording evidence."

"Evidence?" Bob said, looking round the kitchen. "Since when is any of this evidence?"

Darrowby ignored Bob's comment. "I'll have one of my men safeguard Knudson's personal effects."

"Is this really necessary?" Bob said. "I don't want a police officer standing guard outside the Roadhouse Blues bedroom door. We have more guests coming in."

Debbie interjected. "Kathleen Knudson is here. I'm sure the personal effects will be safe with her. And she can stay here for as long as she wants for no cost."

Bob wrapped his arm around Debbie for support. He knew Darrowby was fuming because he and Debbie were smart enough to challenge his intimidation tactics.

"Jimmy, can you perform an autopsy today," Darrowby asked as the coroner stood from his kneeling position.

"Probably be tomorrow. But you can be sure I'll determine the cause of, as well as the manner and time of death."

"How long do you think it'll take?" Darrowby said, grinning at Bob as if he was still in control. "A week? Maybe less?"

"Oh, I'd say about two weeks at the most."

Darrowby's head spun around to the coroner. "That it? Can't do it sooner?"

"'Fraid not. I'll do the best I can. But we're looking at ten to fourteen days for the results to come back."

The paramedics placed Knudson in a black body bag, zipped it, and set him on a stretcher. Debbie buried her head into Bob's shoulder and tried not to cry. Her chest heaved regardless.

They raised the stretcher and wheeled it out of the kitchen. The sound of the metal wheels rolling over the travertine tile in the living room echoed through the house. The police officers had concluded their work and followed the coroner out the front door.

The now silent kitchen framed the glaring eyes of Darrowby. Bob suddenly missed the noise and controlled chaos of the police investigation. What bothered him most was the constant non-blinking stare of the detective. He knew this was part of his strategy; get him to say something to break the awkward silence, anything that would incriminate himself. Or Debbie. The first person to speak lost.

He felt Debbie wrap her arms righter around his waist. They knew each other well. She sensed the same thing about Darrowby. Together, they would stare him down.

Seconds passed. Then a minute. Darrowby had one of the best poker faces Bob had seen. But he had disrespected Debbie in both visits. First Hill and now Knudson. This was motivation to beat Darrowby at his own game.

After two minutes, Kowalski stood and broke the stalemate. Bob knew Turret Head wanted to save Darrowby's ass from blinking first.

I win this small battle.

"I think we're through here," Kowalski said. "We'll have the coroner's report soon enough."

Darrowby set his pen in his pocket. "Two deaths in two months, Mr. Stevens. You have to admit. This isn't normal. In my twenty years on the force, this is rare. And I'm not a stupid man. So trust me when I say, this isn't over."

"Are you treating these as homicides?"

"No. Not yet anyway. Let's see what the coroner's report tells us. We'll go from there. Until then, try not to let anyone else die under your watch at Murcat Manor."

Chapter 25   Spiritual Insight

Bob sat again at the kitchen table, his heart hitting rock bottom as he hit *Enter* on his keyboard, sending the refund for Kathleen Knudson. An invoice printed and he passed it to her while Debbie handed her a tissue to wipe her eyes.

"Mrs. Knudson, I'm so sorry."

The grieving widow held her palm up, cutting Debbie off. "No, you're not sorry. If you were, you never would have provoked my husband. You knew he had a bad temper."

Bob was incredulous. He could barely sputter out the words. "What? He attacked me. You were there."

Kathleen wiped another tear and looked at the floor. "If you'd just left him alone, he'd still be here with me."

Bob could see her tears and the cloth had wiped away much of her makeup and mascara, revealing recent bruises on her face and a black eye. "I ... I just don't understand."

"I know what you're thinking. But Paul was all I had. Now he's gone and I'm all alone. I have nowhere to go."

Debbie waved Bob off before he could say anything else. She helped Kathleen to the front porch for fresh air. Bob sat still and tried to shake off the disbelief of what just happened. Murcat Manor was empty, except for the summer help Raymond Hettinger and Maria Gonzalez and the last couple standing before him. And thirteen lazy cats lounging in the living room. The house was ghostly quiet.

He looked up at the young newlyweds. They were so full of hope and promise. What were their names again? He looked at the invoice. Right. Robert and Marissa Anderson. They stayed in the Love Machine.

"We're so sorry," Marissa said. "You have such a lovely place. And I'm sure you'll do very well."

Robert stuck his hand out for their invoice. "But you have to understand, we're on our honeymoon. We don't need this kind of drama."

"Where are you going," Debbie asked as she returned to the kitchen.

"We've booked a hotel in Ann Arbor. We wish you well."

Bob and Debbie walked the Andersons to the front door. Raymond had loaded their luggage in the trunk of their Ford Focus.

Bob noticed a man and a woman standing against a Cadillac Escalade parked alongside Oak Hill Road. He recognized them as their neighbors on the west side of the property line, divided by the long row of elm trees.

Debbie held his hand. "Look honey," she said with a hint of hesitance. "It's the Bradys. I wonder what they want."

Bob was suspicious. "Strange. They've never come to visit."

"Yeah. They've avoided us like we're infected with Ebola. They didn't answer the door when we visited, and clearly they were home."

Bob snickered. "I remember. They turned off the lights. As if we wouldn't notice they were on when we stepped up onto their porch."

"They're just staring at us. What do you suppose they want?"

"Not sure." Bob waved goodbye to their last guests as they pulled out of the gravel driveway and drove east toward Ann Arbor. The Bradys approached.

"Friend or foe?"

"Well, since they're not carrying shotguns or torches, I'm guessing friend. I hope."

Debbie nudged Bob. "Stop it. Remember, we're not in the boonies."

"Erm ... kinda think we are."

"Smile. Even if you don't mean it."

Bob forced a warm smile. It wasn't as difficult is he thought. He wondered if he could be a politician someday.

The Bradys were in their mid-fifties. Bob knew they had three kids who had families of their own in nearby towns. They wore jeans. But not like what he expected. They looked expensive, as did their shoes and hair. He wore a blue University of Michigan collared shirt. Bob had trouble discerning their facial expressions. Their professional yet old country appearance gave him confidence he would not be sacrificed to their corn gods. He held out his hand.

"Hello. You're the Bradys, right? I'm Bob Stevens. And this is my wife, Debbie."

"Pleased to meet you. I'm Eddie. This is my wife Alison."

Bob was relieved. The Bradys were not at all like what he thought his neighbors might be. Backwoods. Banjo music playing. Hosting a family reunion and the entire town shows up.

But then, all his neighbors up until now had avoided them. Maybe, they saw him in the same light he imagined them, as someone who was light years from what was considered the norm and couldn't be trusted.

"Mr. Stevens, I—"

"Please, call me Bob."

The Bradys retained their stoic looks. He needed to remove barriers and let them know he wanted to be friends.

"Okay. Bob. We see there was another death here."

Bob sighed deep. "Yeah. One of our guests choked on his breakfast. Or had a heart attack. Or both."

Eddie retained his unreadable face. "And your contractor died a couple—wait—just over a month ago."

Bob shuffled his feet, annoyed he was being questioned again. "That's right. Two deaths in two months."

"Both accidental," Debbie added.

"Is that so," Eddie said, eyeing Bob.

"Yes, that's so," he said, setting his jaw and his fists starting to clench. "Sheeesh. What is it with people around here? A couple accidental deaths and all of a sudden we're serial killers."

Alison shook her head. "Oh, these deaths weren't accidental."

Bob had had enough. First Darrowby. Now his next door neighbors. "Okay, it's been a long day. We're going inside. My head hurts. And we need to sleep."

"Now just hold on," Eddie said, reaching out and tugging on Bob. "We're not accusing you of anything. We just want to talk."

"Won't you come inside," Debbie said, snuggling up to Bob. "I'll make coffee. Or better yet, open a bottle of wine. Maybe two. Like hubby said, it's been a long day. And it's only noon."

Eddie held his hands up in a defensive posture. "No ma'am. No offense, we appreciate the offer. But we don't want to step foot in that house." He looked at his wife, then back to Bob and Debbie. "Fact of the matter is, your place is haunted."

Alison bobbed her head in agreement. "Cursed, actually. And this is as far as we dare to tread on this property. Respectfully."

Bob started to lead Debbie back inside. "Okay, let's go, honey. Looks like these local folk are wearing U of M shirts to make themselves look intelligent."

Eddie blocked Bob's path. "Now just a minute, young man. I'll have you know Alison and I are surgeons. We have our doctorates from the University of Michigan and are members of Mensa. So why don't you slow down a bit and listen to us."

Alison stepped forward. "Please, I know this sounds strange. But we'll be forward with you. This property is indeed cursed. It has been since the Turners owned it in the sixties. And the families before them."

"I don't believe in curses," Bob said as he started to turn and walk toward Murcat Manor.

"Please allow me to expound," Eddie continued. "You just had two deaths in two months. Doesn't that strike you as odd?"

Bob stopped. "Now you're starting to sound like Detective Darrowby and his hooligan partner Kowalski."

"And if you don't pay attention to what we have to say, they might connect you to their deaths. There are plenty of people who think they might have been murdered."

Bob flailed his arms in the air. "But we didn't do anything."

"You have to understand," Alison said. "In their eyes, this is statistically improbable. Yet it happened. So naturally, you both are suspects."

"Well, I can assure you we didn't kill anyone. We moved here to build a house, start a business, and raise a family. Not kill the guests who pay our bills."

185

"Which begs the question, why did you buy this property? The Turner place has been vacant since it burned to the ground almost fifty years ago."

Bob was caught off guard. The entire process had happened so fast. It took only twenty-four hours to find the property and secure Ross and Erma's backing. Thirty days later they owned the land and had hired an architect and general contractor.

"We both lost our jobs in Grand Rapids," Debbie said. "We came across this place. It was cheap. Bob actually had the vision of building ..."

"A vision?"

"Um, yeah," Bob said, feeling a bit embarrassed. "It was a brief but very clear vision of this bed and breakfast."

"A vision," Allison said. "And yet, you said you don't believe in curses."

"A vision is very different than a curse," Bob said. "My mind was probably making connections as a way to make a living and provide for a family. That's a perfectly logical explanation. But curses, they're a thing of folklore. Superstition."

"You can try to explain the two deaths away if you wish. But remember the previous farm house that sat on this same location?"

"The Turner property," Debbie said. "Our realtor told us it burned to the ground. As did the barn, which stood fifty yards away from the house. Twelve people died that night. There were no survivors."

"The causes of the fires were never known," Eddie said. "Don't you find that suspicious?"

Debbie shrugged her shoulders. "Houses burn down every day, more so in the past when there were no fire alarms and electrical codes were far less strict."

Bob remembered the story from the realtor who negotiated the deal. Fragments of the conversation came back. He could see Clark Hodgkins sitting on the other side of the desk asking if they believe in ghosts. He mentioned the locals thought the place was haunted. But since that initial meeting, Bob had not given it much thought.

"That's fourteen deaths, including the two here," Eddie said, and cocked an eyebrow up. "And an Amish family of seven people died when their farmhouse burned to the ground fifty years before the Turners. Most people around here had parents alive when the Turner place burned. My mom and dad owned the house we now live in." Eddie pointed to the western ridge of oak trees that divided their properties.

"They knew the people who lived here. The Turner place was actually a commune. It was a haven for Hippies. A bunch of freaks as my father called them. Anything went. Drugs. Free love. Mini-Woodstock weekends with bands playing rock and roll from mid-morning 'til three in the next morning. Young women going topless in the hot afternoons. And it was pretty well known they were into some kind of dark arts, too. To what degree, no one was quite sure. But, knowing all twelve souls died that night, it was probably something that ran pretty deep."

"Well," Debbie said. "Maybe the hippies had a ritual and started the fire, but were too stoned to leave."

Eddie lifted an eyebrow. "All twelve? Seven in the house and five in the barn? The fact not one person escaped is highly improbable."

Bob didn't know what to think. The Bradys were quite the story tellers. Normally he would dismiss their tale as an older couple spinning a yarn to try to scare younger people. But a total of twenty-one deaths? That number carried weight. His head felt like it had been sledge hammered.

"Do you have anything that can combat evil," Eddie asked.

187

Bob stumbled over his words. This topic was foreign to him.

Debbie stepped forward. "Well, we did have a family heirloom my grandmother gave us. It's a Celtic cross her grandfather made when arriving to America from Ireland. Every generation before me had placed it at the top of their house for good fortune. She gave it to us last summer."

Eddie looked at the front of Murcat Manor. "Where's the cross now?"

Bob shrugged. "Destroyed. It shattered in a hundred pieces when our contractor was placing it to the top of the house."

"That's when he fell," Debbie said.

"That's what your contractor was doing when he fell?" Alison gasped, taking a step back and covering her mouth. "He was placing your blessed family heirloom when he died?"

The Bradys' eyes were the size of saucers. Bob thought it was terror.

"We're going to go now," Eddie said. "Find a priest."

"It's a pleasure to meet you both," Alison said in a most charming but rushed manner.

Eddie turned his head as he took his wife's hand and led her down the driveway. "You both better be aware of your surroundings. Pay attention to what's going on around. Do not take anything for granted."

Bob shook his head as they walked back into the house. "That's an amazing story."

Debbie clutched his arm. "I'm officially creeped out now."

Bob held up his hand and started counting off on his fingers. "Two deaths. All of our guests have left. I had to refund their money. I don't know how this day could get any worse."

Bob heard rubber from tires pulling onto the gravel driveway. He looked out the front window. *Oh hell no* ... now he know how the day could get worse.

Ross and Erma were paying an unexpected visit. Bob squinted to see through the windshield. Erma did not look happy.

Chapter 26   All Is Not Lost

Bob filled his lungs to capacity and blew out, fluttering his lips. He slammed his eyes shut and cleared his head of curses, haunted houses, ghosts, and whispers of the dark arts. An upset Erma, who cosigned on their three and a half million dollar loan, trumped them all.

Debbie joined Bob at the bay window and peered over his shoulder. "It's Grandma and Grandpa. I wonder why they're here."

"You'd think they'd give us a courtesy call, first." Bob took Debbie's hand. "Let's find out."

Bob and Debbie stepped back out onto the front porch. Raymond joined them. Bob donned his newfound politician's smile. Raymond stepped out to the driveway, opened the passenger door for Erma, and helped her walk across the gravel.

"Thank you, Raymond," Erma said, glaring at Bob as if he should be helping her. "You're such a good boy."

"Grandpa. Grandma. It's great to see you," Debbie said, hugging Erma first then Ross, who as usual was laughing jovially. "What a pleasant surprise. What brings you to Murcat Manor?"

Erma looked up at the spindle where the family Celtic cross should be, watching guard over all who enter and leave the bed and breakfast. Her countenance dropped and she hung her head.

"Let's go inside," Ross said to Bob in a more serious tone. "We need to talk."

Erma walked past without saying a word. Bob knew she was more upset than ever. Normally she would never pass up the opportunity to take a verbal potshot at him.

Bob needed to take the lead. His battle with Darrowby was mentally and emotionally draining. And the episode with Eddie and Alison didn't help. But he couldn't let Erma dominate during this precarious time. He speed-walked to take the lead and was first in the front door.

Bob stopped at the kitchen archway. He could kick himself as he remembered too late the floor was littered with broken plates and glasses from Paul Knudson's rampage. Erma gasped and held her hands over her heart.

Ross comforted her. "There, there dear. Let's have a seat in the living room."

"I'll finish cleaning in here," Raymond said, squeezing by Bob.

Maria followed Raymond. "Have a seat, folks. I'll bring some lemonade."

Once everyone was seated around the glass coffee table, Ross folded his hands on his lap and cleared his throat. "Bob, Debbie, we'll get right to the point. We know there was another death here at Murcat Manor."

Bob looked at his watch. Darrowby and the coroner had left less than ten minutes ago. "How? Was it on the news?"

"No," Erma said, holding up her cell phone. "Not on TV or the radio, although I suspect it will be any minute now. We have a Google alert for

191

Murcat Manor. We receive instant text messages if news of this place hits the Internet."

"There was a blog post by one of your guests that left and asked for their money back. We drove right over fast as we could." Ross looked at his watch. "Only took us thirty-four minutes to get here."

Bob cringed at the thought of how little time it took for them to arrive on any given day.

"So what happened," Erma snapped.

Debbie started to speak. But Bob needed to take charge. He was officially the manager of Murcat Manor. He was not going to allow anyone to usurp his authority. Not Darrowby. Not strange superstitious folklore surrounding the property's history. And certainly not Erma.

He cut Debbie off with a hand placed on hers. "One of our guests choked on his food or had a heart attack. He died in the kitchen this morning."

"And the broken plates all over the floor?" Ross said looking through the large arched entry into the kitchen. "Looks like there was a small war in there, my boy."

"His name was Paul Knudson. The man had been drinking all night and was extremely hung over this morning. He went on an obnoxious rampage at the breakfast table. He attacked Debbie verbally and then me physically. It all happened way too fast. Next we knew, Knudson grabbed his throat as if to say he was choking. Then he clutched at his chest, his eyes bulged and rolled back into his head, and he fell onto the table and died. It all took less than a minute—the whole shebang."

Erma looked around. "Where are the guests? You're supposed to be booked solid all summer. All I see are thirteen lazy, good for nothing, flea carrying vermin all staring at me." Erma gave them a short hiss.

Bob noticed the cats scattered across the living room looking at Erma. Strange. He hadn't seen any of them when they sat down.

"Bob," Ross said. "We're starting to get worried. I don't need to remind you we cosigned a three and a half million dollar loan for Murcat Manor. Two deaths and an empty bed and breakfast are making us a bit nervous."

Bet you're more nervous than your cool demeanor's letting on, Bob thought. Although he couldn't show weakness, Bob hadn't had time to recalibrate his senses since the death of Paul Kundson. He needed a few moments to think of something to say. What to do? Bob stood from his chair.

"Ross, believe me. I understand completely. I'm going to the kitchen to get my laptop. Be right back."

Bob took his time at the kitchen table. "Thanks Raymond, for cleaning up. You're a big help."

"My pleasure, Mr. Stevens. I'll stay close by in case you need anything."

"Thanks," Bob whispered. "There's something you could do. Make a diversion. Maybe start a small fire on the stove."

Raymond chuckled. Maria gave him a wink. "Good luck."

Bob reentered the living room and set up his laptop on the coffee table.

"Let's get right to the point," Ross said. "What do you plan on doing to get people back in this place?"

"W-well … there's ahm, there are a number of things we can do."

Ross's hazel eyes locked on Bob's. "Like what?"

"Well," he glanced at Debbie who gave him a look that said she couldn't think of anything.

Erma stood and threw her hands in the air. "Oh, for crying out loud. He has nothing."

"Now, now, don't you two worry," Ross said to Bob, then reaching across and holding Debbie's hand. "Your grandmother and I have everything under control."

"Thank you," Debbie said. "Both of you. Honestly, we're not sure what to do."

"I believe you," Erma replied, but looking at Bob.

Ross directed his attention to Bob and sat next to him. He situated the laptop so they could both see. "You have a new group of guests coming in Monday, right?"

"We do." Bob toggled through a few screens. "So far, no one has cancelled. But that could change once the news gets out."

"Fortunately," Ross said, "seven of the ten rooms are booked by people from outside Michigan. This unfortunate death here today is not a homicide. News stations in Indianapolis, Chicago, Cleveland, Toledo, and in Canada aren't going to broadcast this event. The eighth room is booked by a couple in the Upper Peninsula. The final two are local."

Bob started to say something, but Ross's knowledge of these details was unexpected. "Wait. How did you know …?"

"A three and a half million dollar loan?" Erma spat out the rhetorical question like filthy puss oozing out of a festering wound. "*Really*, Bob?"

Bob scrolled down the page and looked at the cities the next wave of guests lived; all just as Ross called off.

Ross cracked a pernicious grin. "We have to do what we have to do to protect our interests. Surely, you understand."

"Oh, don't act so surprised," Erma said. "You don't think we'd leave all the financial aspects to you."

"You hacked into my Murcat Manor accounts?"

"*Our* Murcat Manor accounts," Ross said. "We're partners. Remember? But let's put this in the past. Moving forward, there can be no more deaths here. Understand?"

First Darrowby. Now Ross. Bob had always like Ross. But at the present, he wanted to throw him head first out the front door.

Erma started crying. "Oh, this is all because our beloved heirloom was destroyed. I don't suppose you can build a new Celtic cross, do you Bob?"

"Um, well, I'm not sure."

"Hmph. Didn't think so."

She placed her hands on Debbie's shoulders. "Don't worry, dear. Your grandfather is going to make a brand new heirloom. It'll be similar to my grandfather's cross, but we'll make a few changes to reflect current times. It will protect all who enter. Of course, we'll have our priest bless it, and ..."

Erma stiffened like a steel rod had replaced her spine. Her nose crunched. Her eyes furrowed. Her head locked forward. She glared at the cats lying around the living room.

"Did I just hear one of your cats hiss?"

Ross hunched one shoulder. "I didn't hear anything."

Debbie looked around the large living room, cats lounging all about. "I didn't hear anything, Grandma. Maybe it's the strain of everything."

Bob looked at the lounging felines. They were more spread out than usual. He had the eerie sense they were surrounding the humans.

Erma snapped out of her rigor mortis and took a wide stance with her hands on her hips. Her eyes swelled.

"Don't patronize me, child. I'm not old and senile. I clearly heard a cat hiss when I mentioned I would have our priest bless the new family heirloom."

Erma first panned the room of cats, then perambulated the room, stopping at each cat, bending over, and studying it.

Bob looked to Debbie and whispered. "See. I'm not the only one who thinks these cats are up to no good."

Erma move in a measured pace from cat to cat. Midnight was lying on the fireplace mantle. Erma stopped and put her face directly in front of the cat.

"Did you just hiss at me?"

Midnight yawned, rolled her head, and closed her eyes.

Erma next stopped at Esther, spread across and over an ottoman like her body was a boneless, fur-encapsulated gelatin.

"Was it you, you feline rodent? Tell me now. Was it? Did you hiss at me?"

Esther casually jumped off the ottoman and onto an empty chair, then lay down and lazily closed her eyes.

The situation was awkward. Bob started to say something, but Ross and Debbie motioned loud and clear with exaggerated hand movements for him to stay silent.

Erma continued moving from cat to cat. Each one seemed to respond in a disrespectful manner; defiant, cocky, indifferent, yawning, preferring sleep to paying the least bit of attention to the annoying woman. A couple of the cats moved to another part of the room just before she reached them.

After grilling the thirteen cats, she returned to the couch. Ross looked at her like she was from Planet Oddball. "Is everything alright, my dearest?"

"No," she sniped. "Everything is not alright. I know what I heard, and it was one of those little rugrats."

Ross slapped his hands on his knees. Bob interpreted the motion as trying to break Erma's cat fit. Time to take it from here.

Bob clapped his hands together as he stood. "Okay. Well, it's Saturday afternoon. The new guests aren't due until Monday. We need to get this place back in order. Time to get busy."

"Right," Debbie said. "But I need to clean the kitchen first. With the police and coroner here, I haven't had time to wash the mountain of dirty dishes."

Ross rubbed his belly. "What's to eat, Debbie? Can't get to work on an empty stomach."

"Um, I don't really feel much like cooking, Grandpa. Someone just died in my kitchen."

Ross snapped his fingers. "Raymond and Maria can finish up. That's what you're paying them for. Right? Let's go to Cornwell's for a turkey dinner. We'll go over our vision of Murcat Manor moving forward. I'll have our accountants and lawyers look at every little detail regarding the financials this week and see what ideas and direction they can offer."

"Don't worry about a thing," Erma said with a smug smile. "We'll take it from here."

Bob was seeing Ross in a new light. He was all about the money. Clearly Debbie and he were still reeling from the death of Paul Knudsen, the visit from Darrowby and Kowalski, and the loss of their guests. At least Raymond and Maria had the decency to show compassion for what they just went through. But all Ross could think about was money and fulfilling his gluttonous appetite for food.

Chapter 27 Expanded Powers

In the basement, Emily again took her favorite spot on the storage shelf directly across from the work table. This issue of canned fruit cocktail was a continuing battle. She knocked over the industrial sized aluminum containers of diced and sliced fruits to make room for herself and Debbie would pick up the dented cans and put them back on the shelf.

Once again, Emily caused the cans to tip over and roll off onto the floor, adding another dent to each one.

Emily was happy. Because Rebecca had opened her eyes to accepting who they really were, she could sleep again. They had begun so young and innocent, with a cause to help people with their gifting and abilities. But since humanity had rejected and persecuted them, Emily and her followers had no choice but to meet out their exclusion from the human race the best way they could.

The burden and recurring nightmares of her sister Sarah had lifted. She could enjoy sleep to the fullest for the first time in four hundred years. Emily knew she was more tolerable with the twelve. This meant they respected her, and fell into line when she needed to lead.

"Well Emily, what do you think?" Rebecca said. "Are we having fun yet?"

Emily looked at her close knit group of associates with an extreme sense of pride. "Yes, Rebecca, we are. All of us. That was well done, ladies." She bowed her head. "I'm proud of you all."

"And let's not forget about Helen," Annie said. "She took care of that creep Knudson with no problem. His wife should send us thank you cards, if she only knew."

"Oh, it was too easy." Helen waved her paw. "Believe me, I can do much better than that."

"Well, this was still a great warm up," Annie said. "But let's not stop now. We now need something more challenging. Like working together. We can coordinate our powers. You know, instead of individually or within our usual groups of three, we can band together as a whole."

Annie looked up to her sister Rebecca for confirmation. Rebecca only needed to nod. This told the rest of the clan they better respect Annie, regardless they were sisters.

"That's a great idea," Emily replied. "And with the information explosion of this generation, let's give it up for Madelyn, who has been studying up on the latest scientific research and discoveries. It's mindboggling how much this understanding helps explain our powers."

The cats erupted in a round of applause.

Rebecca nudged Madelyn to the forefront. "Come on. Don't be shy."

Madelyn stepped forward. "No applause necessary. I humbly accept. In this current society, as a human, I would be called a nerd and a bookworm. An introvert."

"Introvert?" Rebecca said.

"The exact opposite of you. Respectfully."

Rebecca winked. "Got it."

"Today, knowledge is so much more readily available. The Internet its right at our finger tips." Madelyn held up her paw. "Make that paw claws. Anyway, with Bob's touch screen devices, I can touch and swipe and move to just about any site. And I can key in words. It's difficult, but I can do it. I punch in the first few letters, and the computer completes the word or phrase—and most of the time it gets it right, just what I wanted. This information age is nothing short of amazing."

Madelyn's voice had risen to an intensity never before heard by the others, to where they stared at her wide-eyed and speechless. Madelyn noticed, and stopped her elated ramblings with a blush.

"Sorry, I get carried away sometimes."

"No, no," Rebecca said, "It's great to see you this passionate and expressive. Even though," she giggled, "I don't understand any of it, not a word you said." She looked around at the others who nodded in agreement to being equally confused. Rebecca giggled again. "And see? Neither do the rest of us. So we'll just have to take your word for it."

"Fair enough. Trust me when I say I can process and interpret information faster than just about any person alive. If you walk away with anything from what I've said here today, please understand we can combine the knowledge of how the physical world interacts with the mystical."

The other twelve looked at each other, then back to Madelyn with blank stares. "Meaning ...?" Rebecca said.

"Very simply, we're able to couple science with the supernatural. This can only help us increase our abilities as we gain a better understanding of the world we now live in."

"Umm ... example, please," Rebecca said. "I still don't have a clue what you're talking about."

Madelyn sighed. "I'll give you the short version. Energy and mass are two sides of the same coin. One can be turned into another. For example, during fusing of certain elements, if the resulting mass is less than the initial mass, the energy released during the exchange can cause a reaction and an incredible amount of energy is released."

Most of the other cats hesitated and groaned because they didn't understand. Esther, however, raised a paw and interjected.

"She's right. As you know, my unique ability allows me to cause small explosions. I never knew how I was able to perform these acts. Now, I have at least a better understanding of how my powers work. And, thanks to Madelyn, I've discovered I can do much more."

Esther had everyone's attention. Especially Emily, as she possessed all of her follower's individual powers to some degree. Everyone revered Esther as she demonstrated one of the most incredible abilities of all the cats. She could blow stuff up, and to a much larger degree and scale than Emily's similar power. It was damn frightening the potential destruction she could wield. They all tried to stay on her good side.

"Don't keep us in suspense," Emily said. "What else have you discovered?"

"Very simply," Madelyn said, "even air has mass and takes up space. Currents in the air are a form of energy. And this mass and energy can be converted into each other. There is some water in the air and Esther is able to fuse the hydrogen atoms to produce helium. A very small amount of mass is lost and converted to energy. It's not much to be sure, but enough for our sister to have a new toy to play with. Esther, care to give our captive audience a demonstration?"

Before Emily's heart could hit its next beat, a hot burst smacked her hard in the face. She was forced back and hit the cinderblock wall. Her mind went blank and her paws were scurrying in all directions. A moment later, she fell off the shelf, landed on her feet, and ran behind a stack of boxes to hide.

Emily shook her head clear and peered around the crates. Most of the other cats scattered. Only Esther and Madelyn remained.

"It's alright," Esther said. "Come back. That was an energy burst and nothing else."

Emily stepped out, but only after the other cats showed themselves and one by one jumped back up on the work table.

"I know you are all amazed," Madelyn said. "Like the TV infomercial hosts like to say, 'But wait, that's not all.'"

Chloe stepped forward and addressed the clan. "I'm next. I've been listening to Madelyn. At first, I didn't know what she was talking about. Like you all, I thought she was a bit loony." Chloe raised a paw next to her head, spun it in a tight circle, and stuck out her tongue.

"Umm ... thanks," Madelyn said.

"Hear me out. I've been focusing on this science stuff the best I can. And I think it really does work. To prove it, I can levitate up to thirty pounds now."

"You've already told us that," Rebecca scoffed, pawing her singed whiskers. "Big deal. Try to top Esther's display of power. Good luck."

A sly grin spread across Chloe's face. Emily knew that sideways smile. Her cousin was going for flair. She would perform a feat to shock everyone.

"Oh yeah, Rebecca? You say that with no effort to hide your sarcasm. Well, pay attention and check this out. I can move multiple, smaller objects. Not just one large one. I've never been able to do this before. Watch this."

Emily was amazed and proud of her younger cousin. As usual, Chloe didn't disappoint. She watched Rebecca, Scarlett, and Helen, trepidation in their eyes, lifted a few feet off the table. Their feet dangling and Rebecca looking scared out of her wits, which was a first for her, the cats were slowly rotated in a full circle.

Emily jumped back up to her shelf and enjoyed the show. She watched with pleasure as Chloe swung the three cats in a small, slow orbit at first, but with each full turn speeding up a little faster. This was a standoff, four hundred years in the making, between her cousin and the second in command, both of whom had a hubris befitting the queen of a large nation. Chloe had the clear advantage, since she was in charge. After a dozen dizzying mid-air rotations, Rebecca blinked.

"Okay, okay. You win," Rebecca said. "Just let us down. Gently, of course."

Emily watched as the three cats slowly were let back down. The others looked on with awe. The whole event was smooth, and Rebecca had just been knocked down a notch.

"That was amazing," Emily said. "Well done. Clearly, a deeper understanding of our powers is increasing our abilities to use them."

A bit startled and clearly humbled, Rebecca said, "Okay, I'm convinced. That was pretty cool." She stepped to the front of the bench. Emily knew her pride was hurt, and would try to change the subject.

"Moving forward, we should look for more guests to kill. We're able to do far more complex murders now. Like Chloe, we all may be able to find out we can do so much more."

Emily was excited and ready to test Madelyn's theory. No time for arguing or rebuttal. "Like you said, it's what we do best. In fact, let's kill two people this time. A couple."

This got a resounding round of, "Yays!"

"Emily," Rebecca said. "It's great to have you on board again. I've missed my best friend. And now I have her back."

Emily smiled wide. "So who's next?"

"The place is empty. Thanks to us. We'll have to wait for the next group of people."

"What about that snippety old wench Erma?" Helen said. "Scarlett, you can cause madness. What a hoot that would be. I'd pay good money to see that."

"That lady is a real basket case." Scarlett replied. "Not much I can do causing madness. She's already wonkers."

A chorus of laughter ensued. Emily found herself laughing, too. Killing guests at Murcat Manor was the cure for what ailed her. She felt regenerated with a lust for more. And, as the leader, she appreciated her followers' willingness to take chances and expand their horizons.

"Isabella," Emily said. "That was a great idea, hissing inside Erma's mind so only she could hear it."

Isabella tried to refrain from laughter. "She really went off the deep end. I think it made her more upset that we yawned or closed our eyes when she confronted us."

The cats shared in another round of laughter. Emily sat back and let the twelve dictate the flow of the meeting.

"But I'm bored again," Isabella said. "Messing with Erma only fueled my desire for more. I can't wait for new guests. Besides, our next victims may not be in this next group. We might have to wait for the next group. Or the next."

The other cats were agitated. They paced back and forth across the work bench, each complaining of their impatience about having to wait to use their abilities on the next victim. Emily needed to bring them back in focus.

"Okay, everyone take it easy. We need to give a little time between killings. Otherwise, Darrowby will shut this place down. We need to dictate the flow of events. Not the detectives. Not Bob. And certainly not Ross and Erma."

"We can't take it easy," Rebecca said. "Not until we kill someone else."

"I have an idea," Emily said. "To kill time until we identify our next victims, let's mess with Boring bob's head. Angel, dreams are your specialty. Tonight, I want you to get inside his mind. Give him prophetic dreams of events that will unfold at Murcat Manor as the days and weeks go by. Make them generic, but meaningful."

Chapter 28   Three Dreams

Bob woke afresh Monday morning. The sun broke through the slits of their bedroom window shutters and woke him an hour before his alarm was set to go off. He rolled back and forth, trying to find relief—both of his sides throbbed with pain.

His stirring woke Debbie. She turned, her head still buried in her pillow, eyes closed, but somehow managing to give Bob a wide smile. They ended up snuggled deep in their pillows facing each other.

"How did you sleep, sweetie."

Bob ignored his soul mate's morning breath. His was worse, he was sure. "The melatonin really helped. I slept straight through. Thanks for the idea."

Debbie stroked his hair. "We need to take care of ourselves. The stress and physical demands of this place are taking their toll on our bodies and our minds."

"Not to mention the deaths of DeShawn Hill and Paul Knudson."

"Well, let's not dwell on that. We'll go crazy if we do. They're in the past. We need to move forward."

Thanks to Debbie, Bob was ready to face the day with a positive attitude, even though his body felt like it was run over by a truck. He nudged six sleeping cats off the bed and tossed off his coverings. He stood and performed a few stretches, then looked in the mirror as he put on his pants and shirt.

"I had some really weird dreams last night."

"Dreams?"

"Yeah. Three, in fact."

Debbie sat up. "Three dreams? That's interesting. Do you remember them?"

"Clear as day."

"That's memorable. They must mean something. I almost always forget mine. What were they?"

"Not that I give any credibility to dreams, however, I'm eating breakfast and everything in my world is blue. I'm by a lake and there are two guardian angels, one male and one female."

Debbie smiled and nodded. "Okay, and then what?

"Well, that was all for the first one. I know, nothing earth shattering. In the second, I'm on a train or a subway. Everything is gray and I'm eating lunch by myself. I'm traveling forward through time and I can clearly see places to get off and get on. I know that I have the ability to stop, but have no control of where I'm going because I don't where I'm supposed to disembark. I'm speeding forward, faster and faster, all the while passing by people and events I should be enjoying."

Debbie's smile was now forced, Bob knew. Two dreams in, and Bob's concern was his wife thought he was losing his marbles. Might as well finish the third and spare Debbie asking for it.

"In the final dream, it's night time. After a long hard day of work, I arrive home exhausted and park in the driveway. I then walk down a path and only want to go inside and eat dinner. But the path swerves around the house into the backyard. I walk all the way to the fence on the boundary line. Just as I reached out to grab it, I woke up. Oh, and you can lose the forced smile. I know this is all so strange."

Debbie blew Bob a quick kiss. "Well, don't fret over it. Maybe vivid dreams are a side effect of the melatonin."

"Speaking of the sleeping aid," Bob said, "I'm glad I got a great night's sleep. Saturday was such a nightmare. And we worked all day Sunday getting this place back to normal. I still find it hard to believe how much work this place needs every day, even with Raymond and Maria helping. My back and sides are so sore I can hardly move."

Bob brushed a couple more cats off their bed and helped Debbie get up and into her robe. "Let's go to the kitchen. We can make any final preparations for today's guests. There're always those who show up early."

Debbie sniffed the air. "I think I smell bacon."

"Mmmm, I smell it too."

Bob looked at the cats, which were also sniffing the air, now wide awake and pacing the floor. "The cats can smell it too. Maria must be getting breakfast ready for us."

The cats were running at Bob's feet as they walked into the kitchen. "These darn cats. I almost tripped over them," he said, steadying himself against the wall.

"Don't look now," Debbie said as they entered the kitchen. "But here come the rest."

Bob almost tripped again as they ran between his feet. But he made it safely to the table and was happy to see breakfast and coffee waiting for him and Debbie.

"Good morning," Maria said. "I know it's been a rough couple days. Have a seat at the table. I'll feed the cats."

She filled four large bowls with scrambled eggs, bacon, hash browns, and melted cheese and set them on the floor. The cats converged and devoured the food.

"I'll never get over how they eat people food," Maria said. "They won't touch cat food. And they love watermelon, especially since it's been so hot."

Bob looked at the cats gorging down their meal and shook his head. He was half way through his plate of food when he opened his laptop and checked the reservations page.

"The good news is no one cancelled. We'll have a full house. The bad news is we still have a lot of work to do. And, as usual, people will probably arrive early before the two o'clock check in."

Debbie took a sip of her coffee and yawned. "We'd better eat up and get started. Also, I think you should write down the details of your dreams."

"Dreams?" Maria said.

"Bob had three dreams last night," Debbie said. She gave Maria the details.

"Mr. Stevens," Maria said without hesitation, "those are very vivid dreams. You should find someone who can interpret them. If you don't, then I will."

Not another mystic, Bob thought, wondering if he should have screened Maria a little more thoroughly before hiring her. Bob would normally shrug off the suggestion of an interpretation of his dreams, especially as crazy as the ones he had last night. But with all the talk of ghosts and curses and the property being haunted, and now Maria giving him a look saying she could find a dream interpreter, he would at least leave the thought open for consideration.

Chapter 29   Double The Pleasure

Emily, along with her leaders Rebecca, Chloe, Scarlett, and Isabella, stood at the top of the stairs. The rest paced back and forth behind them, waiting for the next group of people to arrive. Raymond was mowing the front and back yards and had a full day of outdoor projects planned. Maria was busy in the upstairs laundry room, washing and drying an enormous heap of bedding and towels.

They watched from a nervous distance as Bob and Debbie each took a strange noisy monster out the dark confines of what they called '*The Forbidden Closet*' and proceeded to push them back and forth across the living room carpet. These were demented creatures surely spawned in the bowels of the Netherworld. Somehow, humans had innate powers that controlled the beastly creatures.

Bob paused and peered out the living room front window. He checked his watch. "Ten after eleven. What'd I tell you, honey. The first guests are almost three hours early. Let's put the vacuum sweepers away and go outside and greet them."

Emily blew out a sigh of relief. Bob and Debbie had once again corralled the hellish fiends and put them back in prison behind the 'Forbidden Door.' Emily had given the cats strict instructions never to open it for fear the devils would escape and swallow them whole. With the beasts now vanquished, the coast was clear to go downstairs. Emily led the charge.

"Okay, ladies. Time to pick out our next victims."

All thirteen cats rushed down the stairs into the living room and spread out on the couches, chairs, and ottomans. The next four and a half hours brought nine more couples, three with two kids each. Emily and the cats studied each adult, looking for anything they could exploit. Weaknesses. Strengths. Habits. Emotions. Fatigue. They were patient and open to anything.

Hours seemed to drag on without mercy. It was hard for Emily to keep her eyes open. They had been awake most of the night and stuffed themselves with a huge breakfast. Scarlett dozed off, as had Angel and Esther.

Emily let her sisterhood catnap for an hour before waking them. She let the others take turns, three sleeping for an hour, while the rest studied the incoming vacationers. But as the day progressed, Emily found she was the only one still awake.

Finally, after five eternal feeling hours, the tenth couple arrived at four o'clock. The woman was loud and talking—more like barking—up a storm. Her boisterous voice penetrated through the walls and double paned windows like weaponized laser beams. Emily could feel her anxiety and nervous intensity. She took a moment to focus on the husband. She was getting nothing, which told her he had a calm demeanor.

They were polar opposites and the energy between them was seriously conflicted. This opened many opportunities where her sisters could be most creative with their powers.

"Everyone. Wake up. I like what I'm feeling about this last couple."

The woman pushed her way in between her husband and Raymond, who was holding a half dozen pieces of their luggage. Her mouth was a locomotive on full steam ahead.

"That's right. You owe me this here vacation. I works hard for my money, 'n all's you do is stay at home all day watchin' yo damn TV."

"Aw, c'mon, baby. I be lookin' for work."

"Ha. You. Look for work? My cocoa brown ass you be lookin' fo' work. Hey, bellboy, drop the suitcases here at the door. Reginald can carry 'em up to the room. Be the first work he done in months."

"Bellboy?" Emily said. "How dare she? I already hate this lady."

"Welcome to Murcat Manor," Debbie said most graciously. "It's a pleasure to have you. Are you the Johnsons?"

"Thas right, sweetie. Reginald and Sophia Johnson. Thas who we are. Come all the way up from Detroit."

Emily applauded Debbie for trying to be so graceful in the face of such a belligerent and obnoxious person.

"I see you've booked the Disco Room," Debbie said. "I just know you're going to love it."

Sophia looked around and let out a slow whistle. "Ooowee, this place's sho' is nice. I'm glad we done booked us a solid week here."

A week, Emily thought. Perfect. She couldn't have scripted a better scenario.

Sophia walked across the living room to the large arched entryway to the kitchen and let out a loud long whistle. "Now this here? This here is

213

whatcha calls a kitchen. How's the food, sweetie?" Sophia slapped at her plump belly. "I'm starving."

Debbie caught up to Sophia. "Ah, we eat dinner in two shifts. You're on the second shift at six-thirty."

Sophia turned and placed her hands on her more than ample hips, her head in a soul-sister neck roll. "Six-thirty? I don' think so, honey. I'm not payin' all this money so I can eat leftovers from the first shift."

"Oh, um ... well, I'm sure we can place you on the first shift. They eat at five o'clock."

"Damn straight. Mmmhmm. I'm on vacation, you hear? Ain't taking no back seat to no one or no thing no how."

Sophia returned to the living room. "Good Lord-a-Mighty. Would you jus' take a look at all these lazy behind cats."

"We have thirteen of them," Bob said. "Want to take one home with you?"

"Nuh uh. Nooooo, honey. I hate cats. Had my way? I'd kill all of the useless varmints. Jus' what kinda place you be running here? Thirteen crazy ass cats?"

Rebecca was glaring at Sophia. "This lady has no respect."

Emily shook her head. "I feel bad for the husband. What a mouth she has. I'm almost willing to kill her and let him live."

"Almost."

"An' hey—why'n the hell's my suitcases still at the bottom of the stairs?" She smacked her palms together. "Let's go, Reginald. Get a move on, brah. This here be my vacation. *Comprendo*? Mines. M-I-N-E-S. And everyone's gone be waitin' hand 'n foot on me fo' the next seven days."

Emily was stunned and speechless. So were the others. Their otherwise chatty mental communication airway was devoid of sound.

"Looks like we have our next victims," Emily said, finally breaking the silence. "All in favor?"

The reply was a unanimous and resounding, "Yay!"

"Okay. We have an entire week. We should wait until the last night. Place a little more time between killing Paul Knudson and these two. If we do it tonight, Darrowby might arrest Boring Bob and shut this place down."

"That's my job," Rebecca said. "When the time comes, I'll know just what to do."

Chapter 30   Star Child

Reginald Vincent Johnson was enjoying a deep sleep. Visions of him in high school thirty years ago, swishing buzzer-beating three pointer after three pointer in slow motion swirled in his head. With every shot his defender went for the fake or couldn't contend with his jump shot. With each swish, the crowd chanted his nickname.

Star Child.

Star Child.

Star Child.

The skinny high school senior from Detroit with an Afro so large it seemed to engulf his head would acknowledge the crowd with a fist pump.

But this was more than a dream. He felt just as much awake as he did asleep. He had free will and could make decisions.

Five seconds left. He could fake left, but decided to dribble one step to the right. Leap, fade back, release … *swish*. Another buzzer beater. More cheers of *Star Child* filled the auditorium.

Damn if he wasn't making decisions in his dream. Time to test his theory and do something his coach told him never to do. Five seconds left. He pump faked his defender then drove the lane, dribbling past three defenders before dunking on the opposing center a foot taller than him. Yes. He was in a dream. Yet he could dictate the outcome on his own accord.

But why stop with the continuous game winners?

The crowd went wild after the center fell on his back and Reginald landed on the floor. The final buzzer sounded to more chants of *Star Child*. Thirteen drop-dead gorgeous-and-built-like-a-brick-house cheerleaders mobbed him. He could read their names on their uniforms as they rushed him.

Emily.

Rebecca.

Annie.

Jacquelyn.

Chloe.

Midnight.

Helen.

Scarlett.

Angel.

Esther.

Isabella.

Rachel.

Madelyn.

His face was happily stuffed between the lead cheerleader Emily's bountiful breasts. She grabbed him by his head and whispered with a soft sultry voice, "Reginald, dear."

"Yes, my love?"

"Tonight ...." She lolled her tongue in his ear.

"Yes ...." Reginald thought he was going to explode.

"You're going to die."

The final word ended with a booming hiss that echoed through his head. He thought his eardrums were about to explode. Reginald woke in an instant, sitting up in bed and cupping his ears. His head was hammering. Sweat broke out on his brow.

He took a moment to catch his breath. The dream. It was so real.

He looked over at his wife. Sophia was fast asleep, a sleep mask over her eyes and a hair net covering her braid extensions. She drooled on her pillow as she snored.

Reginald sensed he wasn't alone in The Disco Room. He scanned the four walls, the near full moon casting light through the window.

Up above the door were three shelves, one at the apex of the vaulted ceiling and two a little lower on either side. On the top shelf a single cat sat still and stared at Reginald. The red eyes pierced the night and appeared to look right through him. Invading his space. Piercing his mind.

Reginald reached to the nightstand to turn on the light. The disco ball on the ceiling came to life. Balls of color danced across the room.

He toggled the light switch to turn on the regular light. The disco ball continued to spin. He looked to Sophia, still fast asleep. He grabbed his cell phone and shined the flashlight on the feline. It didn't budge. It didn't blink.

There was no way for the cat to jump that high. It would take a tall ladder for someone to put the shelves there and place items on them. How the hell could that cat get up there? It must be eight feet off the floor.

"Hey Babe, wake up."

"No," she snorted through a half snore.

"You gotta check this out."

"You's not having that ol' dream 'bout hittin' them game winnin' shots an being mobbed by those pretty young thang cheerleaders again, is you?"

"Ooooooh yeah, baby."

"I tol' you t' stop havin' them. I don't likes you being mobbed by all them young thangs. Even if it is in yo dreams." She dropped her head back to her pillow.

"C'mon, baby. Wake up."

"No. You take yo black ass back t' sleep. And stop havin' them dreams with them perky boobs fine ass hoes. Or I'll whoop yo ass good. You hear me, now?"

"Forget about the dream, babe. Check out that cat."

Sophia took off her sleeping mask and rubbed her eyes. "I tol' Mrs. Stevens I don't wants no funky cats in my room. Throw it out. And ice them wet dreams, hear me?"

"Babes, this ain't right. How'n the hell did that cat jump all the way up there?

"It's a cat, Reginald. Now takes yo' ass back to sleep."

Reginald got out of bed. He took off his socks, folded them into a ball, and threw them at the cat. To his amazement, the socks seem to deflect back to him as if one of his game winning shots were blocked and swatted away.

The cat didn't blink. It continued to stare down Reginald. He stepped to his left. The head turned and the red eyes followed his movement. He stepped right. The eyes tracked him through the colored lights of the disco ball.

He looked back to his wife. She was starting to snore again. He shook the bed violently. "Wake up, woman."

She threw the covers off, along with her mask. "Das it. I done tol' you to take yo fool coal black ass back to sleep."

Reginald held up his hand to ward her off. "Shhhhh. Just look," he said in a whisper and pointed to the cat. "You tell me, how the hell that cat can git all the way up there by itself."

Sophia leaned forward and squinted. "Yeah. That sho 'nough is weird. Even for a cat. I don't know of no cat that can jump that high."

"And look at those bright red eyes. Thought that only happens in pictures."

She got out of bed and stood up straight. "It's not moving. Maybe it's a decoration."

Sophia reached down and picked up one of her shoes. "Let's see if it's alive. I hope it is. I'll knock dat crazy ass cat off the shelf."

"I tried that with my socks. But it's like it has some—I dunno—some kinda force field around it."

"Are you stupid? Socks? For real? Leave it to me." She reared back to throw.

Reginald and Sophia jumped back when the cat hissed. The sound intensified as it reverberated through the room, growing in volume until it sounded like a jet engine before it stopped.

"Holy shit," Sophia said. "The damn thing *is* alive."

"And that's the loudest hiss I's ever done heard. That shit there could wake the dead."

"Right now, I wants it dead." She bent back to throw the shoe and gave it a heave with a loud grunt. The shoe was deflected back and landed on the floor with a thunk.

"See what I mean?"

"Yeah. That's real freaky. Just look at that thang. Starin' down on us with those red eyes. It's evil. Turn off that disco ball an turn on the normal light. Has to be somethin' in here I can knock it off that shelf with."

Reginald shut off the disco ball, found the light switch by the door, and flipped it up. He blinked in disbelief. Sophia gasped with her hands to her mouth. There were cats sitting, spread out all over their room staring at them.

Reginald counted out loud. "Thirteen. All thirteen cats is in here."

"But the door's closed. So how'n the hell'd they get in here?"

"I don't know. But they's going out right now."

He turned the knob on the door. "Oh, now this here's downright freaky. Door is locked." He gripped and wrenched at it. "I can't open it."

"No worries," Sophia said, picking out a brass poker by the fireplace. "I'm gonna get rid o' these evil thangs right now."

She took a swing at the closest cat sitting on the foot of the bed. It jumped with ease and landed on the floor on the other side of the room where it sat still, staring at Sophia.

"Oh, hell no. I don't think so." Sophia gripped the poker and held it up over her head.

She took more whacks at three cats. The results were the same. Each one deftly moved out of the way and found a new sitting spot where they continued to stare at the Johnsons.

Sophia bent over and grabbed her knees, wheezing and catching her breath. "Well, don't jus' stand there. Get yo ass over to the fireplace and grab somethin' and start swingin'.

Reginald grabbed the cast iron fireplace shovel, took a few practice swings, then whipped it back and forth at the cats.

"Sheeeeet, you's getting old. You be missin' by a mile."

221

"Baby, you talk too much. Get over here and help me."

Together they swung and thrust their weapons, but never came close. The cats jumped out of the way with ease, each time landing safely away, then sitting and staring at them.

Sophia was gasping for air. "It's … like … these here cats," she wheezed, "they know our every move," another wheeze, "Befo' we even make it."

A minute later, Reginald was spent. He lowered the shovel when Sophia glared at him with a crazed look. "I've got you now, you wicked critter from hell. You nev'r should've come here."

Reginald backpedaled. "Hey wait, baby. It's me. Put that poker down."

"I got you. Now die, you hellion."

Before he could react, Sophia thrust the poker deep into his chest.

Reginald's vision started to go dark. He looked at his wife as lights began to fade. "Now why you gone and done that t' me, baby?"

And Reginald Vincent Johnson's world went black.

Chapter 31   Sophia Johnson

Sophia laughed as she yanked back on the poker, the hooked tip tearing through flesh and bones. Her thoughts were hazy. She felt lightheaded and nauseous. But her vision was clear. She looked down on a kneeling cat, paws covering a mortal chest wound, and crying out for mercy.

"Yeah, I got you good, didn't I you little feline freak. Beg alls you want to. But I'm watchin' yo sorry ass die."

As the fog in her head lifted, she saw her husband on his knees, covering the hole in his chest with both hands, blood oozing out between his fingers. He looked up and tried to say something. His mouth moved, but she couldn't hear his words. His eyes rolled back in his head and he fell forward to the orange shag carpet floor.

"Holy Mothah of God! Reginald. O' dear sweet Jesus. Wha—what just happened?"

"You just murdered your husband. What do you think," a pleasant voice vibrated in her head.

Sophia gripped the poker with two hands and held it up in front of her. She looked left, then slowly completed a full turn, searching for someone else in the room.

"Who said dat?"

"I did."

She studied the cats. One jumped up on the foot of the bed. "Please allow me to introduce myself. My name is Isabella. Nice to meet you."

Sophia looked at the name tag on the collar. *Isabella*.

"You can talks?"

"Not exactly. I have the power of telepathy and illusion casting."

"Tele ... telepa *what*?"

"I can transmit information to a human or animal without using any known sensory channels or physical interaction. Just like I'm doing to you now."

Sophia looked at her dead husband, still twitching on the floor. "But how ..."

"That's easy. Scarlett can give people temporary bouts of madness. She caused you to go cuckoo just long enough for me to plant an image in your mind that your husband was one of us."

Sophia, glassy eyed and discombobulated, watched a second cat jump on the bed and waved her paw.

"Scarlett says hi."

Sophia looked at the name on the collar. *Scarlett*. She held the poker up. It had a piece of flesh that was probably part of a lung draped over the end.

"But ... my Reg. I ... I killed him?"

"Believe me. After listening to your mouth all week, he's better off dead. I'm not sure where he goes in the afterlife but, trust me, it has to be a better place."

"Talkin' cats. You gots to be kiddin' me."

Isabella sighed. "We don't talk. We communicate telepathically with each other. And I can communicate telepathically with people like I'm doing with you right now. Anyway, check this out. Angel here, she started this whole episode by invading your husband's dreams. And by the way, we were the cheerleaders."

Another cat joined the two cats on the bed. Sophie looked down at her name tag. *Angel.*

"Wait. Don't try to make sense of this. I doubt you have the cranial capacity to do so. Next up is Chloe. She can levitate things. She'll help Annie come down from the shelf."

A fourth cat jumped up on the bed. Sophia looked at the name tag. *Chloe.* She turned to see the cat up on the shelf float across the room then onto the bed. Sure enough, the nametag read *Annie.*

"Wait. You cats has special powers?"

"My, my, aren't you the perceptive one. Now you're getting it. But we prefer to call them abilities. And we can combine our abilities and work together. You know. To kill people. Just like we're going to kill you."

"I gotsta be losin' my damn mind."

Sophia was shaking badly and almost dropped the black wrought iron rod. She scanned the Disco themed room as she backed up toward the door. The cats sat eerily still, their only movements were their tails swaying back and forth in unison and their eyes following her every move. Sophia aimed the poker to her left, then quickly shifted to the right of the room.

"You crazy ass cats stay the hell away from me. You hear? I'm gettin' outta here. Don't you dare try to stop me."

Sophia, not taking her eyes off the cats, reached behind herself and tried to open the door, but it was locked. She pointed the poker at Isabella. "Unlock this here door, or I swears to God I'll kill you all."

"I'm sure Helen and Chloe will oblige."

A fifth cat jumped up on the bed. Sure enough, the name tag read Helen.

"Helen can reverse things. A lock in this case. And Chloe, who just levitated Annie across the room, can pull the door open. Cool, don't you think?"

"You truly is hell cats. Screw you all."

Sophia's normal heart rhythms shifted to fast uneven heart palpitations pounding inside her chest. So strong were the abnormal pulsations she felt it spreading to the arteries in her neck. An enormous shudder almost caused her to lose control of her bowels. She found herself hyperventilating. The inside of her head gyrated as her knees lost strength. She must be having an anxiety attack. Yeah, she convinced herself, that must be it.

"I'm sure you feel your heartbeat increase and blood racing through your body. That's Annie, doing what she does best. You know, causing your heart to beat faster. Stuff like that."

Behind her, the click of the lock on the door sounded.

"Uh uh. No how, no way. Cain't be happenin'."

Still facing the cats and holding the poker in a death grip, she turned her head to see the door knob turn by itself. The door swung open and smacked her hard in the butt.

That was it. Sophia dropped the poker and ran out the door, screaming as she pulled the hem of her nightgown above her knees and scampered down the hall. At the top of the stairs the cats swarmed her feet, causing her to lose balance.

She felt a burst of heat, as if an enormous bubble of hot air exploded against her back, pushing her forward with incredible force and lifting her feet off the carpet. Sophia flipped in a one-eighty arc and nose-dived down the stairs; her neck snapped on the first step her head landed on.

Sophia was conscious, but had no control of her tumbling body. She could hear the sickening breaks and cracks of her bones as she slammed against the stairs on her downward plummet. She hit the living room hardwood floor nose first, and her life switched off.

Chapter 32   Investigation

Bob sat at the kitchen table. The boarders, still in their pajamas and robes, gawked at the twisted and broken body at the bottom of the stairs. Raymond Hettinger walked over and placed a blanket over the corpse. Maria Gonzalez tried to calm the guests, some who were threatening to leave and demanding a full refund.

Bob was thankful for Raymond and Maria. They had made excruciating circumstances easier to navigate. He reached out for the two cups of coffee Maria handed him and passed one on to Debbie.

"Thanks Maria."

"You're welcomed," she said through tired eyes and a yawn. "I'll offer some to Raymond and the guests, too."

For the third time in less than three months, Bob had yellow police tape on Murcat Manor's property. And, like the previous two occurrences, it wasn't the yellow tape that was the worst of his problems.

"It only took a week for more people to die," a terse Darrowby said, Kowalski at his side. "That's four deaths in nine weeks. You wanna tell me what the hell's going on here?"

Bob was exhausted. But it was the frustration that he was already perceived guilty that gnawed at him. His words blew out of his mouth.

"Clearly, this is a murder suicide," he said, feeling defensive and sounding like it. "This much is clear. Especially, I would think," he took the offense and eyed the two officers up and down, "to two *trained detectives*."

Darrowby gripped the table and rose. "Excuse me. You now have two more dead bodies inside your house. Put yourself in my shoes." He stood and pointed out into the living room where there was a clear view of the dead body underneath the blanket. "Tell me, what am I thinking right about now?"

Bob tried to say something in his defense, but Darrowby cut him off.

"Are you a detective?"

"No. I jus—"

Darrowby stuck out his palm. "Wait. Hold that thought. Let *me* tell *you* who and what you are. Then I'll tell you who and what I am."

He pointed his forefingers at him and Debbie. "You two are average Joe and Jane Citizen. Got that? You spend your evenings watching CSI reruns and honestly believe that you know more than real detectives like Kowalski and me. That's you, in a nutshell."

"We don't watch a lot of TV," Bob said.

Darrowby slammed his fist on the table. "Shut up. I'm not finished. Between Kowalski and me, we have thirty-five years of the best training and experience available to law enforcement anywhere in the world. Together, we've solved forty-seven homicides. *Forty-seven*. With the exception of six who got off because of their slick lawyers, forty-one are currently behind bars in Jackson State Prison."

Darrowby's eyes intensified on Bob. He knew the detective wanted to increase that number by four with him and Debbie as the perps. Bob looked back through the large archway that led into the living room. All of the guests were now staring in at him and Debbie.

"Ah, isn't there a better place we can talk?"

Darrowby was quick with a response. "Sure is. Down at the station."

"Wait. You're not arresting us, are you?"

Darrowby grinned and let Bob's question hang in the air. "No. This is just for questioning. That's all."

Bob was quicker with his reply. "I don't think that's in our best interests."

Kowalski spoke. "Mr. Stevens, I strongly suggest you come with us voluntarily. If you haven't done anything wrong, then you don't have a thing to worry about. And coming in on your own volition will look good for you. Makes it appear like you want to help rather than trying to hide something or obstruct our investigation."

Investigation. There was that word again.

Bob looked back into the living room. "But I need to ..."

"Don't worry about it. I'll have a couple officers keep an eye on the place. And I'm sure your hired help will keep your guests comfortable until you come back."

Darrowby reached for Debbie's elbow. "Shouldn't take long. I promise. C'mon. You can ride in our car."

Bob despised Darrowby. No way was he letting the scumbag touch his wife. He stepped in front of Debbie and pushed the detective's arm away. Darrowby looked insulted and offended, but Bob didn't care.

The caffeine was kicking in. Adrenaline raised his blood pressure. His mind was clear. He knew going to the Battle Creek Police Station and answer questions was the right thing to do. He didn't have anything to hide. He hadn't killed anyone.

But Bob also knew he needed to lawyer up.

"Okay, detective. We'll go. Give us a few minutes to get dressed. But we'll follow you in our car."

Chapter 33   One More Death

Bob pulled out of the driveway and followed Darrowby, who kept his speed at exactly the speed limit. By the book. Fifty miles per hour.

Behind him, a police cruiser kept a safe but close distance. The time on his dash read 3:16 am. They were the only ones on the two lane country road. Bob glanced in his rear view mirror. Murcat Manor disappeared as Oak Hill Road veered west.

"Bob, the police station's twenty minutes way. What are we going to do?"

Debbie was frantic, he knew. Although she'd momentarily freaked out when Sophie Johnson ran through the second floor screaming and they found the Johnsons dead, she had kept her cool while being questioned by the detectives.

But they were in their own domain, at the kitchen table, which was their territory. And Bob had stood up to Darrowby, as usual. But now, they were on their way to the Battle Creek Police Station, where Darrowby ruled supreme. He would have a dominant advantage.

"You know Darrowby wants to arrest us. This might be a one way trip for us. I'm calling grandma and grandpa."

Debbie fumbled for her phone and dropped it. She bent forward and swept her hands across the floorboard and under her seat. The thought of having to tell Erma their situation sent a shiver up and down Bob's spine.

"Slow down, honey. Forget about your phone. We haven't done anything wrong."

"Bob," Debbie snapped, sounding too much like her snarly grandmother, "In case you haven't noticed, four people have died at Murcat Manor in nine weeks. One of them was Darrowby's friend since they were kids. Obviously, he thinks we're behind all of them. Are you listening to me? He thinks we're murdering psychopaths. And with four deaths, I think this categorizes us as serial killers in his eyes. Like he said, put yourself in his shoes. For all he knows, we had nefarious and insidious reasons for opening a bed and breakfast—to lure in people so we can kill them."

Bob took his hands off the steering wheel for a moment to wave Debbie down. "I know. I know. We need help. And I know just who to call."

"Grandma and grandpa, right?"

Hell no, Bob thought. Not those two. "Clark Hodgkins," he said.

"Hogdkins? The guy who sold us the property?" Debbie shot him an incredulous look. "What's he going to do?"

"We need an attorney. Now. Hodgkins has lived here his whole life. He seems to know just about everyone who's anyone. I'm betting he can find us a lawyer to meet us at the station."

Debbie leaned back in her seat and took a deep breath. She smiled for the first time since they woke up to Sophia's maddening screams. "Good thinking." She gripped his knee. "My man. You're right, as usual."

Bob pulled out his cellular device, and spoke "Call Clark Hodgkins" into it. After a few rings a sleepy and disoriented voice answered. "Hello? That you, Mr. Stevens?"

"It's me. Sorry to wake you."

"Is everything okay? It's three-twenty in the morning. A ghost wake you up?"

Funny man, Bob thought … *not*.

"It's a bit more complicated. We're on our way to the Battle Creek Police Station. There have been two deaths at Murcat Manor tonight."

Bob could hear Hodgkins throw the covers off and get out of bed. "Good God Almighty. Two?"

"Yes. A married couple. Seems she took a fire poker and stabbed her husband in the chest, killing him. Then she ran down the hall screaming like a mad woman. She fell down the stairs and tumbled all the way to the first floor. Broke her neck and half the bones in her body."

"That's four deaths in nine weeks."

"Are you keeping score? How'd you know?"

"It's my business to know. What do you need from me?"

"We need a damn good lawyer."

"Don't tell me. You're being escorted by the Battle Creek police for questioning."

"That's right. But we didn't do anything."

"Mr. Stevens, I believe you. You and your wife seem like some of the finest people I've ever met. But you have to admit. This looks suspicious. Especially in this area."

"There have to be murders around here."

"Sure. Battle Creek, Kalamazoo, and Marshall all have homicides. But not four at the same place in a nine week span."

"I know it looks bad ..."

"It does. But I'm here to help. Who's the detective bringing you in for questioning?"

"Detective Thomas Darrowby."

"Ooh." Bob heard Hodgkins smack his forehead. "That's tough. Darrowby's one contemptible asshole if you're outside of his circle of friends. You get on *his* shit list? You're going need serious legal help."

"That's why we're calling you. You know who's who around here. We don't."

"Don't worry one bit. Got your back. Just happen to know an excellent defense attorney who's gone up against Darrowby in court and won. Name of Kenneth Wilson."

"Is he good?"

"Damn good. Trust me on this one. You want this guy in your corner. With him, you'll be home for breakfast. Without him, Darrowby will make sure you eat your next meal in an orange jumpsuit."

Chapter 34   Interrogation

Bob needed to be strong for Debbie. He put his own emotional needs in the storage bin. For the second time in his structured and sheltered life, the reality of losing his posterity was more than a frightening bedtime story. Outside of Rotten Ronnie and that backstabbing family friend Phil McKenzie, he had never faced an adversary that threatened to take away everything he worked for. Believed in. Sacrificed and fought for.

For the first time, with a sense of hesitation, Bob realized, he could add the word 'entitled'.

His parents, church officials, school teachers, and sports coaches had provided a safe, albeit protected, environment for him to thrive in. The most trouble he had experienced was his high school basketball coach yelling at him for not getting back on defense.

But now, Bob was facing an adversary with the backing of the legal system who could shut down their lives. Unlike a competitive basketball game where he could lose yet start anew the next day, his current reality may not refresh into a new day.

As soon as they entered the front doors of the Battle Creek Police Station, Bob and Debbie were searched and patted down; Bob by Kowalski and Debbie by a female officer. Darrowby looked at them as if they were human traffickers. They placed their personal effects in a plastic tub that rolled down a conveyor belt at the security checkpoint.

Bob held Debbie's hand and followed the detectives, who remained silent, down a series of corridors. Two police officers brought up the rear. The last door behind them slammed closed, the clacking of metal locks echoing down the hall.

"Just relax, honey. We're law abiding and taxpaying citizens. This is just a formality. We'll be home before you know it."

Debbie squeezed his hand and looked up at Bob with a genuine smile he loved so much. "I know. You're my Superman. I trust you."

Darrowby stopped in front of a non-descript room where a police officer stood. He opened the door and motioned them in with a wave of his arm.

Bob looked around. The room resembled a jail cell. It had a foreboding sterile smell, much like a doctor's office recently disinfected to kill contaminants from the previous occupants. Or to cover up something maleficent they couldn't get rid of.

The walls were white and devoid of pictures. There were no windows. And it was hot and stuffy. Sweat formed on his forehead. He looked up at three cameras set up high. Bob returned his gaze to the barren walls and thought the police used sensory deprivation and lack of sleep and food to their advantage.

There was no furniture except for a silver metal table and four folding metal chairs, just enough for Darrowby, Kowalski, Debbie, and himself. Obviously, Darrowby had no idea of Bob intending to lawyer up. Your arrogance, Bob thought, will be your undoing.

"Have a seat," Darrowby said in a cold desolate voice while flipping through papers, pushing a chair out for Debbie with his foot. He didn't give Bob the decency to look him in the eyes.

Bob helped Debbie sit and pushed in her chair. Darrowby and Kowalski sat on the other side of the table.

"It's really hot in here," Debbie said, loosening the top button on her blouse and rolling up her sleeves. "Can you turn on the air conditioning?"

"Sure is." Darrowby turned on a tabletop fan. It oscillated back and forth on the two detectives. "Ah, that's better."

Childish ploy, Bob knew, but an effective tactic to further wear them down. Breakfast was only a few hours away and he was already hungry. He took a deep breath and prepared to go toe to toe with Darrowby on an empty stomach. No problem. Coffee and adrenaline was a good substitute for food and a lack of sleep. This was going to be a major battle. Bob was ready.

"Four deaths in nine weeks." Darrowby plopped his pile of papers on the table. "Explain."

"Are we being arrested?"

"I'll ask the questions," Darrowby said as he leaned in. "If there's anything you want to say, Mr. Stevens, just say it. Spare us the time and the taxpayers' money of prolonging the inevitable."

"I don't like what you're insinuating."

"Oh, you don't. And just what the hell do you plan on doing about it?"

Darrowby was interrupted by the sound of knuckles rapping on metal. The door swung open. A Battle Creek police office escorted a dapper dressed man in a deep blue power suit with a brown leather briefcase into the room.

The impeccably attired man moved across the room with confidence. Physically, he could match up with Darrowby. He approached Bob and Debbie, right arm stretched forward, and gave a smile assuring Bob everything was going to be okay.

"Mr. and Mrs. Stevens, my name is Kenneth Wilson. I'm a good friend of Clark Hodgkins and I'll be representing you moving forward."

Wilson looked to Darrowby and nodded, then redirected his attention back to Bob and Debbie. "Let me assure you, you're in the best of hands." He opened his briefcase on what little space was left on the table.

Bob noticed Darrowby's face. If this bozo is mad at me, he's furious with Wilson. So livid, he can't find the words to speak. Bob could read the wonder on his face. How the hell did *you* find Kenneth Wilson?

Wilson broke the awkward silence. "Thomas, it's so good to see you again."

"Stuff it," Darrowby said, composing himself and standing. "And that's Detective Darrowby to you. I don't know how the hell you ended up here. But trust me. The Stevens are up to their assholes in trouble." He punched a finger on top of the file of papers. "That's four deaths at their place in nine weeks. Understand? This doesn't just … *happen*."

Wilson, with a casual air of intended annoyance to Darrowby, took out a pad of paper and a pen from his suitcase. "My, my, sounds like a lot of work for you to sift through. Four deaths, you say?"

Darrowby's eyes narrowed into viper slits. "I'll only have to prove one. And you can bet your slick suited ass they're going down, Wilson. You lose this time, you get me?"

Wilson yawned and brought a hand up to his open mouth as he leaned against the wall. "It's so early. How about getting us some coffee,

Darrowby? That sound good to everyone?" He gave an aside wink to Bob and Debbie, then fixed his feigned earnest gaze at Darrowby.

Darrowby smirked back, said nothing.

"No? No Coffee?" Wilson shrugged, pulled on his ear while looking down and away, then paced in measured steps as if he were in front of a jury. "Fair enough, detective. So why don't you give me your strongest case."

Darrowby gripped the edge of his desk and leaned forward. "We'll start with the first. DeShawn Hill. Our investigation, using a neutral third party, proves conclusively he must have been pushed backwards while standing on top of a ladder. He was three stories up while working at Murcat Manor. Hill was a big man. A contractor with decades of experience. It would have to take another man—a strong one—to push him back. And someone he would trust to get that close to him three stories up."

Darrowby's eyes laser-focused on Bob. "No one else around could have done that. Except you."

"And I would have to assume then, that there are witnesses Bob or Debbie pushed him?"

Darrowby seethed while he hesitated, then said, "No."

Wilson chuckled, making a note. "Moving on, then? Surely you have more than this on my clients? Please tell me you didn't haul all of us into this little box of a room and try to pin a murder on them with no more than some," he snort-giggled, "little notion of yours?"

If Darrowby's eyes were weaponized, Wilson would have been shot dead. "Sure's hell do. The second death, Paul Knudson. Ten days ago at the breakfast table inside Murcat Manor. The kitchen was practically destroyed in a violent fight involving Bob and Debbie Stevens. Guests, including Knudson's wife, stated in sworn depositions Bob was fighting

Knudson hand to hand while Debbie jumped on his back and tried to claw his eyes out."

He pointed to Bob and said in an accusatory voice, "Both confessed to fighting Knudsen. The autopsy reports are due back this morning."

Darrowby looked at his watch. "In just over three hours, one of the reports is a DNA test of skin particles found under Debbie's fingernails. I'm confident that will turn up a positive match to Knudson. And that's all I need to positively connect Debbie contributing directly to Paul Knudson's death. She attacked him while he was eating. He choked and had a heart attack. All because the Stevens violently attacked him."

"And you've determined who the aggressor was, and who was defending themselves?" Wilson said, cool as chilled guacamole.

Darrowby clenched his fists and posted them on the table. "Guests reported there was a heated discussion at the breakfast table. Bob was yelling at Knudson. Telling him to shut up or get out of his house because he insulted his wife. Mrs. Knudson has given a sworn statement of the event. Yeah, I'd say your client was the aggressor. And so do some of the guests."

"That's your interpretation of what the guests have said. In a court of law, which I can assure you we will never reach, cross examination will conclude otherwise."

Wilson nonchalantly looked at his cell phone and yawned. "Good. The Tigers won last night. Okay. Anything else? Anything of any substance?" he said, not bothering to look the detective's way.

Darrowby stopped for a minute. Bob could see he was calming himself down as he wiped sweat off his forehead and ran his hands over his shirt to smooth out wrinkles. "I like my chances. And I'll say in advance, I accept your challenge."

"Looking for a rematch in court?"

"No. I'm looking for justice."

Darrowby pointed to Bob, but yelled at Wilson. "And don't think for a minute because you got three murderers off because of technicalities you can do the same with the Stevens. Four deaths on their property? You'll have to defend them all. And like I said, I only need to prove one," he said, lifting his middle finger and holding it up prominently in defiance. "Just one. Oh yeah, I really like my chances."

This guy is a real nutcase, Bob thought. Wilson better be real good, or we're going to be in a world of trouble.

"And you say the autopsy reports for Knudson will be here this morning?"

"That's right."

"Hmmmm. That's only a week and a half from the time of death."

Wilson looked to Bob and Debbie. "Obviously, the detectives planned to keep you here until the reports come in." He looked at his watch. "That's just a few hours from now. I do believe Darrowby was going to arrest you. This was indeed a one way trip for you both."

Wilson returned to Darrowby with a steely gaze. "Shame on you for trying to railroad these two decent people through the system."

Darrowby smirked and kept pace. "A few more hours and the autopsy reports will be here. Complete with the DNA results."

Wilson, again leaning coolly against the cinder block wall, turned to Bob. "Mr. Stevens, was Knudson drinking the night before?"

Bob felt rejuvenation in his heart. He wasn't sure what direction his attorney was taking him, but he liked his style. "Was he *drinking?* That's the understatement of the year. They stayed in the Roadhouse Blues room.

For some reason, that room attracts the wild beer drinkers. Guy was so drunk he still reeked of alcohol the next morning at the breakfast table."

Wilson smiled and stepped toward Darrowby as if they were head to head in front of a jury. "Tell me, Detective, among the reports you requested—was there a toxicology report on Mr. Knudson's condition?"

Darrowby's jaw set. His left eye twitched.

"I see. Obviously, not. No toxicology reports were asked for. Must have slipped your mind, eh detective?"

Wilson returned to Bob and Debbie. "The reason Darrowby did not order a toxicology report is that these can take weeks or even months to come back. I'll have to request them myself. They probably won't arrive until after Labor Day. This will give us plenty of time to sort through everything. And not," his eyes shot over to Darrowby, "while you're stowed away in a six by eight jail cell."

Darrowby looked like he might explode in a wall to wall, floor to ceiling splat of boiling plasma. *"I'm not finished.* Finally, tonight two more people died inside Murcat Manor."

Wilson spread his palms out, wide, and up, cocked one eyebrow, and said with mirth, "And my clients are implicated … *how?*"

Darrowby remained silent, clenching his teeth, a human steam kettle with its lid rattling against the pressure.

"Mmhmm—that's what I thought. You don't have anything of substance, Detective, and we both know it. Now if you don't mind, I'd like to take my clients home. This has been a long and stressful night for everyone. Let's go, folks. Back to Murcat Manor. Back you go to your home."

Wilson winked at the flush-faced detective. "Stay classy, Darrowby, surely your chance to solve a fabulously renowned and televised-the-world-over case will come along for you one day, catapulting you into the fame you so desperately desire. But this is not with the case."

Bob felt vindicated. As Wilson helped Debbie out of her chair, a second rapped knuckle sound filled the room. The police officer outside opened the door and stuck his head in. "Detective Darrowby, line one is for you."

Darrowby picked up the phone in a huff. "What is it?" he snarled. After a minute, a calm came across his face. He laid the phone back down and stared at Wilson.

"Well, what is it, detective?" Wilson said.

Darrowby looked like he had lost his center. "I think that's a … yeah, that's a good idea. Let's go back to Murcat Manor."

"What do you mean, *let's*? You're coming too?"

Darrowby stood and put on his jacket. "Yes. I am. Have to. There's been another death at Murcat Manor while we were here."

Bob and Debbie stared at each other, aghast.

"I don't understand," Bob said. "We've only been gone just over an hour. Another guest has died?"

"Not this time. The fifth person to die is your hired help, Maria Gonzalez."

Debbie covered her mouth, but still managed to say, "Maria? How?"

"That's what we're going to find out."

Darrowby looked at Wilson and pointed toward the door. "After you, counselor."

Chapter 35   Maria Gonzalez

Bob took his eyes off the red tail lights in front of him and squeezed the sleep out of his eyes. Fifty yards ahead, Darrowby drove steady at fifty-five miles per hour. The allotted speed limit on this country road. By the book.

The rolling hills, the rhythmic hum of his engine, and the interrogation from Darrowby and his goon Kowalski had drained most of his vigor. Now, Bob had to deal with one more unexpected death at Murcat Manor. Maria Rodriguez.

He looked over at his twenty-six year old, beautiful blonde haired wife. She was stunning as the first day he met her their junior year in high school, even with no makeup and three hours of sleep. Debbie stared out the front window, looking at the morning sun breaking over the rows of elm trees that formed property lines between their neighbors' properties.

Her silence spoke more than words. Debbie was reeling from the five deaths at Murcat Manor, as was he. Life was moving fast at the bed and breakfast, and the stress of paying the twenty-five thousand dollar monthly bills weighed heavily on them. The week before, lying in bed with what precious free time they had, Debbie had confided there was not enough time to properly mourn the recent passing DeShawn Hill. Bob agreed.

For whatever reason, Maria's death hit them with an immense sense of loss. Like their recently deceased contractor, they'd gotten to know Maria intimately, although she had only been employed for a month. Along with the hired hand Raymond Hettinger, the foursome saw each other every day except for their days off work—which were few. They worked together, laughed, and found a common bond that united them. Debbie wanted to keep the duo full time throughout the year, but Bob reminded her the numbers didn't add up.

Bob looked at the digital clock on the radio. 6:12 a.m. It was the dawn of a new day, and he was practically slumping onto the steering wheel, his head slowly nodding forward as he caught himself from falling asleep. Only adrenaline kept him awake, fueled by a mixture of emotions. Some were natural. Others had a toxic origin that invaded his mind, driving him to think of drastic measures to protect Debbie and their future.

Bob gripped the steering wheel so he could brace himself and sit up straight. In his rear view mirror he confirmed Kenneth Wilson, the one person who could protect them, was still behind him. A patrol car with two Battle Creek police officers brought up the rear.

"Bob, honey. We need to keep our cool. Events are spiraling out of control. We can't allow Darrowby to get the better of us."

Bob looked at his wife. Her shoulder length blonde hair was a disaster. Mascara was everywhere but around her eyes. But he would never tell her that. She was still gorgeous, and he was madly in love with her more than ever.

"Maybe we need Kenneth Wilson to stay at Murcat Manor full time."

Debbie let loose a small sideways smirk. "I know you said that facetiously. But it's not a bad idea."

Bob squeezed his eyes again and shook his head as the car swayed toward the center yellow double lines dividing Oak Hill Road. "I'm trying to keep my cool. But I'm really struggling here."

"What are you feeling? Other than being tired."

"Anger. I want to punch Darrowby in the face as hard as I can."

"So do I. Actually, I want to scratch his eyes out. But we can't do that. We have to rise above. What else?"

Bob blurted out before he could stop the words. "Well, I'm scared and not afraid to admit it. There are three more dead bodies in Murcat Manor tonight and we're being escorted back by a pair of overzealous detectives who want to arrest us for murder. Not good, Debbie. Not good at all. Do you understand?"

He felt Debbie squeeze, then rub his knee. "Anything else?"

Bob leaned over and gave her a quick kiss, careful not to take his eyes off the road. "Sadness. Up until now, we didn't know any of these people. Well, except for DeShawn Hill. That was difficult. And honestly, I don't think either one of us are over it. I mean, we saw that man every day but Sunday for eight months. Now add to this madness Maria Rodriguez. She was one of the most innocent people I ever met."

Debbie hung her head and sighed, then looked out the passenger window. "I was thinking the same thing. Maria, she had such a bright future. Her life was taken far too early. Who knows what she would have given to the world? All she wanted to do was become a doctor and help people less fortunate then herself."

The twenty minute ride home allowed Bob to access the more important framework of their relationship. He thought of their personal well-being. But that wasn't all that was on his mind.

"Debbie. Honey. We need time to heal. Just like you said. We simply can't keep up with things. Kenneth Wilson, he can help. But ..."

"But?" Debbie returned her gaze to Bob. He knew that stare. She was looking to him for direction and leadership.

"I'll just say it. I feel like our lives have been invaded by your grandparents, no offense, by Darrowby and his thug partner Kowalski, and now our neighbors Eddie and Alison Brady. I thought we escaped to the country to avoid all of this."

Debbie formed a smile. "Listen to me. I know you don't want to hear this right now, but grandma and grandpa will help us. They always have an answer. Trust me. I've got this. We've got this."

Up ahead, the yellow and white spindles of Murcat Manor came into view. As Bob lowered his speed, he could see crowds of people lining the side of Oak Hill Road.

"I can't tell you how mad I am. Murcat Manor is more than just our place of business where we clock in and out. This is our house. This is our home. This is where we'll raise our four children. I'm not allowing Darrowby to ruin everything."

"Boy, girl, boy, girl," Debbie said softly through teary eyes. "Four kids within eight years. Then you get the ol' snip snip."

Bob felt a buzzing in his pocket. "I'm getting a text from Raymond."

3 fams leaving

Murcat Manor smells bad

I opened windows

Hurry back

"Smells bad? That can't be good. And I don't want to sound like Scrooge, but that means I'll have to refund people their money."

Debbie hunched her shoulders, then let them fall. "That's the least of our worries. The news crews are back."

Bob took a deep breath. "Darrowby. That son-of-a-bitch. He did this. He called the news stations. There's no other way so many would be gathered this early in front of our house. He loves the media attention. And he's trying to bring pressure on us. Make us squirm. We haven't killed anyone. No way am I letting him ruin our lives."

Bob slammed his palm against the steering wheel, hit the horn by mistake, and jumped in his seat. It was embarrassing, but also brought a bit more consciousness to his groggy state of mind.

Bob followed Darrowby into the driveway. His neighbors stared into the windows as if they were peeking in on some bizarre freak show. Then the news teams descended on his car.

"We'll have to make this quick. Get out and make a beeline for the house. Wait for me. I'll get out first."

Bob exited his door, put a hand on the hood, and vaulted over it to the passenger side. He opened Debbie's door and pulled her in tight, forging a passage way to the front door. Three reporters tried to block their path. Crews with shoulder mounted cameras and booms followed close. A middle aged male reporter who Bob recognized from Channel Six muscled his way through the crowd and stuck a microphone in his face.

"Mr. Stevens, what can you tell us about the three people who were killed under mysterious circumstances inside Murcat Manor just a few hours ago?"

Before Bob could react, Kenneth Wilson plowed his way to his side and wrapped his arms around him and Debbie. He helped speed their way to the front door.

"Don't say a word," he said as he craned his neck back and forth into their ears. "Let's get inside. We'll sort things out there, away from the cameras."

Two Battle Creek police officers had the front door open. Bob, Debbie, Kenneth Wilson, Darrowby and Kowalski piled in. The two police officers who brought up the rear kept the news crews at bay.

Bob walked past the guests in the living room. Darrowby was already inside taking control.

"What do we have?" Darrowby barked to the police officers.

"Right this way." They led him toward the back of the house. Darrowby looked over his shoulder and motioned Bob and Debbie to follow.

Bob saw the same coroner working over Sophia Johnson at the bottom of the stairs; the sheet was now off her body. Her head twisted at an ungodly angle, staring at the ceiling, her eyes froze open in what could only be described as pure terror. Bob glanced a second look. Those wide opened eyes, they looked like crazy eyes, as if she had lost all sense of sanity. No other way to explain them.

Inside the kitchen, Raymond was waiting. He was visibly shaking.

"What happened?" Darrowby said.

"I-it was t-terrible. I was. Right here, getting," he shook all over, "w-water for the guests when I smelled it."

"Smelled what?"

Raymond looked at Darrowby, his nose crinkled up and his face distorted like a squeezed lemon. "Burning hair and flesh. I ran to the back laundry room and saw Maria."

Darrowby cocked an eyebrow. "And?"

Kowalski tapped Raymond on the shoulder. "Get a grip, man, this is important. We need facts. Details. Pull it together, okay?"

Raymond closed his eyes, breathed in long, and let out a slow, low-whistling exhalation. He repeated the process, then opened his eyes, his expression now calm, with a fatalistic undertone. He pointed to the deep laundry sink, just a few feet from the dead body of Maria Gonzalez.

"She was standing there, her hands in the water, and she was quivering from head to toe. Her hair was standing on end, and I could swear she was trying to scream, but couldn't. Suddenly there was a deafening snapping sound, and a flash of light—more like a lightning bolt—and she flew backward, landing on her back, there. Her hair was on fire, her eyes rolled all the way back in her head, and her hands looked like they'd been in the deep fryer."

Raymond's countenance withered, as though he'd accomplished a duteous and prodigious mission, and was now sapped dry.

Kowalski stepped over to the laundry sink and looked down. "Radio," he said.

Darrowby looked his way. "Come again?"

Kowalski whipped around with his hands held up in a 'stay back' motion. "Everybody stay clear of this sink. There's a radio in the water, my guess is that it's on, and this water, not being pure water, conducted the electricity to, and through, this poor lady here. The juice grounded through her to the concrete floor and locked her in its death flow until she died from cardio arrest."

Kowalski reached over the sink and unplugged the radio from the wall, then stepped back and shook his head, looking back and forth between Bob and Darrowby. "Poor girl. Looks like she suffered terribly. I don't know

251

what it is about this place. But after seeing and smelling this, I'm convinced this property is cursed."

Chapter 36   The Media

Bob looked at the farm-themed clock on the kitchen wall. Eleven 11:53 a.m. He watched Raymond close the front door as Kenneth Wilson, Darrowby, and Kowalski were the last to leave. Darrowby gave Bob one more dubious look over his shoulder. Bob clenched his teeth and balled his fists. If only he could have one open shot to smash him right in his smug jib.

The door closed. Murcat Manor was once again empty. Darrowby had made it a point to drive every last guest out, demanding a full refund, by creating a dramatic crime scene. Kowalski didn't help with his repeated insinuations the bed and breakfast must be haunted.

Bob looked up at Raymond as he entered the kitchen. "You sure you don't want the rest the day off?"

Raymond rubbed his bloodshot eyes. "Thank you, Mr. Stevens. But I'm fine. I'll finish up a few things, then take a nap."

Bob was relieved. He looked at Raymond as a sentry guarding the place while he and Debbie caught up on much needed sleep.

"Thanks again. I'll triple your pay today. If the news crews knock on the door, don't open it. That especially goes for Ross and Erma, too."

Bob let his shoulders slump and he trudged to his bedroom with a bottle of Merlot in each hand. Debbie followed with two wine glasses. Lying on the bed were thirteen sleeping cats spread out across the comforter and pillows.

Bob threw his arms in the air. "Oh—of course."

Debbie lovingly transferred the felines to cat beds on the floor where they continued their mid-day slumber. She then took the bottles of wine from Bob, popped the cork on one, and poured two glasses.

"Look at them," Debbie said with a bitter-sweet tone. "So innocent. They have no idea what's going on. Or maybe they do, but can't communicate to us how five people died in our home." She patted Emily on the head. "Sleep tight in your own beds, little ones. Sweet dreams."

Little fur coated turds, Bob thought. He kicked off his shoes and pulled the blankets back, grabbed the television remote and lay down, then took the wineglass Debbie handed him.

"I was sure Darrowby would take his time and torment us well into the afternoon with his endless questioning," Debbie said.

"Wilson's a great attorney. He kept the detectives in line and expedited the process."

"And Hodgkins really came through for us. Without him recommending Wilson, we'd be sitting in separate jail cells calling Grandma and Grandpa for help."

"Those two goons in suits. How can they continue to blame us for these, these obviously accidental—albeit bizarre—deaths? I mean, we weren't even in the house when that frickin' radio must have somehow fallen into that tub sink, right?"

"I didn't know that about water and electricity," Debbie said, looking away at nothing in particular.

"Huh?"

"About electricity not able to conduct through pure water."

"Oh, that." Bob sipped his glass of Merlot. "Yeah, I read that somewhere, gosh—think it was back in college." Another drink, then a gulp. "Most people don't know, but it's the impurities in water that allow electricity to pass through. Like salt, for instance."

Debbie snapped her fingers. "We have a water softener that uses salt."

"Bingo was his name-oh." Bob pointed a finger at her and gave an ironic chuckle. He took the last gulp of wine from his glass and said, like a lecturing university professor, "When salts are dissolved in water, they separate into positive sodium ions and negative chlorine ions. These opposite charges, like the opposite poles of a battery, create the potential for the conductive effect. Water's conductive properties make it very dangerous as it allows an electric current to travel through it rapidly and shock any unsuspecting person in contact with the water."

Bob turned on the TV. There were still two news crews in the front of Murcat Manor. Darrowby was live talking with one reporter. The seasoned Battle Creek detective's face filled the seventy-two inch wall mounted TV screen.

How Bob despised this man. He couldn't remember wishing death on anyone, but today he wondered; if he could push Darrowby over a cliff and get away with it, would he? Bob had to be careful not to crush the wine glass in his hand.

"Yes, the three deaths here early this morning were of suspicious nature," Darrowby said into the camera using his usual unblinking stare. "As were the previous two."

"The son-of-a-bitch. I can't believe that guy," Bob said, handing his glass to Debbie for a refill. "I should go out there and punch him in the face for the entire world to see."

Debbie downed her wine and gave herself a refill as well. "I'm mad as hell at Darrowby, too. Look at him hamming it up for the cameras. And right in our driveway live to the world. He really thinks he's all that. Like he's some big shot local celebrity."

"He's gunning for national celeb status the way he's throwing gasoline on the fire."

A tall brunette jostled for position among the reporters. "Records show Robert and Debbie Stevens, along with her grandparents, Ross and Erma Dempsey, are owners of Murcat Manor. Are they suspects? Are you investigating these deaths as possible crimes? Or even Murders?"

"I can neither confirm nor deny at this time. But stay tuned. If there has been any foul play, the good people of this area can rest assured I will arrest any and all appropriate person or persons involved."

Bob gulped down his second glass of wine. "He certainly isn't doing us any favors, leaving it wide open for viewers' speculation that we're involved."

"We've also found," the brunette reporter said, "that the two previous homes built on this property burned to the ground, killing everyone that lived here. Once in nineteen sixty-seven, and before that in nineteen-seventeen. Rumors around here are that this property is cursed or haunted."

"That's correct," Darrowby said. "Murcat Manor is the third property to stand here in the last century. And the five deaths here bring the grand total to twenty-four deaths."

"Are you friggin' kiddin' me?" Bob downed his second glass of wine. "He's sensationalizing the story through the media."

"Ugh. Turn the channel."

Bob turned to all the local channels from his satellite dish from Cleveland to Detroit to Grand Rapids to Chicago. They were all carrying the same story from their sister stations in Battle Creek and Kalamazoo.

"So Murcat Manor is now a regional story spreading to surrounding states, which by the way, is our market. Next up, CNN will make this a national story."

Bob turned to one of the news channels in Lansing. They watched as they were filmed arriving back to Murcat Manor early in the morning. Darrowby exited his car and led the way, posturing like a demigod to the media.

The camera panned to Bob and Debbie as they got out. Bob was beyond pissed off. One thing was a sure bet, he'd lay the money for next month's mortgage payment on it; Ross and Erma were watching the same stories.

"Oh my God. We look terrible." Debbie seized her face in both hands. My mascara. It's running down my cheeks from crying. And look at my hair. It's messy and matted. But that's because we had like, what—three hours' sleep before the Johnsons died? And the interrogation room at the police station was a sauna."

Bob had his hand out, waving off the cameras as Wilson plowed a path for them into the front door.

"Un. Frickin'. Believable." Bob shook his head, smacked his forehead. "No way. This can't be happening to us. Our dream is turning into a nightmare. And we've been open barely two months."

Debbie poured Bob another glass, pried the remote from his hand, and turned off the TV. "Time to wind down, lover. Drink up."

"I'm turning off my cell phone. And yours," Bob said. "I know Ross and Erma will be calling. And I sure as hell don't want that rooster alarm app waking me up tomorrow."

**

Thomas Darrowby lay in his bed with wife. He sipped his scotch with pleasure as he navigated the late night news stations.

"Thomas, that wasn't fair. Calling the media out to the Stevens' place like that. You don't know they killed any of those people."

Darrowby didn't take his eyes off the TV. "Oh, they did. Trust me on this one, Laura. Those two, they're guilty as sin."

Laura Darrowby studied Bob and Debbie as the camera zoomed in on them. "But just look at them. So young. So innocent looking. You know what I think? These deaths have to be a series of unfortunate accidents."

Darrowby laughed in a loud boisterous way. He looked over to his wife. "You're the innocent one. So trusting. That's why I married you, sweetheart. To balance out the overbearing alpha male in me. In my line of work, we call that a trail of evidence. Oh, don't let their Happy Days or Brady Bunch appearance fool you. Those two," Darrowby pointed to the TV with his glass in his hand, the ice cubes clinking, "they're not who they seem to be. They're pure evil. I can sense it when I'm in the house."

"Are you sure it's coming from them?"

"Where else could it come from? Murcat Manor's not built on an old Indian burial ground." Darrowby laughed at the preposterous thought. "The only other things in the house are thirteen lazy cats."

"Well, thirteen is an unlucky number."

Darrowby laughed so hard he spilled part of his scotch on the bed. "Sorry, honey. Yeah. Sure. The cats. They killed them."

Darrowby slowed his laugh.

"What's the matter?"

"Now that we're talking about the cats, Bob Stevens did mention three were on the roof where DeShawn Hill was working when he fell backwards."

"Well, maybe the cats spooked DeShawn. That's plausible. Did you think of that?"

Darrowby downed his drink and poured another. "Aack—nah, no way. Impossible. Anyway, this story's plastered all over TV. It's gone viral on the internet. This is golden for me. That's what I'm after."

"And just what do you hope to gain from all of this?"

"This will place more pressure on Bob and Debbie. It's just the thing to help counteract their hiring of that slickster of an attorney, Kenneth Wilson. He's beaten me in court on a number of occasions. This time around, I hope reporters can dig something up that will help me convict the Stevens of at least one murder."

Darrowby felt Laura's fingers now combing through his wavy black hair. "Well, I'm sure you know what you're doing. It's just that the Stevens, well, they don't look anything like killers."

"Hmph. Oh they are, dear. I have four of my best men interviewing all the former guests in person and over the phone. There have been hundreds who stayed there since the place opened Memorial Day Weekend. It's a lot of work, but mark my words. As surely as the sun will rise tomorrow, there has to be at least a few people who can shed light on the Stevens and the five deaths that happened under their watch."

Darrowby relaxed and took another long drink. "I swear, I'll see them both behind bars for the rest of their lives."

Chapter 37   Winds of Change

Bob was standing in his gray world again, riding the same neutral-colored speeding bullet train. He gripped a handle that controlled where the train could stop. Looking out the windows, he saw countless terminals where people got on and off. Bob was never more stressed. He needed to disembark and move forward with his life. But which station was his? It was all so baffling. Until he knew, he couldn't stop the train.

Bob woke without the sound of a rooster crowing from his cell phone alarm. He turned his head and looked at the clock. It was barely seven in the morning. The sleep was healing. He was no longer exhausted.

But he was drained: mentally, physically, and emotionally. As his head cleared from his dream and he saw the two, no three bottles of empty wine on Debbie's nightstand, he realized he was also financially drained.

He bolted upright in bed, three sleepy cats grousing and rolling off his chest. Murcat Manor was empty again.

Debbie emerged from the sheets and mumbled something.

Bob looked at the elongated lump under the sheets. "I think you asked what time it is. It's a little after seven."

"Evening or morning?"

Bob found enough humor in his wife's innocence to form a chuckle. "Morning. It's Monday morning."

Debbie sat up and held her head. "How long did we sleep?"

"Let's see. We came home early yesterday morning. Darrowby left around noon. Then we drank a lot of wine and crashed about five. That's fourteen straight hours of sleep."

Debbie shook her head and rubbed her eyes. "Wait ... the guests. I have to cook breakfast and ..."

Bob placed his hand on her shoulder. "Don't worry about it. The place is empty. Again. I'll give you a few minutes to wake up."

Debbie gently pushed three sleeping cats off her and crawled out of bed. She looked in the mirror, tried in vain to make sense of her hair, then stuck out her tongue.

"That's right. I remember now. Bob, just what the hell is happening to us? To Murcat Manor? Three more people died, including Maria. And guests are leaving like a flock of flies."

Debbie was interrupted by muffled pounding from above. Bob looked up at the ceiling. "What the heck is that?"

"I don't know."

Bob walked over the bedroom window and opened the shutters. "Strange. I see three pickup trucks in the driveway. They have Hill Construction on the doors."

"Now that is weird. I didn't think they liked us. Anything else?"

His chest caved in a deep sigh. "Ross and Erma's car."

"Grandma and Grandpa. Thank God. They can help us." She tossed Bob his robe. "Put this on."

Salem's Daughters

"This can't be good," he grumbled as he thrust his arms through the sleeves.

"As dark as things seem, don't be too sure. Grandma and Grandpa, they always have the solution. We need to trust them."

Bob knew Debbie was right. But he did need something to help take off the edge of Erma before leaving the sanctity of their bedroom. He turned on his cell phone and used Voice Command to text Raymond Hettinger.

We're coming out now

I see Ross and Erma's car in the driveway

Need fresh java

Thanks

Bob then went to the bathroom and opened the medicine cabinet. He found what he was looking for. Advil. After popping four into his mouth, he turned on the faucet and cupped his hands to capture water and swallow the gel caps.

Knowing relief was minutes away, he walked back into the bedroom. Debbie had put on her white cotton robe and was fixing her hair with her hands while slipping her feet into slippers. "What a way to wake up. My head is pounding."

Bob held up the Advil. "How many?"

"Three. Thanks."

Bob found a wine glass half full and handed it to Debbie, who used it to wash down the pills.

"I think we're ready. After five deaths, what's the worst that can happen? Let's go."

He took Debbie by the hand and entered the kitchen. Ross and Erma sat at the table. Their laptops were open. Raymond was brewing fresh coffee.

263

"Well, good morning, sleepy heads." Ross made a vain attempt to display his usual jovial way as he stood and gave Bob and Debbie a hug. But the smile was forced. It wasn't close to the traditional Ross smile and laugh.

Erma remained seated, looking down at her laptop. She was reserved. Bob had never seen them this way. It was as if a spell of despondency had fallen on them. Things were far worse than he'd expected.

"Grandma," Debbie said as Bob pulled out a chair for her to sit. "I'm so sorry. I don't know what to say. I don't know what to do. But now that you're here, everything's going to be okay. I just know it."

"There, there child," Erma said in a soft, comforting tone. "There's nothing you, or Bob, can do at this point. Just leave everything to us. Again."

Erma ignored Bob, and that was fine with him. She remained silent as she raised her arm, aimed the remote at the kitchen TV, and flipped through various channels airing morning news shows. The leading stories were the same: *Murder at Murcat Manor. Is Murcat Manor haunted? Murcat Manor, Not What It Seems To Be.*

"Please. Remain seated," she said, her expression flat, voice even. "Both of you. Coffee's finished."

Raymond brought two cups and set them in front of Bob and Debbie.

Ross again tried, with marginal success, to don a smile. "I know this has been all too traumatic on you. But you have to understand we have a lot of work to do. We can't stop. You both slept all yesterday afternoon through this morning. It's now time to get right back to work."

"Not only is Murcat Manor empty once again," Erma said in a calm but lifeless monotone. "There have been many cancellations through August and well into September. Do you know what this means?"

She lowered her arm and turned off the TV. "I don't think I need to go to any more channels. We all get it."

Ross folded his hands on the table and leaned in. "Bob. Debbie. You realize at this rate, we will begin to miss monthly payments. That's eighteen thousand to the bank. Five thousand in food bills. And another two thousand in utilities."

Although Bob's brain was mush, he still needed to try to take the lead. Can't let Ross and Erma run the entire show.

"We won't have the huge food bills while we're empty. But yeah—we just need to get people back in here. Once we show the banks we have full occupancy again, they'll work with us."

Erma closed her eyes and rubbed her forehead. "No, no Bob. No. The bank will not help us. Since there have been three more deaths, I doubt they will restructure the loan. And we have to think of the insurance on the place. A total of five deaths in just a few months? Think about it. They could cancel the policy on Murcat Manor at any time."

Debbie did what she usually would do when overwhelmed by stress. She folded her arms on the table and buried her head in them. A muffled voice escaped. "I'm sorry. I don't know what to do."

Ross patted Debbie's hands and stroked her hair. "But we do, sweetie. Once again, it's Grandpa and Grandma to the rescue."

Bob could hear more noise upstairs. Hammering. Cordless drills. Nail guns firing off. More miscellaneous banging. Footsteps walking back and forth. Orders shouted out.

"I saw the pickup trucks in the driveway. What's going on up there?"

Ross stood, sucked in his gut, stuck out his barrel chest, and took an exaggerated breath. That was his way of taking control when changes were needed.

"Bob, we need to do something drastic to save Murcat Manor."

"How?" Debbie said, lifting her head. "Guests are dying here. Five people in nine weeks. I'm starting to believe the rumors this place is haunted."

"Precisely, my dear. Precisely."

Ross's jovial smile returned. But this time, his expression was different. Bob discerned there was something sinister behind the face. "Now you're onto something. And this, we will turn to our advantage."

Bob didn't know what Ross and Erma had in mind. But he didn't like whatever was coming. Ross continued to stand, chuckling, as if he had lost a portion of his sanity. Jared Leto's portrayal of The Joker in *The Suicide Squad* came to Bob's mind. Ross seemed maniacal. And money—the one thing that Ross could get maniacal over—was always the driver behind his decision making processes.

The banging from upstairs became louder, the pace of work faster. Bob craned his neck to look through the living room at the front door. Carpenters and painters came down the stairs and exited the front door.

"Who are they?"

Ross pursed his lips, sequence-tapping his fingers against his chest. "Men from Hills Construction, my boy."

"What are they doing here? With Hill's death, I didn't think they'd step foot on our property. They thought we had something to do with his accident."

Bob noticed Erma staring at him with an incredulous look when he said the word *accident*. Ross gave Bob a stern look. His lip quivered. Bob could see spittle coming from his mouth. He felt he was back in the board room being stared down by a really pissed off CEO. Ross was quickly rising to the level of detest Darrowby had so far held all by himself.

"I have my ways, Bob. I have connections. Okay?" He pointed toward the front door where two workers entered while locking eyes with Bob. "DeShawn Hill's wife and brother have kept the company in business. So I brought in those familiar with building Murcat Manor to help with the changes."

"Changes? What kind of changes?"

"We're converting the themes on some of the rooms," Erma said with little reflection in her voice.

Bob didn't like change. Major changes meant he failed and was no longer in control. He stood and stepped into Ross. "Whatever you've concocted, just stop. Okay? I don't like any of this."

Ross was relentless. He stuck his forefinger in Bob's chest. "Listen to me, my boy. As of today, Murcat Manor is a sinking ship. If we stay the course we're all going down. This bed and breakfast is a post-iceberg-collision Titanic, and we need to make a serious transformation. Right now."

Two more workers entered the front door, loaded down with—what? Bob couldn't make the items out.

"Where do you want these, Mr. Dempsey?"

Ross stepped away from Bob. "Upstairs. You'll see the rest of the crew. Just join up with them."

"Yes, sir."

Bob stepped through the open arced kitchen door to get a better look. "What are they carrying? Did I see whips, chains, and, is that a *thumbscrew?* I'm not following. How's this going to change our fortunes? And just what the heck are those things the guys are taking upstairs?"

"Bob, we need to fill rooms. Fast. As in yesterday. Capish?"

267

Bob watched as another worker bring in what appeared to be a straightjacket. "Well, yeah. But I don't think bringing in instruments of torture and death is the answer. Just how do you expect to fill the rooms this way?"

Erma shook her head. Ross continued his sneer. "Not how do we, my boy, but how *did* we."

Bob turned back to Ross. "You've filled the rooms with reservations?"

Ross spread his arms wide, his genuine jovial smile returned. "Many of them. But don't you worry. We'll pack 'em in again."

By now, Bob knew Ross's earlier dour demeanor had just been a setup, a ruse and ploy to manipulate the situation to his advantage. The sly old dog had been setting him up like a world class pool hustler.

Bob looked at the clock. "Fourteen hours. That's how long Debbie and I slept. That's not much time to ... how did you manage—"

Ross held up an open palm. "I can accomplish more during that amount of time than most men can do in a week. That's how I got in life to where I am. Understand? I get things done. I do them fast and finish them right the first time."

"Allow me to get to the point," Erma said. "We're now appealing to the fringe element."

Bob didn't like what he'd already seen or heard. But this was beyond sanity. The fringe element? Inside his house? His mind raced as he envisioned every possible form of life from a freak show invading Murcat Manor. Sitting at their kitchen table. Lounging in the living room. Breeding in the upstairs rooms. He shuddered.

Bob glanced around Ross to see workers bring in what looked like an operating table and chainsaws. "Are those what I think they are?"

Ross turned around, a relaxed smile on his face. "Yes, they certainly are. The Victorian Room will be renamed the Insane Asylum. It'll be a creepy lab inside a white padded room. The operating table is the bed, complete with fake blood stained sheets. Dissected body parts will be arranged around the room. Pretty cool, don't you think?"

Bob struggled for words. Debbie raised her head. Erma pulled out her flask, took a long swig, and handed it to Debbie, who also took a long drink.

Debbie, drinking whiskey for breakfast? Erma? Yes. But Debbie? Never. She was stressed more than ever, and now Ross was sitting at the kitchen table demonstrating tools of medieval punishment.

Bob shook his head. "And the torture machines?"

Ross laughed, which gave Bob a most uncomfortable feeling. "Those are for the Egyptian Room, which is now the Medieval Torture Chamber. Complete with stage props of just about every known usage of torture from that time."

Ross flagged down one of the workers, waving for him to come over. He did, and Ross took a strange looking implement from the man and held it up with pride.

"Did my homework, too, and found this little beauty. It's called a Heretic Fork. See?"

Ross turned it this way and that for observation. It had a two pronged sharp fork on each end with a leather collar attached in the middle of the connecting steel stem.

Ross explained, "You strap this device around the victim's neck, positioning the forks, one jabbed tight under the chin and the other poked into the sternum. Then you hang the poor sap by his hands to where just his toes are touching the floor. Idea is, you have to stay awake—conscious,

269

anyway. If you fall asleep, or pass out, your chin will drop, and ....” Ross paused long, that Joker-like malevolent grin on his face. “Basically, you're skewered.”

Now Bob was thinking of taking a swig from Erma's flask. “That's ... that's just plain ... grotesque. Weirdo occult nut-bag crap.”

Ross was laughing hard. "Hold that thought. It only gets better, Bob my boy. The Safari Room is now officially the Paranormal Room."

Ross was alive with words. Bob found it vexing he could get so excited over the morbid makeover themes.

“The Disco Room is now the Serial Killer Room. That's what the chainsaws are for. Dolls will be hung from the ceiling like puppets. We needed some extra ummphh, so we added machetes and other such weapons of choice from horror flicks. They're props, but I have to admit they look so real.”

“You've got to be kidding.”

Ross held up his hand. "But wait. That's not all. Finally, there's the Skull and Crossbones Room. This will replace the Neptune Room, or Under the Sea. It'll be black and gray and complete with its very own graveyard. A zombie wasteland with an underworld theme on Earth. The bed is a giant coffin. Fog is pumped in for special effects. This is meant to strike fear in the hearts of visitors.

Bob had to ask. “Just out of curiosity. What about the Roadhouse Blues?”

Ross waved off Bob's question. “Two deaths are attributed to that room. It'll book solid as is.”

Bob's head was swirling vortex of maddening images and thoughts. He had to somehow stand his ground. “Look. I understand you feel you need to take drastic measures. The four of us could soon owe a lot of money we may not be able to repay. But changing half the rooms to these bizarre themes? This is outright demented."

"Maybe so," Erma said. "But do you have a better idea? Because we sure don't."

Ross patted Bob on the shoulders. "Sit down, Bob. We have more to discuss than theme changes."

Ross paced back and forth with the leadership of a CEO and the showmanship of P.T. Barnum. He used his charm, smile, and hand gestures as he continued. All of which Bob despised as he knew he was going to be sold something he didn't want.

"You'll love this. The Paranormal Room was a last minute decision. Erma and I did online research and came up with the other themes. But last night, the cast from *American Ghost Stories* called us. Can you believe it?"

Debbie took another swig from Erma's flask. "I've seen them on TV. They set up in abandoned and so-called haunted places and look for evidence of ghosts."

Ross stopped and spread his arms wide. "And guess what. They want to spend a few nights here. At Murcat Manor. Can you believe it?"

Bob shot out of his chair. "No. Absolutely not. You're turning this into a freak show."

Debbie stood next to Bob. "Grandpa, as much as I love and respect you, I have to back up my husband. We forbid this."

Ross's smile got bigger, if that were possible. "We don't have a choice. They offered us a hundred thousand dollars to do their show live. It'll be broadcast to over two million viewers in real time. Right here at Murcat Manor."

Debbie fell silent. Bob's jaw dropped.

"And it's a check I can deposit as soon as they leave."

271

"We need that money," Erma said. "We talked to the people at the bank. They're not messing around. They're getting panicky, thinking this place will go out of business before the summer is over. They want their money."

"So we accepted *American Ghost Stories*' offer." Ross accentuated his statement with a loud clap of his hands.

"This is short term," Erma said. "Just to get people coming back. I'm sure once a year or so passes, we can go back to the original themes. But for now, we're promoting like hell, no pun intended, to the fringe element."

Bob took a longing look at Erma's flask, but resisted the urge and instead had a drink from his coffee. It helped clear the after effects of the wine from the day before. "I know you're trying to help, but this is an awful idea."

Ross's grin disappeared. "No, Bob. I'll tell you what's awful. Having all these bills due with no way to pay them."

"This'll never work," Bob countered.

"Wanna bet," Erma said, turning her laptop to Bob and scrolling down the page. "There have been over one hundred new reservations, and that's just in the last few hours."

"Overnight," Ross said, "Murcat Manor is gaining a reputation as one of the few real haunted Bed and Breakfasts. Can you believe it? Thanks to us, of course. Bob, we can exploit this. The possibilities are better than they've ever been."

Bob had to laugh. "People won't buy into this ... this rubbish."

"Oh? Five deaths in nine weeks? Nineteen deaths from the previous homes here? Wouldn't you say by now everyone thinks something's going on here? Something strange? Macabre? Even sinister? My boy, this reputation will either make or break Murcat Manor. It's up to us to decide which direction we take this."

Erma took one more swig from her flask. She offered Debbie another drink, who emptied the flat metal container Erma called *Old Faithful*.

"Now Bob, there is one more problem. Darrowby's just waiting to bust you. Good thing you lawyered up with that Wilson guy. Not sure how you found him, but consider yourself lucky."

Bob knew he shouldn't be surprised, but had to ask. "How did you know?"

"Remember," Erma said. "We cosigned on a three and a half million dollar loan. We're not about to let you run this place into the ground."

Bob had the fleeting thought that Ross and Erma would do well as CIA agents with an Eagle Eye global privacy invasion computer at their disposal.

Ross put on a gentle demeanor. But he placed his hand on Bob's shoulder, gripping it with surety.

"Listen up. I need to level with you. If this doesn't go well, we'll have to bring in a new manager for Murcat Manor."

"Translation," Erma said, stiffening upright in her seat. "You'll be out if things don't turn around."

Bob stepped away from Ross's manipulative constraint. "You can't do that. We're part owners. If I go down, you go down."

Erma glared at Bob. "Do you think we're stupid? It wouldn't take much to push Darrowby over the edge. He wants to arrest you for murder. And who's to say you're not somehow involved. You have to admit, five deaths makes you look very suspicious."

"Now Erma, darling, let's not be too hasty. I say we give Bob another chance."

Unbelievable, Bob thought. They're playing bad cop good cop with me. He wondered if they rehearsed their routine driving to Murcat Manor.

Erma maintained her stare. "This is not a request. It's a statement. Take it or leave it."

Erma started to squirm uncomfortably. Bob looked down at the cats rubbing up against her ankles. Scarlett jumped up on her lap. Two more cats were now on the table, nestling their heads into her chest. Bob welcomed the unexpected interruption.

Erma brushed them off and kicked at the ones on the floor. "Get away from me, you good for nothing disease ridden varmints. Go shed somewhere else."

"Well, I think we're clear on what we have to do," Ross said. "Erma and I need to go home and sleep. We've been up all night planning this. Then, it's right back to business."

"Remember," Erma said as she stood and stomped her foot to scare the cats away. "This is it. Make it work or we bring in new management."

Erma gave Debbie a hug and kiss, then took Ross's arm as they walked to the front door. She looked back into the kitchen.

"Have a good day, Bob."

Go to hell, Erma. Bob's wish followed her out the door.

Chapter 38   American Ghost Stories

Emily lounged on an ottoman in the center of the living room, soaking up the late morning sun light streaming through the open plantation shutters. Her twelve followers lay scattered around the living room on various pieces of furniture.

Emily was more excited than she could remember in this, her sixth life. The novelty of performing the double murder of Sophia and Reginald Johnson with pinpoint precision and the spur-of-the-moment killing of Maria Gonzalez had worn off.

Emily loved the creativity Madelyn conceptualized while watching Maria fill a tub sink in the downstairs laundry room to soak the blood-stained shag carpet rugs from the Disco Room. Jacqueline dropped Maria's core body temperature to the point she stood still. Chloe levitated a radio above the sink and plugged it into a socket. Then she simply let the radio fall.

Now they needed a new and bigger challenge to satisfy their lust for more terror.

The energy given off by the wave of new guests surpassed any of the prior visitors. Unlike previous weeks when one or two guests showed up early, today the parking lot was full by eleven o'clock.

Emily looked for, identified, and fed off what people emanated. She wasn't sure what to expect with the new promotions the Ross and Erma had in mind. But she looked forward to the possibilities of the darker elements invading the bed and breakfast.

She sat up to take notice while her following dozed off. Typical.

A young eclectic group of people strolled through the front door. Disrespectful would be an understatement. The young punks, who looked like they were barely out of high school, acted as if they owned the place. Two girls walked straight to the kitchen and rummaged through the refrigerators.

Raymond Hettinger, as was part of his job description, hauled their luggage from their cars into the bed and breakfast, then up the stairs to their rooms. Not one had the courtesy to say thank you.

Emily studied the freakish group who were unlike anything she had seen. The incoming guests had pale skin that didn't look natural. They contrasted their skin tone with stark black clothes and hair that seemed to be the norm within their circle.

"Madelyn, wake up. You've been researching these fringe elements Ross and Erma described. Expound on this morbid looking group."

The splotchy black, brown, and white cat yawned and raised her head. She studied two young couples.

Bob looked like he wanted to frisk them for contraband.

"These persons are what are commonly known as Goth. This is a subculture that is dark and mysterious to the outsider—like Bob, for instance. He wouldn't have a clue what makes them the way they are.

Basically, it's counter culture to the one that preceded it, the Disco era of the nineteen-seventies."

Madelyn stood and stretched, then looked through the living room arched door. "The two in the kitchen rummaging through the refrigerators, they think they're vampires."

An inward shiver caused Emily to cringe as she glanced at the pair. "Those two genuinely scare me. Are they really vampires?"

Madelyn half suppressed a chuckle. "No. Not to worry. There are no such things as vampires."

"Says you. I'm not so sure. They look the part."

The discussion was interrupted by the sound of two vans pulling into the gravel driveway. It was this group that got Emily's heart pumping. This is what she was waiting for. Emily cast a wakeup call loud and clear.

"Everyone, this is it. Rise and shine."

The sleeping cats jumped to attention, confused and groggy, looking around the living room.

"What's going on?" Jacqueline said. "Why the five alarm wakeup call? Did Rebecca set the house on fire?"

"Not yet," Rebecca said. "But I just might. Emily, don't ever wake us up like that again."

"Sorry 'bout that. But the folks from the TV reality show, they're here."

Emily focused her senses. She heard the side doors of the vans open, followed by six individual voices. Five males. One female. Raymond came down the stairs and stepped out to help bring in their gear.

Angel and Scarlett jumped to the top of a sofa to get a better look. Midnight, Chloe and Helen pretended to be interested in Bob and rubbed up against his legs as he stared out the bay window in disbelief. Emily laughed inwardly, knowing Bob thought members of a traveling circus escaped and just invaded Murcat Manor.

"There are two brothers," Madelyn continued. "Ned and Henry Leeds. They're twins, but not identical. The pretty young female with rust colored hair, Denise Forsythe, is the face of the show."

Emily jumped onto the floor and strolled toward the front door. Madelyn followed. "Who are the other three?"

"The scrawny looking one wearing a blue jeans and a white T-shirt is the producer, Johnny Rocket. He's young and this is only his second year with the group. But he's very talented and comes from a long line of Hollywood big wigs. He coordinates and arranges everything from financing the program to advertising through all phases of filming and development. He's taken this show to new heights. It has a huge following and is one of the most watched shows on Cable TV."

"Fascinating. What about the others?"

"The two cameramen? I don't know who they are, specifically."

"What rooms are they staying in," Emily asked as the crew entered the foyer.

"The Paranormal Room and the Serial Killer Room."

Rebecca laughed. "They all walked right past us. We didn't register so much as a blip with them. They can't be that good at what they do."

"Don't you think we should go for an easier target?" Midnight said. "Like the Goths?"

Emily instantly hated the Goths and Vamps. They were so disrespectful, and they didn't strike her as the brightest crayons in the box. But the crew from *American Ghost Stories*, now these people would present not only a challenge, but a threat.

Emily's heart was still pounding. This could be their biggest score in all of their previous lives. The Turner place was all too easy to burn down. Everyone was stoned out of their minds and offered little resistance. The Amish family was sleeping when Rebecca did her work.

But the crew of *American Ghost Stories*, they offered high risk and high reward. Her following always complained about how bored they were. Problem solved. They just hit the lottery.

"We have to think big here, ladies. Remember, we discussed how we've been able to increase our powers as we better understand and use them in more difficult opportunities. Well, look no further than right in front of us. Oh, we're going to have a great time. Sisters, meet our next targets."

"Which ones," Esther asked.

"All of them."

Emily followed Bob and Debbie into the kitchen. They sat at the table and checked in who she knew Bob thought were really weird guests. The rest of the cats followed and spread out. Rachel, as usual, made her way to Bob's lap. Isabella and Jacqueline walked across the keyboard of his laptop. Emily chuckled, watching Bob as he digested this dark and diverse group of guests as they overran Murcat Manor.

More than a dozen Goths and Vamps were now raiding the refrigerator and rummaging through the cupboards and pantry. Bob did not look happy.

"Dinner's at five o'clock for the first crew," Debbie said, using a merry homecoming tone. "Six thirty for the second. You're on your own for lunch."

"I don't care," a male Goth said, closing a freezer. "There's nothing good here. Just a bunch of healthy food. Got any Hot Pockets?"

Bob closed his laptop and stood. "What's your name?"

"Um, Phil."

Bob pointed out into the living room. "Get out of my kitchen, Phil."

"Is it true five people were murdered here," a second young male asked, who looked barely old enough to drive. He was dressed in a black leather jacket with countless studs and pins. Ink black hair fell over his forehead and covered one eye.

Bob placed his hands on hips and looked at the delinquents dressed completely in black. Their faces were covered with white makeup. Their dark hair, black lipstick, eye liner, and fingernails made them look like death microwaved. He was clearly disturbed this was the kid's first question.

"Five people died here. Yes. But they were not murdered," Bob said deadpanned. "Don't believe everything you read."

Phil made a disrespectful facial expression and looked around the kitchen, then out to the living room. "This house, it's not so scary," he said in a sniveling tone. "Looks like my mom's home. Only bigger."

A female elbowed her way in front of him. "Hi. I'm Brooke. Phil and I are staying in the Medieval Torture Chamber." There was much excitement her voice. "How many people died there?"

Bob looked down into dark yet anticipating eyes. She wore a spiked dog collar and matching wrist bands.

"None."

Their faces and shoulders dropped.

A sneer formed across Bob's mouth. "Tell you what. You two can be the first, okay?"

That wisecrack remark appeared to re-excite them, much to Bob's consternation.

Debbie gave an askance look at Bob, then handed the guests their room keys. "Raymond already took your luggage upstairs. Your rooms are at the far end of the hall."

Emily sat upright just inside the kitchen door and watched with vigilance. Next to check in were the six people from *American Ghost Stories*. The Goths and Vamps remained, mesmerized as the crew entered the kitchen. It was as if they were in the presences of demigods.

Madelyn researched the group, and had set up Bob's laptop while he slept so they all could watch episodes on YouTube. Was the crew for real? Or were they all show and in it for the money?

Emily's verdict: inconclusive. The fact they initially walked past without noticing her didn't help their credibility.

But Emily wasn't letting her guard down. They may have supernatural gifts of discernment. Regardless, she would remain patient. Since *American Ghost Stories* was broadcasting their show live, Emily and the others would give their two million viewers a show they would never forget.

The producer stepped forward and shook Bob's hand. "Hello Mr. and Mrs. Stevens. My name is Johnny Rocket. Thank you for allowing us to stay here. We're truly grateful, especially on such short notice."

Johnny introduced the rest of the crew. "This is Ned Leeds. To his left is his brother Henry. And this is Denise Forsythe."

Bob received Ned's handshake. "We've seen your show. Welcome to Murcat Manor."

"You and your crew will stay in the Paranormal Room and the Serial Killer Room," Debbie said with more enthusiasm. "I still find it hard to believe you're taping a live show here. After seeing you in person, I have to admit this is so exciting."

Johnny Rocket scrolled through notes in his iPad without looking up. "The Paranormal Room is where the Johnsons died last week. It used to be the Disco Room, right?"

Emily could see Bob fighting the urge to throw up. "That's right."

"Very good. We'll get right to work," Johnny said. "Now Mr. Stevens, I assure you we won't disrupt your normal business. We use two cameramen that follow us around. That's it. Just the six of us. We'll be as discreet and respectful to your property and guests as possible."

"Thank you," Debbie said. "As much as we'd like to be a part of this, Bob and I are locking ourselves in our bedroom with a couple bottles of wine. We don't want to get in the way of your show."

Denise Forsythe smiled approvingly. But Emily sensed she was glad Bob and Debbie would be secluded in their room. The first thing Emily discerned about the incredibly popular hostess of one of Cable TVs biggest shows was Denise had an immense problem with pride. Emily had found a great weakness, and would exploit this against her and the crew in incredible ways.

"I understand," Denise continued, brushing her fingers through her long flowing rust colored hair. "Just be sure to watch the show. After all, you live here. If there's anything paranormal going on, you'll want to see me and my cast expose it."

Bob let out a laugh but caught himself. "I'm not superstitious. No offense, but I really don't expect anything to happen here tonight."

Ned Leeds, the main host of the show, stepped forward. "Mr. Stevens, we're a lot alike. We're skeptics at heart, as are most paranormal detectives. We do our best to weed out the instances of people imagining— or even staging, making up—what they've experienced as real. Then, if anything remains, we'll explore that as possible paranormal activity."

Bob sat and fidgeted in his chair, staring into his half empty glass of Coca Cola. Emily knew he was trying to be polite, while at the same time letting the crew know he thought they were full of shit. Emily appreciated the conflict. Sometimes, Boring Bob surprised her.

"Well, I'm still not a believer," Bob continued. "I mean, I am. But, just not in what you're promoting."

"I can understand your reluctance," Denise said. "But there is far more to our world than what we can perceive with our five senses."

Bob lifted his glass in salutation. "If you can prove that tonight and present your findings to Detective Darrowby, I'd greatly appreciate it."

Johnny Rocket brought his hands together in a loud clap. "We'd better set up. We have a lot of work to do," followed by two more quick claps in rhythm. "Chop-chop. Let's go."

Emily needed to know more about the crew since the show was being shown live in just nine hours. Especially Denise. Ned Leeds was clearly the leader, at least with the studio and Johnny Rocket. But the energy emanating from the TV hostess was much stronger than the rest.

Johnny also had a dominating personality that competed with Ned and Denise. He was now trying to shift gears and keep the crew moving. Emily planted a question in Debbie's head.

"I have to admit," Debbie said as she stepped in front of Johnny and addressed Denise. "I'm a little more open than my husband to spectral incidents. What's your background, if you don't mind me asking?"

Denise, never one to shun the spotlight regardless of the audience, was happy to oblige.

"I was raised in Happy Valley, Pennsylvania. My father's a Pentecostal preacher. You could call him a holy roller." She laughed. "Heck, if—you know those Picture Dictionaries they have now? Heh. Look up 'Holy

Roller' and my dad's image will be the meaning. His brothers were the church elders. They believed in healing, casting out demons, and miracles."

Johnny raised his wrist in the air and tapped his watch with an impatient dramatic flair. Denise smiled as she purposely ignored her producer and recollected her childhood in a succinct manner.

"Dad and his anointed elders did things that, to this day, I can't explain by logic or normal physics. People would come up to the stage, get prayed over and have hands laid on them, and then toss aside crutches and rise out of wheelchairs, dancing and running across the sanctuary of our church. I've seen just about every type of phenomena that falls outside of the traditionally accepted realm of the five senses. The blind saw. The deaf heard. Limbs grew where before they were stunted. The healed laughed for the first time in years and spoke with new tongues. My father, well, I can assure you he had no fear. He didn't care what the skeptics thought about him. Their results healed and converted people."

Debbie's nod was slow and somber. Emily had to keep the questions and answers coming. She planted a second question.

"That is certainly interesting," Debbie said. "Fascinating, actually. How did you three meet?"

Denise's eyes darted to the two twins. "I met Ned and Henry in college while at Penn State. We were in a philosophy class together.

"Unlike Denise," Ned interjected, "I don't believe in any particular religion. I do, however, believe in the existence of extra dimensions. This is where angelic and demonic spirits could live. These living beings could convert from energy to mass and then back to energy, freely crossing back and forth from their realms into ours."

Bob squelched a grin by pressing his lips into a firm straight line. "Um ... okay."

Emily looked up at Ned's brother. He was the quiet one. Okay Henry, you're next.

Debbie shook her head and laughed "Amazing. You lead such intriguing lives. A far cry from anything I've done. What about you, Henry?"

"When I was sixteen, I was out with friends and we were in a horrible car accident. They died. Three of them. I had a near death and out of body experience. I remember vividly looking down on myself as the ambulance took me to the hospital. I saw the doctors and nurses working on my broken body. I died three times on the operating table. But, miraculously, they were able to save me. After the third revival, I reentered my body."

"That's ... that's just ... wow, I mean that is truly incredible."

Bob sighed and looked away.

"It took me a full year to recover from my injuries. I had plenty of time to read and research out of body experiences. I know they're real. I'm living proof."

"So that's our story," Denise said. "We have different backgrounds and belief systems. But the one common thing we want to do is show the world life exists in a miraculous and elegant manner beyond the confines of what most people have been brainwashed into thinking is the one and only reality—that which we see on the surface. And worse?—duped into believing this," she banged her hand on the hard wall surface, "this material 'real' world is all that there is, and nothing else can exist beyond their man-made intellectual borders—borders?—hell ... more like conceptual imprisonment."

Johnny shoved his way between the much stockier Leeds brothers. "Okay, people. We really need to get a move on. We got us a ton of work to do before tonight's show."

Emily started to get up and leave, but … *wait* … Denise, what's she doing? The atmosphere and collective mood in the room became charged. Denise had her eyes closed, her head tilted back, and took a slow deep breath as she leaned over backward. Her hair rolled off her back and seemed to flow as she swayed back and forth in place. She began humming a barely audible tune, beautiful and melodic.

Emily thought the scene was mesmerizing, almost hypnotic, the way Denise swayed to and fro with her hair following a moment after; like a weeping willow with its long branches swinging in a gentle breeze. She was amazed the woman held the pose and didn't fall. Both cameramen turned on their hand held cameras and zoomed in on the emerging starlet.

Emily focused on Denise Forsythe, trying to discern what was transpiring in Debbie's kitchen. Was she a fraud, acting out for the audience? Or did she possess paranormal gifts that helped discern elements beyond her normal five senses. She strolled around the table and settled in one of the cat beds for a better look.

Bob started to say something. Ned put his forefinger to his lips to signal silence. Even the Goths and vampire wannabes were held spellbound, eyes and mouths wide open. Anticipation replaced Emily's usually patient demeanor. After a few minutes she planted a thought in Bob's head to break the silence.

"Is she okay," Bob whispered.

Ned let out a near silent laugh. "Yes. Denise does this when she senses something supernatural."

Debbie looked worried. She grabbed Bob's arm tight. "Does she perceive something out of the ordinary?"

"Some people would think this is very normal," Denise responded, keeping her eyes closed.

Ned spoke. "What is it? Are you getting something?"

"That would be a definite yes. There's a major disturbance in the basement. It took a few minutes to recalibrate my senses. But trust me, my insides are on fire. One thing is for sure. Murcat Manor is the mother lode of supernatural activity."

Denise maintained her swaying posture, but her head cocked to the side and her forehead creased. "Strange. I'm not sure what it—that—means."

"What do you see," Ned asked.

"I'm embarrassed to even say it. It sounds so stupid."

"Don't keep us in suspense. Just blurt it out."

Denise scoffed as she spoke. "I see large dented cans of fruit cocktail. Lots of them strewn across a concrete floor. It's as if they were pushed from a higher elevation. Repeatedly."

Emily's senses were on fire. Denise wasn't a fraud; she was now officially a threat.

Bob turned to Debbie, who was already locked onto him. She looked petrified when Denise mentioned the dented cans.

Bob shook his head, as if this was the dumbest thing he had ever heard. "Well, there's nothing down there except supplies."

"Heh heh ... and thirteen cats that often congregate there," Debbie added.

Denise opened one eye. "Thirteen?"

"Um, yes. That's right."

The hostess stood up straight and fixed her hair with her fingers. "What a convenient number," she said through a sly grin.

Denise panned the kitchen, looking at the cats, then, to Emily's surprise, focused on her. Denise's grin widened as if she had exposed an evil hidden secret the house was trying to hide. She nodded her head and let out a subtle laugh as if to tell Emily *checkmate*.

"Guys," she continued, "we need to set up cameras in the basement, too. Tonight, we find out what's causing all these deaths at Murcat Manor. And, if we're lucky, what caused the fires on the two previous properties here."

Emily didn't need to see anything else. "Emergency meeting. Everyone. But not in the basement. Once the crowd disperses, we'll make our way to Bob and Debbie's bedroom."

Emily waited as Raymond helped the crew to their rooms. The Goths and Vamps followed up the stairs like zealots in a cult who'd found new idols to worship.

The twelve cats, led by Rebecca, made their way through the animal door into Bob and Debbie's bedroom. Emily felt a sense of relief once the kitchen was quiet. She and her followers would devise a scheme to destroy the cast of *American Ghost Stories*.

As she strutted toward the bedroom, one last guest arrived. An elderly man. Alone.

His presence in the kitchen caused Emily to stop mid stride. She slipped under a chair and studied him from the other side of the kitchen table. Something about him was different, yet very much familiar.

Friend or foe?

It was as if she knew him. But from where? She sensed from when might be a better question.

Chapter 39   Joseph Meicigama

Emily watched from a crouched position as Bob and Debbie welcomed their last guest. Bob extended his right arm and shook the visitor's hand. "Hello. Welcome to Murcat Manor."

"You're the last booking," Debbie said. "You must be Joseph Meicigama. I hope I pronounced that correctly."

"Close enough," the man said with a docile smile as he looked around the kitchen. "You have a wonderful place here."

"Thank you," Debbie said as she spread her arms out. "I call the kitchen my home away from home; I spend so much time here cooking meals for everyone."

The elderly man smiled graciously. "I'm looking forward to some home cooked meals. I've done more than a little research on this place. I understand your dinners are what help make this bed and breakfast a favorite destination."

Emily rolled her eyes when Debbie blushed at the old man's charms.

"Are you local, Mr. Meicigama?"

He winked. "Yes. Generations of family have lived in this area longer than just about anyone else."

"We're happy to have you stay with us," she said with much respect. "You'll be staying in the Frontiersman Room. I'm sure you'll love the accommodations."

Every fiber in Emily came to life. She carefully deliberated the strange man whose presence triggered her internal alarm system. Early to mid-eighties, but in great shape. His mind was clear and sharp. Soft spoken, but dauntless. He had dark, weathered skin, contrasted against ghost white wavy hair. He combed it back over his head behind his ears and tied it into a long lock drawn against the back of his head.

The stranger wore blue jeans and a light blue buttoned up collared denim shirt. Cowboy boots completed his attire. He could fit in any crowd and not stand out. Except the Goths and Vamps. But Emily wasn't fooled. He was trying to conceal himself in plain view as an unassuming, yet charming senior citizen.

But the old man did wear something odd around his neck; a thin silver braided chain. She discerned there was something mystical attached to it hidden under his shirt.

She sent out a communication to her followers. "Hold up, ladies. There's one more arrival. He's alone and trying to fly below the radar. I'm convinced he came in last to avoid attention. I don't trust him."

Back to the old timer. Emily thought hard where she might have met him. And what was the meaning of his silver chain? Time to place another thought in Debbie's head.

Debbie leaned into Joseph. "That's an interesting piece of silver around your neck. May I ask what it is?"

"Oh, this?" Meicigama pulled out a small silver object with a turquoise stone set in the middle. "This is a gift handed down to me from my grandfather," he said with great pride. "It helps me to interpret dreams."

"Are you Indian?" Debbie caught herself. "I mean, Native American. Not the East Indian, of course."

His smile was congenial. "Yes, ma'am. I'm a native, of Ojibway descent. But you know us better as Chippewas."

The hairs on Emily's back went porcupine in alarm mode.

Meicigama continued, "I'm retired now, but I held a tenured professorate at Western Michigan University for thirty years, teaching general Native American Culture, as well as more specific subjects like Shamanism, the Ancient Practice of Strong Medicine, Shaman Dream Weaving and Interpretive Practices."

Had Emily been a porcupine, her quivers would have launched in fright and flight mode. But she stayed put, riveted by what she was hearing.

"You don't say," Debbie said, with obvious intense interest. "You know, Mr. Meicigama, Bob had a really strange dream a couple weeks ago."

Bob flinched. "Debbie, please, don't bother our guests with my dreams, I—"

Joseph Meicigama cut Bob off. "It's no bother. Trust me, Mr. Stevens. It's a gift my family has developed over many generations."

"Honey, I really don't want to do this."

"Actually," Debbie said, undeterred. "It was three dreams. Do you think you can tell us their meanings?"

Joseph rubbed the amulet between his fingers as he looked at Bob. "Yes, I do. Tell me the first of the three."

Bob hesitated, but Debbie elbowed him. "Go on. Tell him."

"Okay. I'm eating breakfast and everything in my world is blue. I'm sitting by a lake and there are two guardian angels, one male and one female."

Joseph nodded his head. "That's it?"

"Yeah. Sorry, it's not much. But it was so vivid. I can see everything just as if I dreamt it last night."

Another nod from Joseph. "That's enough. And the second?"

Bob looked down, his eyebrows furrowed. "Everything is gray. I'm eating lunch and I'm alone, traveling back and forth through time. I see places to get off, as if I'm on a train or subway."

He looked back up, straight at Joseph. "But I don't know which exit I need. So, even though I have the ability to stop, I have no control of where I'm going because I don't where to get off. I'm speeding forward, faster and faster, all the while passing by people and events I should be enjoying."

Meicigama gave a sagacious tilt of his head. "I see. And the third dream."

"It's night time. After a long hard day of back-breaking work, I'm in my driveway leaving my car. I walk down a path and I want to go into my house and eat dinner. But the path swerves around the house into the backyard where I walk to the fence on the boundary line. Just before I reached out to grab it, I woke up."

"What do you suppose they mean," Debbie asked.

Meicigama put his hands on his hips and stared at the floor. Emily knew the interpretation was not going to be good news for Boring Bob.

"These dreams, they are absolute and straight forward in their essence. But I hesitate to tell you what they mean."

"To be honest," Bob chuckled and shrugged his shoulders, "I'm not much of a believer in dreams forecasting my future. So hey—take your best shot."

Emily was on edge, waiting for the shaman's next words. This was no ordinary man. Although Boring Bob and Debbie welcomed him as a docile guest, Emily knew he presented a serious threat. To what extent, she wasn't sure. She stayed under a chair, listening.

Joseph stared at Bob, looking as though he was assessing the man's ability to take what he was about to say. He blew out a breath of resignation and complied with the request.

"Your first dream is easy to interpret. The guardian angels represent your parents who act as spiritual guides. Blue represents grace, hope, heaven, truth, and wisdom. These are what your mother and father imparted for your young life's journey. And the setting is breakfast. This tells of your youth until you left home."

"Bob had wonderful parents," Debbie said with pride. "His father's gone now. But his mother lives in Auburn Hills."

Joseph smiled, brief, then became staid. "Your second dream is your current life, being that the setting is lunch. Gray indicates fear, fright, depression, ill health, ambivalence and confusion."

He paused, again appearing to assess Bob's demeanor, which seemed tenuous, but intent on listening.

"To dream about time and travelling through time tells me something happened to change your world from blue to gray. Your desire is to escape from your present reality. This includes people as well as circumstances. You want to go into the past where life was safe or jump forward to the future where your personal hopes are realized. For the present, your fears are of not being able to cope with the pressures and stresses of everyday life."

"Nailed that one right on the proverbial head," Bob said, looking at Debbie.

Joseph stroked his chin, his visage morphing into somber. "In your third dream, the setting is dinner and represents your future. You want to go home where there is safety. But you are on the wrong path. And the color is black, meaning it is nighttime. And this represents death."

Bob winced—just a quickie—but then didn't seem fazed. "Well, we're all going to die someday."

Meicigama continued to rub his omelet. "Unfortunately, in your dream you reach the boundary line of your property. That you are about to grab the fence, the outermost limits of your property, tells me your time is short."

Bob and Debbie were silent for a laborious and lengthy pause. So was Emily. The Indian could tell a good story. Or, perhaps, he had a gift worth noting, one that could rival *American Ghost Stories*, or even exceed it.

Bob spoke. "Good thing I don't believe in dreams." He chuckled, but it sounded silly, almost goofy.

"I'm not so sure," Debbie said, her hands coming together in a mild wringing. "Mr. Meicigama, is there anything we should do? I don't want my Bob to die."

Bob half-laughed, more of a cough. "Honey, I'm not going to die."

"J-just—stop, Bob," Debbie admonished him with hand up. She turned back to Joseph. "Please, is there anything we can do? You know, just in case the dreams are real."

Joseph laughed. "You? No. There is not. But, perhaps, there is something I can do."

Debbie's countenance lifted. "Well, that sounds promising. Can we help?"

Meicigama made and abrupt turn and started to walk toward the living room. "I'm sorry. I need to rest. I'll show myself to my room."

He stopped short, turned back and looked hard at Bob and Debbie. "I suggest you two leave Murcat Manor tonight. Have a date night. Go to dinner then see a movie. There's a midnight showing of *Ghost Busters* in Jackson."

The old sage walked around the table and past Emily as if she wasn't there. He went out of his way to do this. She was sure he got her attention, then ignored her on purpose. The act was purposeful. He was staying at Murcat Manor for a reason. And Emily was convinced his visitation involved something to do with her.

Chapter 40   The Witching Hour

Denise Forsythe looked at her watch. 11:55 p.m. Her heart always beat faster in the minutes proceeding the filming of an episode of *American Ghost Stories*. But she was always in control of her emotions because they had an editing room. They could retake shots. Cut scenes out. Splice something in later. Heck, Johnny Rocket could modify her hair using computer graphics if it wasn't looking good.

But tonight was live. There would be no re-dos. No second chances to get the show right the first time. The entire crew looked nervous. The anxiety caused her to stutter slightly as Johnny walked through the final instructions.

But she had faith in 'The Kid' as she affectionately called Johnny Rocket. Only twenty-three and one year out of UCLA's famed Westwood-based film school, he was young to be a producer. Yet he was one of the best at his craft.

The Kid was scary organized. And he didn't bother Denise or the Leeds brothers with countless back end details that made *American Ghost Stories* one of the highest rated shows on cable television. He allowed them do their show in front of the cameras while he handled the particulars behind the scenes.

Johnny spoke with a hint of a squeak in his voice that Denise would playfully tease him about. "You're all a little nervous. So am I. But we've had a couple walkthroughs, so we'll be fine. Slow goes it, okay? Three hours is plenty of time to cover the house and the outside property. We don't gotta rush nothin'."

Denise smiled at him, adoring the way he intentionally abused the English language, like some uneducated buffoon when he was as brilliant a guy as any she had known.

"An' most of all?" he continued, "Just have fun. Lotsa fun. And we'll have us a frickin' awesome show."

"And remember," Ned said, hands on his hips with a stern look as he turned to each member of the crew. "We're not mentioning the Stevens are under investigation by the Battle Creek Police. We're here to explore any observable phenomena that cannot be explained using scientific methods. That is all."

Ned looked around the living room then into the kitchen. "And judging from Denise's vibes earlier today, I feel strongly we're going find the holy grail of paranormal activity. Something evil that's been around for generations is active once again and killing people on this property."

The cameramen were in place. The skinny, still pimple-faced but self-assured producer stood off to the side and looked at Ned, counting off with his fingers. "Five, four, three, two, and ... we're live."

Ned clasped his hands and said with much enthusiasm, "Thank you for tuning in, and welcome to our very first live showing of *American Ghost Stories*."

He turned to the rest of the crew and Denise donned her signature wry, but incredibly sexy smile for their fans. "With me, as usual, are my twin brother Henry and the lovely Denise Forsythe. We're in the living room at Murcat Manor, a popular ten room bed and breakfast located in south central Michigan in the rolling countryside between Battle Creek and Marshall."

Ned spread his arms wide as the cameramen stepped back to give the audience a comprehensive image of the living room. "Although the outside of this bed and breakfast is fashioned after a Grand Victorian house, and can give a person the appearance of a house that might harbor metaphysical activity, the inside is very much different. It's modern in every sense, from the recessed lighting to the contemporary furniture and decor."

Ned dropped his smile that gave way to a serious demeanor. "But don't let this modern day setting fool you. The history of this property tells us there's something evil living here that goes back generations. Trust me. This promises to be our best show ever."

Ned led everyone toward the front door. He opened it and stepped out onto the porch. One cameraman followed while Johnny aimed a handheld floodlight and highlighted the white latticed gazebo in the front yard.

"If you've seen the previews, you know five people have died here during the past nine weeks. In late April, a month before Murcat Manor opened for business, probably the most mysterious and dramatic death occurred when the general contractor in charge of the building Murcat Manor was killed. The ladder he was on, three stories tall, fell backwards. His body was crushed and impaled on the gazebo's metal spire peak."

Ned and the cameraman came back into the foyer. He stopped at the base of the stairs and pointed up. "Earlier this month, a man from Detroit was killed upstairs in his room by his wife after she thrust a fire poker into his chest. According to accounts from that night, she then ran down the hall in her nightgown, her blood curdling screams waking the guests. She fell down the stairs and broke half the bones in her body, including her neck. She died right here at the bottom of the stairs."

Denise followed Ned as he walked back through the living room and into the kitchen, careful to stay in the picture. Ned was the leader, and he was great at working the audience.

But she was the eye candy who received the most social media attention. Her Facebook Fan Page had hundreds of thousands of fans, and she had millions of followers on Twitter. A large segment of their viewers—especially men—tuned in just to get a load of her off-the-charts sexy gorgeousness.

"Another guest," Ned continued, "died in the kitchen while eating. Cause of death: a simultaneous combination of choking and a heart attack. A very strange way to die. And finally, one of the helpers hired for the summer was electrocuted in the laundry room behind the kitchen."

"That's right," Henry said, taking his cue from The Kid. "That's five deaths on this very property in a little over two months. Now, the owners of Murcat Manor, Bob and Debbie Stevens, declined to be filmed and are not here for the show. But we thank them just the same for allowing us to stay the entire night here and bring to you, our awesome viewing audience of two million people, *American Ghost Stories*. Live and uncensored."

Denise looked at Johnny, who pointed at her, signaling she was to deliver her line. She sashayed around the massive oak kitchen table for effect as the cameramen followed. Her hips and walk were sensuous. Her eyes bespoke deadly seriousness.

"As if five deaths on this singular property are not enough to make a believer out of the biggest skeptic that something strange is happening on these grounds, there have been an additional nineteen deaths in two previous houses and barns that once stood here. They burned to the ground under mysterious circumstances. Seven poor souls in nineteen-seventeen, then twelve more in nineteen sixty-seven, perished here."

Denise couldn't contain her excitement as she talked with her arms and hands, speaking with the grandest of smiles. She was in her glory. "As Henry claimed, this promises to be our best show ever. Three hours. Live. And it's midnight with a full moon. What more can we ask for?"

Denise was pumped and had volumes to say, more so than on any previous episode. The nervousness in her stomach was gone. She was a skeptic, as were Ned and Henry. It was vital to ferret out false leads and phony people who staged a paranormal setting just to get on their show. Credibility with their faithful and growing audience was what helped make their cable program so popular.

But tonight, she was sure of one thing. Murcat Manor was the real deal. She could feel it. The tingling on her skin. The burning in her bones. And she was barely starting to ramp up.

"We've set up cameras," Ned continued. "Small devices in all the downstairs rooms, except Bob and Debbie's bedroom. We'll respect their privacy. Unless, of course, they come home during the show and we detect activity behind the door." Ned winked and chuckled.

Henry moved toward the basement door. "We even have the front and back doors covered." He paused for dramatic effect. "And the basement. We feel we may be saving the very best for last. You'll want to stay awake for that.

"We can go in our two rooms we rented for the night, the Paranormal Room and the Serial Killer Room. The first was once the Disco Room where a married couple from Detroit died. There are eight more themed rooms upstairs. Murcat Manor is a full house tonight. If we're lucky, some of the guests may allow us in to visit their rooms."

Denise waved to Johnny, then pointed at the Goths and Vamps trying, with pathetic results, to hide in the background behind couches and chairs. She motioned the cameramen to make sure they got them in their shots.

After a quick pan of the living room, Ned stepped toward the back door, leading the crew. He lifted his left arm and tapped his watch. "It's midnight. So let's get started, shall we?"

Chapter 41 Generational Curses

Tonight at Murcat Manor is the best possible scenario for our fans, Denise thought, wringing her hands in glee and anticipation. And a full moon to boot? She shook her head in awe. It just doesn't get any better than this.

All the hard work and sacrifice seemed to line up for this one special night. She felt is if this event was foreordained just for her and this one live episode.

Denise loved the Goths and Vamps peeking around the corners, running back and forth to get a better view but staying well in the background, jockeying for position and examining her every move. This was adding quality production value for the live viewing audience. And if paranormal activity did happen, the many cameras arrayed around the property would certainly capture the events.

She followed as Ned and Henry took turns talking to their audience as they explored the backyard. Even though the Leeds Brothers were not identical twins, internally, they always knew what the other was thinking. They often finished each other's sentences and answered for one another. Denise thought doing a show on their lives would be more than a little interesting. She had always been a little freaked out over how twins and triplets could do this.

Ned turned to her and spoke. "Denise, are you feeling anything?"

"Yes, I am," she said in a low soft tone. "Where do I begin?"

Denise wracked her brain to compartmentalize all the information she was receiving, then place it in some logical progression through space and time that would make sense to her and the viewing audience. Images, voices, a few screams, and other random signals competed for her attention. It was as if the people who died here were crying out to her, trying to tell their story of the injustices that happened to them.

As fascinating as these communications were, she also detected elements of revenge. They grew louder, more intense, as if she was their only hope to help escape the hell that held them captive and attached to this property. This particular aspect disturbed her the most.

Denise tossed out her thoughts the best she could as she composed herself, looking at the cameras. The show must go on. "So much has happened here, layered over three generations and a century of time. It's difficult to sort through all the activity."

Ned spoke. "Can you go back to the first property that burned down, killing seven people?"

Denise had performed her due diligence. She was prepared with facts and figures that needed no pomp and ceremony to fascinate the audience.

"Let's go back to the summer of the year nineteen-seventeen. The day was Thursday, June twenty-sixth. Jonathan and Elizabeth Jacobson owned this land. They were Amish and had five children. Three boys and two girls, ages four to seventeen. They, with the help of their Amish community, erected a house and barn. They farmed these twenty-five acres with corn and lima beans. On one fateful night, all members of the

303

Jacobson's family died while the house and barn burned down to smoldering ashes. There was no explanation as to how the fires started. By the time neighbors arrived to help, both structures were hopelessly engulfed in flames."

Denise looked at Ned and Henry as they walked beside her, engrossed with her story. She walked up to and around the large shed.

"This was where the first barn was built. As was the second. The property exchanged hands five times until nineteen sixty-four, when a young couple named Kevin and Barbara Turner bought the property. A second house and barn had been built by one of the previous owners in nineteen twenty-seven."

Denise kept a slow but steady pace across the lawn, ignoring the humidity that made breathing difficult. She felt this was the best way to deal with the barrage of communications battling for her attention. She envisioned a rope lassoed around both houses, linking them together through the fifty years that separated the terrible events killing nineteen people. She expected to find that same linkage moving forward to Murcat Manor.

"The Turners turned the place into a commune: a classic Sixties hippie haven. Many people came and went over the next three years. Stories of wild parties, drugs, free love, backyard rock concerts for days at a time—like mini-Woodstocks—and anti-establishment signs and banners everywhere."

She took a breath. "Basically, everything the Sixties are remembered for defined the Turner place. Anything went. There were rumors some people of the commune were also into the dark arts. To what degree is not known. But neighbors who lived in this community back then, whom we interviewed earlier this evening, tell stories that most of the locals stayed away from the Turner place. They all knew strange things were occurring here and wanted nothing to do with the steady pace of hippies and vagabonds that frequented the property."

Denise continued across the midnight moonlit lawn. "There's no reason to walk to the boundaries of these twenty-five acres. All the activity occurred, and is occurring, in the house. And, there is a strong sense that what happened in nineteen-seventeen, and again a half-century later, is at work once again. The questions are, what, and where is it?"

Denise found herself at the backdoor of Murcat Manor. She realized she was being drawn back into the house, as if whatever presence inhabiting the bed and breakfast was not afraid of her. It wanted her to return. She was being challenged. This had never happened. Most presences tried to detour her from continuing. She stared at the door knob, trying unsuccessfully to conceal a gasp.

Denise felt a hand on her shoulder. She jumped, but somehow suppressed a terrifying scream fighting to leave her mouth.

"Hey. Take it easy."

Ned's voice and words were calm. She looked into the two cameras while the men filmed her. Henry and Johnny stood speechless.

"Are you all right?" Ned said. "Do you want me to take the lead for a while?"

Denise, sharp as ever, broke the awkward moment with a fake laugh. "Sure. I'm fine. There's just a lot of activity here. That's all. It's hard to wrap my head around everything that's going on right now. Come on. Let's go back inside."

Ned was genuinely concerned. She could see it in his eyes. Both his hands were now on her shoulders.

"Are you sure?" He looked at his watch. "We still have over two hours. There's no need to rush."

Denise dismissed Ned's suggestion with a second phony giggle and reached for the door. "The only place left to explore is the basement," she said with a guileful smile to the cameramen. "Let's go."

Chapter 42   The Basement

Emily Livingston lay quietly, rolled up on her belly, her head buried in her soft folded paws. The perfect pillow. She waited patiently in the darkness of Murcat Manor's basement. It had been her turn to be the sentry and let most of the other cats rest. As nocturnal beings, they would normally be up and about by now. But they needed to conserve their energy for this special night's hunt, which was about to begin.

But Joseph Meci ... Mec ... oh, forget it. Indian Joe it is. She sensed she'd seen him before. But she was only in the second year of her sixth life. The only explanation was they had met during her past life. Could he have visited the Turner place?

She searched her memories, which were quite coherent, over the past four centuries. There were hundreds of diverse people of all ages, race, religions and spiritual beliefs—or no beliefs at all—that came to the commune. Some sought enlightenment or they wanted to become 'turned on' into the world of psychedelic drug culture. Most were, to some degree, ready to "tune in, turn on, and drop out"—the call of the generation to snub their noses and turn away from status quo society, in search of wider more liberated horizons.

Others were attracted to the dark arts that some practiced. It was a community where anything was acceptable. It was a 'happening' of searching for meaning in life and spiritual awareness, through the new and exciting Holy Trinity: sex, drugs, and rock and roll. For the happy hippies, it just didn't get any better than the Turner place. The farmhouse was as close to Nirvana as could be found anywhere on earth.

Until Rebecca torched and cauterized the place into smoldering smithereens, killing everyone, including Emily and the rest of the cats.

Scores of faces scrolled across Emily's mind, but she failed to connect any to Indian Joe. In the commune, people shared interests, possessions, and resources. There was a blending that discouraged individuals to be conspicuous outside of physical features.

When he had entered Murcat Manor earlier that day, the stranger displayed no distinctive mannerisms such as an accent or a limp that would make him stand out. With each successive non-match, the more concerned she became. In fact, she was becoming downright scared.

The man harnessed powers. She perceived they were ancient, mystical, and powerful. Abilities she was not familiar with and could be difficult, if not impossible, to combat. He was a threat to her and the rest. That much she was sure.

But so far, all he had managed to do since his arrival was go to The Frontiersman Room and sleep. Perhaps, he was just an old timer losing his mind, alone and lost in the present and trying to relive the traditions of ancestors long since passed.

Regardless, she couldn't let her guard down. Not tonight. She had to take preemptive measures to ensure he would not be trouble.

Emily summoned Isabella, Angel, and Rachel, who had agreed to forego the extra sleep and monitor his room. They were stationed at the top of the stairs where they could see the door to the Frontiersman Room.

"Anything yet?"

"Nothing," Isabella said. "Do you want us to wake him? Could be a lot of fun to throw him into the mix."

"No. Better that he rests. He's pretty old and might sleep through the night. We'll deal with him tomorrow. For now, I don't want him to interfere with what we have planned for the cast of *American Ghost Stories*."

Across the basement, along the familiar and empty work bench Raymond Hettinger had promised to do work on but never found the time, Annie, Chloe, Scarlett, Helen, and Jacqueline also waited in silence. Emily designated Annie second in charge of this event and was confident she could lead. Together, they would take out the cast of *American Ghost Stories*.

Her second in command, Rebecca, was stubborn and difficult to manage. Emily needed those involved in this scheme to know their parts and follow through as a team. This was not the time for one of them to take an independent stand at the last moment. She could not afford the chance Rebecca might again start a fire and bring Murcat Manor down in a murderous gigantic bonfire of wood and mammal flesh.

Rebecca, who had torched the Allen's house in Battle Creek a month earlier when Bob gave her to the young couple the first week they were open. And the Turner place almost fifty years ago. And the Amish farm before that.

No. Emily would not allow for a repeat performance tonight. She left the extremely talented but rebellious cat upstairs to be in charge there

309

along with Midnight, Esther, and Madelyn. They were to lounge in the living room where they could see what, if anything, was happening on the ground level.

Time to check in upstairs. "Rebecca, how are things up there?"

The reply came quick and snappy. "More boring than spending an evening alone with Bob balancing his checkbook. I'm so frustrated. How could you put my sister second in command, while abandoning me up here? What am I supposed to do?"

"Absolutely nothing. That's the point. You haven't burned down the place tonight."

"Night's not over, yet."

"What about the freaks?"

"The Goths and vampire wannabes are scattered across the house, hoping for the best place to be should a metaphysical event take place. Can I set them on fire?"

"Honestly, I can't tell if you're kidding or serious. To be safe, the answer is no."

Directly above, Emily heard the back door to the kitchen open. Footsteps shuffled onto the wooden floor. Muffled voices were laughing and having too good of a time. The energy increased as the crew walked overhead toward the basement door.

Emily had an idea. She thought of Esther sending the burst of energy that sent Sophia Johnson flying head first down the stairs. Since she possessed all the individual abilities, she should be able to do something similar.

Emily squeezed her eyes shut and cleared he mind, then sent a quick burst of energy upward. Nothing special. Just a little something to cause a jolt and let Denise know there was something waiting for her through the basement door.

She knew her strike found its mark when there was a stutter in their steps and the voices fell silent.

Time to alert the rest of her feline friends. Emily sent a soft but stern call. "Look sharp, sisters. It's time."

Emily stood and performed a quick stretch. "Annie. Chloe. Scarlett. Helen. Jacqueline. Ready to go?"

"We're ready," Annie said.

"Remember, we have the advantage and the element of surprise. We've gone over our plan. You all know your parts. We're on the offensive. Denise will lead in a defensive manner. At least until she sorts through her surroundings. Then, she'll attempt to be the aggressor. We'll have to strike before she's able to do that. Helen, you disabled the cameras they set up here in the basement?"

"Sure did. It was easy. The only live cameras will be the ones the cameramen have on their shoulders."

"Excellent. And remember to leave the cameramen alone until the very end. We need them to film everything. After that, they're fair game. Feel free to be creative with them."

Above, the doorknob to the basement door turned and a sliver of light stabbed through the darkness. It expanded into a portal as the door opened, illuminating the flight of steps descending into the cellar. At the top the stairs, the cast of *American Ghost Stories* combined a single long shadow down into Murcat Manor's subterranean world that was the cats' domain.

"I have a last minute idea. I'll disable the main light to the basement," Helen said.

"Nice."

Emily loved the unrestricted improvising her sisters added to her structured scheme. She could hear the *click-click-click* as Ned flicked the light switch up and down.

"Not working. Weird. Murcat Manor is a newly built residence with all the modern technology. I'm surprised a simple light switch isn't working."

Denise peered over Ned's shoulder. "Nice touch. But typical," she mocked. "We've seen this before. Whatever's down here, this is child's play. As was that little burst you sent us in the kitchen, whatever that was. Try as you might, I'm not frightened by you."

Ned turned on his flashlight and swept the beam back and forth across the basement. Denise craned her head and bent down, looking around. "I see six pairs of shiny green orbs down there. Hello, kitty cats."

"Flashlights on," Ned said. "Everyone. Let's go. Stay close and follow me."

A cameraman took the first steps down, walking backward to film the crew. Ned's beacon of light was followed by three more luminous torches piercing the darkness. The second cameraman brought up the rear. Johnny was the last to enter.

"It's getting stronger," Denise said with much excitement. "I can feel the energy everywhere on this property. Outside. Around the tool shed, which is the former barn. Certainly inside the house. But no more so than right here in the basement."

Denise maneuvered between Ned and Henry to take the lead as they stepped onto the cement floor. She walked down one long wall and shined her flashlight on herself, her fingertips touching the cinderblocks, and turning her head for the camera.

"This is a haven of activity unlike anything I've ever felt. I'm not sure we can cover everything in three hours. The activity here in Murcat Manor is truly astounding."

Denise pranced back to the work bench, almost dancing, snapping her fingers as if she found her groove. Her head bobbed as if following the beat in a nightclub. She strutted like the finest looking babe in a singles' club and knew everyone—the guys because she was so hot, and the gals because they were jealous—was looking to see what she would do next. She grinned wide and shone her flashlight on the work bench, then on the shelf Emily laid on.

"Six lazy cats. Sleeping in the dark basement at one o'clock in the morning. What's wrong with this picture?"

Henry shrugged his shoulders. "Um, they're just lazy good for nothing cats."

Denise shot him a look of despise. "That was a rhetorical question." She slapped Henry's forehead. "This is exactly why I have millions of Twitter followers and yours could be counted on your fingers."

Emily was enjoying the conflict forming between the crew. She knew it was there, latent underneath the smiling for the cameras. She discerned Denise had a problem with pride—too much of it. And once the cameras rolled, she didn't like to be challenged.

Denise spun on her heels and shone her flashlight at Emily, challenging her, and invading her space. "And here we have Debbie's favorite cat. The one who seems to be the queen of Murcat Manor's feline clan."

She gave Emily a brief but distinctive disrespectful smirk. Emily stared back, laughing inwardly, allowing Denise to think she was the queen bee tonight. The anticipation was almost as good as what the grand finale would be.

Pride in an opponent was the greatest weakness one could display. Vanity upon vanities, Emily thought. Denise Forsythe was so young and beautiful. She enjoyed much success at such an early age and had an emerging audience of adoring and lusting fans. But, in Emily's eyes, this only made Denise typical and predictable.

Oh, I'm going to enjoy this beyond measure.

Denise smiled triumphantly, presenting the contents of the shelf like a game show model. "And take a look at this, guys. Commercial sized dented cans of fruit cocktail. Hah! I have to admit even I'm amazed at the vision of these dented cans from earlier today. I mean, what are the odds. Damn, I'm good."

Denise turned her head, flung her hair from side to side, and treated the audience with her wicked sexy smile. "One aspect of being a paranormal investigator is that I'm also a numerologist. We focus on specific digits and their order, values, and their sums. We look for interpretations of their derived values, while attempting to determine their meaning in our cosmos and how they vary throughout different cultures. For the sake of tonight's show, I'll present my knowledge and experience and tell you what I think they mean."

Denise cleared her throat. "There are six cats here in the basement with us. The number six has various meanings, depending on the culture and the time period. But what I'm getting, right here right now, is six is the number of man. More specifically, the sixth commandment of the Old Testament comes to mind: Thou Shalt Not Murder. And that commandment has been broken at least nineteen times on this property in the past, and five times recently at Murcat Manor. If we can conclude one of the many evil elements that has its roots in Murcat Manor, it carries the name of Murder."

Denise reached out and petted Emily.

Oh this is just too rich, Emily thought. She's trying to control the situation. Tell me I'm no more of a threat to her than any normal harmless cute little kitty would be. Pathetic. I have four hundred years and five previous lives of roguery and murder to stack up against you. Six, counting my earthly human existence.

Emily purred for the cameras and allowed her eyelids to droop, reveling in the immensity of her pernicious and insidious ruse.

"There are thirteen cats total in this bed and breakfast. The number thirteen is associated with corruption and disintegration that results in revolts. So we have identified a second root that has its tentacles wrapped around this bed and breakfast. Rebellion."

Emily yawned and closed her eyes for the cameras, playing completely bored with the research and lecture.

Denise spoke directly into the camera. "But let's not stop with numerical concepts. Over history, cats were mystical characters that have delighted and terrified people for thousands of years."

Emily rolled on her back and playfully patted her paws in the air, mimicking batting at a piece of yarn.

"Recent research shows cats may have been first domesticated in Mesopotamia. They lived in close association with humans in Egypt four thousand years ago. In ancient Upper and Lower Egypt, religious acts were centered on animals, including cats. The females were revered as goddesses and received the same mummification rites as humans. Cats controlled vermin and snake populations, although that would be difficult to tell by looking at these six lazy felines."

Just keep talking sweet cakes, Emily thought as she yawned again.

"They were highly regarded in Rome and Greece, but not worshipped. However, in China, the myth was that the gods appointed cats to oversee the beginning of the world and they were granted the power to speak."

Denise turned back to Emily. "Tell me, my purring fluffy little friend, can you speak?"

Henry poked at Emily. "Well, this one looks completely bored. Like a total waste of a life. I don't think she's listening to a word you're saying."

Denise slapped Henry's probing arm aside. "Don't be fooled. Cats are nocturnal. It's already past midnight." Denise pointed at Emily. "This cat should be out prowling. Why, Henry, is she and five other cats down in the basement sleeping?"

Before Henry could answer, Denise motioned for one of the cameraman to step up and focus in on Emily.

"Oh, I'm getting strong vibes from this one. What's your name, little kitty?"

Emily calmly lifted her head and stared at Denise through wide open eyes. She placed the thought loud in Denise's mind.

Emily.

Denise jerked upright and rubbed her ears.

"What's the matter," Ned asked.

"That was almost deafening. I thought ... I thought I heard her say her name was Emily. Didn't ... didn't any of you hear it?"

Ned and Henry looked at each other. "No," Henry said. He reached out and held Emily's name tag from her collar in his fingers. "But this tag clearly states her name is Emily. Maybe you noticed this and thought you heard it."

"I'm not stupid. And by the way Henry, you're an idiot."

Denise placed her fingers in her ears and massaged them. "My eardrums nearly exploded." She looked at the crew. "Really? No one heard that?"

As both cameramen turned their attention on Denise, Emily took advantage of the distraction and jumped down to the floor.

Denise, now infuriated, looked around for Emily. "Hey, where'd that cat go?"

She trotted around the basement shining her flashlight back and forth across the floor. "Here, kitty kitty kitty. Come out, come out, wherever you are, you little shit."

Denise looked behind a stack of boxes marked Industrial Cleaning Products. "You can't hide from me. I'm not fooled by your calm and mushy demeanor. Everyone else may be. But not me."

"Um, are you alright," Ned said. "You've never acted like this. It's just a cat."

Henry added, "For the first time, I'm a little creeped out. I thought we're looking for active paranormal activity. Not lazy cats."

"We are," Denise snapped. "It's the cats, you stupid sack of monkey nuts. Haven't you figured it out yet? Do I have to do all the work?"

"Whoa. Take it easy. No need to snap at us."

Denise gave Henry a dismissive sweep of her arm. She moved to another corner of the basement. "Just keep the cameras rolling and follow me. The trail ends here. I promise you, tonight will be our biggest night."

The cameramen followed Denise as she talked, broke away to pan the basement, then focused again on the female star. Emily waited until Denise made her way to the south wall and jumped back up on the shelf with the dented cans of fruit cocktail.

"There you are. Look at you. I'm not fooled, *Emily*. You think you're so coy. But I know you're the epicenter of everything that's evil about Murcat Manor."

Emily sat and stared, then licked her paws for the viewing audience as she was now in the background behind Denise. Now was the time. She gave the order.

"Chloe, do your thing."

Chapter 43   Confrontation

Before Denise could say another word, her hair started to lift and float, as if it had broken free from Earth's gravity. First, the bottom ends curled up. Next, entire sections bobbled and rose. They lifted and fanned out in a fantastic display, swaying as though a gentle breeze casually blew through them.

The cameramen, mouths agape, filmed Denise from both sides. Ned and Henry simply pointed, unable to utter a word.

Denise was so engaged with Emily she didn't know her hair, live for a viewing audience of over two million people, had left its rightful place off her shoulders and back. It swayed back and forth, forming a two foot aura that framed her smug face.

Emily glanced over at the other cats. "It's begun."

Denise was now mocking Emily, oblivious to her rising hair. Emily stared at the TV hostess, raised her right paw, and made a sweeping motion. Five large cans of fruit cocktail fell on their sides and rolled off the shelf and onto the floor. She repeated the process with her left paw. Five more cans joined the mess on the concrete below.

Denise turned to face her crew. "Hey, are you morons getting this?"

"Whoa," Henry said, *"your hair."*

"My hair? What about it?"

"It's … it's like," he made a billowing gesture with his arms, *"floating?"*

"Floating? Look, numb nuts, I don't know what the hell you're talking about, but turn those cameras around. That cat, Emily, she's doing magical things."

The two cameramen focused on Denise as she pointed at Emily, then the ruined cans of fruit on the floor.

"Yes. Your hair," one of the cameramen said. "It's … I've never seen anything like this in my three seasons on this show. Have to admit, up until now I thought you three were full of shit. This was the only job I could get and you paid well and treated me right. But right now, I'm a believer. This place is haunted."

Denise stuttered over her words as she looked up. Her initial response was she was spellbound, but still trying to lead the show for the live audience. She frantically matted down her prized hair, only to have it drift up again. She ran her fingers through it, then swatted at the billowing tresses. After a few more failed attempts, she gave up and focused back on Emily.

"Guys, get your cameras on Emily. I know she's the source of the evil at Murcat Manor."

Denis tried again to pull her hair down, only to watch it leave her shoulders and drift above her head.

"They're just messing with me. Playing their immature games. My hair, this is just a distraction. Focus on that stupid good for nothing cat."

"Stupid, are we? Nobody calls me stupid," Emily shouted to Denise. The hostess stood ramrod stiff at Emily's second internal communication.

"Helen, your turn."

Emily stared at Denise with proud satisfaction as Helen cross-switched the thoughts of Ned and Henry's brains. The process occurred in an instant. There was no outward motion from either of the brothers. No jerking of the shoulders or twitching of the mouths. Their eyes didn't bulge. They didn't cough or buckle over. But Emily knew the maternal twins now thought they were each other.

"Are you crazy," Henry said. "You're the star of the show. Look at your hair. I've never seen anything like this."

Denise fired back. "I don't take orders from you. Ned's the leader. It's his show."

"I am Ned. Denise, as much as I respect you and your abilities, I think I need to take you upstairs. It's getting the better of you. Henry can take over."

"No. You're Henry. And I never liked you. You're a loser and here only because of your brother Ned. Damn it Johnny, don't just stand there fondling your balls. Do something."

She aimed her flashlight at the five cats on Raymond's workbench. "And don't forget about the rest of those cats. I want those cameras on them. Now."

Emily knew the floating hair gimmick would keep the cameramen's attention on Denise, the star of the show. Time to move forward.

"Annie, you're up."

Behind the cameramen on the workbench, Chloe levitated Scarlett, Helen, and Jacqueline. Emily's cousin once again demonstrated her ability to raise three cats, circle them in a tight orbit, then gently lower them back down.

With the cameras still aimed at Denise, and the Leeds brothers and Johnny Rocket staring at her, the female hostess was the only one seeing the airborne wonder. She stared in awe, trying to formulate words. All she could do was point her flashlight at them, her long bushy red hair still floating around her head like it had a will of its own.

Johnny's words were squeamish as he looked on Denise's hair with an open jaw. "Guys ..." Johnny cleared his throat and came back in with a slightly deeper tone. "Do what she says. Turn around and get a shot at that cat."

The basement fell silent. All cameras, eyes, and flashlights, were now on Emily. She rolled over on her back and lifted a leg, licking herself in places that were sure to give the television audience something to laugh at.

"Okay Chloe, mission accomplished with Ned and Henry," she said as she began playing with her white socks feet for the cameras, then batted her paws in the air. "Their minds have been officially switched. Scarlett, take care of Johnny Rocket. Don't hold back."

The silence was shattered as Johnny grabbed his head, dug his fingernails deep into his scalp, and let out a horrible, deafening scream that echoed off the basement walls. The cameramen turned to their producer. Denise jumped back, visibly terrified for the first time tonight.

Johnny Rocket, the man who brainstormed the idea of filming live at Murcat Manor, their fearless leader, now whipped his arms at anyone close to him. He connected with one of the cameramen and knocked the camera out of his hands.

Jacqueline dropped Johnny's core body temperature to a threatening ninety degrees, causing extreme shivering and mental confusion, adding to his bout of madness. The chance of his heart stopping increased to an alarming rate.

Johnny Rocket gave the viewing audience what they were looking for. His breakdown, accompanied by burrowing his fingernails into his head then pulling out large chunks of blood-soaked scalp and hair, attested to this not being an act. Ned and Henry each grabbed an arm and pulled him to the ground so he couldn't further hurt himself.

"What the hell is happening to him," Denise screamed, frantically pulling her hair in. She shone her flashlight where Emily should have been. "And where's that damned evil cat?"

Johnny screamed in ghoulish howls. He began to beat his head on the pavement. The Leeds brothers fought to control him.

"Time to go in for the kill," Emily said. "Annie, raise Johnny's blood pressure as high and fast as you can. Explode his heart. And bring the noise."

The much thinner Johnny Rocket continued to flail on the ground as Ned and Henry fought hard to contain him. Both now had bloody noses and busted lips. Ned spit out a tooth.

"Annie. Do it now."

Johnny continued to wail and punch and kick.

"Annie, what's going on?"

A telepathic scream filled Emily's head. "Chloe. Was that you?"

"Yes. Annie, she's dead."

Emily ran to the work bench and jumped to where Annie lay on her side. Emily didn't need to investigate. She knew her soul had departed her feline body. Annie was certainly dead.

"Chloe, what just happened?"

Emily heard the fear in her own cracked voice. Terrified not only at her friend's death, she discerned something had been unleashed that she couldn't see, attacking her and her sisters.

"Chloe. Answer me."

Helen's head was hung, her voice somber. "She can't. Chloe's dead too."

"That can't be ... what, how ..."

"I don't know. Like Annie, she just fell over."

Across the room, Johnny broke free. The cameramen aimed their flashlights and filmed him as he ran across the side of the basement, arms out like sideswipers, bashing the shelves free of their contents. He screamed and punched at Ned who tried to tackle him. Denise stood, shining her flashlight on her hair, again trying in vain to pull it in. Her pride and joy, like liquid vanity, slithered like snakes and escaped through her fingers.

Emily went to Chloe, but tripped over another cat. It was Jacqueline. She also lay dead. She had simply dropped without a fight.

"What the hell's going on?" Emily screamed.

But her voice was lost. Her last words echoed between the reality she departed and the strange place she was thrust into. Emily Livingston had been ripped out of her body with a terrible force. The searing pain was akin to being turned inside out. She had passed out, if only for a few moments.

She floated aimlessly with no purpose. One moment, her arms swung over her head. Next, her legs were on top and she fought to regain control of her body, her movement, and the direction she was going. Sensory deprivation prevented her from gaining any restraint, not only from her bodily movements, but her will.

Silence wailed.

The absence of noise was anything but peaceful. Now that she had attained a natural reduction of physical stimuli she once had believed would bring her peace, she was instead filled with terror. Rather than a serenity that would heal the wounds of her past, she now had no control over her ... *world?* Was this a world? Emily was at the mercy of whatever, or whoever, had brought her here in dreadful violence.

She was in a void of darkness. There was no sense of up or down. She cried out, but struggled to discern the sound of her voice. Emily hadn't been this terrified since the night four hundred years ago when the mob chased her through the Boston countryside.

A voice spoke. Vague at first, but as clarity set in and the pain diminished, she recognized the tone and pitch.

"I have you right where I want you. Don't try to fight. It will only make things worse for you."

Emily struggled to get away. She moved her feet to run. But she was suspended. There was no ground. Her torso and arms were caught in a sticky net or possibly a spider's web.

She gulped in air and shouted out, "Where am I? Why did you bring me here?"

"I'm an old friend from the Turner place. I was a much younger man then. But with all the people coming and going, I'm not surprised you do not remember me."

The voice was now crisp and clear.

Indian Joe.

"Oh, and in response to your question, where are you? Very simply, you're in my Soul Catcher."

Soul Catcher?

"Let me enlighten you."

325

A light shone on Emily. She could see her arms. Her hands. She wiggled her fingers, but she didn't feel like flesh and blood. Yet somehow she had her original pinkish and frail human form.

"Some of your friends are here, too."

Emily looked around. As she tuned into her present reality, she began to make out their forms to her left. Their screams became clearer. Louder.

Annie.

Chloe.

Jacqueline.

"What is it you want?" Emily cried out, struggling with her wrists, trying with all her might to escape her entrapment.

"It's not what I want. It's what needs to be done. You are true evil, as are your twelve friends. You killed the Amish family. Then, somehow, by a magical power I've never seen, you came back and killed everyone at the Turner place. And now, you've returned again and killed five innocent people at Murcat Manor.

"I saw the reports on the news, and I knew the same wickedness that worked on this property when I was a young man is back. Now, I'm going to stop you once and for all so you can no longer continue this cycle of murder."

Emily strained against her imprisonment. But the more she moved, the more she became entangled. She looked up at a figure descending upon her with a long knife that looked more like a short sword.

"You're going to kill us with that?"

Indian Joe's voice was calm and calculated. "No. I'm not a murder, like you. What remains of my life is short, and I do not want to have to account for your shed blood at my day of judgment."

The man wielded his long knife above his head as if it were an extension of his arm. "You are truly witches whose souls inhabit cats. The fact I saw you fifty years ago at the Turner Place tells me you have tapped into strong magic that has given you nine lives. And I detect a mixture of English and New England accent in your voice, so I conclude you came out of Colonial America. I can only hope this life is as close to if not your final life, and that you never again leave the Netherworld. With any luck, you will go straight to your final judgment."

Indian Joe, not fully flesh and blood, but very much real, was not willing to negotiate. Emily had but a few moments to hatch an escape plan. Or die.

Chapter 44   Strong Magic

Emily tried to make sense of her desperate situation. She didn't know where she was. The shaman-like powers Indian Joe used were far beyond anything she had experienced over her four centuries. The terrifying screams of Annie, Chloe, and Jacqueline howling in undiluted panic for her help only added to the confusion.

To further intensify their plight, her abilities, along with her sisters, were useless in the steely interlaced threads. For one short second, Emily chided herself for not having Madelyn research spiritual matters in addition to the scientific.

They had four centuries to do so. Emily and her following were professionals in her own tight knit realm. But now, she was thrust out of her element. She was completely ignorant and at the mercy of a foe she damn sure should have been prepared for.

Emily had to summon the cats roaming Murcat Manor. They were her only option. But would her sisters be able to hear her telepathic beseeching?

"Rebecca. Scarlett. Isabella," she screamed at her leaders.

"What is it?" a faint utterance echoed. Emily couldn't discern what direction it came. But it was clear the voice belonged to Rebecca.

"We've got trouble."

"I'll say. We can hear the ruckus up here. Great job. Whatever it is you're doing in the basement, don't stop."

"Listen to me." The horror and intensity in her voice was good. If her leaders could hear her, they'd understand the urgency.

"It's Indian Joe. He's using a strange magic. He's ripped our souls from our bodies. We're no longer in the basement."

Rebecca's voice was now clear. "Where are you?"

"We're ... I'm not sure where we are. Somewhere between you and the Netherworld. We're trapped in some kind of sticky netting. Indian Joe's going to kill me along with Annie, Chloe, and Jacqueline. Only Helen and Scarlett are left alive in the basement."

Screaming filled her ears. Rebecca wailed over the news Annie her sister was gone.

"Rebecca. Get control of yourself. We're going to die if you don't help. That includes Annie."

Emily wasn't sure if the others could hear her over Rebecca's mournful banshee screams. Her worst fear, beside the shadowy human-like figure approaching with a very long knife, was Rebecca setting Murcat Manor on fire and killing any chance she had of returning home.

"Somebody shut Rebecca up. Now!"

An instant later there was silence.

"Rebecca's under control," Isabella said. "I gave her a vision of Indian Joe's trap you described. She's now focusing on how she can help. Rebecca's ready. We're all ready."

"Isabella. You, Rachel and Angel are guarding The Frontiersman. You have to get inside. Indian Joe's soul is here. But his body is in his room. You have to get in there and kill him right now."

"I'm leaving my body now," Rachel said. "I'll teleport into his room. But there's nothing I can do except give a report what's happening inside. I need Helen to unlock the door for the others to come in."

"I'm on my way up now," Helen said. "I'm dodging the crew of lunatics down here in the basement and running up the stairs into the kitchen. I'll be with you in seconds."

To Emily's left, the ghostly shade of gray approached a struggling and screaming Annie. His visage became clearer the closer he came. The outline was that of an older man. But he was in great shape. Broad shoulders. Thin waist. Strong sinewy arms gripping his long knife with surety.

After four hundred years of living a disembodied existence, she had forgotten what her sisters had looked like. Annie. Tall and thin. Light complexion. Her narrow face framed by the blackest of long straight hair. She and her sister Rebecca were beautiful in their human lives.

"Don't do it," Emily cried out. "What do you want from us? We'll leave Murcat Manor. Just let us go."

Indian Joe let loose a mocking laugh. "No. You won't. You are who you are. It's in your blood. You'll eventually kill undeserving people again. I'm the only one who can stop this generational curse of madness."

Emily cried out. "Anyone, I need an update. What's going on? We're going to die here."

"We're in," Helen said. "Wow! This place looks like a museum of Indian artifacts of every sort. I see Indian Joe. He's lying on his bed. He's in a white leather-skinned outfit of some kind. His hands are folded on his chest. Incense is burning and there are crazy native relics all over the room."

"Specifically," Madelyn said, "I see Soul Catchers. These are the prominent items. Some are as large as a flower vase. Others are small. It looks like he's placed them in a strategic pattern facing the four corners of the Earth. It's as if he's cast a net across Murcat Manor."

"Stay low. You don't want to get caught up in—"

More screaming. It came from Helen. "It's Angel. She fell over. I think she's dead. Just like Annie, Chloe, and Jacqueline in the basement."

Emily saw a female figure approaching, spinning out of control. It was Angel. She crashed into the net next to the others still yelling and struggling to free themselves.

"Ah, I see my Soul Catchers have caught one more of you. In a few minutes, most if not all of you will be here. And I will destroy you one by one. Starting with this one."

Indian Joe was now upon them. He stood in front of Annie and raised his knife. Emily tried to force herself between them, but she only became more entangled.

"Don't you touch me," Annie spat, trying to kick at the shaman. "Get the hell away."

Indian Joe shouted something in a native tongue Emily didn't recognize. He let fly with a viscous sweep of his arm. He didn't gut Annie, as Emily expected. Rather, he cut the netting holding her left wrist.

A few more skillful thrusts and swipes of his knife, and Annie floated off. At first, it was a slow and graceful freefall. Seconds later, she picked up speed, tumbling end over end, off into the darkness, like being sucked into a vacuum. Her humanlike appearance disappeared, her screams following, muffled and absorbed into the dark silence.

Emily tried to calm the others trapped in the net. But the fear and mayhem prevented her from communicating anything to them. Here, trapped in the bowels of the Soul Catcher, they were utterly powerless.

"Do not be concerned regarding your friend. She's gone now."

"Isabella. Talk to me. What's happening in the Frontiersman Room?"

"Esther's trying to charge some of the objects around his body and explode them. Rebecca's working on a small fire to burn his brain."

"And ..."

"Nothing. He's using a magic we don't know about. We'll be able to break through eventually. The question is, can we do it before we're all caught in his Soul Catchers."

Indian Joe moved on to Jacqueline, slicing his way through the netting holding her. She soon followed Annie, screaming into the dark abyss. He then moved on to Chloe.

"Hurry. Do something. Or he'll kill us all."

As Jacqueline disappeared, another female figure appeared on the horizon, then slammed into the netting to Emily's right.

It was Rachel.

"So," Indian Joe said, so much more interested in Rachel that he left Chloe and bypassed Emily and the rest and moved on to her. He marveled as he studied the newcomer.

"You have the ability to leave your body and travel around in just your soul. Rare is the person who can do this and successfully reenter their body, although this made it that much easier for my Soul Catcher to capture you."

"It's impossible," Helen said frantically. "And I feel the pull. I think I'll be next. What do we do?"

Emily racked her brain. She needed more time.

"We have to do something different. You've all tried your abilities. But he's blocked them. Madelyn, use your logic. It's up to you."

"I'm a step ahead of you."

"I hope so."

"We haven't seen this magic. I have heard tell of it, the Native Americans had shamans—medicine men—and Indian Joe is obviously one with what is called 'strong medicine'. But the real trick, I believe, is this is all a diversion. He wants us to waste our time here. What we see lying in the bed is not Indian Joe. It's a hologram of sorts. A technique where ..."

"*English,*" Rebecca shouted.

"It's an illusion. He wants us to stay here so he can capture our souls. All the while preserving his body."

"What are you talking about?"

"Think about it. Why would he risk his body? He knows if we find and destroy it, he dies and we live. Clearly, this is a diversion."

"So where is his body?" Rebecca demanded.

"In the only place it can be safely stored. Remember, he's the one who recommended Bob and Debbie leave Murcat Manor tonight and go see a movie. So, logically, his body is in their bedroom."

Emily watched helplessly as Indian Joe fronted Rachel. He gripped the leather bound handle with both hands and held his knife high, almost in a sacrificial manner. He wasn't laughing or mocking his prey. The shaman was all business. This was his mission.

"Get down there. Now! He's about to cut Rachel loose."

It took less than fifteen seconds until Emily heard Madelyn's voice again.

"We're here outside Bob's bedroom door," Rebecca said. "But we can't penetrate the animal door. Indian Joe must have a spell on it. He's prepared we'd figure out his trick. We're trying. Believe me. But we can't get in."

Emily was beside herself. Strange magic. Strong medicine. A supernatural barrier. No time to figure out how to get past it. Emily stopped struggling and tried to catch her breath.

Indian Joe had won.

She watched as he swung his long knife. Rachel was freed of the soul catcher. She spun off into the darkness, screaming madly like Annie and Jacqueline before her.

"Wait," Madelyn said. "Indian Joe probably didn't have a lot of time to prepare. He arrived twelve hours earlier. I think he's using smoke and mirrors."

"What are you talking about?" Emily cried out.

"I bet he only covered the animal door with a spell. I doubt he thought about us using the doorknob since we lack opposable digits. Helen, quick—unlock the deadbolt and doorknob."

The telepathic connection between the cats was clear. Emily heard a few clicks from the tumblers inside the locks, the doorknob turning, and the door creaking open.

"We're in. He's on the bed. And this time, I'm positive that's really his body. There are soul catchers here along with other artifacts. We'll have to take our chances and take him out."

Emily watched as Indian Joe cut Angel loose. Four of her sisters were banished to the Netherworld. She was next. Her cousin Chloe would follow. She closed her eyes and braced for the inevitable.

The steely bands that bound her wrists and ankles melted away. She began to feel the sensation of a slow rolling fall. Her legs were above her head. Then she felt upright.

But instead of being consumed with fear, a smile formed. Indian Joe had not cut the bands that bound her. They'd simply ceased to exist. Her sisters had succeeded. She wasn't destined for the Netherworld. Rather, she was going home. As was her cousin, Chloe.

Madelyn had cracked the code, as she liked to say. Emily wasn't sure what that meant. It was a technical term only Madelyn cared to understand. And that was okay, she thought, as she opened her eyes to see Indian Joe soaring off in the opposite direction with a look of total shock.

Madelyn, the shy one who shunned the spotlight, was the heroine today.

Chapter 45   Home Again

Emily tumbled, feeling like her insides were crawling up her throat. She still had no idea which way was up or where she had been. Indian Joe had not revealed those specifics. But he was gone and she was free, as was Chloe.

Emily picked up speed. She was sucked into a space devoid of matter that could only be a portal to her feline body. A bittersweet thought overwhelmed her. She was happy to be alive. But in a few moments she would have to explain to her sisters why she failed to save Annie, Jacqueline, Angel, and Rachel.

But what would be the most troubling; telling Rebecca her sister Annie was not returning—she was trapped in the Netherworld and would have to wait until their seventh life to come back.

Her velocity increased. For an instant she wondered where Indian Joe would end up. Obviously, he was not coming back to join his earthly fleshy body. He could go to a much better place. Or a far worse one. Emily wasn't sure and she didn't care.

Her sisters won the battle with an exceptional Indian shaman-warrior. He had generations of mystical magic on his side which neither she nor the others recognized. They'd gotten lucky, Emily knew, thanks entirely to an unexpected outcome. Emily would bestow much honor upon Madelyn, who used logic rather than magic to gain the victory. This honorable attention, of course, the introvert of the clan would shun.

Images were blurred as she hurtled toward her realm within the bowels of Murcat Manor. She took one last look at her fingers and toes, which she had not seen in four hundred years. After a few wiggles of her pink appendages and a brief giggle, her time apart from her physical feline form was over.

Muffled voices became distinct. Colors separated. Individuals took their own unique forms. Up ahead, is that Denise Forsythe? And is she holding my cat body?

Emily crash landed into her corpse. The collision was violent and almost as agonizing as when she was tore from her body. She fought to keep from passing out. But she was in. But she needed to put on her skin. Emily couldn't breathe, which didn't help her stay conscious. If she didn't fit into her cat body in a swift and proper hurry, she would suffocate.

Emily felt around with her right foot and found an opening. She slid into the right leg of her carcass. The fit was snug. She put her left leg in with one quick smooth movement and tried to maneuver it. She was groggy from the impact, but Emily felt as if her soft furry little hind paws could move.

A male voice echoed in her head. It was clearer than the muffled noises a few moments ago.

"Look, its foot moved. I thought you said it was dead."

"Of course it's dead," followed Denise's condescending voice. "Just like the other cats on the work bench. Guys, keep the cameras on me. And forget about my levitating hair. Focus in on this lifeless cat."

Denise held Emily's body high in the air, like a warrior presenting a hard earned victorious prize to a cheering crowd.

"Hmph. Not much of a leader," she said to the cameras. "I bet she died of fright. Just like a scaredy-cat. Get it? Scaredy-cat?"

Having Denise hold her body was unacceptable, Emily thought. But the mocking? Making jokes for the cameras at her expense? What's she doing now?

Tossing me up and down in her hand like some rag doll? Oh hell, no. I don't think so.

Emily shoved both arms into the limp cat's sleeves. She thrust her face into the lifeless fur-lined shell of the head and was now all the way in. She gulped a deep lungful of air. Her insides came to life. Energy flowed outward from her lungs and heart, spreading through her internal organs. Her senses connected her to the world with each successive breath.

Her muscles twitched, sporadic at first, then with a symphony of movements. Emily was alive. She screamed and jumped. It was all pure instinct. One moment she's laying limp in Denise's hands, looking up into two cameras shoved in her face, and next …

Denise Forsythe, the drop dead sexy face of *American Ghost Stories*, let out a blood clotting scream. Emily's claws dug, slashed and gashed into the entertainer's face. Emily's head and eyes were now level with television hostess. She saw the cable emcee's unadulterated terror and shock at the sight of Emily now alive, along with what must be unspeakable pain as her claws gouged in deeper, her one-inch curved nails penetrating all the way to Denise's cheekbones.

She clamped her teeth down on Denise's nose with a savage blood-drawing bite, then yanked her claws from her face, making sure to rip some flesh.

Time to split. And fast. The element of surprise had given Emily time to inflict immense pain and terror. But she wasn't about to wait for the counter attack. Emily scampered off as Denise began flailing her arms and kicking her legs in a mad frenzy.

Emily had to run upstairs. To tarry meant certain death at the hands of an enraged psycho-diva. She was followed by Chloe, who'd also entered her physical cat body. Scarlett, the only cat in the basement other than Helen who had escaped the Soul Catcher, followed. The three ran through the legs of the Goths and Vamps at the top of the basement stairs and through the animal door into Bob and Debbie's bedroom.

There on the bed, surrounded by Madelyn, Esther, Helen, and Midnight was Indian Joe. The mood was solemn. Not because Indian Joe lay silent, but because of their fallen sisters. Rebecca sat on Indian Joe's chest, her head hung low, their noses almost touching. Emily knew she was crying.

Madelyn broke the awkward silence. "He's dressed in funeral clothes, and in a way that is open where his spirit can depart his body. While he was alive, I suspect there were spells that would keep all of us from approaching except Rebecca, who can start fires."

Emily was confused. "Why would he do that?"

"I believe he planned to kill as many of us as possible. But clearly, Indian Joe didn't think he would kill all thirteen of us. He expected one would kill him. Since Rebecca is now sitting on his chest, he chose her as the one to lead him into the afterlife."

"By fire?" Emily said.

"More specifically, cremation. A common rite of passage into the afterlife practiced by many Native American tribes."

"Is it safe to go up there now," Emily asked.

"Oh yes. He's very much dead."

339

"How did it happen?"

"I sizzled his brain," Rebecca said in a low somber tone. "Like Madelyn said, Indian Joe knew he would die tonight. He discerned some of our powers and, according to his ancient customs, thought I should be the one to kill him. But, instead of consuming the bed in flames, I decided to go internally and cook the inside of his head. Who knows, without cremating his body, he may be floating in purgatory forever. Serves him right for killing my sister, Annie."

Chapter 46 Head Count

Emily jumped up on the bed and sat next to Rebecca. She stepped on Indian Joe's chest and rubbed her paws into him, searching for a heartbeat. His eyes were closed. He looked at rest, as if he had already made peace with his maker.

"He was able to do what we did four centuries ago. Separate his soul from his body."

Madelyn's tone and posture was disassociated. "The shaman one-upped us. He was also able to separate our souls from our bodies. Although I should have, I didn't know this was possible."

Emily scanned Bob and Debbie's bedroom. "These artifacts, are they what he used to perform his magic?"

Wooden and turquoise implements, carved and painted with hideous faces, were placed throughout the room. They faced the four corners of Murcat Manor's property. Incense filled the room with strange but oddly pleasant aromas.

"Indian Joe must have worked right after Bob and Debbie left for dinner and the movies, and the cast of *American Ghost Stories* were interviewing the neighbors. The freaks were trailing them and we were in the basement planning our strategy. He had free reign of Murcat Manor for at least a couple hours. Then he filled Bob and Debbie's bedroom with two things. First, the Soul Catchers, then assorted amulets used by North American shamans."

"Soul Catchers." Emily shuddered. "He mentioned that's what we were caught in." She looked around again at the artifacts. "Get down. Those things might still be active."

"Not to worry," Madelyn said, walking back and forth between the multiple-headed objects. "These are handmade tools characteristic of his culture from a time gone by. The Soul Catchers' powers were tied to their owner. As long as he was alive, his magic—strong medicine he'd call it— would work. But now that he's dead, these are useless relics—mere chunks of wood, really. The only thing they're good for now is to put on display at museums."

Screaming came from below. Things were crashing and breaking. Emily heard Denise swearing she would personally kill the rest of the cats. Especially her.

"Looks like *American Ghost Stories* is still having fits," Chloe said.

Emily turned to Rebecca, still staring down at Indian Joe. She brushed up against her grieving sister and snuggled her. "I'm so sorry. I don't know what to say. Everything happened so fast. There was nothing I could do."

Chloe sighed, crestfallen. "There was nothing any of us could do." A tear dripped down her cheek, her head in a slow wag. "Indian Joe caught us all by surprise. He ambushed us with strange magic we've never seen."

Rebecca heaved a deep breath. "I don't blame you. Any one of us could have died tonight. Not just my sister Annie." She turned to Madelyn. "I know I often made fun of you. And I apologize for that. Tonight, you saved us. Thank you."

Approaching sirens, competing with the screaming and arguing from the basement, broke the solemn moment.

"Darrowby," Emily said. "He must have been watching the show."

"What do we do?" Rebecca said, with a humility Emily had never heard from her second in command. "I understand how you felt when you lost your sister Sarah that night outside Boston. I'm sorry for how I've acted since then."

The sirens grew louder.

"Don't worry about it. We'll discuss this later."

"Okay. Just know I'm here for you. You're our leader. And I'll follow and respectfully do whatever you say."

Emily was happy Rebecca had a change of heart, even if it was under the most trying of circumstances. Time to move forward. "Okay. We have four dead sisters. Rachel and Angel's bodies are upstairs. Annie and Jacqueline's are in the basement. Any ideas?"

"The bodies. We should hide them," Helen said.

Chloe shook her head. "How? Why? They're spread over three floors. We'll never get to them in the next couple minutes. And even if we were able to hide them, the police are going to tear this place apart. They'll find them."

"Listen up," Emily said. "We've been found out. Twice. And in one night. Once by *American Ghost Stories* and then Indian Joe. I agree with Chloe the police will find our sisters' bodies regardless what we do with them. This will cause Darrowby to have to a good long look at us. We have to protect ourselves moving forward."

"Actually," Madelyn said, "We've been found out three times, if you count Erma."

"That's right," Isabella said. "The day I hissed inside her head. She went nuts. She walked up to each of us, asking if we did it."

"Exactly," Emily said, police sirens now wailing directly in front of Murcat Manor. "No one else heard it but that batty old lady. Oh yeah, I'm sure in the back of her mind, she hasn't forgotten about that. I have to say she's making connections, too."

More bellowing and shrieking erupted from the basement.

Rebecca huffed. "Can't anyone make them shut up? They're scaring the hell out of me. And we're supposed to be the ones doing that."

Scarlett raised a paw. "Believe me, I'm trying. But it's not working."

"Why not?"

"I don't know. This has never happened before."

Rebecca winced and cupped her paws over her ears. "Emily, you have the same abilities we all have. Can't you flip the off switch? That guy's incoherent babbling has to stop."

Emily closed her eyes tight. Johnny Rocket continued to wail. The Leeds brothers were also yelling.

"I'm trying. But ... nothing."

"I think I know why," Scarlett said. "While everyone else in the basement was caught up in the Soul Catcher, I watched Johnny smashing his head against the cement walls and floor."

"That's it," Madelyn said. "He probably has serious physical brain trauma. You may never be able to turn it off."

Rebecca turned to Helen. "At least you can switch Ned and Henry back, right?"

"Of course I can."

"Well ...."

Helen started to move, then stopped. "Ah ... no. I think I'll leave them like that. What about Denise's hair?"

Chloe was laughing. Rebecca had to chuckle.

Emily shrugged. "Good question. It may float forever. Who cares? Certainly not me. I hate that uppity bitch."

Rebecca nodded in agreement. "Okay. What to do. We can't wait around until someone else finds us out then tries to kill us. That seems to be the pattern."

"We'll think of a plan," Emily said. "But first, we need to make sure Darrowby doesn't begin to have his doubts about us. Four dead cats could lead him in that direction."

"And Erma?"

"We'll have to devise a scheme to take care of her, too."

"What about Bob and Debbie? Bob may be boring, but he's not stupid. He'll figure things out sooner rather than later."

Madelyn sighed. "The answer is simple. Once again, we leave evidence Boring Bob had something to do with another death at Murcat Manor."

"Brilliant. Madelyn, where have you been all this time."

"I've been here all along, helping far more than you'll ever know. But I shun the spotlight and you never notice me."

Emily brushed up against Madelyn and hugger her with her tail. "I'm sorry. Really, I am."

"Not to worry. I'm an introvert. I prefer to work behind the scenes. Okay, time to link Bob and Debbie to Indian Joe's death."

Rebecca spoke. "But how? This is their room. Any evidence we leave would belong here."

"Except," Madelyn said, walking over and into the walk-in closet. "There. See? Bob has some old baseball equipment. A couple bats, glove, and baseballs. Now, any infliction will be post mortem. But, since Indian Joe's only been dead for a few minutes, we can still cause damage on and below his skin that will lead Darrowby to suspect foul play. Eventually, forensics will conclude he was already dead. But this will give us some breathing room."

"Perfect," Emily said, "Chloe, levitate one of those hardballs, and hurl it as hard as you can directly into Indian Joe's temple."

"With pleasure," Chloe said, a ball rising from the closet shelf. "Taking aim, and wooooshh!"

The baseball flashed across the room and slammed into Joseph Meicigama's temple with a resounding smack, then tumbled off the bed onto the floor with a soft thud.

Emily inspected the wound as it swelled and turned a dark brownish-blue color. A few drops of blood trickled from his ear.

"Excellent. And surely Bob's prints will be all over the ball. Good job, Madelyn and Chloe. Now let's go."

"Wait," Rebecca interjected. "I want to see Annie one more time."

Emily listened to the noise from the basement. Johnny Rocket was still putting up a hell of a fight. At the front of the house, footsteps pounded up the porch steps. The front door was forced open and slammed against the wall.

"I'm sorry for your loss. Our loss," Emily said. "But we have to wait for the basement to clear out. Darrowby's here and Murcat Manor will once again be a crime scene. He and his goon sidekick aren't going to allow anyone in the basement. Not even us."

Chapter 47 The Aftermath

Bob wondered if he should be used to this setting. He sat, once again, at the enormous oak kitchen table at a crazy hour of the morning when he should be sleeping with his gorgeous and voluptuous wife. But the same scenario playing out was becoming routine. Raymond made coffee for him and Debbie. Oh, and also, ho-hum, there was another dead guest at Murcat Manor.

And let's not forget attorney Kenneth Wilson, Bob thought, chin cupped in his hand as his elbow rested on the table. As counsel, Wilson is there to ensure he and Debbie were not arrested for a horrific crime they did not commit.

Next up are Detectives Darrowby and Kowalski. What death at Murcat Manor would be complete without these two thugs in suits looking for any reason to take him away in cuffs?

Then there were the Battle Creek police offers. Bob watched as they ran yellow police tape back and forth across certain sections of his bed and breakfast.

But the paramedics taking away a still screaming Johnny Rocket strapped to a gurney; now *that* was a new twist. Bob was relieved when they gave him a shot of something in the arm. By the time the producer of *American Ghost Stories* reached the living room, he was sedated.

Ah yes, next up are the Leeds brothers, adamant they were each other. Yeah, Bob hadn't seen that one. Not be outdone, there was Denise Forsythe, her face still bleeding from a really pissed off cat and her unexplainable ever-flowing-heavenward hair.

Bob wasn't sure if that was part of their act to gain new viewers. Or, he finally had to consider as the paramedics turned their attention to Denise' hemorrhaging face, if all four had lost their minds and Murcat Manor truly was haunted and cursed.

"Is Johnny going to be okay," Debbie asked one of the police officers walking in from the living room.

"He'll be held for a seventy-two hour psychiatric evaluation. After that, I'm not sure."

Bob looked at the time on his cell phone. 3:30 a.m. He was physically and emotionally spent, and he was fed up with Darrowby's bullshit. This time, he had an alibi. He and Debbie were at the late showing of *Ghost Busters* in nearby Jackson.

"What part of *we weren't here* don't you understand?" Bob didn't try to hide his disdain or sarcasm as he responded to Darrowby's questioning him for the umpteenth time.

Bob despised Darrowby's non-blinking stare. His glaring hazel eyes, set under a pair of black bushy eyebrows, only exemplified the fact the detective was a zealous fiend wearing a cheap Brioni Vanquish II knockoff. Further exacerbating the disgusting situation was the fact he possessed an authority while lacking the mentality to make rational judgment calls. Power being wielded by a man with a double digit IQ was not a good combination.

"I see a dead Indian in your bed, Mr. Stevens."

Bob couldn't resist. "That's Native American. *Sir.*"

Darrowby tensed. His left eye twitched. Bob knew the detective was this close to taking a swing at him. Likewise, Bob thought, wishing his thoughts could be conveyed telepathically. Take your best shot, shit for brains. I'm ready.

"Not to mention a cable television crew, all who have completely lost their marbles."

"Could be part of their act," Bob said as he feigned a yawn and glanced over Darrowby's shoulder.

Denise Forsythe was in the living room, standing in front of the mirror centered above the fireplace. She cried as she tried to pull her hair down, only to have it again and again float up and spread out with each attempt. The paramedics tried to coax her to sit down so they could clean, numb, and stitch the deep wounds on her face.

No cameras were filming. The cameramen had long since left. Both swore they would never come back. What if this wasn't an act?

Darrowby snapped his fingers loud. "Stay with me, Mr. Stevens. And finally, we have four dead cats. Two in the basement. Two upstairs."

Bob gulped. That was strange. He thought back to DeShawn Hill and the three cats on the rooftop when the fatal *accident* occurred.

Bob hunched his shoulders then let them drop. "I don't know what to say." He reached for his wallet.

Darrowby reached for his gun.

"Hold your horses, cowboy. I'm just showing you the receipts and movie stubs. Proof we were not here."

"Actually, that's proof you showed up at the theatres at midnight. A near perfect alibi. You could have snuck out, came back here, and had plenty of time to kill the Indian."

"That's Native American," Debbie said. "You will address him as such as long as you are in my house."

Darrowby's slammed his fists on the table and bellowed, "Shut up."

The words were loud and mean and echoed in the confines of the cavernous kitchen. Bob might tolerate this jerk of a human being speaking to him this way. But Debbie?

No way in hell.

Bob acted without thinking. He stepped up onto the table and punched Darrowby square in the jaw with a left uppercut as the detective leapt up to meet him. By the time Bob was fully conscious of his actions, Kowalski had pile-driven him to the floor and four other police officers each grabbed one of his limbs.

Bob was picked up and thrust face first against the wall. Kowalski yanked his hands behind his back and cuffed him, intentionally tight. Kenneth Wilson was yelling at everyone to stop. Debbie was in a fit of uncontrolled hysterics.

Wilson stepped between Bob and Darrowby, who was picking himself up off the floor. His hands stretched out chest high kept the two separated. "Whoa. Just stop, everyone."

"You struck an officer of the law," Kowalski hollered, grabbing Bob's wrists and shoving him back toward the table. "That's a felony."

"Your *boyfriend* told my wife to shut up. Nobody does that. You people have no respect."

Bob again found himself heaved down, this time face first on the kitchen table. He felt his nose break and blackness threatened to overtake him. Blood poured from both nostrils.

"And you struck a civilian who was not resisting arrest," Wilson said. "That's also a felony. I'll have your badge handed to you in a criminal lawsuit."

Bob was helped up by Wilson and Debbie. His head spun. He swallowed blood through the back of his nasal passage.

"You ... you beast," Debbie screamed.

"And you two are murderers," Darrowby yelled back.

"I think you broke my husband's nose." Debbie snatched a dish towel and wiped the crimson flow running down Bob's face and off his chin.

Darrowby stepped into Bob and rammed his finger into his chest. "And you almost broke my jaw. But here, let me fix your schnoz for you."

Before Bob could react, Darrowby pinched the bridge of his nose between his fore and middle fingers. He gripped and wrung it, resetting the nose with an awful sounding crunch.

Hideous pain shot through Bob's head. For a moment he saw hot white flashes against a dark background. But his anger overrode any physical pain. He locked his knees and stood his ground. Robert Jeremy Stevens wasn't allowing Darrowby any satisfaction by showing weakness.

It seemed to work. Darrowby looked stunned. Now Bob was the one glaring down on him, eyes wide open and steadfast. Darrowby needed an out. He stepped back and donned a bad actor's attempt at a sincere smile.

"You got lucky my partner has a short fuse. I guess these two events cancel each other out."

"The Stevens were in Jackson watching a movie," Kenneth Wilson said. "So I suggest you take the cuffs off my client and let the police officers finish their work. You and your goon partner may leave. Now."

Kowalski took the cuffs off Bob while Darrowby held up a large Ziplock bag containing a single item: a baseball. He looked at Bob, then to Debbie. "There's a dead Indian in your bed with a bruise on his left temple. I'm confident this piece of evidence will be your downfall. If your prints are on this ball, and why wouldn't they, and autopsy results show this ball is what killed him, that's all I'll need to shut this place down and put you and your wife behind bars for the rest of your lives."

Chapter 48   Ross and Erma

Bob opened his eyes, scratched himself, then stared at the ceiling covered in country western album sleeves. He and Debbie had fallen asleep in the Roadhouse Blues Room. Their personal bedroom was a crime scene—some rubbish about one of his baseballs being a possible murder weapon. Their door had yellow police tape blocking anyone from entering, even though Joseph Meicigama's body had been taken away and the police officers were gone.

Darrowby again, playing his mind games.

Bob guessed it was around lunchtime. His stomach usually rumbled around noon. And right now his gut was howling.

His mind flashed back to last night when Darrowby told Debbie to shut up. He was glad he busted Darrowby in the jaw, even if he got a broken nose in return and was almost arrested.

He picked up his cell phone off the nightstand. 11:58 a.m. Bob sighed, knowing who would be sitting at the kitchen table: Ross and Erma. He didn't need to look out the window to see their car in his driveway.

Bob glanced at Debbie, wrapped under a sheet in a fetal position. He gave her a swat. "Wake up, honey. Let's go see your grandparents. I'm sure they're here."

The Roadhouse Blues. How Bob hated this room and its honky-tonk theme. It attracted some of the most undesirable people. He thought back to the socially challenged people who slept here.

The first guests to walk through Murcat Manor's front door; Eugene and Beatrice Barnett the toilet cloggers, and their red headed triplet boys who terrorized the cats and broke half the lamps and vases in Murcat Manor.

Paul Knudson, who simultaneously had a heart attack and choked to death, if that were even possible.

The bikers.

The drunkards.

The drifters.

The derelicts.

Half probably had warrants for their arrest, others rap sheets the length of a rugby field, and the rest most likely had been lucky and were never found out about their crimes.

He shuddered, thinking he needed a shower after just being in this room.

Routine. The word seemed to be implanted in his mind as he relieved himself in the restroom of a suite Willie Nelson would be proud to call home. Bob was concerned he was becoming numb to these events. He thought back to his dream of riding the gray train. Faster and faster it went, passing stops and people he knew, but never able to find a place to stop and get off.

Is that what happens, Bob deliberated, when the same events consistently occur? The developments speed up and there's nothing you can do to change them. You grow a little more incapable of feeling emotion as each new episode become part of a pattern. A routine.

But four dead cats? Bob couldn't shake that. And Joseph Meicigama had died in his bedroom, in his very bed. This was not a stranger who died in The Frontiersman room he rented. This was personal.

Out of all the guests he'd met, many he had already forgotten their names, Bob liked Joseph the best. He checked his heart. He missed that man. His death was a loss, even though he'd told Bob he was going to die soon. Bob edited that out of his thoughts. The rest of his interpretations of his dreams seemed to be accurate.

Debbie yawned as she rose from the bed and put on her robe. Bob took her by the hand and smiled soft and warm. "Let's go downstairs and get some coffee. I'm sure your grandparents are waiting for us."

Bob had to chuckle as they entered the kitchen. Sure enough, there were Ross and Erma Dempsey with their laptops open.

But a third person sat at the table talking to them was a total shocker. On the near side of the table sat a plump man with suspenders, wiping his forehead with a red hankie. It was their realtor, Clark Hodgkins.

Bob nodded to Ross, who was once again wearing a subtle plaid suit along with his trademark contemptible jovial smile. Erma stared off. She seemed distant and disconnected, as if she was lost in her own world. Bob had never seen the family matriarch like this. He wondered if she too was becoming calloused to yet another death. Perhaps, this was just another routine day for her, as it was for him. Bob found himself feeling uneasy about her wellbeing.

Also present were the Goths and Vamps. Raymond served the remaining guests leftover turkey sandwiches. Seeing them in full makeup and attire, Bob thought the Roadhouse Blues wasn't so bad.

Clark stood and reached out to shake Bob's hand. "Mr. and Mrs. Stevens, so glad to see you again. Wow, looks like Darrowby's bozo of a partner really did a number on your nose. Sorry to hear about last night."

Bob was happy Hodgkins was present. He liked the man who had referred Kenneth Wilson as an attorney. But why was he here, now, with Ross and Erma?

"It's great to see you too, Mr. Hodgkins. What brings you to this neck of the woods?"

"Well, Ross and Erma asked me to come here with them."

"Actually," Ross interrupted, "that was Erma's doing. Me, I couldn't be happier with how things are going. But my Erma?" He wrinkled his nose.

Like Darrowby, Bob tired of Ross. He wasn't going to take any more shit from him.

"A man just died here last night. What the hell are you happy for?"

Ross ignored Bob's aggressive comeback. Erma continued to stare off into some remote space. Bob shook his head and chuckled under his breath. These people are more than strange.

Ross held up the cashier's check for one hundred thousand dollars. "Last night could not have gone any better."

Bob was about to climb over the table and throw a well located, high velocity left hook at Ross. It seemed like the right thing to do.

"Oh, yes. That's right. Except for the Indian dying. What was his name? Injun Joe, or something like that?"

That's Native American, you moron. And his name was Joseph Meicigama.

"That was in your bedroom, right?" Ross said, still admiring the check.

Bob was about ready to tear Ross's head off and urinate down his throat. He held back, though, and just glared at the man.

Ross was still enamored with the check to where he didn't notice Bob's looks that would kill if they could. "Whatever. I can't wait to get to the bank and deposit this. What'd you think about that, my boy?"

Ross again held the one hundred-large note above his head and up to the kitchen light. He snapped it a few times, then smiled wide, brought it down and kissed it before putting it away in his wallet.

"Anyway, as usual, the normal guests left demanding a full refund. As expected," Ross presented the dark dressed guests at the table, "the fringe element stayed. And Bob, this is where the money is. It's this element that's booking Murcat Manor solid well after Christmas."

"But what about when the hype dies down?" Erma, still staring off, said. "What then? We'll still be strapped with twenty-five thousand dollar payments each month."

"No. My dear, that episode last night with *American Ghost Stories* was pure twenty-four carat gold. The ratings were the best ever for the show. The cable channel will be repeating that episode from now until eternity."

Erma spoke but didn't move. Her tone was flat and devoid of emotion. "There's something evil in this house. A presence exists on this property that has authority to kill without hesitation. I don't know how to explain it, other than it's alive with a will of its own. I can feel it."

Ross shook his head. "I beg to differ. Things could not be better."

Erma broke her faraway gaze and addressed Ross. "Look at the cast from *American Ghost Stories*. Johnny Rocket is under suicide watch. He's officially bonkers. And the Leeds brothers, Ned and Henry, they're convinced they're each other. They'll surely follow Johnny to the Looney Bin."

Ross dismissed Erma's statements with a wave of his hand. "That's just plain balderdash. Ratings. TV ratings. That's all, my dear. The entire episode, it was planned well in advance."

"What about Denise Forsythe?"

Ross shrugged his shoulders. "The red head? What about her?"

Erma gave Ross a stern look.

"What about her, dear?"

"Her hair. It continued to float, even after the show was over and the cameras were off. It's as if her hair had a will of its own, mocking gravity and any scientific laws of physics."

Ross stared at Erma for a moment, then burst out laughing. "Hogwash. Part of their act. Right Bob? Back me up, my boy."

"This morning," Erma continued, nettled with her husband, but still with the even keeled monotone of a droning monk. "The news said Denise had shaved her head. There was nothing else the dear woman could do. She tried wearing different wigs. Good Lord knows she tried on dozens, is what they're saying. But that hair also floated. Everyone one of them. Now she has to wear a cowboy hat to cover her bare head, with the strap tightened under her chin to keep the hat from levitating off of her."

Erma turned her face enough to level her steely eyes with Ross's. "What do you make of that? *Dear*?"

Ross shook his head. "Don't know. And frankly? Really don't care. We're booked solid through the holidays. Freaks they may be, though."

Ross looked to the Goths picking over their leftover turkey sandwiches. "No offense." The Goths looked like they thought they'd just received a compliment.

"Of course," Ross went on, diverting his attention to Raymond. "We'll have to wait until tomorrow to welcome any new booking. Raymond will need to get this place in ship shape first. You can do that by tomorrow afternoon, right? That's what we pay you for."

Ross, you're a grade A two fisted jerkoff. An ambidextrous wanker-yanker.

Erma turned her attention to Bob. "Tell me, Bob. What do you think?"

"You want to know what I think?" Bob was shocked Erma would ask for his opinion. He glanced to see if she was sneaking swigs from her flask.

"That's right. You're a very smart man. You've had a few months to contemplate events here at Murcat Manor. Six deaths in three months. Not to mention the nineteen poor souls who previously died on this property. The complete destruction of the cast from *American Ghost Stories*. And, for what it's worth, we can add four dead cats to the total."

Bob looked around at Erma, Ross, Debbie, Clark, Raymond, and the Goths staring at him, expecting something, anything, that could help explain the bizarre events at Murcat Manor.

"I'm not sure. At first, I was a skeptic. I thought these were coincidences." Bob took Debbie's hand, knowing she had the same questions.

"But, having someone die in our bedroom. In our bed. I ... we haven't had time to think this through."

Bob noticed his free hand was shaking, and his coffee cup was spilling onto the table. "Although I don't believe in ghosts, now that I had time to about it, this place may very well be cursed."

Bob, waiting for the caffeine to kick in, turned to Clark Hodgkins. "You've been silent. What do you think?"

"It's not what I think as much as what Erma thinks. She hired me."

"The recent surge in reservations from the fringe element is great," Erma said, snapping herself out of her doldrums. "But it's not going to last. Something else will come along to tickle the fans of *American Ghost Stories* and they'll forget all about Murcat Manor." She looked around the table. "Are any of you following me?"

"Then we'll think of something else," Ross said.

Erma shook her head. "That's why I asked Clark Hodgkins to join us today. We have to be realistic. We need a backup plan. An exit strategy. And that's where his expertise can help." Erma stood and looked directly to Bob. "We have to consider selling Murcat Manor."

Ross came around the table and gave Erma a side hug and kiss on her forehead. "Now, now dear, let's not get hasty. No need to hit the panic button."

"I ... I h-have to admit, I'm fear ... really fearful," Debbie said, squeezing Bob's hand in a death grip. "Coming h-home to a ... a—a driveway full of police and," she sighed, "another dead guest, this time in my ... my very own bed, it's just too much. I need a break."

"There, there, sweetie," Ross said, pulling Debbie in with his free arm. "Don't you worry about a thing. There's nothing to be afraid of here. Just a bunch of old silly hooey superstition. That's all. Murcat Manor is our cash cow. We're not going to change anything."

Debbie let go of Bob's hand and pulled away from Ross. She had never fended off a hug from her grandfather. Bob could see Debbie, like Erma, were ready to stand up to Ross and his greedy and demented schemes.

That's my girl.

"Our movie date last night was our first time alone away from this place. And we come home to yet another corpse, this time in our bed."

Debbie looked to Clark Hodgkins. "Do you think you can sell Murcat Manor? I don't want to live here anymore."

Clark didn't hesitate. "Don't you worry, Mrs. Stevens. I'll put together what I think I can realistically list it for. After that, the four of you will have to sit down and decide what you want to do."

Ross pushed out his belly and patted it with both hands. "Well, you all can go on and worry about a bunch of superstitious nonsense. Me, I'm getting hungry." He looked at Debbie with a manipulative smile. "Nothing a good old fashioned turkey meal from Cornwell's won't do to fix what's ailing you."

Debbie looked up at her Grandfather, a glint of a smile forming. "Well, I guess so. A few hours away from this place will help. Thanks Grandpa."

Ross took Debbie by the hand. He walked around the table to Erma and tried to lead her to the front door. "Coming, dear?"

Erma shook her head. "No. I'm feeling a bit under the weather. And my arthritis is acting up again. You all go. I'll relax on the sofa in the living room."

"Are you sure?"

Erma smiled and stood on her toes to kiss Ross. "Yes. You can bring me back a To-Go plate. I'm going to take a nap. I'll feel better after that."

"That leaves you, Bob. Coming?"

Again with the big, annoying, commercial smile. Ross was the last person, outside of Darrowby, he wanted to be with. And things were moving too fast. Bob needed time alone to recalibrate his senses and think things through. As mad as he was at Ross, he welcomed the break in events. He could use this time alone to his advantage. Ross and Erma, they were only slowing him down.

Aside from that, Bob needed time to research the history of the property. Toss in four dead cats? He couldn't shake the thought of some unforeseen activity at work. For once, he was in agreement with Erma. There was a presence in Murcat Manor he felt was hiding in plain view. Now that he admitted there was a force at his bed and breakfast he had no control over, it was time to uncover what it was and what he needed to do to take back authority of his bed and breakfast.

"Thanks, but no thanks. I'm going to Western Michigan University's library. I think I need to dig deeper into this property's past. I know you can find a lot on the Internet, but I have a hunch there are occult types of occurrences, and strange bits of history, that could better be found—if they still exist anywhere at all—in the archives of a good library."

Ross was already halfway through the arched door and into the living room. "Suit yourself. But you're wasting your time, my boy."

Debbie glanced back to the Goths and Vamps. "I'm not sure what time we'll be back. There's more leftovers from the refrigerator. Just be sure to clean up the dishes."

One of the Vamps tossed her sandwich on the table. "I hate turkey. And I'm bored. Murcat Manor sucks. I still haven't seen a ghost. This place is false advertising. No one's died today."

Before Bob could kick the freaks out of the kitchen, Erma gave the unruly brat a devious grin. "Day's not over, yet."

Chapter 49   Old Faithful

Erma Dempsey awoke to a stampeding rush of feet descending the stairs. She opened one eye to see the Goths and Vamps leaping the final few steps and pouring out into the foyer. Their black boots stomped across the travertine tile floor as they laughed and headed for the front door.

Erma would have slapped the snot out of her kids if they'd run through her house like that.

She took a deep breath and lifted her head. They were kids, barely eighteen. She surmised they lived off their parents' money. No way these lost souls, looking and behaving in such a foolish manner, could find a job and support themselves.

"The food here sucks," the alpha male Goth said as he opened the front door.

His girlfriend smacked him on the butt, all smiles. "Mickey Dees, here we come."

Erma sat up straight and put on a smile as she ran her hands through her hair and matted down her blouse. Perhaps, these kids, they've been neglected. Maybe they never received the love and discipline from their parents she gave to her kids. Erma thought there was something good inside most people. The spark of the divine simply needed to be massaged to the surface. Then pummeled into submission, if necessary.

She'd raised four children. Surely, these youngsters were not much different, regardless of their choice of clothing and makeup. And oh my goodness, all those absurd tattoos and body piercings. Their counter cultural preferences clearly told her they were desperate for someone, anyone, to notice them. That's all.

Erma would attempt to say something nice to them.

"See ya, granny," one of the Vamps said, pointing at her. "Don't try to get up without your walker."

Erma's words froze before they could roll off her tongue. The audacity of the delinquents' actions stunned her. It was as if there were no repercussions to their actions. Her kids had never spoken to her in that way. They knew the consequences.

But these weren't her kids. She couldn't whack them with a switch, so she blurted out the first word that came to her mind.

"Chill. I'm just trying to be cool, that's all."

The Vamp looked over her shoulder as she opened the front door. "Granny, the only time you should say chill and cool is in reference to a sweater."

The rest laughed as they piled out onto the front porch. Not one of the eerie and mysterious lot bothered to close the door.

Erma could only stare and mutter the words, "Disrespectful little bastards."

Erma had a good nap. But the afternoon was getting late. Ross and Debbie would be back soon. She opened her purse, knowing where to reach. Left side. Just behind her wallet. It was there in the same place. Just as it had been in every purse she owned over the past fifty years.

Her trusty flask. A family heirloom, handed down to her from her grandmother on her wedding day. This precious gift was old school, where heritage and personality trumped mass production. A deep tan leather body molded by her grandfather's hands stretched over the sterling silver container. A green Celtic cross with their family crest was imprinted into the aged parchment.

She had a name for her flask: *Old Faithful*. Her best friend was always there to give courage and make her laugh during the most challenging of times. And today, she would need her companion's help more than ever.

Erma Dempsey had to take control of matters. Ross was blinded by the hope that false gimmicks would keep Murcat Manor packed.

But Bob, she was beginning to realize, now he was one smart cookie. As much as Erma made fun of Bob she had developed a respect for him, incrementally at first, but lately exponentially. She knew once he committed to a task, he would see it through. Tonight, Robert Jeremy Stevens would expose whatever dark secrets lurked behind the history of Murcat Manor.

Unfortunately, Bob took calculated risks. And Erma didn't have the time that Bob's risk management mindset would offer.

She pulled out *Old Faithful* and twisted off the cap. She closed her eyes and took a careful sniff of the Balvenie Single Malt fifteen year old scotch, saluted her old friend, and took three large gulps. A quick shudder and flapping of the lips as the whiskey passed her esophagus brought her senses back to full charge.

Erma placed the flask back in her shoulder purse and stepped to the front porch. The Goths backed their cars out of their parking spaces and drove past, staring at her, and making insolent faces and jabbing fingers her way while laughing.

Erma gave each carload of brats a grin and a stiff high wave of her middle finger, breaking their mocking expressions into surprised deadpanned faces.

The aging yet conniving matriarch closed the front door and walked through the living room and into the kitchen. Now, she needed to get rid of Raymond. Erma came prepared with a plan.

"Raymond," she called out.

The Murcat Manor handyman came from the basement, wiping his hands with a towel. "Hi Mrs. Dempsey. What can I do for you?"

Erma handed him a prescription from her purse and faked a cough. "Be a dear, and run over to the pharmacy for me. I forgot to fill this. And Ross is still out at Cornwell's with Debbie. They won't be back for a while."

Raymond offered a wink. "Sure thing. I'm just finishing up some odd jobs. Anything else you need?"

Erma placed her hand on his cheek. "No. Just the prescription. Thank you for helping me out." She donned a bewildered look. "Sometimes, I just don't know where I leave my brain. Let me tell you, getting old, it's not fun."

As soon as Raymond left, closing the front door, Erma took a few more swigs. She patted *Old Faithful* as if they were kindred souls.

She stood at the head of the large custom oak table and looked around the Debbie's domain. How proud she was of her only granddaughter. Debbie Elaine Stevens was not short on vision. She had accomplished so much at such a young age and was living her dream in a way far beyond most women could ever conceive.

Erma took a deep breath and looked across the table, Debbie's centerpiece and pride and joy of Murcat Manor. The door to the basement stood on the far side of the kitchen. The pet door at the bottom allowed the cats free range in and out of the cellar.

Those damned cats. They were not in the living room. Nor were they in the kitchen. Bob and Debbie's bedroom was sealed with yellow police tape, including the animal door. And they hated the outdoors. Spoiled little vermin, they were. They could only be one place.

The basement.

Erma took a moment and allowed the Irish whiskey to absorb into her bloodstream. Satisfied *Old Faithful* had not let her down, and why would she now, Erma walked around the oak table and stood at the door to what she believed was a portal to the underworld. This was a place where the metaphysical world converged with the physical. It wasn't necessary to understand or explain the malevolent evil that had the authority to kill as it pleased. That it existed, and endured for generations underneath Murcat Manor, would suffice.

Erma took another lung full of air and gripped the door knob. She despised the cats and the mayhem they inflicted on innocent people. That's what overrode the fear that would turn most people away. In one swift move, she stood at the top of the stairs. Erma had a grand view of the basement and a good idea what to expect.

There were nine hellish cats left after last night's *American Ghost Stories* fiasco. If she could kill at least five, that would be considered a victory. She would pick off the rest later, one at a time.

Chapter 50   Tables Turned

Emily Livingston could scarcely believe her luck. She'd eavesdropped when Erma got rid of Ross and Debbie. Her husband was such a glutton. He would finish lunch at Cornwell's, then munch on the buffet, staying until it was time to eat dinner.

Bob Stevens would be out late, researching the history of Murcat Manor at a local college. Raymond Hettinger was playing errand boy. Those freakish Goths and Vamps were not a threat as they were off to McDonalds for dinner.

It was just Erma now.

Poor little Erma. She must be drunk. Why else would she be foolish enough to challenge Emily and her sisterhood? But Emily decided to never again underestimate an opponent. There was much strange magic they had never seen. Indian Joe had taught her that.

Erma Dempsey had no special powers like Indian Joe. She was elderly, although sprite for her age. And she was petite. If the young and vibrant cast from *American Ghost Stories* were powerless to do anything, what could tipsy little old Erma possible do to harm them?

There she stood, now at the bottom of the stairs, all five feet two inches and barely one hundred and twenty pounds. Emily could take her down in a second—a mere thought implant would take her out. But why draw more unneeded attention to her and the rest of the cats?

Darrowby would be back. Four dead cats may not be the main thrust of his systematic probing. But he had to be asking questions about the feline clan. And a dead family matriarch in the basement would pour gas onto the fire that was Darrowby's investigation.

Emily sat on her favorite shelf amidst the industrial sized banged up cans of fruit cocktail and laughed inwardly as Erma studied her surroundings. Her following lounged around, not too worried.

"Well ladies, what do you think?"

Rebecca, sitting on a stack of boxes of cleaning supplies, with Madelyn at her side, was the first to respond. "I think AARP's confused. She's examining the basement. We're all in plain sight. What's she looking for?"

"Another bottle of Irish whiskey?" Helen said.

That elicited a round of soft laughter.

Erma stepped forward and zeroed in on the work table. She passed by Chloe and Midnight, who were lying in the center, without looking at them.

"Maybe she's sleep walking," Midnight said.

Emily watched as Erma found a small piece of drywall, then picked up a cordless drill from Raymond's tools and a hand full of screws. Emily laughed again as the aged woman looked peculiar carrying a power tool. Erma walked back to the stairs and climbed to the top. She turned her head over her shoulder and looked down on the cats with a leer.

"I've got you now, you disease carrying miscreants."

Erma knelt, her back to Emily, blocking her movements. But the sound of the drill confirmed what Emily suspected. Erma was sealing the animal door shut.

"Um, I think we should confirm Erma as a threat," Chloe said. "No vote needed."

Erma stood on the top step and looked down on Emily. Her smirk grew to a full smile as she gave an underhand toss of the drill.

The tool seemed to take its time as it followed its parabolic arch before banging onto the work table. The violent noisy impact scattered smaller tools onto the floor as it slid to the far end and disappeared over the side. Chloe and Midnight barely escaped its path. They jumped off the table with a screech and disappeared behind a row of folding chairs.

"Yep. She's a threat," Esther said.

Erma walked with confidence down the stairs, one step at a time. Her smile never wavered. Halfway down, she unzipped her shoulder purse.

"Careful," Emily said, holding her breath and realizing her pulse had risen. "We don't know what's in her bag."

"She could have a gun," Helen added.

To Emily's relief, and amusement, Erma pulled out a foot long cross. She gripped it tight by the long base and held it in front of her. Once on the basement floor, she panned the room with it, as if creating a defense around her the cats would not be able to penetrate.

"Is this some kind of joke?" a chuckling Esther said. "We destroyed her family heirloom, that giant Celtic cross, when we killed DeShawn Hill. Does she think that puny little Crucifix is going to hurt us?"

Emily exhaled. She collected her thoughts and felt sorry for Erma. It pained her to see the family matriarch stoop to such a ridiculous act.

She imagined Erma in her youth. Strong. Smart. A leader. But fast forward to today, it was, well, kind of sad. The queen of the Dempsey clan was a hollow stump where a glorious tree once stood. Emily would try to put an end to this before Erma further humiliated herself and got hurt.

"Hello, Erma."

Erma snickered as she began a slow and steady pace across the basement. "Yeah, I knew there was something evil about you cats when one of you hissed inside my head and made me look foolish in front of my family. Remember that? I do. No one else heard it. But I did."

Erma scanned the room of cats. "Which one of you flea bags was it?"

Isabella jumped up on the work table and waved her paw. "It was me."

Erma's grin turned into a scowl. "I don't know how you did it. And I really don't care."

"I'll tell you anyway," Isabella said, maintaining her stare at Erma and again waving her paw. "Please allow me to gloat. I have the power of telepathy. I can transmit information from and to a human or any other animal without using any known sensory channels or physical interaction."

Emily couldn't resist. "Or maybe you're crazy and imagining cats are talking to you."

Erma continued her pace as she pulled out her flask and took a few gulps, still holding her cross. She wiped her mouth with her sleeve and put the flask back in her purse.

"Oh, I'm not crazy. I can assure you that. In fact, I'm smarter than anyone in this family. In case you haven't realized it, I'm the only one who's figured you smelly rodents out."

"Well then, maybe you're drunk. And for the record, we're felines. Not rodents."

"I know what you are," Erma spat out. "Don't get smart with me. I don't tolerate sass talk."

"Listen to me," Emily said. "Why don't you turn around and go back upstairs. Just leave. Pretend none of this happened. We've already killed one elderly person in Indian Joe. We don't want to hurt you."

Erma regained her wicked smile. She approached Isabella and Esther, waving the cross in their faces. Then she moved on to Helen and did the same.

"I've got you lazy good for nothing regurgitated fur balls right where I want you."

As the other cats did their best to act as if they didn't care, Emily watched Erma as she trotted back to Isabella.

It happened fast. Erma spun the cross in her hand with speed and precision. She now held the short end of the cross and tore the covering off what was the long base.

An elongated shiny steel blade gleamed in the basement light overhead. The Celtic cross had become a dagger—similar to the knife Indian Joe used. Only this time, Erma intended to use it on gutting the cats. Once again, Emily and her sisterhood had let their guard down. And now, another elderly person had turned the tables on them.

Chapter 51   Erma Unleashed

Emily sprang to her feet and tried to shout out a warning. But a thrust of Erma's arm, a few slicing motions of her hand, and within seconds, Isabella lay dead on her side, her entrails spilled out across the work bench.

Erma stepped back and raised her dagger in triumph. "That's for planting the hissing inside my head and making me to look foolish in front of my family. And for smart mouthing me."

There was nothing Emily could do to save Isabella. One of her leaders, and best friends, let out a ghastly shriek as she was ripped from inside her pelt and sucked into the Netherworld. She had to act quickly and take the offensive before Erma could pull another surprise from her handbag. A massive energy burst would put an end to this.

Too late. For a senior citizen, Erma was quick and agile. With one nimble move, she turned and whipped out a can of pepper spray from her handbag, directing a stream at Emily. Before Emily could move, she was hit on the left side of her face.

The pain was immediate and unbearable. Her eyes slammed shut. Tears filled her inflamed face. With only the use of one blurry eye, she jumped off her shelf and hot footed to the other side of the basement.

"Everyone take cover." Emily said, frantically wiping her face with her paws. "Erma's been practicing. She got me with a direct hit to my face."

"What's our plan?" Esther shouted out.

Emily could hear paws scurrying for cover. She peered around a stack of boxes. Her left eye was closed, but with her right she could see cloudy images. Erma kicked over a stack of boxes and sprayed at Helen and Midnight. Both cats sprinted off in separate directions.

"There's nowhere you mangy parasites can hide," Erma shouted. With surprising speed she moved through the basement, knocking over anything that could be used as a hiding place.

Emily needed to physically see Erma to cast an energy burst. But the golden-ager disappeared from her view. Someone else would have to take her out.

"Scarlett, hit her with a bout of madness."

"Are you sure that's a good idea? She's half nuts as it is. And I really don't want to expose myself."

"Just do it."

"I can't see," Midnight said as she ran into the base of the work bench. "I need help. I don't know where I'm going."

"She's right behind you," Chloe said. "Just run."

Midnight came back into Emily's view and ran into a cinderblock wall. She got up and stumbled forward, an easy target for an enraged Erma.

"Helen," Emily said. "Turn off the lights."

A second later the basement was pitch black.

Emily, trying to cope with the burning sensation in her eyes and nostrils, needed to coordinate a counterattack while they had the advantage of darkness. "Scarlett, how's that dose of nutso coming? Better make it a double"

"I need to see her to get a direct hit."

The sound of a purse being unzipped was followed by a beacon of light moving back and forth across the basement. "I came prepared for you rotten creatures from hell."

Emily squinted, trying to ignore the searing pain. "Look for the flashlight. Aim a couple feet above it."

"Got her," Scarlett said with much gusto. "She's stunned, but still looking around."

Erma took a few swigs of her flask. "I'm not sure what just hit me, but it's not going to work. That only pissed me off more."

"Hit her again."

"Done. But she's still moving. Why isn't it working?"

"I think I can answer that," Madelyn said. "In the human brain, information from one neuron flows to another neuron across a synapse. However, alcohol interferes with the brain's communication pathways. These disruptions can affect the way the brain works."

"English," Rebecca yelled out.

"Since she's drunk, the alcohol is actually guarding her brain, at least to an extent, from Scarlett's bout of madness."

"So it's having no effect on her?"

More boxes came crashing down. Cats screeched as they ran for new cover.

"Actually, I think it made her worse. Now she's half mad and half drunk, but coherent enough to know she's on a mission to kill us."

"Erma got me with her pepper spray," Helen said. "I tried to get a clear view to shut off her flashlight, but she saw me. Now I can't see a thing."

"Don't try to rub it off," Madelyn said. "That'll only increase the inflammation."

"What can I do?"

"Milk," Madelyn said. "You have to get to our bowls of milk upstairs. That'll help take the sting away."

"I've got you cornered," Erma said to a cat. "Take this."

Pepper spray noise again. Damn, Emily thought, this is way out of hand. "Someone's in trouble. I'm not sure which one of us it is."

"And now for the grand finale," Erma said.

Emily heard another screech. It was the brains of the group. She had been torn apart from her feline body and joined Isabella in the Netherworld.

"It's Madelyn. Erma got Madelyn."

"That's it," Rebecca said. "I'm torching this loon."

With the one blurry eye Emily could make out Rebecca running in a circle. A flash of fire burst in the middle.

"Oh, you like to start fires, do you? Well, two can play at that game." Erma ran to Raymond's work table and grabbed a large monkey wrench. She took a few hard swings at an overhead gas pipe. A small hiss could be heard. She darted across the basement and whacked a second pipe. More hissing.

"Go ahead. Start a fire. That actually saves me the trouble of burning this cursed place to the ground for insurance money. No way am I losing my ass to this money pit. And sweet mother of mercy, I'll be damned if I let you freaks from hell kill again."

Emily needed to end this before they and half of Murcat Manor went up in a spectacular ball of flames. "That crazy woman's going to kill us all. Chloe and Esther. It's up to you. Do something."

"I'm trying to blow something up," Esther said. "But I need to look at an object for at least a few full seconds."

"How about her flask?" Emily said.

"Great idea. She's stopped to take a few sips and standing long enough for me to get a good look. C'mon Erma. Keep your flashlight still and take another swig, you lush. Hold that pose, and ..."

A loud sound like the crack of a whip echoed in the basement. Erma dropped the flask and fell on her butt.

"That's a good start. Hit her again. Use her flashlight."

Once more, the whip-like crack sounded loud. "Bullseye. But the flashlight's shattered. I can't see her."

The smell of gas was getting worse. Things were moving too fast. Erma was unpredictable and could take out everyone with her next attack. Someone had to kill the dame of the Dempsey clan now.

"We don't have a choice. There's nowhere for the gas to escape. We've got to get out of here. Helen, turn the lights back on."

"Let there be light," Helen said.

The well-lit basement revealed Erma. Emily watched a half mad, half-drunk elderly woman as she staggered to her feet. Her hair stood up and was blown back, as if she had stuck her finger in a light socket. There were ghastly burn marks on her hands and face, proof Esther found her mark with at two direct hits. But Erma advanced, undeterred, looking for another cat to kill.

"Damn. Do we need a tank to stop this crazy woman?"

Erma looked left and right, showering pepper spray in a wide arc, moving her arm up and down, trying to hit any cat unfortunate not to get out of the way. The can emptied, and Erma hurled it toward Esther. She picked up anything she could grab and threw them at the cats.

"Die, you ugly little beasts."

A ball peen hammer flew at Emily, spinning end over end. She jumped left, only to have a crow bar hit the cement floor inches from her. She dove for cover behind a pile of toppled boxes.

"Somebody has to stop her now. Sparks from the tools she's throwing could cause the gas to explode."

"I can't get a good shot," Esther said. "She's pulled out another can of pepper spray and is spraying it everywhere."

"Let me try," Midnight said.

Midnight teleported herself behind Erma, then clamped down on her left ankle with her teeth and claws. Erma froze, her eyes looking like they would explode from her head.

"That was great," Emily said. "Esther, your turn."

Esther stepped out and zeroed in on Erma's pepper spray. It exploded in her hand. Emily shuddered as Erma held up her arm, staring at her right hand, now missing two fingers. Two more dangled by thin strands of skin, like little blood sausages stitched to a clump of raw hamburger.

Pepper spray covered her face. Erma dropped to her knees in the center of the basement, incapacitated. She sucked in air and let out a scream of agony that could wake the dead.

Emily could see a little better. Erma thrashed about on the ground, yelling curses at the cats. Anything she could grab with her left hand became an airborne missile.

"Everyone, just stay away from her. Follow me and start making your way to the stairs. Helen, can you do anything about the gas?

"The pipes are cracked. Nothing I can do about that."

"Chloe, lift towels up onto the pipes and cover the leaks. That'll at least slow down the flow of escaping gas."

Emily led the cats to the top of the stairs, then took one last look at the raving madwoman on her knees and one hand, still trying to feel her way across the basement.

"Erma, I really wish you would have just left. But now we have to kill you. And by the way, you never trapped us in here. Helen, do your thing."

One by one, the drywall screws Erma used to cover their animal door began to unscrew.

"Um, Helen, forget about the drywall. Just open the door. We need to move fast."

"Oh, right."

Helen easily turned the knob and the door opened. Emily led her flock into the kitchen. She kicked the door shut and Helen locked it. The clan took a minute to catch their breath. Next to the door were two bowls of milk. Emily buried her face in one, Helen in the other.

"This is beyond comprehension," Rebecca said, starting to run around in circles and worrying Emily she'd start a fire. "We lost two more sisters: Isabella and Madelyn. That's six of us gone in less than twenty-four hours."

Emily raised her head from the milk. "Shhh. Quiet, everyone."

"What is it," Rebecca said.

"I thought I heard something."

"I don't hear anything."

"Neither do I," Helen said.

An instant later, with a loud grunt, Erma's head crashed through the drywall covering the pet door. Her right arm emerged from the small square. She took a swipe with her good hand and just missed grabbing Midnight by her back paws.

"I swear I'll kill you all," she screeched through blistered lips. "You hear me? Just wait until I get my hands on flea-infested hellions."

Erma was a mess. Her hair was soaked with sweat. Her eyes were shut tight. Her face was raw and swollen and peeled with puss-oozing blisters.

"That's enough. I'm ending this," Chloe said.

A cast iron frying pan took flight off the main stove and hit Erma between the eyes. A clang echoed through the kitchen, then a soft thud as Erma's head plopped on the floor.

"Wow. Quick and decisive," Rebecca said. "Nicely done."

A hushed silence prevailed as the cats gathered around Erma's zombie looking head.

"Do you think she's dead?" Scarlett said.

Midnight swatted Erma's nose with her paw, then jerked back. "I don't know. Someone, poke her in the eye with something and see if she moves."

"Wait," Emily said. "Someone's here. They just came in the front door."

"Mrs. Dempsey, I have your prescription."

Midnight peered into the living room. "It's Raymond. What do we do?"

"Cover Erma with something."

"I got this one," Chloe said. She levitated one of the four red and white checkered tablecloths off the twenty-four foot long oak table and it lowered over Erma's head. "Perfect."

Emily heard his footsteps approaching. "That's the best we can do. Let's take care of Raymond. Bob and the rest will be home any time."

Chapter 52   Dark Secrets Revealed

Bob looked up from his laptop as three buxom young female students approached with their fabulous breasts at attention. One had a tablet and a pen ready. The second scrolled through her cell phone. The third snapped an image of him. This was his fifth interruption. He would need to move to a new table.

The lead female, a blonde with a smile and figure that would remain in his memory a long time, was bolder than Bob cared a woman to be.

"Hey, you're that guy who owns the haunted bed and breakfast," she said with a look of absolute fascination. "My name's Susan. Wow. I've never met a celebrity. And what happened to your nose? Did a poltergeist do that to you?"

"I've seen you on the news," the second said, still taking pictures of him. "What's it like to live in a haunted mansion? Oh, I'm Francine."

"Can I have your autograph?" the third said. "You can call me, ummm ... how about Tina?"

The lead girl looked ready to slap the other two. "You're no more Tina than I'm Susan or she's Francine."

Bob closed his laptop and tucked a stack of old newspapers under his arm. "You're mistaken," he said, trying with all his might to not stare at any of the three's ample bosoms.

"No we're not," Francine said. "I have YouTube clips right here." She shoved her cell phone in Bob's face. "That's you."

Bob started to rise. "Not me. But I get that a lot."

"Then who are you?" Susan said. "You're too old to be a student."

I'm not that old, Bob thought. "I'm a professor."

"You look too young to be a professor. And why haven't I seen you?"

"Look, just leave me alone, okay?"

Bob lowered his head and shoulders and plowed his way through the group of gawking would-be groupies. He found an empty table in the corner and plopped down in a chair with his back to the wall.

Bob rubbed his temples in frustration. His head was starting to pound. Acid from five cups of coffee began to rise up his esophagus.

An entire afternoon researching the Internet, old newspapers, and Microphish revealed little more than what Denise Forsythe uncovered about the Turner place. It was a commune where hippies escaped the world and partied twenty-four seven.

The old fashioned wooden chairs added a stiff back to Bob's fatigue. The wear on the seat told him this chair was generations old. Sturdy. Durable. But incredibly uncomfortable. The campus was well over a hundred years old. Bob figured the chair was an original.

He closed his eyes and slowly rolled his head, easing the tensions building up in his neck. He felt he could hold this pose all night when a gentle hand fell on his shoulder.

"Hello," a calm and soothing female voice serenaded him.

Bob turned to see a lady in her mid-fifties standing over him and offering a pleasant kind smile. She wore a laminated nametag. Bob glanced at the name: Ellen Martin - Head Librarian.

"You're the owner of Murcat Manor. I've watched that episode of *American Ghost Stories* twice. They're showing it nonstop. I have to say, you're a local celebrity now."

Great. That's the last thing Bob wanted to hear. "Yes. I'm Bob Stevens. Nice to meet you."

"I see you're researching the history of the property."

Bob didn't think Ellen wanted his autograph. She looked supportive. No need to get up again and find a new seat. "Yeah. There's definitely something far beyond normal going on at the grounds."

"I'm sorry for the deaths. I can't imagine what you're going through."

"Thanks. It's been rough for my wife and me. She's at the point where she doesn't want to stay there. I have to admit, so am I."

Ellen flipped through the newspapers stacked on the table and stopped to point out one particular headline, tapping it with her finger. "I recall that night. I was in elementary school. It was big news that summer. I remember my father driving by the burned down house and barn. It was quite the attraction."

"Well, so far I've come up with nothing. Just the same old story over and over: house burns down, everyone dies, cause of fire unknown."

She formed a knowing smile and said with a wink, "You're right about the newspapers and Microphish. That's all common knowledge. Maybe I can help."

"Are you saying you have other material?"

383

Ellen now donned a subtle smile that told Bob she had information everyone else was not privy to. But, she was willing to share with the right person.

"I have access to copies of student research papers from nineteen sixty-seven."

"And you think some of them did their research on the Turner place?"

"Perhaps. But more specifically, many of the papers in the late sixties focused on the counter culture of the time."

"But what information would students have that wasn't already here in the library?"

Ellen laughed. "Trust me. Many of them frequented the Turner place. That was the era leading up to the Summer of Love. Woodstock happened just two years later, in nineteen sixty-nine. Murcat Manor was a haven for hippies and, of course, lots of drugs. There was steady traffic back and forth from this campus to the Turner place."

Bob was already standing. "Can I see them?"

"Sure. I have access to a database of scanned research papers." She turned and flung her hand over her shoulder, index finger wagging 'come hither', with the look of someone letting you know you were about to be granted initiation into a secret, elite society. "Come with me."

Bob followed Ellen as they crossed the cavernous library. He took one last look over his shoulder. Summer students scattered across the library were pointing and staring at him.

Bob followed Ellen into a back office room. She took a seat behind a computer, pulled up a database, and entered her user ID and password.

"I'll do a few simple searches. We'll focus on the year proceeding as well as the year of and the year after the fire."

After a few short minutes, Ellen stood and presented the chair to Bob.

"There are scores of papers you can scroll through. Take your time. Can I get you anything?"

"Water. And Advil. Thanks."

"Sure thing. Be right back."

Bob was beside himself. This was luck like he'd never anticipated. Before him was a goldmine of information no one had seen in decades. He scrolled through paper after paper. After a few minutes, Ellen returned and handed him bottled water and a plastic container of Advil.

Bob poured four gel caps in his mouth and guzzled the water. "Thanks so much."

"Any luck?"

Bob sighed, feeling discouraged. "Nothing. I've sped read through dozens of research papers. I'm feeling stymied. They don't tell me anything new."

Ellen reached for the mouse and made a few clicks. "Let me see something. Ah. Here are some pictures students took of the Turner place. Of course, they didn't appear in the actual papers. But they were part of their research. We saved them because they captured so much of that era. If anything, I think you'll enjoy the nostalgia."

Bob regained a little hope. "They say a picture is worth a thousand words. Let's see."

Ellen turned to go back to her work. "Let me know if you need anything else."

Bob clicked on various black and white and color images. He had to chuckle, looking at the hair and clothing from the era. People from all walks of life were sporting long braids and huge afros. They wore tie-dyed tee shirts, miniskirts, striped pants, bell bottom jeans, beads, copious handcrafted jewelry items, and footwear ranging from six inch tall platform

385

shoes all the way down to sandals and bare feet. More than a few of the girls were unashamedly topless, with just a drape of beads and necklaces adorning the upper part of their breasts.

There was even a psychedelic painted bus in the front yard—a classic 'Hippie Bus'. He studied the faces for a while. There must be close to a hundred hippies leaning out the windows and sitting on the top, posing for the picture.

Bob was full-on laughing when we opened another color image. The scene depicted was in the living room. About twenty people crowded the sofa and chairs. Others sat or laid on large pillows and bean bags on the floor.

He almost clicked away to another page, but ... *what in the* ...?

Bob's heart almost stopped, then banged against his rib cage. There were cats in the picture. On the laps of the people were what appeared to be lots of very spoiled felines.

"Thirteen," he said in a slow whisper to himself, "to be exact."

He increased the size of the image. Bob went around the room and zoomed in further on each cat. He recognized each one by the color of their fur and the patterns of their spots and stripes.

Emily.

Rebecca.

Annie.

Chloe.

Midnight.

Helen.

Jacqueline.

Scarlett.

Esther.

Angel.

Isabella.

Rachel.

Even Madelyn, with the dark circles around her eyes that looked like nerdy glasses.

Bob nearly levitated out of his chair. He opened more images. More pictures of hippies with cats on their laps. Emily was with a young lady in a yellow summer dress. Rebecca, Annie, and Jacqueline slept by the fireplace.

Chloe, Midnight, and Helen eating scrambled eggs and hash browns on the kitchen table. Isabella, Rachel, and Madelyn devouring watermelon. They even gathered in the same clusters as at Murcat Manor.

"No way. It's not possible."

"What's not possible," Ellen asked as she stuck her head in the door.

"What? Oh, nothing. Just their clothes and hair. It's such a crazy scene."

"That was the late Sixties. They would have called it groovy. Is everything going okay?"

"Fine, I guess. Hey, can you email me some of these pictures?"

Ellen gave a frowny face. "I'm afraid I can't do that. They're property of the school. We actually have the copyrights on them. But I'm sure you can request copies. There's probably a form somewhere. I'll take a look and be back."

Bob couldn't wait to fill out paperwork. He fumbled for his cell phone, then took pictures of the images. Eight in all. There were more, but it wasn't necessary to go any further. He tapped each picture and texted them to Debbie, then grabbed his laptop and walked out.

"Mr. Stevens, are you leaving now," Ellen asked.

"Yes. I need to get home for dinner. Thanks for your help. Really. I mean it."

As soon as Bob stepped out of the library, he called Debbie.

Her voice was like honey. "Hi sweetie. Still at the library?"

"Are you with your grandfather?"

"Yes. We're at Cornwell's eating dinner. You know Granddad. He'll do anything to eat here. Twice in one day if he can."

"Listen to me, but be very discreet. Do not show any visible reactions to what I'm about to tell you."

"Why? What's up?

"Are you being discreet?"

"Um, yeah, sure. I guess."

"Get up and go to the bathroom. I texted you pictures of the Turner place."

"Bob, what did you find?"

Bob heard the change in her tone. She was concerned. "Debbie. Your voice just rose. Discreet, remember? Get up now, and act normal."

Bob could hear Debbie excuse herself from the table. Thirty seconds later, she was back on the phone.

"Okay. I'm scrolling through the pictures. Talk to me. What's this about?"

"You tell me. What do you see?"

"I see a bunch of hippies. And ... cats."

There was a pause. Bob allowed Debbie to arrive at making the connections. He could hear her gasp. She muttered his same words from the library.

"Uh-uh. No. No, this can't be."

"It is. It's the same damned cats. Emily. Rebecca. Chloe. All of them. Even Madelyn with the glasses."

"Oh ... my ... God. Bob. What do we do?"

"The answer's obvious. Meet me at Murcat Manor. We're going to kill those cats."

"Bob, my grandmother's there."

"Yeah. Alone. Call her. Make sure she's okay. I'm pulling out of the parking lot now. It's forty miles to Murcat Manor. I'll get on the I-94 and be home in thirty minutes."

"We'll be there in fifteen. And Bob, drive safe. I love you."

Chapter 53   Epiphany

Detective Thomas Darrowby paced the industrial gray vinyl flooring of his office at the Battle Creek Police Department. He knew somewhere in the stacks of files he and his partner, Sergeant Detective Kowalski, and a host of other police officers were sifting through, was someone or something that would break the Murcat Manor case wide open. They needed to be relentless in their search. He knew their work would pay off. It always did.

He rubbed his jaw, still sore from the left hook Bob connected. Darrowby hated to lose. One more reason to bust Bob and send him to Jackson State Prison for the rest of his life.

Darrowby looked at his watch, then to Kowalski. "I'm tired. And hungry. Let's grab something to eat. We're going to be here late into the night."

Kowalski closed the file he was working and slapped it onto his desk. "I'm frankly befuddled, partner. Every lead ends up going nowhere. The Stevens' attorney will dismiss everything we have as circumstantial evidence."

Darrowby kept pacing, still rubbing his jaw. "There's something here. I can feel it. We just need to keep interviewing previous guests at Murcat

Manor. Six deaths and hundreds of guests over the past two months? Somebody had to have seen something."

A knock on the door got his attention.

"Come in. And you'd better have something to tell me."

Two police officers let themselves in. "Sure do, Cap'n. We just came back from that interview you sent us to have with Patrick and Marian Allen. They stayed at Murcat Manor the first week it opened."

Darrowby ran the timeline through his head. That was after DeShawn Hill died but before the first guest, Paul Knudson, died of simultaneous choking and a heart attack.

"Yeah? And?"

"Turned out, there wasn't an interview. Least, not with them. They're dead."

"Dead? How?"

"Remember that house fire in early June on the other side of Battle Creek? A young couple died. It was ruled arson, but so far investigators haven't determined the cause."

"That was the Allens?"

"Sure's hell was."

"Whaddaya got?"

"We interviewed their family and neighbors. Nothing out of the ordinary. Except this."

The officer held up his cell phone. "I had Mrs. Allen's mother forward me these pictures."

Darrowby snatched the phone and scrolled through them. "I recognize that cat." Darrowby tapped the image to enlarge it, then focused on the collar tag. "Rebecca. That's one of the Stevens' cats."

"Bingo. The Stevens gave it to them when they left. A few days later their house burned down to the ground."

"The cat must have found its way back to Murcat Manor."

Kowalski frowned, pulling on his ear. "That has to be twenty miles away."

"You read stories all the time about pets finding their way back home."

"So the death toll just went up from six to eight."

"Kowalski, let's go. We're paying the Stevens another visit."

Darrowby thought back to when Bob told him he saw three cats on roof when DeShawn Hill fell backward and was skewered on the spike of the front lawn gazebo. For the first time, he considered there might be more to the cats than he wanted to acknowledge.

In the parking lot, Darrowby tossed Kowalski the keys. "You drive. I need to think a few things through."

"Sirens on?"

"Not this time. I want to surprise the Stevens."

Darrowby had a few minutes to sort through what he previously dismissed as unreasonable, that the thirteen cats at Murcat Manor were more than lazy pets. Could they have played a part in the eight deaths? Or, God forbid—the commissioner would have his badge if he pursued the matter—could the cats be the center of supernatural activity linked not only Murcat Manor, but also the Turner place and the Amish family?

"It's weird how that cat was able to walk all the way back," Kowalski said, intruding on Darrowby's thoughts.

"Huhn? Oh yeah. Right. Sure is. I've hear of dogs doing that. But not cats."

"Give me a dog over a cat any day. Dogs'll listen. They obey. And they come when you call. But a cat? Fuggedaboudit. They have a mind and a will all their own. You can't train 'em. They do what they want, when they want to."

His partner's words struck a chord. Cats do have a will of their own. Darrowby didn't trust cats and never paid any attention to them. Until now. But he had a case to solve. Multiple cases, actually. He had to consider his career as well as his sanity. No way could he mention cats as accomplices. Any chance of moving up the political ladder would surely stop.

What to do? Continue the investigation under the rules his superiors would judge him by? Or Begin to delve into matters that expanded far beyond his training and the results expected of him.

Chapter 54   Ross's Last Words

Murcat Manor came into view as Ross Dempsey passed the last rolling hill on Oak Hill Drive. Debbie looked at the dashboard clock. 7:45 p.m. Bob wouldn't be home for another fifteen minutes. Debbie clutched her cell phone and again called her grandmother. Again, no answer. She sent another text. No response.

"Here we are," Ross said. "There's nothing to worry about. She's probably sleeping on the couch, sweetie. Trust me. My Erma's okay."

Ross pulled into the driveway. "See? What'd I tell you? Everyone is here. There's your Ford Explorer. And I see the freaks' cars too. And there," Ross pointed. "Raymond parked his truck furthest in the back. Everyone's here. Just like they should be."

Ross parked close to the front door. Debbie got out and viewed Murcat Manor. She sensed something was terribly wrong.

"Well, let's go inside," Ross said, taking Debbie's hand. "What's wrong? You're shaking like a leaf on a wind-blown tree."

Debbie pulled back and looked at all the windows on the front of the house. What she expected to see, she wasn't sure. There was movement upstairs. The lights were on in the Goths' and Vamps' rooms. Shadows passed back and forth through the blinds. The Ramones blared loud enough to be heard in the driveway.

But downstairs, she could not detect any activity. Even though it was still daylight, the sun was beginning to set toward the western horizon. She thought there should be a few lights on. And no way would her grandmother tolerate the Ramones to be played that loud. She'd surely put a stop to that.

"Okay. Let's go. I want to make sure Grandma's okay."

"Pish posh. Erma's fine."

Ross opened the front door and Debbie rushed through the foyer into the living room, hoping to see Erma sleeping on the couch. The place was empty of people and cats.

"Grandma," Debbie cried out.

No reply.

"She's probably in the kitchen."

Debbie ran up to the arch entry of the kitchen. No lights were on and there was no sign of Erma or the cats.

Debbie turned in a full circle and gave a shout that could be heard throughout Murcat Manor. "Raymond, are you here?"

Her only reply was the Ramones being turned up louder.

Ross tossed Erma's To-Go dinner, wrapped in a plastic bag, on the table. "No offense, sweetie. Your turkey leftovers are delicious. But Cornwell's, well, you can't beat seventy years of greatness."

"Grandpa, I'm really worried. Where's Grandma? And Raymond?"

"I don't know. Maybe the freaks have them tied up in the backyard and are sacrificing them." Ross almost laughed himself silly.

"Okay, that's totally not funny."

"You're right. I'm sorry. Maybe Erma's upstairs scolding those punks. I bet she has one by the ear and putting the switch to the others."

Debbie ignored his insipid attempts at humor. It was eerily quiet, even with the rebellious rock music from upstairs.

"Grandma. Where are you?"

Ross resumed laughing. "She's locked herself in the storage closet."

"How do you know that?"

Ross stopped and looked at her. "You didn't hear her shouting she's in the closet?"

"No. I didn't hear anything."

Ross grabbed his belly and laughed harder as he walked back through the living room and down the hall toward the pantries and storage closets. "She just yelled out again. Oh, that Erma. She must be taking a few swigs from *Old Faithful* again. Wouldn't be the first time. She's locked herself out of our house and cars too many times to remember."

Debbie cupped her hands around her mouth and yelled out one more time at the top of her lungs, "Grandma. Where are you?"

Ross turned and gave her an indignant look. "Stop shouting. You could wake up a graveyard. She's right here. In this very closet."

Ross reached for the door knob. Debbie imagined the worst. Emily and the other cats had set a trap. She lunged at him. "No. Don't open the door."

Ross gave Debbie a cavalier flip of his hand and opened the closet. He stepped in and split a swath through winter coats on hangers with his right arm.

"Erma? Where in tarnation are y—"

Ross's last words were drowned out by a wail from Debbie as a bowling ball crashed into the center of his head, collapsing his skull.

He sank to a kneeling position and stayed in a slumped, although upright posture, the bowling ball firmly implanted into the top of his head. His eyes bulged out of their sockets. His tongue stuck out at an awkward left angle. His chin was buried into the top of his chest.

Inside, Chloe, Midnight and Helen sat on the top shelf. Debbie knew they had somehow managed to extricate the blue bowling ball from its usual place in the bowling bag on the floor, levitate it up to the top shelf, then wait. As soon as Ross was in position, they pushed it over the edge, plummeting down on its trajectory of death.

Debbie felt a complete sensory deprivation, a whiteout that while still conscious, blocked out communication from her five senses to her brain.

She didn't know for how long, but when she came to she was still standing, staring down on her grandfather. One of the most powerful men she had known was reduced to a heap of wobbly flesh and bones. He looked like the smallest disturbance would cause him to tip over. Chloe, Midnight and Helen were nowhere to be seen.

Unwillingly, her mind replayed the scene in great detail. She thought it would stop after the first time. But the event repeated itself over and over—as if the thoughts were implanted in her head, like the sound of Erma's voice that only Ross could hear.

Debbie knew her free will had been invaded. She shook her head and covered her eyes.

"No more," she screamed out. "Whoever or whatever is planting this in my mind has to stop. Now."

Debbie continued to shake her head and took a quick breath. She had freedom and control over her mind. But she could feel the tug of another presence, an unhallowed force that'd had its way far too many times on the property.

But not this time. This was her house. She would fight.

What would Grandma do? Debbie never took martial arts or boxing lessons. She looked at her open hands. What she needed were weapons. She turned and marched into her kitchen. Here in her bailiwick an arsenal awaited.

There was no shortage of knives and things she could throw. Each counter and island had a set of steel forged Japanese Chubo kitchen knives. Small cast iron skillets hung from the ceiling. Vases and mugs were everywhere. The chairs at the kitchen table could be broken into smaller pieces and used.

Debbie reached for the knives when a blast of heat hit her, knocking her down. It was as if a massive bubble of hot air burst in front of her.

"What the hell," was all she could manage as she stumbled to her feet, gobsmacked at the unforeseen force that blindsided her. But it was the heat on her face that scared her most. She felt her cheeks, glad her skin was still attached.

A second blast leveled her, sending her back to the floor. Frantic to escape a third burst, she stayed low and crab-walked backward on all fours. Her kitchen table would provide refuge, if only for a few moments. Once on the other side she backed into something. Her hands and feet gave out and she collapsed, on, what's this? The table cloth. What's it covering?

Debbie lifted a corner to reveal a badly damaged hand and forearm. She jumped to her feet, tearing off the fabric. Between her legs lay her beloved grandmother, stuck halfway through the animal door and staring up at her through vacuous eyes. A frying pan lay by her head.

"Oh, good God Almighty. This ... this can't be."

Debbie was too appalled to scream, although she realized she had assumed the position with her hands grabbing both sides of her head and her mouth wide open. Forget about the knives. She needed firepower.

She steadied herself on the table and walls, making her way through the back of the kitchen and down the hall to their bedroom. She ripped off the yellow police tape from the door. The officers had performed a meticulous search of her bedroom when Joseph Meicigama was found dead in their bed the previous night. But not thorough enough.

Debbie leapt up onto the bed. She balled her fingers and reared her fists up and over her head. With a forward thrust she smashed her fists into the wall above their headboard and tore off a large chunk of drywall.

There, strapped to the inner wall, was a loaded Mossberg 500 pump-action twelve gauge shotgun and a Ruger SR9 9mm semi-automatic handgun. A hunting knife with a leather and Velcro leg strap complemented the firepower. A satchel full of shotgun shells hanging from a nail completed the mini arsenal. Compliments of their architect Michael Fronteria and builder DeShawn Hill who, when they said they had thought of everything, really meant it.

Security was a top priority, and both insisted Bob and Debbie sign off on this detail. Hill claimed the shotgun was one of the most efficient close range killing machines. He made a convincing argument, as ten rooms filled over a year's time would allow for at least a few unsavory characters. The past residents of The Roadhouse Blues alone confirmed Hill's concerns.

Just above the headboard, covering the space between two wall studs, he had installed ¼" thick drywall, rather than the 5/8" thick material used throughout the rest of the house, making it easier to punch a hole in the wall. With the thinner material shimmed out flush with the rest of the wall, it made a perfect hiding place.

Debbie confirmed the safety was on and tucked the handgun in her belt under the small of her back. She wrapped the leather leg strap above her right ankle and secured the hunting knife. The satchel of twelve gauge shotgun shells was now slung over her left shoulder. The shotgun in her right hand, safety on, Debbie Stevens was ready to go.

Although not an expert in firearms, Debbie was raised with three brothers. She did know how to aim straight and shoot. With a fully loaded shotgun in close quarters, that's all she needed.

Debbie composed herself the best she could and moved forward with a determined steady pace. She glanced at her Grandmother on her way back through the kitchen. "Don't worry. I'll get those hellions for you. I promise you that."

She entered the living room. To her right and down the hall she could see her grandfather's corpse. He was dead. There was nothing she could do to bring him back. But she would certainly kill the cats. She turned off the safety. Left hand holding the hand stock. Right hand on the grip behind the trigger. Shotgun held low.

What to do? And where were the cats? Surely they were organized and ready to ambush. And she was alone.

With no definitive plan, the only option was to wait. The clock on the wall told her Bob would be home in a few minutes. Until then, she could only pace back and forth between the living room and kitchen, ready to blast any cat foolish enough to challenge her.

Chapter 55   Final Preparations

Emily crouched at the top of the stairs. She hid behind the top post and stared down into the living room. Rebecca, Midnight, Chloe, Helen, Esther, and Scarlett sat patiently a few feet behind her.

They could make their move now. She could simply give the order to any of her remaining followers to kill Debbie. It would happen in a matter of moments, much as it had when Helen killed Paul Knudsen in the kitchen by a simultaneous choking and heart attack.

Or the process could be drawn out indefinitely—like when they all teamed up to kill Reginald and Sophia Johnson, the couple from Detroit in the Disco Room. After all, cats do like to play with their prey before killing it.

Then she'd allow Rebecca to perform what she did best: burn the house to a pile of smoldering ashes while they escaped.

Debbie wiped her eyes and ran her hands through her hair, then tugged down on the bottom of her blouse, as if that would help make her presentable for this final confrontation. Emily was impressed the way Debbie composed herself, even though she looked a nervous wreck. But, considering she'd witnessed her beloved grandparents dead, killed in a hideous, gory display thanks to their group effort, Emily wouldn't hold it against her.

Debbie pulled out her cell phone for the twentieth time and tried to call Bob. Emily nodded to Helen, who ended the call, as she had all previous attempts. Emily laughed inwardly. Little tortures. Simple things, like cutting off cell phone communications, they provided some laughs. It was a nice way to assuage the mounting tension, now that they were fast approaching the Grand Finale—the *coup de grâce!* She smirked, relishing the last few moments leading up to the bed and breakfasts' annihilation.

Debbie still looked bewildered. But Emily knew she had a crazed and mounting focus for revenge—a factor that drove her to remain inside and not run for safety. She knew Debbie was consumed with one driving thought; she was hell bent on killing her and the rest of the damned cats.

"She's alone," Rebecca said. "And she's outnumbered seven to one. Just look at her, with no special powers and scared as can be. But I have to hand it to her. She's one determined lady."

"Challenge accepted," Emily said. "I think I'll send her a couple little energy bursts. Nothing too big. Just to see the look on her face."

Emily aimed one at the small of her back.

Debbie jumped then swung the shotgun around. "Who's there," she said with a hint of terror.

This was cause for a round of laughter. Emily followed up with another to her backside. Debbie spun around again, looking for the source of the blasts, the cats laughing more.

"Who's doing that," Debbie said with more force. "Show yourselves now, you cowards."

"My turn," Midnight said. The black cat disappeared, then materialized in the kitchen archway. Emily snickered as Midnight would meow, then disappear when Debbie turned to look. Midnight performed her trick five more times around the living room.

Emily had one final chuckle before calling Midnight back. "That's enough. Save your energy for the real battle that's about to take place."

At the rear of the upstairs hallway, the Goths and Vamps partied behind closed doors. They laughed stupidly. The Ramones played loud. Some of the girls sang along with the lyrics. Poorly.

Emily continued to study Debbie, while behind her, small talk among her clan rambled on as they awaited the inevitable final showdown.

"I'm glad Ross came back," Chloe said. "He was such a greedy glutton. I had no respect for him."

"But you have to admit crazy Erma was different," Scarlett said. "Like Indian Joe, she was wise enough to secretly plot, challenge, and kill two of us."

"Sure. I'll give Erma that," Midnight said. "I'm amazed she didn't take out more of us."

Rebecca, skittish and restless, paced back and forth. Emily knew it took all of her strength to hold off on setting Murcat Manor ablaze.

Emily craned her neck. "Rebecca, please. You're making me nervous. Relax for a few minutes. I need to focus on Debbie."

Rebecca continued to pace. "You know I can't. My sister Annie, she's gone. I never had the chance to see her one last time."

Emily returned her attention to Debbie, who remained in the living room, stuffing her cell phone into her pocket after another failed call to Bob and unsure what to do next.

"I'm sorry. Believe me, I understand all about losing a sister. But stay with me. It's almost time. Just follow my lead."

Rebecca relented. She took her place beside Emily and peered down on Debbie. "I'm with you. You know I am. I always look forward to this part. But I have to admit, I'm fidgety. You know how this is going to turn out."

Emily kept her gaze on Debbie. "This time, wait for the rest of us to get out of the house before you burn it down. Anyway, we need to wait for Bob to come home. We have some time to kill. But it shouldn't be long."

Rebecca bounced and started pacing again. "I can't wait."

Emily sighed, tired of Rebecca's hyperactivity. "Then go. Burn down the neighbors' house. The Bradys."

Rebecca stood at attention and raised her paw in salute. "Now that I can do. I remember they told Bob and Debbie to find a priest, because this place is cursed. Well, time to go and show them what it's like to have a property that's bedeviled."

Scarlett stepped between Emily and Rebecca. "Are you sure that's a good idea? I think we should stay together. Half of us are now dead. We lost six in less than one day and night. That's a big hit to take so fast."

Emily motioned for Chloe to open the front door. "The fire department and police will be sure to come here as the evening unfolds. The fire will make for a great distraction. Be discreet. Wait for the opportunity and don't let Debbie see you leave."

Chloe stood at the top riser and focused on the front door. It opened just enough for a cat to squeeze through. Debbie turned her attention again to the hall where Ross was. Within seconds, Rebecca was down the stairs and outside.

Less than a minute later, a car sped up the road, skidded wildly into the driveway, and screeched to a stop.

"That would be Bob," Emily said. "Ladies, it's time."

Chapter 56   Bob's Back

A car fast approaching from the west brought Debbie back from her disheveled thoughts. She didn't have a plan. But Bob would. She ran to the front porch. The sight of her hubby's SUV charging over the hill was her game changer. Bob veered across both lanes of country road as he sped toward Murcat Manor, then hit the brakes a hundred feet before reaching the property entrance.

The tires screeched as they gripped the pavement, leaving long black skid marks across the gray asphalt as Bob brought the car into a sideways skid. He swerved into the gravel driveway, clipping the rear bumper of Ross and Erma's Cadillac Escalade and tearing it off as he pulled to a stop.

Bob jumped out of his car, bolted to the porch and cleared the eight steps in two leaps. Debbie, with shotgun swung low, grabbed him in a mighty one-armed bear hug and pulled him into the house.

Her spirits were lifted high as Bob gripped her tight to him, lifting her off her feet. Her man was here. All was well.

"Debbie. Thank God you're alright."

Debbie started to close her eyes, feeling safe in the security Bob had always provided. She could almost disengage from the madness and fall asleep in his arms, knowing he would fix everything.

"Who else is here? I hear rock music from upstairs. And where are Ross and Erma?"

Thoughts of her grandparents' destroyed heads and lifeless eyes stabbed her safe feelings to death. Her feet were back on the foyer floor. She rose on her toes, balled Bob's shirt with both hands and pulled herself up eye to eye with him.

"Things are bad here," she blurted out. "Grandma and grandpa, they're dead."

Bob looked over her shoulders and surveyed the expansive living room. "Dead? How?"

"Follow me."

Debbie stormed into the living room and kicked over an end table, aiming the shotgun in case Emily or one of her cohorts had taken refuge underneath it.

"Those cursed cats. They're not normal. Anything but—they have ... *abilities*."

She scanned the living room, looking for a furry tail sticking out from behind a piece of furniture or a cat making a break for the kitchen. "There's some kind of magical powers attached to this property that can only come from the bowels of hell. I can't believe we didn't see this sooner."

"I see that now," Bob said. "This place is cursed. We didn't recognize it or heed the warnings, which, in retrospect, were many. And now we're trying to catch up and somehow defeat something we can't see or hear."

Debbie embraced the Mossberg 500 twelve gauge shotgun to her chest. "It's as if they have a certain level of power to operate. Like they can come and go and do whatever they want, regardless that we're the legal property owners of Murcat Manor. They're thieves, taking away an authority that rightfully belongs to us."

Bob took the shotgun from Debbie. "That's what I was thinking on the way home. If they were able to come back from the dead, and kill our guests in the gruesome ways they did, we're dealing with serious dark forces far beyond the physical realm we live in."

He tilted the gun on its side. "Five shotgun shells in the magazine tube and one in the chamber."

Without saying a word, Debbie swung the satchel slung around her neck and opened it for Bob to see, revealing a steady supply of ammo.

"Good. This helps. But we need to find out what powers they have if we're going to find and kill them." He held the shotgun up. "I don't think firepower alone will be enough."

Debbie flipped over one of the sofas with a deep grunt, then grabbed matching long back chairs and threw them across the room. They tumbled end over end and crashed against the wall.

"For starters, they can plant thoughts and voices in peoples' minds. When we came home," Debbie fought back a sob, then gritted her teeth. "They placed Grandma's voice in Granddad's head."

Debbie hooked Bob by the hand and led him toward the hallway to the utility rooms. "The cats made it sound like Grandma was drunk and had locked herself in one of the closets. But I couldn't hear anything. I knew something was terribly wrong and tried to stop Grandpa. But he opened the closet door and ...."

Debbie stopped, buried her head in Bob's chest, and motioned for him to look around the corner. "Be careful there are no cats there."

Bob peeked down the hall and swung the shotgun into position at his waist. "Oh. My. God. Ross."

"I know. I saw it happen. Midnight, Chloe, and Helen were in the closet when he opened the door. The bowling ball you keep on the floor zipped up in its leather case? They somehow had it on the top shelf. When Grandpa opened the door, they rolled it off onto his head. It all happened so fast. I tried t—"

Bob held Debbie's face in his hands. "Shhh. Stop. There's nothing we can do for him now. I'm very sorry. He's gone. But we need to be strong. We have to kill those cats before they can harm us or anyone else."

Debbie kept her head close to Bob's chest and eyes closed as he led her into the kitchen. She knew what question was coming.

"Where's your grandmother?"

Debbie let go and pointed toward the basement door. Bob walked around the oak centerpiece of the kitchen. Once on the other side, he pulled up and vomited.

"I'm trying to explain what happened," Debbie said. "But I have no idea how Grandma got trapped in the animal door. Or why her face and hand are so badly burned."

Bob shook his head as he picked up the frying pan and set it on one of the stoves. "They couldn't just kill them. They really had to work hard to do this in such a horrendous way."

Debbie remained on the other side of the table. "I can't look at Grandma. Not like that. I pulled the table cloth off her. Can you put it back over her and find something to cover Grandpa?"

Bob bent over and respectfully pulled the napery back over Erma. Without a word he took a second red and white checkered covering off the kitchen table and walked through the living room to the storage closet and laid it over Ross.

Bob came back to the kitchen and sniffed the air. "Is that …?" He turned to Debbie, his eyebrows bunched together, and sniffed again. "Honey, do you smell gas?"

Debbie inhaled slowly, closing her eyes and blocking out her other senses screaming at her, competing for her attention. The sight of her dead grandparents. The sickening sound of the bowling ball crushing her grandfather's skull. The Ramones, still blaring from upstairs. It was hard to focus on any one thing.

She felt Bob's hands on her shoulders, helping her get centered as he repeated the question: "Hon, I'm sure I smell gas. Don't you?"

She shook her head. "No. I don't smell anything."

Bob looked around the kitchen. "Well, I smell it. It's faint. But I can't tell where it's coming from."

"Yeah, okay, sure. Whatever. Now, back to the cats?"

"You said they planted Erma's voice in Ross's head?"

"No," came a voice in Debbie's mind, as she went stiff, her eyes turning into glazed saucers. *"They didn't plant her voice. I did."*

Chapter 57   The Revealing

A female voice. Debbie detected a slight mix of a New England and British accent. She felt like it came from within her ears. But she couldn't be sure.

"I must be losing my mind," was all Debbie could say as she peered into the living room.

"No, you haven't lost your mind. Yet."

She spun on her heels and looked around. "Who said that?"

"It's me. Emily."

Debbie turned back to Bob. "Did you hear that?"

Bob looked into the living room and took a few measured steps. "Sure did. A young female voice with a slight accent from a time gone by. But I have no idea what direction it came from."

Debbie felt a bit more relieved when Bob confirmed the safety from the twelve gauge Mossberg 500 was off. With a little more to be courageous about, she called out, "Emily. Is that really you?"

"Oh, it's me, alright," the voice resounded in her head. "I'm surprised you haven't made the connections by now. There have been so many deaths right under your nose, and still you're distracted by all of Darrowby's bullshit of an investigation. You deserve to go to prison for our crimes."

"Who are you? Really," Debbie blurted out as she followed Bob, looking around and behind any furniture still standing. She flipped the second sofa over, kicked over the end tables, and toppled the remaining chairs.

With no more furniture to overturn, she grabbed fixtures and pictures off the wall and heaved them in all directions. The added frustration of an opponent she could not see, taunting her, was driving her to the edge of hysteria.

"How are you doing this?" she shouted. "And why are you killing everyone? You had no right to murder my grandparents. They're decent, innocent people who never hurt anyone."

The patronizing laughter of the young woman filled Debbie's head. It was a haunted sound of amusement that echoed. As soon as one wave of laughter faded, a new one replaced it.

"I seriously doubt that. I bet Ross spent a lifetime screwing other people over so he could get ahead. He was a glutton who had no control over himself or his lusts. He'd do anything to get ahead in life and bring himself satisfaction of any kind."

"At least my grandparents didn't murder innocent people. Like you. So don't judge my family, you freak from hell."

The empty chilling laughter continued. "You're a spirited one, Debbie. I'll give you that. But it's not enough to save you."

Debbie had to give a brief audible chuckle, adding a smirk with a sideways smile. Something to counteract Emily's offensive if she was watching. She wasn't afraid anymore. The confusion faded, like weights lifting from her eyes. There was now a voice to place with the force behind the evil, even if it wasn't audible; something personified she could identify with rather than a cowardly foe who refused to show herself. Her smirk turned into a full grin.

"Where are you, Emily?" She emulated her adversary's condescending pitch that said *bring it, bitch.*

"Over here. On the sofa."

The tone was calm, as if she was being spoken to as a child. Debbie walked around the toppled sofa twice, Bob beside her, shotgun ready to unload. She turned the furniture right side up, but no Emily.

"I don't see you."

In an instant, a black cat with three large white spots appeared on the center cushion. Bob stepped back, visibly confounded by what just happened. But Debbie would not be intimidated.

"I know you're trying for a grand entrance to try to scare me. But it's not going to work. I don't fear you."

Bob spoke. "What the hell are you disgusting creatures? You're not from this world."

Emily sat still, her head moving back and forth between Debbie and Bob. Her words came, but her mouth remained closed.

"Oh, we most certainly are from this world. Born and raised."

Debbie was disgusted by the pretentious manner in which Emily addressed them. "Bob. Don't allow her to talk down to us. We're in control here. This is our house. And we're going to blast these stupid cats into oblivion."

Debbie heard the laughter a third time. It was clear Emily believed she was above them.

"Don't ever call me stupid. This is your one and only warning. Do it again and I'll kill you where you stand. That being said, please allow me to give you a brief rundown on who we are and how we ended up as your *pets*. I use that term so loosely. Anyway, each of us has an individual and unique ability."

"Had," Debbie responded without hesitation. "By my recollections, at least four of you are dead."

413

Emily continued without skipping a beat. "Forget about the abilities. Think of it as a gifting, if you will. For example, Midnight, she who despises Bob more than any of us for giving her that stupid name when I clearly told you to call her Amy, can teleport. She can transfer herself from one place to another in an instant. And as leader of my clan, I possess all of the gifts to varying degrees. So naturally, I can teleport myself as well. We can only move short distances, like across the house. But it's a great ability to have, wouldn't you agree?"

Emily disappeared. Debbie looked to her left and right, then into the kitchen.

"I'm behind you," Emily said through a sigh, as if a cat were bored with a new toy after playing with it for a brief minute.

Debbie turned around. Emily was sitting on the overturned coffee table.

"How did you ... how, I don't understand. You're cats."

"Not exactly," Emily's voice resonated in Debbie's head. She looked to Bob, who nodded he could also hear.

"I won't waste any time. Yours, or ours. We're daughters of the women hung at the Salem Witch Trials and various other witch hunts you won't read about in your history books. Fifteen years later, the same mob and their sons, came after us."

Debbie wasn't sure if she should be wasting her time talking to Emily. But the past few months had been nothing less than traumatic. Tonight she lost her grandparents. She needed to know.

"Came after you? Why?"

"Ugh. Just shut up and listen. We're their offspring. Now do you understand? Of course, the male descendants were not persecuted. I guess that was a sign of the times four hundred years ago. Anyway, the women, including myself, had no choice but to escape. We had a plan. Otherwise, we'd have died a very brutal human death. So we prepared to separate our souls from our bodies. This was an ancient and most difficult magic within our craft. As our physical bodies fell to the ground in a heap, our souls entered a litter of young cats in the first of their nine lives."

"I don't believe it," Bob finally said.

"Ah, Boring Bob. I'm not surprised. Here. Brace yourself. Maybe this will help."

Debbie felt something, or someone, invading her mind. Numbness began to dull her will. She could only explain it as a presence penetrating the defenses of her resolve. It controlled her thoughts while leaving her free will to wonder and question the events unfolding inside her head.

Debbie wretched and clutched her head in defiance. But she couldn't stop the stream of thoughts entering from the left and parading across her mind.

The images came swiftly. Sound followed. It was as if she were watching a movie, then sucked into the scene. The landscape was vivid and laden with emotion. Emily's bitterness and hatred consumed Debbie to the point she felt she was living in the event. She could feel the cool temperatures and a mist in the air.

An auburn haired woman of seventeen led dozens of young women racing down a muddy moonlit two-wheel path through a heavily wooded area. They desperately tried to outrun a mob with torches and pitchforks. With the clothes everyone wore, the muskets and flintlock pistols the pursuers fired, Debbie discerned this had to be Colonial America.

"That would be me," Emily said, the words hostile and bitter. "Trying to save my people from a mob of drunken idiots."

Debbie saw some fall in midstride. Three horsemen rode to the front of the riotous throng and chopped down the women with pistols and hatchets.

"See that innocent young girl," Emily spat out. "She's my beloved sister, Sarah. She was only fifteen. Sarah had her whole life ahead of her. I promised my mother I would watch over her."

Debbie couldn't move. She felt like her vocal cords were rusted shut. Her eyes were forced to stay open and watch the madness and carnage unfold. Her focus zeroed in on Sarah as she saved Emily's life, but was cut down by a hatchet to the center of her back.

Then she plunged deeper into the vision. Debbie felt the hooves of horses thundering on the ground. An intense pain of the cold night air being forced in and out of Emily's lungs as she ran for her life was overwhelming.

More young women were gashed down to the left and right. Up ahead, a barn stood. The doors opened on their own. Emily led the women in with the three horsemen, then the doors closed moments before the mob could reach them.

The scene fast forwarded to two of the horsemen dead on the ground. The third was naked and babbling like a madman to his horse.

There were over twenty women in the barn. One, a dark haired beautiful girl about the same age as Emily, began running in a circle. A younger woman, the spitting image of the circling girl, and most likely a younger sister, encouraged her on. A small fire started in the center.

"Rebecca," Debbie managed to eke out.

"That's right," Emily said, the repulsive vile still in her voice. "That's Rebecca. And Annie was her younger sister."

Oh, shit, was all Debbie could think. No wonder Annie always followed Rebecca around Murcat Manor. Annie, who died in the basement last night during the filming of *American Ghost Stories*.

Rebecca stopped, looked to the top of the barn, and threw her arms in the air. Four streams of fire arched upward then dropped into the four corners of the barn. Livestock became restless. Horses and cows looked dangerous as they panicked. Within moments, the enormous building was ablaze with light as smoke filled the air.

A searing pain consumed Debbie's being, as if she were one of them. She felt like she was being turned inside out as she left her body and entered a cat. She watched through the wildcat's eyes as the women collapsed on the dirt floor, eyes wide open. Their souls escaped from their mouths and fought for a feline host as they kicked the souls of the host cats out of their respective bodies with a quick but powerful hex. The battle for a host was intense but brief. Some would win and live to breathe another day. The rest would die.

Debbie snapped back to reality. Bob. He was shaking her. She was breathing heavily. Her head was soaked with sweat.

"Only thirteen of the original thirty-nine survived that night."

Emily. She was sitting on the center cushion of the sofa again. Her voice was calm with a hint of superiority.

"Twenty-six of my sisters died in the forest between Salem and Boston four hundred years ago. Thirteen of us escaped. Long story short, we were adopted by families over the first six of our nine lives, the most recent being you and Bob. In our third life, our adopted family moved westward across New England, through Pennsylvania into Ohio, and then Michigan. And here we now are."

Debbie's evening had been a roller coaster ride of emotions. She felt overwhelmed and on the verge of fainting. But she had to be strong. And Bob, her strength, was beside her. Together they would kill Emily and whoever remained from her four hundred year old coven.

Emily continued to laugh and mock them. "Murcat Manor is going to burn. *Burn*, do you hear me? Leveled into a festering heap of smoking ashes. And we'll frame you and Boring Bob for the murder of your grandparents. Isn't that right, ladies?"

Debbie was unable to express any words as she watched the other cats, one by one, file into the living room. They lined up on each side of Emily. Debbie did the math. Six cats in front of her. Four dead that she knew of. That left three missing. Isabella. Madelyn. But the most disturbing absence was Rebecca. Not good.

"We must be imagining this," Bob said. "The stress. That has to be it."

Emily sighed. Her condescending voice returned.

"Boring Bob, will you ever be a believer? Maybe this will help. I'll get right to the point so not to lose your attention. These are our powers. Listen up. Pay attention. This is important. Especially since you're going to die. Midnight, she can teleport herself."

Midnight disappeared from the overturned sofa. Debbie looked left and right, then saw the black cat materialize on the other side of the room. Before Debbie could process the impossible feat, Midnight was gone, only to emerge from behind the sofa. She jumped back up and took her place next to Emily.

"Okay, okay. That's enough. Thank you, Midnight. Save some of your energy for later. Moving on, Helen can lock, unlock, and reverse the flow of solids, liquids, and electricity. And for the record, she killed Paul Knudson at the breakfast table by causing him to gag and have a heart attack at the same time. She also cross-switched the Leeds brothers minds."

Debbie tried to say something. Anything. But Emily cut her off.

"Please, don't interrupt. It's rude. Next, we have Esther. Let's just say she can blow things up. And it was Esther, along with Scarlett and Angel, who killed DeShawn Hill. Darrowby thinks it was Bob on the roof and pushed the ladder backward. But it was Esther who caused the energy explosion to thrust the ladder backward and send him to his death."

Debbie again attempted to interrupt, but Emily looked her off and continued.

"Rebecca isn't here at the moment. She starts fires. But you saw that in our little trip back in time. She's the loose cannon of the group. And it was Rebecca who torched the Turner place and the Amish farm. She also melted Indian Joe's brain."

Emily had the momentum. Her speech sped up, her ego and bitterness from the past dictating the pace of the conversation.

Debbie again wanted to interrupt and ask where Isabella and Madelyn were. But she thought better of trying to take the momentum away from Emily. Let her talk. The only option Debbie had was to extract information that would help find their strengths and weaknesses. Then she would have to find a way to exploit them and send the witches to hell where they belonged.

Talk away, Emily. Your pride will be your downfall.

Bob started to raise the shotgun. Debbie placed her hand on his forearm and eased it down. She gave him a sideways glance telling him to let Emily talk.

"What else, Emily? Now that I think about it, our guests died in diverse ways. But I think you'd consider them cunning and clever."

"You're so pathetically naïve. I mean, come on. You're only now making the connections? And even then, only after I have to explain them to you, as if you're a child."

Debbie fired back. "Don't underestimate me. I'm a lot smarter than you take me for."

Emily rolled her eyes. "Whatever. Moving on. Next, we have Chloe."

The ginger cat to her right raised and waved her paw as if to say hello.

"Chloe is my cousin in our human lives four hundred years ago. She can levitate things, drop them, or fire them across the room. Like Bob's fifteen pound bowling ball, which," she gave Bob a sly wink and a pernicious grin, "we all know is just covered with your fingerprints. Yes Debbie, the ball that smashed your grandfather's head. The shameless pig. Chloe, show Debbie and Boring Bob what you can do."

Debbie could only watch as again, there were no words to describe what she was seeing. Midnight and Helen were lifted four feet off the sofa, then reversed positions and lowered back on the cushions.

With each new revelation, Debbie's world unraveled just a little more. But she had to accept that her perceived existence, the universe she was indoctrinated in through public schools, college, and a conservative church was failing her. There was more to the reality she lived in, and Emily and the rest had tapped into it, albeit in a dark way.

"Do you want to see more?" Emily continued. "Oh, I'm not finished yet. This gets so much better."

Debbie heard Emily's tone and pitch again increase. It oozed with pride and arrogance.

"Scarlett, she's truly amazing. Say hello Scarlett."

The brown and white striped cat raised her right paw and waved it back and forth.

"Scarlet says hi. She can toss a bout of madness on a person. This makes it easy to not only plant thoughts like I'm doing now, but to nudge someone to carry out, under our influence, acts they would never commit on their own.

Debbie thought back to Sophia Johnson, who impaled her husband with an iron fireplace poker. "Sophia. You got into her mind and made her kill her husband."

"That crazy lady from Detroit in the Disco room. You bet. And Scarlett totally messed with Johnny Rocket from *American Ghost Stories* last night. Poor ol' Johnny. He'll never be the same."

Debbie remembered Erma's follow up report earlier in the day on the cast from *American Ghost Stories*. Johnny Rocket had been committed to a mental hospital. The Leeds Brothers were sure to follow.

Emily's voice crackled. "Care for a personal demonstration?"

No, Debbie thought. Don't you dare, you aberration from the Bottomless Pit.

Bob gulped in air and gripped the shotgun tight. Debbie averted her attention from Emily to her husband. His knees buckled. He trembled as his knuckles turned white. He fought to keep the shotgun pointed to the floor.

Debbie didn't like what was coming next.

"Honey, the gun. I ... help me. Make it stop."

Debbie snapped her head back. "Emily, stop it now," she commanded. "Bob, just shoot her."

"I can't. I'm trying to. But, I ... I just want to shoot those stupid punk kids upstairs."

Two blasts boomed in the living room. Debbie ducked, then looked up at large matching holes in the ceiling. She could look directly into the Roadhouse blues. Fortunately, the Goths were on the other end of the upstairs hall.

"Oh, here's the real kicker in all of this," Emily said. "Since I possess each individual power I can team up with Scarlett and better break down Bob's will, then control his thoughts and actions."

The Ramones abruptly stopped. The sound of a door opening upstairs and boots running in a disorderly haste rumbled overhead. The Goths and Vamps ran down the hall and poured down the stairs.

They screamed and shouted and fought each other as they descended to the first floor. The group ended in a heap of twisted arms and legs at the bottom of the stairs as Bob waved the shotgun at them.

Some untangled themselves and ran out the front door. Others headed toward the kitchen for the back door. A few remained frozen in fear, unsure of what to do next.

"I ... can't control ... Debbie, you have to help me."

Debbie reached for the gun, but Bob brought it level with her head. Debbie ducked a second before he fired; the heat from the blast singed her scalp.

Bob swept the gun left toward the front door. Debbie saw his finger squeezing the trigger against his will. Tears streamed down his cheeks as he fought the urge to kill. He jerked the gun upward and destroyed the chandelier in the living room. Glass rained down on the escapees heading for the back door.

More laughter reverberated in Debbie's mind. Emily. The hilarity was hysterical. She was intensely entertained by this.

"You're both losers," Emily mocked. "Look at us. We have such amazing abilities you know nothing of. We've had four hundred years to perfect our craft. All you have is a stupid shotgun that we can control through Bob. You're both as good as dead.

"In this life and the past life, during the nineteen-sixties, Madelyn, who is one of the world's greatest geniuses, has researched the discoveries and breakthroughs of energy and matter. She studied Albert Einstein and other great scientists of your time using books, magazines, and your laptops.

"Energy and matter. They're the same thing. Once we understood that, we discovered we could increase our powers. And here's one trick I've learned during this lifetime. We used this on your grandmother in the basement. And on you in the kitchen. It totally confused both of you."

Debbie thought of the times she'd found Madelyn staring at their laptops. She'd thought it was cute. Now she understood the cats were learning how to increase their powers to a degree they never knew possible until now.

Another invisible burst of heat knocked her on her back. Debbie staggered to her feet and shuffled toward Bob, trying to step into him and take the gun. But Bob again turned and aimed for her head. She hit the floor as Bob fired off a round, then returned his attention to the last Goth. It was one of the girls.

"Emily, you don't have to do this. Just leave."

Debbie expected Emily to laugh at her. At least say something that would put her down. Instead, there was silence.

Debbie looked up from the floor. Bob was tiring. The physical and emotional energy he'd spent to fight off the spell was exhausting him.

"Emily, this is our property. Not yours. I command you to stop this roguishness now."

Again, there was silence from Emily.

Why was she quiet during this crucial moment? Ever since Emily had introduced herself, she couldn't stop talking.

Debbie had an epiphany. What if the battle for Bob's mind was also expending Emily and Scarlett's energy? It took energy to use energy. If Bob was tiring to the point of exhaustion, then so must be Emily and the rest of the cats.

That's why Emily had become strangely silent rather than boasting of their superiority. Emily must be tiring, too.

This insight jump-started Debbie. Emily wasn't invincible. She had weaknesses. And it was time to exploit them.

"You can do this, Bob. Fight the urge. Emily and Scarlett have to be getting weak too. This will come down to whoever quits first. You can do this."

Tears streamed down Bob's face. "I ... I'm trying. But ..."

"I'm here for you. Don't give in. You can do this. We can do this. Together."

Bob closed his eyes. "I'm so sorry."

The final Goth had run for the front door. The young woman who was the only civil one of the bunch—the lead Goth's girlfriend named Brooke—was the last to leave.

For all Bob's might, he couldn't resist Emily and Scarlett's control. All he could do was shout, "Look out."

Sounds of crashing and breaking glass came from the coffee table. Feline screeches, the eeriest she had ever heard, filled the room, then went silent. Bob jerked the gun toward the floor and fired. A hole appeared. Debbie could see into the basement.

Bob once again had full control of himself. He turned to Debbie, looked down at the coffee table, and grinned.

"Nice job," he said between breaths. "Thanks honey,"

Debbie stood by the table with a large serrated hunting knife in her hand. On the floor, a cat lay in a pool of her own blood, her entrails spilled out through several wide open cuts.

"I killed Scarlett," Debbie said, her body shaking and voice cracked. "Emily and Scarlett were so focused on you, as were the others cats, I was able to grab the hunting knife I had strapped to my ankle and gutted the hellion."

Debbie pulled up her pant leg and showed Bob the Velcro knife holder around her ankle, then re-strapped the knife. "I wish DeShawn Hill were still alive, if only to thank him for the guns and knife he placed behind the drywall in our bedroom."

Bob, still out of breath, found a way to huff out, "Thanks again ... honey. I'm back. We're back." Bob gave Debbie a quick but deep kiss. "Now let's kill ... some time traveling sorceresses."

Chapter 58   The Hunt is On

Debbie took the lead. Not because she didn't trust Bob or his leadership. She respected him more than any man in the world. But Bob was exhausted after his battle with Emily and Scarlett. His skin was drained of color. His shoulders were hunched and he had trouble standing up straight. His words were spoken in broken phrases. She'd give him a few minutes to recover.

Debbie scanned the living room. Emily and her disciples had disappeared. Except Midnight. She sat on the fireplace mantle, staring at them.

"There." Debbie nudged Bob with her elbow. "Midnight. She's on the mantle fireplace. She looks tired and disoriented."

Debbie tried to make sense why Midnight was in plain sight. The jet black feline stayed in place and breathed heavily.

"She's trying ... to catch her ... breath," Bob said, himself still winded.

Debbie fished in her satchel and handed Bob more shells. He turned the safety on, pointed the barrel away from them, chambered a shell, then loaded the rest into the magazine.

"She looks scared and stressed," Debbie said. "Did the others desert her because she can't keep up?"

"Maybe she's a decoy," Bob replied. "A diversion ... to trick us."

Debbie leaned into Bob. "I'm thinking the same thing. The other cats can attack in a way we're not prepared for."

Bob took a deep breath, still feeling the effects of his battle with Emily and Scarlett. "But we don't have time to debate this." Another deep breath. "I'm taking Midnight out."

Debbie bobbed her head. "Shoot her."

Bob aimed the shotgun and fired. But Midnight vanished just before he pulled trigger.

A small smoky hole appeared in the wall six inches above the wooden fireplace mantle. Chunks of drywall and dust littered the mantle and the tile floor. Debbie stepped forward and squatted down twelve inches, looking into their bedroom. She could see their headboard, sprayed with hundreds of small pellets spread out over a much larger two foot radius.

"Holy shit... did you see that? Midnight disappeared." Bob placed his hand through the hole, then pulled back and ran his fingers across the wall. "There should be splattered remains of cat on the wall."

"Shhhh," Debbie said. "Less talking, more hunting."

Bob turned and walked backward, shotgun at the ready, Debbie close in tow looking for cats to blast. Now that there was a lull in the action and the momentum had swung their way, she was able to get a good look at the expansive living room.

What was once a place of socializing among the guests and their kids now looked like a war zone. Two large sofas, a love seat, four chairs, six ottomans, a coffee table, and four end tables were overturned. Shotgun blasts tore holes in the floor, ceiling, and walls. The chandelier was

427

destroyed. Broken glass littered the travertine tile. And Scarlett lay dead in the center of the room.

"No more rogues in here," Bob said. "Next up, the kitchen. Let's go."

Debbie hesitated. "Wait. I need to do something."

She locked the front door, then secured the living room windows. "We can't allow them to escape. If I have to, I'll torch this place myself to kill them."

Debbie grasped Bob's hand and pulled him into the kitchen. She made a quick pass around the kitchen table, opening pantry doors and looking in cupboards and under the sinks.

"They're not in the living room," Bob said. "We don't see any in the kitchen." He took a deep breath and pointed the shotgun at the basement door. "Down there. That's the next obvious place to look."

Bob stepped in front of Debbie and took the lead. "Turn around and don't look. I need to pull your Grandmother out from the pet door."

Debbie turned her back and closed her eyes. Bob grunted and wheezed as he tried to pull her out. "She's really stuck. I can't get her out."

"I'm so sorry, Grandma," Debbie said, bending down and gripping Erma by her arm. "Bob, I'll pull while you open the door."

Bob opened the door as Erma's body was scrunched into the adjoining wall head first. The sight and sound was disturbing, but they could now squeeze through.

"I definitely smell gas," Bob said as the descended the stairs.

"I smell it now," Debbie said. "Let's make this quick."

Once in the basement, Bob surveyed the mess. "Looks like a small war took place here. Everything's knocked over. There're boxes thrown about everywhere. And look over there. Two more dead cats."

"It's Isabella and Madelyn," Debbie said, adding the names to the list of Annie, Jacqueline, Rachel, Angel, and Scarlet. "That makes seven dead cats, five live ones, and Rebecca still missing."

She leaned over and picked up a dagger. "I recognize this. It belongs to Grandma. At least she got a couple of the she-devils."

Bob pointed. "On the other side of those boxes is a mangled can of pepper spray. Looks like it exploded."

"Chloe. Emily said she could make things explode. That would explain Grandma's burnt skin on her face and hand. These cats are some sick psychopaths."

"They're people," Bob said. "Just like us. Only now they're living in a cat's body. And it looks like Erma was onto them and came here with a plan. She sure did put up one hell of a fight. She tore this place apart." Bob gave a brief salute. "God bless your grandmother."

Debbie performed the four way sign of the cross over her chest. "I'm not Catholic, at least in the traditional sense. But Grandma deserves this. I'm glad she took out two of those witches. Way to go, Grandma. You're amazing, as always, in life and in death."

Debbie placed Erma's dagger in her belt. "Be ready. I'm going to start throwing aside anything a cat can hide behind. If we see one, I'll step back and you blast it."

Bob set the shotgun against the wall and picked up a sawed off two-by-four piece of wood. "I don't want to shoot down here. The pellets could ricochet off the walls and hit us. That, and the gas leak."

Debbie nodded in agreement, then grabbed the work bench and gave it a heave. It tumbled to the floor as the tools spilled over in a loud crash of metal on concrete. She covered her ears at the sound.

"No cats under there," Bob said.

429

Debbie moved swiftly and efficiently through the basement, walking up one aisle of cleaning supplies, then down another with stacks of cloth linens, table clothes, and napkins for the kitchen. She knocked over four foot stacks of boxes of laundry detergent and stepped out of the way.

No cats.

She moved on to clear plastic bins filled with blankets and sheets piled four feet high. She used her shoulder and pushed with her legs to knock them over.

Still no cats.

"I don't think we'll find any down here," Bob said. "Let's go back upstairs. We need to check the bedrooms one at a time."

Debbie snared Bob by his pants waistline and pulled him back. "Wait. I'm not convinced. This was one of their favorite places to hang out."

Debbie let go of Bob and looked up at the ceiling. She had a hunch.

"Where's the fireplace in the living room? Right about there, wouldn't you say?" Debbie pointed up ten feet away from them.

Bob's eyes followed Debbie's finger. "Yeah. Okay. Why?"

"In the process of Emily and Scarlett trying to control your mind, you became exhausted fighting them."

"Sure. It took all my strength. I'm only now catching my breath."

"And that's what I'm thinking happened to them. They're exhausted too. I bet they have to expend much of their stamina to do what they do."

Bob smiled wide. "And you think Midnight teleporting off the mantle used up much of the strength she had."

"My guess is it takes a lot of energy to teleport. Or perform anything they do. While I was waiting for you to come home, Midnight was playing tricks, appearing and disappearing in my peripheral vision. Then she was showing off in the living room, and Emily told her to save energy for later.

I think Midnight tried to teleport off the couch and out of the living room as Emily and the rest of the cats ran for cover. But the fireplace mantle is as far as she got. Each of her successive attempts will probably be a shorter distance."

Bob pointed to the ceiling where the fireplace would be, then dropped his arm to three large storage bins. As Debbie reached out she heard a rustling. She grabbed the bottom container and jerked it out.

Midnight was there.

Debbie stepped back. Bob jumped in and took a swing. The cat disappeared.

"Damned thing teleported again."

Debbie continued knocking over what remained of the any boxes and crates stacked more than two high. "She's not far. I bet she's ... there. Right there. She's behind those folded chairs."

Debbie swept them aside with a mighty sweep of her left arm. The metal chairs skidded and scattered across the cement floor.

The silky black cat disappeared again, only to reappear ten feet away. She jumped over the toppled chairs and tried to run up the stairs.

But she moved lethargically and stumbled. Midnight looked wearied. Bob ran to her and took an exaggerated swing, catching the pitch black feline and smashing it flat to the stair tread. He snatched the cat by the neck, tossed it in the air like a softball and swung again, sending the cat flying across the basement. She hit the cinder wall hard and flopped to the floor.

"I think she's dead." Bob was smiling wide. "That, my dear, was a home run swing."

"Just to be sure," Debbie said, stepping over strewn boxes and picking up the limp cat. She twisted its head. A snap resonated through the basement.

"That's for Grandma and Grandpa, you bitch from hell."

Debbie felt the tug on her sleeve. "Get back to the kitchen," Bob said. "I'll get the shotgun and try to stop that gas leak."

Debbie stumbled over more boxes as she ran up the stairs. She had to step over Erma's bottom half then squeezed through the narrow opening.

"Sorry again, Grandma." Debbie kissed her fingers then touched Erma's forehead. "Nice job taking out Isabella and Madelyn. We got Scarlett and Midnight. We'd make a great team if you were still here."

Debbie reached down and pulled out *Old Faithful* from Erma's handbag. She unscrewed the cap and took three long drinks. "Thanks again, Grandma. Here's to you. You did great." She gulped what was left, then slid the flask in her back pocket.

Debbie closed her eyes and shuddered, letting the burning from the aged Scotch subside as it made its way down the hatch. She kept her eyes closed, allowing the alcohol to penetrate her stomach and make its way to her coursing veins. She already missed her time with Grandma. For a brief moment, she forgot about Bob and was with her grandparents once again.

A scraping sound on the kitchen floor and Debbie was right back in the present. She looked down as Erma's burned and boiled arm slid over her feet. She turned to see the basement door shutting by itself.

No. Freaking. Way. She planted on foot on Erma's chest and the other on the floor, reached for the knob, and pulled back with all her might.

"Bob, get up here now. They're trying to lock you down there."

Debbie couldn't look through what opening was left without losing her grip. She leaned her weight back and heaved. She could hear Bob's feet jumping many stairs at a time.

"Hurry. I can't hold the door back."

Bob's right arm, holding the shotgun, was all that made it through as the door continued to close. A loud crack echoed through the kitchen as Bob screamed a hideous cry. The shotgun fell to the floor and Bob's arm retreated.

Debbie gripped the edge of the door and tried to wedge her arm between it and the casing, sacrifice her own body. Anything for Bob.

The door latch was closing. Her efforts were puny compared to the force she was trying to counter. Her fingers slipped out. The door shut and the lock turned.

"My arm. It's broken." Bob's voice penetrated through the solid oak barrier, but it was a vapid echo of itself by the time it reached Debbie.

Debbie turned, pulled, and rattled the knob. "The door. It's locked. I can't open it."

Three more hard tugs and Debbie knew it was useless from her side. She was wasting precious energy. "I can't open it. Ram the door with your shoulder."

After a few loud thuds and the door not budging, Bob said, "No luck. The door's solid hard oak. So is the jamb. It's not giving an inch."

Debbie stepped off Erma, grabbed the shotgun, and looked around the kitchen. "Damn it. Emily, open this door now."

Again, Emily's laughter rang inside Debbie's head. She blocked it out and slammed her boot to the ground.

"That's it," Debbie shouted. "No more. This is my house. I'm in control. In case you haven't noticed, you're on the losing side. Let's take

433

an inventory and see how many of you died in the last twenty-four hours. In the basement are the carcasses of Isabella and Madelyn my grandma killed. God rest her soul. And Bob and I just killed Midnight."

Silence.

"Last night Annie, Jacqueline, Rachel, and Angel died during the taping of *American Ghost Stories*."

"For the record, it was Indian Joe who killed them," Emily said. "I also died. So did Scarlett. I won't bore you with details your feeble mind cannot comprehend. But long story short, Scarlett and I were able to come back."

Debbie fired back. "Speaking of Scarlett, I just gutted her in the living room. And since I don't see Rebecca, I'm assuming she's dead. That's nine cats down. Four to go."

Debbie stepped into the living room, shotgun at the ready, and looked behind the overturned furniture. "There's nowhere to go. You can't hide. I know you have to be close to me if you want to do your dirty work. That'll make it easy to hunt you down one by one and blast the living hell out of you."

"Sheeesh, Chill out. We don't want to escape. We could, though. Helen, do your thing."

Clicking noises came from the front door. Debbie watched as the locks turned by themselves. The door swung open, then slammed shut, locking again.

"Let's be clear. It's you who can't leave."

Debbie ran around the living room, looking for any trace of the remaining cats. "Show yourselves, you cowards. Nine of you are dead. That leaves Chloe, Helen, Esther and you."

"We're all here. Except Rebecca. And that makes five of us still alive."

Debbie stopped to recalibrate. "Rebecca. Is she dead?"

"Nope."

"Where is she?"

"She's busy."

"Stop playing games."

"Rebecca got bored so she stepped out for a little adventure. Look out the window toward your neighbor's house. Now that I think of it, we should have burned that place down along with the Turner home. The Brady family has always been a bunch of pompous assholes who think they're better than everyone else."

Debbie backed toward the window on the west side of the room and peered over her shoulder, all the while swinging the shotgun back and forth, ready for an attack from the cats.

In the grass at her property's edge, four volleys of fire arced a hundred feet up in the air, then descended on Eddie and Alison Brady's house. In moments, the wood shingled roof was engulfed in flames.

"Rebecca will be back in a few minutes. She'll want to burn this place to ashes. It's her thing. It's what she does. Might as well raise the white flag and accept the inevitable. You're going to die. My remaining sisters and I, we'll live on in this life, then join our fallen comrades in our seventh life sometime in the future."

Debbie backed up toward the front door, stumbling over her feet, and reached for the knob.

"I'm sorry. But we can't let you leave."

Debbie tried door. It wouldn't open. She tried turning the three locks, only to see them lock again.

"What the hell?"

"There are three locks on the front door. Having only two hands, you'll never be able to unlock all three at the same time and escape. You can thank Helen for her expertise in locking and unlocking things."

Debbie looked through the living room into the kitchen to the basement door.

"Forget about Bob. Only Helen can unlock what she's locked. Helen, do you want to let Boring Bob out?"

Debbie could hear Bob still pounding away with one fist. Her heart felt like it was squashed flat and all vital fluids were leaking out. Her soul mate's voice was cracked and weak. She could hear the indescribable pain from his crushed arm in his voice.

"So sorry. Helen said no."

Debbie tried a few windows. She couldn't open any. She picked up a candy bowl and reared back to throw and break a front window. It exploded in her hand, burning her fingers. Shards of crystalline glass hit her face.

Debbie couldn't lose her mind. It was her against Emily. No time to show weakness, to the cats or herself. She cocked a grin and picked out embedded pieces from her cheek and hair, flicking them in the air. There was some blood, but not a lot.

"By the way, that was Esther. She can make inanimate objects explode by converting some of its mass into energy. Much more efficient than a shotgun, wouldn't you agree?"

"You listen to me," Debbie said, shaking her wounded hand. "I know you don't want to die. If Bob and I go, then so do you."

"We've been through this before. And make no mistake we're in control. Although this is the first time some of us have been killed before the grand finale. We usually all go up in flames together. Oh, speaking of going up in flames, Rebecca's back."

The locks on the front door clicked in unison and the door opened. Rebecca proudly strutted in, her tail wagging in the air. The door slammed shut behind her and the locks clicked to the locked position.

Debbie had an idea. It's now or never. She took one more glance out the window at the Brady's house, now completely consumed in flames. The fire department would be arriving any minute. Instead of blasting Rebecca, she had to get her to start a fire. That would bring emergency vehicles to Murcat Manor.

"Go ahead. Set this cursed place on fire. I think you're bluffing. You're too much of a coward to give the order."

"We'll do that. But first, let's play a game of hide and seek. We're already hiding. I'll give you a hint. We're all here in the living room. Find us and kill us, and you live. Fail, and you die."

Debbie needed to be brave. But she was terrified for Bob. She needed his help. He needed hers. Bob's pounding and thumps became softer, yet more desperate. His strength was spent.

"Bob, talk to me," Debbie shouted. "It's just a door."

She could hear his voice but not make out what he said. She pulled out her cell phone and called him.

"Bob, are you okay? I need your help."

"I can't get past the locked door."

"Use power tools. The basement's full of them."

"Trying. But ..."

The phone went dead. She called back.

"Every time I plug in a power saw, it shuts off seconds after I turn it on. Same with my cell phone. I call you but it disconnects as soon as—"

Dead again.

Emily was laughing hysterically.

It only took Debbie a moment to make the connection.

Helen.

Emily said she could lock and unlock doors. And turn things on and off. Debbie's mind was whirling faster. Emily, in all her arrogance, had given away too many clues as to how they operated. The cats had to be close by, or able to look at what they influenced.

This was all a trick. She had wondered if Emily would try to use a diversion. Orchestrate something so obvious, Debbie wouldn't see, or pay any attention if she did.

And here it was. Emily drew Debbie and her shotgun away from Bob. Helen had to be in the kitchen where she could see the front and basement doors. The other cats also there, planning on killing Bob.

Debbie turned and sprinted toward the kitchen. On the other side of the table she heard the pitter patter of pawed feet scattering across the wooden floor. She jumped onto and rolled across the table and landed on the other side, catching the sneaky conspirators by surprise.

She swept the shotgun around and saw three cats run off. Chloe and Esther disappeared around the table. Helen was not so fortunate. Debbie squeezed the trigger. An incredibly loud boom and a viscous kickback, and the hellcat was blasted into bloody pieces.

Debbie landed on her butt but quickly recovered.

Bob was shouting at her. "What's going on? Did you get one?"

"Helen. I just blasted Helen. That leaves four more. Hold on, honey. I'll get you out."

"Mrs. Stevens. What's going on here? Did you just shoot that in the house?"

A familiar voice emerged from behind. Raymond Hettinger. The bulky summer help stumbled into the kitchen from the backdoor. He had to steady himself as he rubbed his forehead. Dried blood covered the left side of his head, neck, and shoulder.

Debbie ran to and helped steady him. "Raymond. Thank God you're alive. What happened?"

"Your grandmother asked me to go the pharmacy and pick up a prescription. When I came back, I saw her lying on the floor. The cats were gathered around her. I think they were mourning her. I bent over to see if she was alive or dead. There was a small frying pan on the floor. Somehow, and I know this sounds crazy, but it lifted by itself and floated in the air, then hit me in the head. I stumbled out the back door. That's the last I remember. I think *American Ghost Stories* was right. This place is haunted. There has to be a poltergeist in here."

Debbie, still holding the shotgun, grabbed Raymond by the chin with her free hand and pulled him in. "Don't be. Those cats gathered around my grandmother, they're possessed and spawned from the pits of hell. They killed her."

Raymond gave a look of disbelief. "Those cute furry little cats I play with all the time?"

He looked down on the shotgun Debbie gripped, down at Erma, then back to Debbie. Raymond broke free of Debbie's grip and put a little space between them.

"Raymond, you have to trust me. There's no time to explain. Bob is locked in the basement. There's no way to unlock it."

Bob continued to pound and hit the door. "Is that Raymond I hear?"

"It's me, Mr. Stevens. I'm here to help."

Raymond reached for the knob, placed his right foot on the wall, and pulled. Nothing. The six foot four handy man couldn't get the door to budge. Bob was still pounding with his one good hand.

"We've got to get him out," Debbie said.

A disheveled look came across Raymond's face. He paused, then said, "An ax. There's one in the shed. I'll be back in thirty seconds."

Debbie knew the scene looked far too suspicious. But she had to get Bob out. Together, they would try to explain what happened. Raymond rushed back into the kitchen with the ax poised over his shoulder.

He stumbled forward, still reeling from being hit in the head with a cast iron skillet. "The Brady's house next door is totally on fire. I hear lots of sirens. Must be the Fire Department."

Although disoriented, he looked coherent enough to do the job. "Stand back, Mr. Stevens."

Raymond, not taking his eyes off Debbie and her shotgun, took a violent swing. He was right handed, but swung from his left side. Debbie knew this was so he didn't turn his back to her.

The ax dug deep into the door. He had to fight to pull it out.

"A few more whacks and I'll have you out, Mr. Stevens."

Behind her, metallic clinking and clanging filled the air. Debbie turned to see a dozen knives from one of her cutlery sets leave their wooden holders and hover, suspended in air. The blue-and-white-steel forged Japanese Chubo kitchen knives looked as menacing as weaponized drones.

Debbie knew what would happen. She opened her mouth and inhaled. But before she could speak, the knives shot across the kitchen. They found their mark. Every one embedded deep into Raymond. Most were in his back. A steak knife found its mark in his neck. Two went into his left thigh. One dug deep into his right shoulder.

Raymond froze, then fell forward. His head bashed against the floor and the ax fell harmlessly beside him. Raymond didn't move. Behind Debbie, Emily and Chloe sat. They raised their paws and clapped in a high five, then ran off in separate directions.

There were more sirens. But these did not stop at their neighbors. They were passing the Brady farmhouse and nearing Murcat Manor.

Chapter 59   A Jinx is a Jinx

Debbie was flabbergasted. How could this happen. The cats found one more person to kill. Grandma. Grandpa. Now big strapping Raymond Hettinger lay dead on her kitchen floor. No way could anyone survive an onslaught like, she shuddered, aghast at the sight of him … *that.*

There's nothing I can do for Raymond. Get it together, girl. Let's go.

Back to Bob. He's still pounding on the basement door. If she didn't get him and herself out, she was sure, Emily would bring today's body count to five—including hers and Bob's. As Debbie picked up the ax, what looked like a liquid stream of fire glided past her. It hit the doorknob, spread across the six solid oak door panels, then jumped to the walls. The flames crawled like advancing demons to the ceiling.

Rebecca.

"Hey," Bob's muffled voice made its way through the door. "I smell the smoke from the other side. And the knob is blistering hot."

"It's Rebecca. She set the door on fire."

"You need to get me out. Now. Otherwise, Deb," he sighed in resignation, "save yourself."

On the wall was a fire extinguisher. She pulled it from its holder and aimed at the door. A few moments later the fire was out, although smoke and discharge from the extinguisher filled the kitchen. The fire alarms blared, their high-pitched beeps only multiplying the tension.

Debbie took a few more whacks with the ax, focusing on the door knob and lock. She wasn't strong enough to break it. On the counter was a stack of dish towels. She wrapped her hand with one and tried to turn the red hot knob.

"It won't work," the deadpanned voice said.

Emily again.

"The only one who can undo a jinx is the one who performed it. And you just blasted Helen into a million pieces."

Debbie looked around. Again, there was no way to tell which direction the voice was coming from. But she knew the cats were close and watching her. They were not going to miss this, the climatic conclusion of their sixth life.

"But you can. You said you have all their powers."

"Doesn't work that way." Emily's tone was harsh and acrid. "I mimic my follower's powers, but only as long as they're alive. They reside with me for a few minutes after they die. I can feel Helen's power slipping away as we speak.

"And you do realize, don't you, that your fingerprints are all over those knives that are plunged into poor dead Raymond's back? Your fate is sealed in a one-way package to prison, should we decide to let you live."

"Please. I beg of you. You've killed enough people. You don't need us."

"You're right. I don't need you. But this is what we do. This is what we've done for our previous five lives."

"I'm sorry for what happened to you. To your sister. But that's in the past. You can't go back and change it."

"I know that—you think I don't know that?" Emily was now in a full rage. "But I can seek out revenge the only way I know how. The only way the rest of us know how. And thanks to you and Boring Bob, our sixth life has been the best ever. I take a bow and thank you both."

"Oh, screw this. Bob, step away from the door. I'm blasting it into smithereens."

A moment later Bob's faint voice could be heard. "I'm safe. Blast away."

Debbie felt the gun getting hot in her hands. "What the ...?"

She stared, dumbfounded, at the end of the barrel bending sideways. Then the screws holding the trigger undid themselves and the device came apart in her hand.

"Give it up. We've had five lives, spread over four hundred years, of doing this. There's nothing you can do. Admit it."

She's right, Debbie knew in her sunken heart. But she still had to fight. The Mossberg 500 was useless as a shotgun. But she could still swing it like a baseball bat. And she still had the ax.

Debbie prepared to attack but, before she could do anything, the back door opened. Through the smoke and fog a shadow appeared.

"Drop the shotgun, Mrs. Stevens."

Shit. Darrowby.

Chapter 60   Blazing Inferno

Debbie went stiff as a board. Her breathing was stifled, erratic. What else could go wrong? Take a deep breath, she told herself. Darrowby won't hesitate to shoot.

Through the haze-filled kitchen the distinct outline of a man stood on the other side of the large oak table. He had a handgun pointed at her chest.

"I was already on my way here when those kids your psychotic husband tried to blow away called us. Thank the good Lord above they all escaped this house of horrors. Now drop the shotgun. Or I swear to God I'll drop you."

Debbie's mind was in a 100 meter dash-to-the-death-line. Bob in the basement. Four cats still loose. Darrowby ready to shoot. What to do?

"Don't tempt me," Darrowby shouted, his voice monotone, with a pause between each word, "Drop. The. Gun."

"Listen to me. My husband Bob, he's trapped in the basement. You have to help me get him out."

"This is your last warning. Five. Four. Three ..."

A blow hit her right arm. Her left wrist was grabbed by a meaty hand and thrust behind her back. The ruined shotgun fell to the floor.

"Don't make any stupid moves," Kowalski shouted in her ear.

"Hold her there, partner. Pin her to the floor. I'll secure the rest of the house."

A minute later Darrowby reappeared. Kowalski pulled Debbie to her feet.

"Debbie Eileen Stevens. You're under arrest for the murder of Ross Dempsey. Your very own grandfather. With a bowling ball, no less. So whatsamattah, huh? Run out of guests to kill? Kowalski? Cuff this cold blooded killer."

Debbie was fast afoot and twisted free, evading Kowalski's lurch at her with the handcuffs. Darrowby, ignoring her pathetic attempts at dodging the inevitable, walked sure footed around the table. He tripped. Debbie knew on what. Or rather, whom.

"Is that your hired help, Raymond Hettinger?"

Darrowby shone his flashlight through the smoky air on the corpse. The detective looked like a ghost through the haze, but his image became clearer as he approached. Debbie now had both arms pinned against her back. Darrowby brushed past her, then stopped short at the front of the basement door.

"Holy .... shit ... sweet ... mother of ... mercy. Another dead person."

Darrowby pulled the towel off Erma's head and nudged the grey skinned head with his foot. The head turned and expressionless eyes stared up at him through her burned and scarred face.

Debbie struggled against Kowalski's steely grip. "It's not what you think."

"Both your grandparents. And your hired help. What'd you do to your grandmother, light her face on fire? My God, you really are sick. You know that?"

Darrowby coughed from the smoke, pulled out a hankie, and covered his nose and mouth. He pointed toward the basement door.

"Bob's down there? Why? Is he hiding from me? Is he armed?"

Debbie looked up at Darrowby, appearing in control and as dapper as ever. She was powerless under Kowalski's restraint to do anything. Darrowby looked down on her and cracked a grin. God, how she despised this arrogant bastard.

"No. That's not it. He's trapped in the basement."

"Trapped? Trapped, as in you locked him down there? Planning to let him burn with the house? What happened here? The basement door and the walls around it are charred. I can add pyromaniac to your resume of violent crimes."

"What? No, you stupid baboon. The cats ..."

Debbie caught herself.

Darrowby stuffed his hankie into his pocket and stepped toward her. "Ah. The cats. Translation, you're the cats. You killed all the guests here. You're Rebecca, who starts fires, including burning down the Allen's house with them in it."

"What are you talking about? I never burned down a house."

"Don't play stupid. Patrick and Marian Allen. Young couple from Battle Creek. Stayed here the first week you were opened. You gave them one of your cats. Rebecca. Ring a bell?"

"I remember them. But, I didn't know they died."

Darrowby raised an eye. "Sure about that?" He brought his face close to hers. "Know what I think? You went to their house in the middle of the

447

night to take back your cat. Then, you set fire to their home, killing them in the process."

Rebecca. That damned cat Bob gave them torched their house and murdered them before finding her way back to Murcat Manor.

Debbie continued to struggle. She planted her feet and bent forward, trying to wriggle free. But Kowalski was too strong. He easily pulled her off balance, taking away any leverage she could muster.

Debbie looked out the kitchen window. Across the field, her neighbor's house was fully consumed in flames. She wondered if the Bradys were able to escape the inferno. Hell, no. Rebecca would have seen to that.

Now, Rebecca was running loose in Murcat Manor. She had to get free and kill her. Debbie glanced into the living room. Where were the remaining cats?

A flare flashed in the living room, followed a split-second later by an awful explosion. A ball of blistering heat billowed over Debbie. She was blown against the brick wall, then slumped to the floor. The entire living room was ablaze. Moments later, the fire sucked the oxygen out of the kitchen and fed the inferno.

Debbie was on the floor gasping for air—Darrowby was quick to his feet. Kowalski crawled to Debbie and seized her again.

"Brilliant."

Emily again. This time she was ecstatic, her words laced with laughing madness.

"Why didn't I think of this before? Combine Esther and Rebecca's powers of fire and explosions. I mean, did you see that? Wow! Most of your living room and half the upstairs are gone."

Debbie knew Emily was completely demented. But she wasn't stupid. Emily needed to kill her and Bob, and now Darrowby and Kowalski, yet leave a way to escape. There was only one way out. The back door.

Darrowby tried unsuccessfully to unlock the basement door. He bent over, seized Erma by the wrists, and gave a few determined pulls.

"Kowalski, I need help. I can't get the old bag out. She's really stuck."

Darrowby took control of Debbie. Kowalski grabbed Erma by the arm pits while sticking his foot against the bottom of the door. After a few heaves she came loose. He let her body fall into a crumpled heap in the corner of the kitchen.

"Good job. Here's Mrs. Stevens. Now to take care of Bob once and for all. He's not leaving here. I'll make sure of that."

Darrowby shoved Debbie into Kowalski, who spun her around and secured her wrists together behind her back. He snatched his handcuffs and slapped one side shut on her left wrist.

Debbie lost it. She became a fury of arms and legs—head butting, scratching, clawing and biting.

"Bob. It's a trick."

Kowalski's hand covered her mouth. She had to watch as Darrowby tried to open the door, but couldn't unlock it. He picked up the ax lying next to Raymond and heaved a mighty swing. A hole opened.

A few more swings and the hole enlarged, but not big enough for a person to step through. Darrowby kicked at the wood around the opening and broke off large sections. Much of the door now was scattered in chunks on the floor.

Darrowby motioned through the gaping hole. "Mr. Stevens. Hurry up. This place is coming down. I've got to get you out of here."

Debbie planted one foot and gave a reverse kick to Kowalski's shin. But his hand remained over her mouth. All she could do was give off audible grunts. Debbie watched with angst as Bob ran up the stairs. Darrowby reached his hand out to him.

"Detective," Bob said. "I never thought I'd be happy to see you. But thanks."

A fist slammed just below Bob's sternum knocked him half way down the stairs.

"Whaddaya think I'm stupid? That ass-hat attorney Wilson will find some frickin' loophole and allow you and your murderous wife to walk. And make me look like a public idiot in the process. Can't take that chance. No way, Mr. Stevens. You're gonna pay for your sins. Tonight. Right now. Just wanted to say it to your face and remember your expression."

Debbie strained but was helpless as Bob lurched up the stairs and tried to swoop past Darrowby. But with a broken arm, there was not much he could do. A furious kick to Bob's chest sent him tumbling butt first down the stairs to the bottom.

"That's for killing my good friend DeShawn Hill."

More laughing. Emily was having the time of her sixth life. "This is so much better than *American Ghost Stories*. And now your precious little bed and breakfast is on fire. This has been by far and away our best life. But wait. The best is yet to come."

Chloe sauntered around the table and sat on Raymond's back. As if it had a will of its own, a ten inch butcher's knife struggled to free itself from his back. It pulled out with a sickening slurping sound.

Debbie flew into a fury of flying fists and feet. An elbow found Kowalski's chin. She scratched and bit and clawed at him. They spun in place, Debbie battling to break free and Kowalski trying to restrain her.

"How's it going over there, partner? She's just a girl. Sheeesh. You have one cuff on her. Slap on the other and take her outside."

Darrowby returned to Bob, knocking him back down the stairs a third time.

The crimson stained knife rose and hovered five feet off the ground. Chloe licked her right paw and pointed to the center of Kowalski's back. The projectile hurtled across the roof and embedded itself into its new host.

Debbie felt his grip on her loosen. He stumbled forward and laid his hand on Darrowby's shoulder. Kowalski blinked a few times and sputtered out his last words.

"Damndest. Thing. Darrowby. You won't ... believe it."

"Yeah? What is it? A cat attack you?"

Kowalski dropped in a heap. Darrowby reached down, pulled the knife out and rolled his partner over. He kept his eyes on Debbie as he felt for a pulse on Kowalski's neck and wrist.

Nothing.

The look in Darrowby's eyes glaring up at her. Emily sitting on the kitchen table with Chloe, Rebecca and Esther, watching as if this was their favorite TV sitcom. Bob unconscious in the basement. Three corpses on the kitchen floor. Half of Murcat Manor blown to bits. Smoke rolling into the kitchen. Emily's taunting laugh echoing in her head. What to do?

Debbie gauged the path to the back door. If she sprinted fast enough, she just might make it.

Chapter 61   Grand Finale

With one fluid movement, Darrowby stepped in front of Debbie and assumed a linebacker's upright stance, ready to blitz. The detective's unblinking eyes revealed a state of concentration so intense he could pile-drive Debbie through the floor like a pneumatic hammer drill.

"You crazy treacherous freak. First you kill DeShawn Hill, who I've known since we were kids. Now you murder my best friend and partner with a knife—*in the back*, no less. You're nothing but a crazed coward. You deserve to die with your husband. Wait, hang that thought. I'll torch what's left of this place with you in it."

Debbie tried to retreat, her hands up and out. "No ... wait. That's not what happened."

Darrowby looked at the four cats sitting on the table. "It was the cats, right?"

"Yes, I—no, but ... wait, you don—"

Darrowby snared a fistful of Debbie's hair and pulled her head back, shoving his gun under her chin. "Go ahead. Say it was the damn cats. Say it. I dare you."

Debbie understood she had lost everything. Bob. Her grandparents. Murcat Manor. Her vision of raising a family of four kids. There was nothing she could do to bring back any of her lifelong dreams.

But Debbie Elaine Stevens held on to the one thing no one could take away from her. She still held the truth in her heart. She would not to succumb to Emily's manipulative madness. Regardless of Darrowby's handgun shoved against the underside of her chin, Emily Livingston was the real enemy. Darrowby, he was no more than an inept, stupid pawn caught up in her sadistic game.

Too bad, Debbie thought, Emily didn't deem Darrowby worthy of hearing her voice. That would make her life so much easier.

Debbie, her head cranked back and locked against her shoulders, rolled her eyes to meet Darrowby. "Sorry for Kowalski. But I didn't kill him."

"You should die here tonight with your homicidal husband. I should toss you down in the basement with him and let the house burn down and collapse on you."

Darrowby spun Debbie against the wall. He kicked her feet apart, almost causing her to fall. He pulled up the back of her shirt and hauled the Ruger SR9 9mm semi-automatic handgun out from her belt.

"What's this? This meant for me?"

"No."

"Always walk around your burning house with a shotgun and handgun, do you?"

"No. I swear. It's not like that."

"And what do we have here? A dagger, it seems? Hmm, almost missed that. You could do a lot of damage with this baby."

Debbie wanted to puke as he pawed her all over, feeling for more weapons. He found the hunting knife strapped to her ankle and yanked it out.

"You're a real sicko. Worst I've ever seen." Darrowby threw the Ruger and knives through the archway and into the burning living room.

Emily continued to laugh. "Weeeee win. As soon as Darrowby opens the back door to take you to a waiting patrol car, we'll also leave. Ha! He won't care if we also run outside."

Debbie looked on as the cats sat on her table and stared. Their tails rose in the air and wagged back and forth in unison. This was entertainment in its best form to them.

Rebecca got up and ran in a small circle. As she sped up, a small fire came to life in the center. Two streams jumped to the kitchen curtains and whisked onto the walls.

Emily's voice resonated in Debbie's head. "Rebecca says one more fire for the road. A parting gift. From us, to you."

Debbie turned and stepped into Darrowby. She shoved both her arms under his right armpit and swept him off her. He stumbled but recovered and snared Debbie by the waist, picking her up. She was parallel to the floor, her legs stretched out and kicking wildly in the air.

Debbie Elaine Stevens took one final look at the cats. "No way, Emily. This is still my house. My kitchen. My domain. And I'm going to prove it right now."

With one swift move she reached around Darrowby's waist and unclipped his gun belt. She seized his semi-automatic handgun and aimed it at the cats. Safety off, she unloaded.

One round.

Two rounds.

The foursome ran in a panic.

Three rounds.

Rebecca was hit and flipped backward and off the table.

Four rounds.

Five rounds.

Six rounds.

Chloe took two hits and crumpled on the table.

Seven rounds.

Esther flattened out like a punctured balloon.

Debbie aimed at Emily and fired off two more rounds before Darrowby ripped his gun from her hand.

Emily leapt off the table. The flames from what was left of the living room invaded the kitchen. She stepped toward the back door.

As Darrowby pinned Debbie to the floor with his knee in the small of her back, she saw terror in Emily. The high priestess of her feline clan was confused. She was now alone.

Debbie grinned. "That's it, Emily. You lose. All your friends are dead. And I get the sense you don't want to be here by yourself."

Darrowby shouted in her ear. "Stop talking to the cats, you insane freak."

Debbie winced as Darrowby slapped the cuffs on her other wrist far too tight. The slowing of circulation made her hands numb.

"Bob. Please, you have to help him. Let me die. But for the love of God, let my Bob live."

Darrowby pulled Debbie to her feet. "Not a chance. I'm getting out of here now. This hellhole is coming down in a pile of smoldering rubble."

As Darrowby said this, the rest of the upstairs and what remained of the living room caved in. Debris, fire, and heat exploded into the kitchen.

"Let me try to save Bob. At least give me that."

"Not a chance. Much as I despise the thought, I do need at least one of you alive. You know. For the media and publicity. A trial of this magnitude will attract nationwide media attention. And guess who'll be answering their questions? Me."

Debbie dropped to her knees and screamed out, "Bob. Can you hear me?"

Nothing.

"He's not getting up from that last fall down the stairs. Now let's go."

"Bob."

Darrowby shoved Debbie to her feet. Pain shot up her arms toward her shoulders. By the back door, Emily sat, staring at Debbie. She clapped her paws.

"Bravo. Well done. You certainly are an opponent worthy of congratulating. I give you that. But you have to understand this escapade will end on my terms. I can't allow you or that moron Darrowby to leave. So I'm taking all three of us out."

Debbie struggled to gain her balance. "No, Emily. You can't do that."

"Shut up," Darrowby shouted, balling her shirt in one hand and pulling her up and into him. They were nose to nose. He pointed back at the lone surviving cat. "That's just a dumb. Stupid. Cat."

"Oh, dumb and stupid, am I? Nobody calls me that."

Darrowby tensed as he loosened his grip on Debbie and stared back at Emily. Debbie knew she was talking to him as well.

"I get the last laugh. I can't allow you to escape. That would mean you won."

Debbie saw Darrowby's stunned eyes as he leaned toward Emily. He started to take a step toward the cat, but stopped, looked back at Debbie, then again to Emily.

"What ... the ... hell ..."

Emily continued, sitting calmly and staring carefree at Debbie. "And you're right. I don't want to be in this world alone. But I have the solution to both. Directly below me are two gas leaks in the basement, compliments of your grandmother Erma. I need to set them off now as I feel Esther's powers leaving me."

"Don't do it."

Darrowby started to backpedal as the black and white spotted cat raised a paw and waved. "We'll be back. All thirteen of us. We still have three more lives. Too bad the same can't be said about you and Detective Dickhead. Good bye, Debbie."

Emily closed her eyes and tightened her shoulders. A giant explosion erupted from the basement. The wooden floor lifted with the eruption of smoke and fire. Large and small chunks of wood exploded across the kitchen.

A large plank spun through the air and hit Debbie in the head. Her world was shutting off. She realized she was on her back. Darrowby lay on top of her, motionless. Looking up, flames danced to the smoke rock and rolling across the ceiling. The sight, sound, and smell of Murcat Manor burning was terrible. Part of the ceiling above the kitchen gave way and crumpled in flames to the floor. A rafter crashed next to her head.

Debbie's last thoughts were of Bob ...

I love you. I'm sorry I failed you, my dearest.

And of forevermore ...

Now, sweet Jesus Almighty, receive us. We're coming home.

457

Stephen Tremp

Chapter 62   Heaven or Hell

Debbie Steven's world was one of isolation and sensory deprivation, where darkness and silence governed her will. She drifted aimlessly with no sense of direction, regardless of her determination to control her surroundings. A swirling sensation hindered any ability to coordinate her five senses.

She could not discern up or down. Her universe was devoid of left and right. Back and forth did not exist. Even so, she was aware, again, that she at least existed.

My name is Debbie Elaine Stevens. This much I'm sure of.

She had been aware a few times, but had soon meandered back to sleep. This time, she was stronger and determined to break through.

But her thoughts were disorganized, random and scattered. Where am I? Could I be dead? If so, which place did I end up?

Take it easy, girl. Relax. No need to hurry. Proceed at a comfortable pace. Take an accounting of what you have and go from there.

Debbie sensed the presence of someone else—or some entity—with her. A friendly kindred spirit that protected her. A veil of sorts seemed to fall from her mind, opening up the world around her just a little bit.

From this, Debbie deduced she didn't end up in that place with Emily.

Emily.

That evil black cat with three large white spots jumped back into her memory. Debbie gasped as fear flooded in. Desperate to escape, she took a deep breath and tried to move her arms and legs as a current swept her back. She tumbled and spun, not knowing where she was or if that damned cat was in pursuit.

But the image of Emily opened the floodgates of new remembrances. Memories of people and events poured into her mind, in a scrambled cacophony of bewildering images and sounds. Ross and Erma Dempsey. Grandma turned and hissed at Emily who had tried to sneak up on them, causing that malicious cat to turn and run so fast she was no longer in Debbie's world.

There they stood; an angelic duo if there ever was one, suspended against a blanket of white. Grandma smiled. Her skin was no longer horribly burned and scarred. She looked just like Debbie remembered, wearing a nice solid matching outfit of blue and white with a cute matching hat.

Grandpa, his head back as it should be, wore a brown suit with a slight plaid pattern. He held his belly and laughed. They brought her pleasure and reassurance.

Only the promise of new perfect bodies heaven promised could explain this. Erma spoke, but only her mouth moved. Debbie knew she communicated Emily was no longer a threat. Surely she was in heaven. Another veil lifted, and she felt a little more alive.

Debbie tried to speak. But no words came out. No matter. She could wave to her beloved grandparents. Her heart jumped. She raised her arms to wave them back and forth.

One arm was free. But, her left wrist was constrained. She could move it a few inches and that was all. A cold metal ring enclosed her wrist.

Strange. But at least she could feel again, although this was not what she expected. Her confusion lifted a bit more. The swirling slowed.

Grandma and Grandpa held out their loving arms to her. They called to her and extended their unconditional love with the purest smiles and laughter. Surely this was heaven. They didn't have white feathery wings or halos. But they were here and Emily was not.

Debbie tried to wave both hands three more times. Again, her left wrist was restrained.

Clank.

Clank.

Clank.

What is that awful sound echoing in my ear? It's giving me a headache.

At least she could hear now. A second sense returned, jumpstarting hope within her heart.

With two senses recovered, it was natural to go for sight. The effort to open her eyes shot a pulsating wave of pain deep into her head. After a few moments the misery subsided. Shadowy figures hovered above, blurred and blended with light.

Debbie forced her chapped lips open. The pain to move her bottom jaw was intense. Her mouth was so dry, her tongue snappy and crackly. Worst morning breath ever. Something small, cold, and wet was placed in her mouth as she tried to speak. Crushed ice?

As her lips and tongue sprang to life, the incredible scent of a perfume she had never experienced infiltrated her nose. So peaceful and calming, confirming this could not be hell.

All her senses had returned, at least in part. She knew her right hand was being held and gently stroked. She rolled her head. Her hand came into view, held between to larger, darker hands.

But her left hand. She tried to lift it, but again could only raise it a few inches.

Clank.

Clank.

Clank.

More crushed ice was placed in her mouth. Not much, but enough to help increase her senses.

Debbie tried to speak. Only dry guttural sounds escaped.

"Shhhh. You just relax, you hear me, now?" The gentle stroking moved to her forehead.

Debbie squeezed her eyes shut, then opened them a little. She could perceive much more. But the lights, they were too bright. And the beeping noises, so loud and confusing. The pulsating pain in her head returned.

"You just let good ol' Latasha take care of you. Stop squirming. I know you can hear me."

Debbie blinked a few times, then looked up at a staring, smiling face. Dark hair. Ebony skin. Individual features still too blurry to make out. More of Debbie's surroundings came into focus. Her senses separated. Sight and sound became distinct from each other. She took in a slow deep gulp of air that made her dizzy. She almost passed out.

"There, there now. You just rest up, child."

No. This can't be. I'm in a hospital. And that's a nurse looming over me.

Grandma and Grandpa, still smiling and laughing, disappeared like a wisp of smoke in the wind.

Debbie tried to move her left arm again.

Clank.

Clank.

Clank.

That noise is driving me crazy.

"Now don't you go and try something foolish, Mrs. Stevens. You shouldn't try and move, or I'll have to give you something to put you right back to sleep. You hear me?"

Debbie closed her eyes. She needed to relax and let things come to her.

Bob.

Images of her soul mate came once, twice, then overwhelmed her. She wept. But the nurse saying she would give something to put her back to sleep caused Debbie to gather the strength to stop, if only for a few moments.

Debbie needed answers. She composed herself, and muttered a word. It came out before realizing that's what she needed.

"Ice."

"You just rest, honey child."

"Ice ... please."

More crushed ice was placed between her lips. It melted and flowed across her tongue. Refreshing. She was now able to speak more words.

"Bob. Where is ... Bob?"

Debbie clenched her fists and flailed her wrists. One hand was free. Her left, still bound.

"Now you listen up and stop this foolishness right now or I'll put you down for your own good. I'm not messing around. Understand?"

Debbie relaxed and nodded her head. She focused her eyes on a middle aged African American woman, somewhat heavy with age, and gray roots shooting off a dark Afro in every direction.

"Okay. Now I have your attention. You seem to be coming around pretty good. So allow me to give you a brief rundown. Your name is Debbie Elaine Stevens. Do you understand?"

Debbie nodded her head.

"Robert Jeremy Stevens. That's your husband."

Debbie again nodded, holding back tears.

"Well, I hate to be the bearer of bad news. But your husband, and I'm sure he was a mighty fine man, he … well, honey, he died."

Darrowby. That maniac killed my husband. Debbie blotted out his face.

"Yes, ma'am. He died in a fire that also killed your grandparents. And a few more people. Honey child, you should thank the good Lord above you're still alive."

A flashback of those who were murdered by Emily and those cursed cats rolled across her mind, this time slower, organized, and in chronological order.

DeShawn Hill.

Patrick and Marian Allen.

Paul Knudson.

Reginald and Sophia Johnson.

Maria Rodriguez.

Joseph Meicigama.

Her grandparents.

Eddie and Alison Brady.

Raymond Hettinger.

Detective Kowalski.

Bob.

She could now control her senses and her thoughts, but not her emotions. Her arms and legs began to shake. She let out a long loud wail.

Latasha's hands gently covered her mouth. Debbie grabbed her wrist with her free hand and tried to pull it off.

"Honey child, I told you to relax. Your heartbeat on the monitor just sped up to unacceptable levels. And your grip, it's mighty tight for someone who's been in a coma for three days."

Debbie remembered grabbing Darrowby's semi-automatic handgun. Rebecca, Chloe, and Esther were ripped apart by bullets as she nearly emptied the clip. Emily briefly escaping, then standing above a broken gas pipe, only to blow herself up in an attempt to kill Debbie and Darrowby while bringing down the rest of Murcat Manor in a fiery heap. Debbie let go of Latasha's wrist, and the image of Darrowby's gun faded.

"As I said, my name is Latasha. I'm the head nurse of this floor. You're at the Trauma Burn Center at the University of Michigan Hospital here in Ann Arbor."

Debbie's worst fear as a child was realized; being burned alive. So much for being in heaven.

Latasha placed some more crushed ice in her mouth.

"I'm ... I'm burned? How bad?"

"Not so bad as you might think. You have second degree burns over thirty percent of your body, mainly your arms and legs. You also have a broken right leg and three cracked ribs from your bed and breakfast falling down on you. Oh, and you have a concussion. That'd help explain your three day coma."

Latasha reached for something on a steel table next to the bed. "Now, I'm gonna hold a mirror so you can see your pretty little face."

Debbie looked. Her head was covered in bandages. Holes allowed for her eyes, nose, and mouth to be seen.

"Like I said, it's not as bad as you think. Your face has lots of small cuts. They was a couple gas explosions. You have twenty-seven stitches. But don't you worry none. Your face will have some minor scarring, but nothing a little makeup won't cover. But in general, your body's been severely traumatized. You'll need plenty of time to heal."

Debbie tried to lift her left hand again.

Clank.

She looked. It was handcuffed to the rail of her hospital bed.

"What ... what's this?"

Latasha's smiling face now became stern. "Compliments of Detective Darrowby."

"Darr ... Darrowby?"

"Yes, ma'am. You and him are the only ones made it out alive. He had a group of police officers wheel him here and he read you your rights. 'Course, it don't mean nothing since you were unconscious. But he'll be back now that you're awake. I guarantee you that. Again, I'm sorry about your husband. And your grandparents. God rest they souls."

"Bob ..."

"Fire department found him in the rubble of the basement. Again, I'm so ... oh, honey child." Latasha smiled at her like a mother would her long lost and found again baby.

Debbie looked at her wrist again and tried to raise her head.

"I'll fill you in on what's happening. Then I'll have to induce you back to sleep. Long story short, Darrowby is charging you for a whole lot of murders. Everyone who died at Murcat Manor, including your late husband. And your neighbors whose house also burned same time as yours. Fifteen deaths in all, yes ma'am."

Debbie tried to say something in her defense. The only words she could spill out were, "Cats. Those ... damned ... cats."

Latasha shrugged off the words. "This is big news, honey. It's all over televisions. Fifteen people dead? Makes you out a serial killer to the media. And this is the third time the houses on this property burned to the ground, killing everyone. People are stopping by in droves and taking pictures. Oh yeah, it's big news, honey."

Debbie collapsed on the pillow and closed her eyes.

"But don't you worry none. Your attorney, he's been on TV a lot. He's taking Darrowby to town, making him look for sure like some fish-eyed fool. And you? Child, he's got folks thinking you're like some second coming of Mother Theresa."

"Darrowby. Where ... where is he?"

Latasha smiled wide. "Oh, he's here. But don't you worry. He's on another floor. He's awake and in lots better shape than you. But good lawd, that man," she rolled her eyes and feigned fanning her neck. "He's madder than a wet hornet. I can tell you, as soon as you're up and about, they're gonna formally charge you," she tapped the bed's side rail. "Right here in your bed."

No. No, no, no. This can't be happening. Debbie's world started to swirl again as she tried to break her shackled arm free of the cuff.

"Hey, didn't I say don't you fret none? Your lawman, he be on top of things. He's making an impressive case for you for the country to see. According to news polls, half the folks think you're guilty as sin. Yes, ma'am, they sure do. But there are plenty of others, like myself, be

467

thinking you didn't have nothing to do with killing any of those poor folks."

Debbie gave up trying to free herself. Her heart pounded. Her head felt like it would detonate any second in a big bang splat of wall to wall, floor to ceiling plasma. And the anxiety she felt over Bob and her grandparents now gone was too much to bear.

"I'm gonna to let the doctor know you're awake. He'll probably put you back to sleep for a day or two until you stabilize a little more."

Debbie didn't need the doctor for that. Her world spun back into darkness. She lost all feeling. Her remaining thoughts were of Bob. Good thoughts. Pleasant memories. No better way to end the horrific day and get a good night's sleep.

Chapter 63   No Way Out

Debbie Elaine Stevens folded her arms on the table, leaned in, and buried her head. The lonely and insignificant feelings she had were incomparable. Although she'd only been in the office a few minutes, she already hated the place.

Debbie closed her eyes. Darkness was not only her friend, but a place of comfort away from her sorrow where she could hide from the violent events of the previous month, if only for a few moments.

Heavy narcotics helped alleviate the pain from her broken right leg, various cracked ribs, a major concussion, and second degree burns. Though she was able to endure the continuous and agonizing misery from her physical injuries, the OxyContin could not dull the heartache due to the loss of those closest to her. Escape, even for a few brief moments, seemed her best alternative.

Robert Jeremy Stevens, her husband and one true soul mate, was gone from her life at the young age of twenty-six. Her self-worth had plummeted like a thermometer in post-midnight Antarctica. She would never again see

Grandma and Grandpa Dempsey. Even her parents had refused to show for the legal discussion that would determine the course for the rest of her life.

Debbie raised her head and looked around the refined yet stale boardroom. Although the ceiling loomed twelve feet above her head, she felt like it and everything above was about to cave in. Just like her last thoughts of a burning Murcat Manor crashing down around her and destroying her aspirations of a happy and fulfilled life.

In front of her, the rectangular table with thirty high-back, black leather chairs stretched across the room. On the far end, her legal team conferred. Voices talked over each other in hushed whispers. But the acoustics in this room were incredible. She could hear each word her counsel spoke.

The group of five individuals stopped talking and stared at her. Debbie wondered if they thought she was too stupid to understand what they were discussing, or if it was the meds messing with her mind. Was Kenneth Wilson laughing at her, or simply smiling?

The side effects of the pain-killers impaired her mental and emotional functions. To try and focus was too much work. She had to trust Wilson, and decided to let their words blend together and float off somewhere. Where? She cared not.

Debbie nervously rubbed her hands across the rich, stylish table. It was polished to where she could see her reflection as if looking in a mirror. The prominence of the centerpiece reminded her of the custom oak kitchen table in Murcat Manor. A fond memory assuaged her beleaguered head of how that nice man, DeShawn Hill, had custom made it especially for her. It wasn't polished like this table. She couldn't use it as a mirror, but it was the central gathering place where she'd prepared over sixty meals a day.

Ah, my dream kitchen, Debbie reminisced. My happy place, full of life and laughter, and the place I made countless new friends. People guffawed and drank wine, forgetting about their problems if only for a few days. My kingdom where I ruled supreme and felt most fulfilled. Bob and I spent more time at that table than anywhere else in the bed and breakfast.

But this board room, it was cold and sterile. The walls were off-white. Missing were windows opening to the great outdoors, allowing the outside to enter the drab and dreary room. There were no pictures adorning the walls such as rustic barns from local artists, or western horizon sunsets, or hunters shooting mallard ducks. No mirrors. And the overhead lights, why were they so bright? And did they have to buzz so loud?

A chill ran up and down Debbie's back. The air conditioning was set too high. She shivered as she crisscrossed her arms and covered her shoulders with her hands. Beyond the glass walls stood a long white hallway that seemed to extend forever in both directions. She had known doctors' offices and hospitals with that gross smelly sanitary smell to have more life.

Worse, Debbie thought, and this was the real ass-kicker; she was not only back in Grand Rapids but was in the very same downtown high rise office building she swore last year to never again enter.

American Credit Services and Bernie Butthead ... errrrr, Bernie Mortenson, was four stories below. Ugh. Debbie's stomach turned as she thought of her former manager so physically close to her. Thank God they had not run into each other on the elevator ride up.

Life's a funny thing when you go through a full circle phase.

Debbie, though, would treat her former boss with dignity, giving Bob respect—he'd always insisted she do so. But she would draw the line at calling him Mr. Mortenson. A chuckle escaped at the thought of calling him Bernie Butthead to his face.

"Mrs. Stevens. Are you still with us? Is there something humorous you'd like to share with the rest of us?"

"No. It's nothing. Really. Just the pain-killers making me light-headed. That's all. Heh heh."

Kenneth Wilson was an imposing figure. Not only because he was tall and well built. He had a stately appearance that was dignified and elegant. When he walked into a room or rose to speak, his presence commanded attention.

Straighten up girl and pay attention, Debbie told herself. *Right now, this is the only family you have. Your salvation rests in their hands. You don't want to spend the rest of your life in an orange jumpsuit rotting away in prison.*

Wilson gave Debbie a soft warm smile. He walked across the room to her, his team in tow. Four attorneys each wearing designer suits that cost more than what many people made in a month. One legal secretary rounded out his group. Debbie guessed TJ Maxx for her.

"Mrs. Stevens," Wilson began. "I understand events at Murcat Manor last month have been traumatic, to say the least. You've lost your husband and your grandparents. Now, you've been charged with fifteen murders. To the outside world, your situation may look bleak. But, I can say with complete confidence, you can trust me and the legal team I've assembled."

Behind him stood what appeared to be a formidable group. Debbie was glad they were on her side. She felt her worries and depression lift as Wilson's confidence melted away some of her fears.

Wilson turned to his affiliates and presented them proudly. "I assure you these are some of the best at their craft. Please allow me to first introduce Ethan Kennedy. He's an experienced and respected criminal defense attorney and twice has been Defense Counsel of the Year. Mr.

Kennedy is a natural born negotiator who can craft deals most attorneys can only dream of. He's well liked and he's a fan of the media. Like myself, he holds a lot of press conferences. He loves the camera and the camera loves him."

Debbie recognized Kennedy from various news television stories over the years. She liked the man right away. He oozed competence, determination, and tenacity.

But the words 'negotiator' and 'craft deals' were unexpected.

Debbie looked back and forth between her counsels. "I'm sorry. Did you say something about negotiating a deal? I thought we were going to trial? Should be a slam dunk. Right? I didn't kill anyone."

Ethan Kennedy bent down to greet her properly, shaking her hand. "It's a pleasure to meet you, Mrs. Stevens. Like Kenneth stated, he's assembled the best team possible. I'm grateful to be here working on your behalf. We're here for you."

Kennedy stepped back and Wilson continued. "This is Emma Stanley. She has a reputation as one of the best high stakes attorneys in the Midwest. She's won many high profile cases, including sports personalities, political figures, and very wealthy people."

Debbie felt better with a female in Wilson's circle. An immediate bond of trust was formed without a word spoken. Debbie sat straight up when Wilson said she'd won high profile cases. Fifteen deaths in a bed and breakfast? It didn't get any higher profile than this.

"Finally, we have Logan Thomas. He's a former prosecutor and forensics expert. His main job will be to twofold; establish that you did not start the fires that burned down Murcat Manor and prove you didn't kill anyone, especially your husband."

Wilson paused to take a breath and consider his next words. This scared Debbie. Pauses were generally a prelude to 'but ...'

"But, in all honestly, Logan Thomas is the backup plan in case we do go to trial."

Backup plan? What the hell is Wilson talking about?

Wilson drew another measured breath. "Now I know we discussed going to trial. But I honestly believe, with the advice from Mr. Kennedy and Miss Stanley, we'll have to move in a different direction. In all probability, if we do go to trial, you will not receive a not guilty verdict. In which case, you would spend the rest of your life behind bars without the possibility of parole. Michigan does not have the death penalty."

Debbie glanced back and forth at the five sets of eyes staring back. "No ... wait. I don't understand. A different direction than going to trial? What do you mean?"

Wilson continued. "It's my duty, as your council, to advise you what your options are and what we believe is the best path to take. Now, after hearing everything, both from you and from what we know of Darrowby and the prosecutor, here's what we're up against. Debbie, you are officially charged with fifteen murders—DeShawn Hill, Patrick and Marian Allen, Paul Knudson, Reginald and Sophia Johnson, Maria Rodriguez, Joseph Meicigama, Eddie and Alison Brady who lived next door to you, your grandparents, Raymond Hettinger, Sergeant Detective David Kowalski, and your husband Bob Stevens.

Debbie tried not to break down. *Those damned cats.* They haunted her even after their demise.

"Darrowby swears he saw you lock your husband in basement, then set Murcat Manor on fire and causing two gas explosions. While he tried to free Bob, you stabbed Kowalski in the back with a knife."

Just the name Darrowby caused Debbie to shoot up from her chair. The pain in her broken leg, still in a cast, was indescribable and she almost fainted and fell. Emma Stanley was quick to grab her and help her sit back in the chair.

Debbie reached in her purse, fumbled with her pain killers, and took two with a drink of water. "That's a bald-faced lie. That Darrowby, he's a stinking liar. He killed my Bob. He's the murderer. Not me. He should be on trial for his life."

Wilson stood his ground with his hands locked behind his back. "Mrs. Stevens, please calm down. It's his word, a decorated and respected detective, against yours. And that'll go a long way with a jury."

Ethan Kennedy put documents he was reading back into a folder and leaned into the table. "Darrowby stated in his reports he personally witnessed you murder Detective Kowalski with a ten inch butcher's knife. Fire investigators who recovered his body found the knife in his back, exactly as Darrowby described."

Darrowby again, making life a living hell for Debbie.

"Making matters worse, you had an empty flask of whiskey in your back pocket with the words *Old Faithful* engraved in the leather covering. This is not good for you in the eyes of a jury."

Ethan Kennedy picked up a second folder and opened it. "It doesn't help Raymond Hettinger was also found with eleven knives in his backside in the kitchen where Darrowby found you."

Debbie looked back and forth at the attorneys. No one spoke. In Kennedy's eyes, she was the only one who could have stuck all those knives in Hettinger. She picked up on the other attorneys shuddering, and understood they came to the same conclusion.

"And Debbie, your grandparents also died there. Darrowby swore he saw Ross with a crushed skull. Erma was burned horribly, beyond recognition. When he entered, he found you walking through the kitchen with a shotgun. You also had an automatic handgun, a knife strapped to your ankle, and a dagger in your belt."

Debbie looked down on her reflection in the table again. It was as if she was on trial here and her defense was the prosecution. She felt hope slipping away.

"Yes, that's true," she murmured.

Kenneth Wilson stood and paced the floor. "Okay, here it is. Darrowby's sworn testimony is going to be difficult if not impossible to beat in court. We have two options. Go to trial and go for a not guilty verdict, which is highly unlikely, or ..."

Another measured breath. Debbie hated those.

"We go for an insanity defense."

Debbie tried to interrupt. But she couldn't find the words. Maybe, she thought, because she couldn't believe what she was hearing. Emma Stanley sat next to her. They had rehearsed this. All she could do was try to stand again and protest.

This time, Emma Stanley was ready and coaxed her back down. Her stare penetrated. "Honestly, your only real hope is the latter."

Debbie waved her hands in front of her, as if this would clear the madness from the air. "No. Stop. I'm not crazy. Darrowby, he's the real killer of my husband. Him, and those damned cats who ..."

Debbie cut herself off. Her eyes bulged as she slapped her hands over her mouth, as if she could pull the words back.

Wilson smirked and stepped away from the table. "Exactly."

He resumed his pacing. "There are two options we can pursue. We can go for cognitive insanity. Basically, this means you were impaired by a mental disease and you did not know the act was wrong."

He stuck his finger in the air for effect, as if he were in front of a jury. "But, I don't think that will work. You would need to establish you had a long history of mental illness. And you do not have any history whatsoever. At least," he said with a sigh, "leading up to the opening of Murcat Manor."

"Yes. That's right. I have no history of mental illness." Debbie folded her arms tight and glared at the lot of them. "Because I'm not crazy. So let's go to trial. I'm not guilty of anything. Darrowby, he's the real killer. What are we waiting for?"

Wilson continued, unhampered by Debbie's interruptions. "Next, there is incompetency."

"Hey," Debbie fixed her stare on Wilson and tapped the table like a schoolteacher wanting a daydreaming student to focus. "The guy in the suit, yes, you. Are you even listening to me?"

Wilson gave the same condescending smile. Only this time, it looked patronizing. He maintained his pacing.

"Very simply, under Michigan law, you performed a crime that is a result of a mental illness wherein you lacked the substantial capacity to either appreciate the nature and quality or the wrongfulness, or you were unable to conduct yourself to the requirements of the law."

"Wait ... what? I didn't perform any crime."

"Please, Mrs. Stevens. Let me get through this." He spun on his heal and faced Debbie. "Case in point. Darrowby stated you blamed the deaths of your patrons on the cats and supernatural powers they possessed. You did personify your cats, right? You gave them names of people, rather than animals, such as Tabby or Shadow or Tigger."

"That's right. Well, all except one. Midnight. But Bob named her. But it wasn't really me who named the cats."

Emma Stanley spoke with a soft comforting voice. "It wasn't you? Who then did name the cats?"

Debbie vividly recalled the first day of building Murcat Manor when they found thirteen little kittens in the rubble. "Their names just popped into my head as I picked them up. One at a time. It was like they were telling me their names. Amy, the one Bob named Midnight, hissed and scratched me when he named her." Debbie chuckled a bit at the thought. "I don't think she liked being called Midnight."

Debbie realized her mistake. Must be the meds. The attorneys stared at her like she was from another dimension.

"Forget about the cat's names," Debbie said. "Look, I'm not sure where you're going with all of this, but ...."

Wilson shot an open palm in the air. He looked at Debbie, and she could swear she saw pity in his eyes as he continued.

"You had a mental breakdown because of the stress of running the bed and breakfast, the twenty-five thousand dollar monthly bills, and each additional death of your guests. Factor in Darrowby's aggressive approach to you and your husband as the prime and only suspects, and, well, you can clearly see how that would only have added to your mental anguish."

Debbie balled her fists and tried to stand again. "No. No, no, no, no, no. You're my attorneys. You work for me. See how that works. I pay you—"

"Correction," Wilson said. "It's your parents, as executors of your grandparents' estate, who are paying us. They used cash and sold assets to pay for your defense. But most of your grandparents' wealth, including the equity in their house, was used as collateral to secure the three and a half million dollar loan to finance the building of Murcat Manor. Going to trial, which I believe would not go well for you, would cost far more than what money is left over from the Dempsey estate."

Emma continued with her soft, soothing voice. "And as much as you or I don't want to say this, your parents think you're mentally ill in some capacity. They also believed you killed your grandparents, their parents, as evidenced by their not being here today. Their absence speaks volumes. But they also lean in the direction that the stress did get the better of you and that, at least to an extent, you are not responsible for your actions. I don't know how to say this other than simply tell you, although they do not want you to go to prison for the rest of your life, they do want you committed."

That was it. Those words left Debbie feeling as if she was slammed in the gut with a nail-embedded two by four. Her breath left. Her soul died. She now understood she was truly alone in this world. All she had left was Kenneth Wilson and his dispassionate team. It was his way and nothing else.

Debbie quietly sat and relented. "What does this entail?"

"First, we file a motion for a competency hearing. Then, there'll be a psychiatric or psychological evaluation for you. Finally, the competency hearing will take place. After that, if you are deemed incompetent to stand trial, you will be handed over to a state mental facility until your competence can be reestablished."

Debbie did what she knew best in overwhelming stressful situations. She folded her arms on the table and buried her head. "Mental facility? You mean a loony bin."

Ethan Kennedy's whisper was clearly heard. "She really does believe the cats performed the killings. I think she'll pass a lie detector test if we stick to this story."

One of Debbie's eyes popped open just above her forearm. "Ummm, I'm still in the room and can hear you."

Debbie knew her only way out was to go in deeper. Tell the truth. The cats killed everyone. Be convincing. Pass a lie detector test. Be declared incompetent to stand trial, then committed to an institution. This outcome was not what she expected coming into the meeting, but it was better than rotting the rest of her life rotting away in prison.

Wilson continued talking.

Debbie refused to look at him. Darkness and pain killers were her solace.

"Understand, this does not mean you will never be tried. You will be reevaluated many times and quite possibly tried at a later date if you are found competent to stand trial. Darrowby's relentless. He'll be pressing for the rest of your life."

Debbie would raise a white flag if she had one. She accepted the inevitable. She peered between her arms at Wilson. "Don't worry about that. The cats really did kill all those people. The only regret I have is that they didn't kill Darrowby, too. That would make everything so much easier. Those hellcats truly are haunting me from ashes of Murcat Manor."

Chapter 64   Thirty-Three Years Later

Debbie Elaine Stevens stood behind one of the dozen large counters lining the puke-pink colored walls of the kitchen cafeteria. Her job today, as it was for the other eleven females working at their respective stations, was to bake five Thanksgiving Day turkeys and prepare side dishes for the staff at the Southern Michigan Correctional Center. They were also making holiday meals for local homeless shelters the prison helped support with cheap inmate labor. The prisoner population would be served their normal tasteless cafeteria slop.

With uncanny speed and the precision of a culinary artist a skilled chef would be proud to watch, Debbie chopped celery and onions for her homemade bread stuffing. She wasn't in the privacy of the amazing kitchen in Murcat Manor, her personal domain where she had once ruled supreme.

But Debbie was in her natural element. Although she would not be in charge of serving and entertaining hundreds of people every week, she retained a sense of normalcy that helped her feel human while living out her life in a most horrible place.

She glanced to her right where her new cell mate, Madison La Croix, finished cutting a case of cabbage and carrots into a mound of shredded produce. Madison had been transferred from another facility earlier in the week. She had killed her abusive husband in a last ditch effort to save herself two decades ago.

The jobless parasite had come home to their trailer in a drunken rage and, as his custom was, would handcuff her to the hot water radiator and beat her. She overheard him tell someone on his cell phone that he would be finished once and for all, and to come over in fifteen minutes and help clean up.

Unfortunately for the now silver haired mother of three, the state did not see this as a case of justifiable homicide, since Madison was not actually cuffed and beaten at the time she stabbed him thirty-one times with a pair of fabric scissors.

But a Battered Women's Assistance League paid for a legal defense that saw to it she was incompetent to stand trial due to the years of mental and physical abuse she endured. A paper trail of prescription psychiatric drugs for ADHD and a few minor episodes of rebellion from her youth was all her legal team needed to exploit her *history of mental problems and inability to discern right from wrong.*

Like Debbie, Madison had been moved through numerous facilities over the past three decades, due to the state reclassifying the criminally insane and figuring out how best to house and rehabilitate them. The most recent decision, because of massive budget cuts, resulted in her being relocated to this facility in Battle Creek.

The Southern Michigan Correctional Center housed hundreds of convicts as well as those deemed criminally insane and incompetent to stand trial. Everyone was lumped together in one place, with those incompetent to stand trial isolated from the Level 2 more dangerous criminals, and the Level 3 convicts—hardened and volatile people, most of whom were serving life sentences with nothing to lose and would kill for any small reason, including fun. Debbie was certainly glad to be kept apart from those creeps.

Madison ended up here and not with the general population of prisoners. Debbie related to having a top rate legal team beating the system and they formed an immediate bond. Debbie had gotten her new cellmate a tryout in the kitchen. This was her first day.

She looked over to Madison. "Hey, how are you holding up? Everything okay?"

Madison gave Debbie a wry sideways smile. "Oh, just fine. As long as I'm in the kitchen, that is. I love it here. Thanks again for the good word and getting me in here. I owe you. And I always pay my debts. I promise you that. You'll see."

Madison took a violent whack with her chopping knife and cut a head of cabbage in near symmetrical halves.

"Ha! See that? A perfect split. I pretend I'm cutting up my asshole of a husband and feeding him bit by bit to the pigeons. This is all I think of. All day. All night. For the past thirty years. You'll see. Now that I know and trust you, we're like sisters now. Right? Of course we are."

Madison clutched the knife handle and split a second head of cabbage, then began chopping again. "I'll tell you every plot I can think of to kill the bastard over and over. I'm a very creative person. You'll see. After all, we have lots of time. It's not like we're going anywhere. I think the time will pass quickly. For both of us. Don't you? You'll see."

Debbie was aghast as she slowed her pace with the knife. This sweet little innocent Madison might not be so virtuous after all. Debbie didn't

483

know what to say, so she remained silent, a trait prison culture instilled in her over the years.

Madison continued. "And you, well little *Miss Beat the System*, let's not forget about you. I know your reputation. To the legal system and in the public's eye, you're known as the most prolific female serial killer of our time. Your story, it's in high demand. And why not? But I can understand why you deny every request for an interview. Oh, there must have been hundreds over the years. The media. Best-selling authors. Television screenwriters. And let's not forget graduate students working on research papers."

Madison was almost as fast as Debbie with a knife as she mowed through more cabbage and carrots, although she resembled more of a greasy spoon hash slinger than a Rodeo Drive gourmet chef. That little insight into Madison's head, along with the gleam in her eye as she chopped and sliced and diced with fervor, gave Debbie reason to believe perhaps her new friend really was crazy after all. She'd have to request a new cell mate.

Debbie sighed as she tossed more celery and onions on the cutting board and picked up her speed. Her right hand was now cutting almost as fast as her left hand could toss the whole vegetables on the table. The holidays were always rough for her. Although surrounded by hundreds of people every day, she knew she was all alone in this world. The staff and inmates were merely faces with a name she memorized and placed together. She had no family to speak of.

Gone were her beloved grandparents, Ross and Erma Dempsey. Her parents had passed five years earlier. Others who had shared her life, like her attorney Kenneth Wilson, had died. Even Clark Hodgkins, the realtor who sold her and Bob the property for Murcat Manor, had passed on.

But what hurt most was Bob, her one and only soul mate, murdered by Detective Thomas Darrowby. The irony? That bastard was not only walking free from a murder he had pinned on her, he was now retired after enjoying fabulous career, having been promoted to Chief of Police not long after Murcat Manor burned. Today, he would enjoy a warm holiday meal with his extended family.

What a bastard.

"Mrs. Stevens, you okay?"

Sergeant Rosie Pyke stood behind her. Debbie despised the sheriff's deputy who took her position as staff leader of the cafeteria far too seriously. Good lord, you'd think Pyke was the Chief Executive Officer of the United States of America barking orders in the White House War Room the way she carried on.

But she knew better than to let Pyke steal her peace she fought so hard to maintain. She had to stay thankful. Content. Focused. Her fate was far better than the alternative, being re-evaluated and deemed fit to stand trial. Surviving with the general prison population was not an option. Her hand picked up more speed as she thought of being housed with common criminals a mere hundred yards away.

Rosie Pyke now stood beside her. She was tall and thick with short black hair. There was never a wrinkle in her uniform. Rosie was fair. But she was always a stickler for strict adherence to the rule book. Debbie tried to hold back a snicker as she imagined her with a thick mustache. She could pass as Darrowby's brother.

Debbie could hear Bob's words as clear as if he were alive and talking to her from across their kitchen table, reprimanding her in a most loving but stern way to treat her superiors with dignity and respect.

Debbie, my love and soul mate, you need to treat people in positions of authority with respect, regardless what you think of them. Sergeant Pyke is your superior, and should be addressed as such.

Bernie Butthead. Detective Dickhead. Pyke the .... No, better not. Thanks Bob. Even now, thirty-three years later, you're there for me with your words of wisdom.

Debbie followed Rosie's glare as she looked down on her handiwork. Debbie followed the path of the eight inch Wusthof Classic Vegetable knife where she had chopped, sliced, and diced the vegetables with synchronized speed. She had cut far more than needed. A small mountain stood piled high.

"Mrs. Stevens. I asked you a question. Are you okay? Are you even listening to me? I hope I don't see an infraction in the works."

Hope my ass. You'd love the chance for another write-up. "Oh, I'm fine. Just, you know, it's the holidays. I miss my family. That's all."

Rosie fixed Debbie a solid glare. "Yeah, sure. Better take it easy with that knife, or I'll have to write it up in my report as an incident. You've been a model patient and you don't want to screw up by having kitchen privileges taken away. Besides, your turkeys are by far the best. I'll be sure to have one directed my way. You can count on that."

Debbie feigned a smile as she pictured Rosie, sitting alone in her tiny office, devouring an entire turkey. She measured five cups of cut vegetables and placed them into a large tin bowl. Slow down, she told herself. It took her years to gain the trust of the staff and be able to work in the kitchen, where her extraordinary culinary skills gained her favor with the warden and the prison staff.

She added the mix to an even larger bowl containing bread cubes. As she sprinkled in thyme, salt, and pepper, the bracelet-like band encircling her left wrist vibrated ever so subtly. She looked at the wristband that, with a tap of her finger, would show a virtual touch screen and monitor on any flat surface.

Ancient technology, long since replaced by tiny interfaces placed behind the ear lobes and operated on the user's electronic impulses caused by thoughts and emotions. But this was the only telecommunications the State allowed her to possess.

Debbie was only interested in one item: a predetermined alert. The developers who bought the twenty-five acre property where Murcat Manor once stood were planning a ground breaking for a major resort. Daily she had prepared herself to receive news. And here it was. She sat the bowl down and called out to Rosie, now on the other side of the kitchen and writing up a female inmate for a minor breach of a ruling ridiculous to begin with.

"Excuse me, Sergeant. I need to use the restroom."

Rosie turned and bellowed, pointing a thick finger at Debbie. "Hurry up. And don't forget to wash your hands. Failing to do so is an infraction."

Debbie pulled off her thin rubber gloves and apron and made her way to the bathroom. Once in the stall, she projected the touch screen and monitor on the inside of the stall door and clicked *Enter* to begin the news story. The anchor man, his hair combed into a high mound at the front of his head, smiled wide for the camera. Debbie convulsed as she couldn't fathom pompadours having come back into fashion with a vengeance.

"And now we have a real feel good story for you this Thanksgiving morning that's sure to make your hearts warm and toasty. Let's go live to our reporter Olivia Nesman in the rolling hills between Battle Creek and Marshall."

A young pretty blonde stared at Debbie, her hair a scaled down beehive, also a reincarnated fashion rage. "Thank you, Arthur. I'm here at the ribbon-cutting ceremony for the exclusive luxury Oakhill Hotel and Resort. This is big news around here."

Debbie gasped loud, hoping Rosie, who she knew had her ear pressed on the other side of the bathroom door, didn't hear. Olivia Beehive continued to talk way too fast and chirpy as she walked across the lawn in front of the sprawling hotel. Behind the reporter stood a dozen men and women dressed in business attire. The man in the center held an oversized pair of gold colored scissors.

"This property had been acquired ten years ago by local developers. Now, three years after breaking ground on this five-star hangout for the rich and famous, the luxury four hundred and eighty-eight room retreat is ready to welcome their first guests. This place is absolutely stunning and booked solid through next summer. The hotel, with its seven restaurants and eighteen-hole golf course, will bring many jobs to the area as this countryside continues to be developed with new housing tracts, malls, and schools. And now, the mayor of Battle Creek, Conner Addison, will cut the ribbon and officially open the resort."

Debbie wasn't sure what hurt more, the memories she shared with Bob or the beautiful serene countryside developed into a planned concrete jungle.

Addison cut the ribbon, then led the group through the front doors. Olivia followed into the posh lobby, adorned with exaggerated opulence that told most viewers they couldn't afford the stay. Olivia continued with her overly chipper, fast paced tone. "But that's not all that this story is about."

Four more suits held something in their hands. The camera zoomed in. "And just this morning, thirteen baby kittens were found by a maintenance crew in the basement."

Oh. My. God.

Olivia picked one up and scratched its belly. Black rings circled the eyes. "Oh, she is so adorable. I just love these little fluffballs. This one looks like a nerd. These circles around her eyes, they resemble thick black glasses."

Conner Addison faced the camera and responded. "We're calling these cute little bundles of joy the Miracle Kitties. If they can survive all alone without a mother, we're confident they can bring the resort good fortune."

Olivia handed the kitten back. "Well, you'll need it—the history of this property seems to be haunted."

Addison and the resort managers laughed in unison. "That's ancient superstition. In today's world of modern physics and technology, there's simply no place for that sort of nonsense. These little kitties will be the perfect pets to greet guests as they arrive for a time to be pampered at our luxury resort, one of the largest and finest in the Great Lakes region."

Olivia leaned in and rubbed a few cats on their underside, her cameraman zooming in from above her shoulder. "Aww, they're so cute. What are you going to call them?"

"Believe it or not, their names just came to me." He rattled off their names while pointing at each individual kitten:

Emily

Rebecca

Annie

Jacquelyn

Chloe

Amy

Helen

Scarlett

Angel

Esther

Isabella

Rachel

He paused, for a second, "Oh yes, and Madeline."

Debbie took a deep breath to gather her bearings. She was a thousand miles deep in a vast valley of sorrow and anger when a rap on the door jerked her mind back.

"Mrs. Stevens, everything okay in there?"

Sheeeesh. Maybe I should have given Rosie a tray of chicken wings to keep her busy, Debbie thought.

"I'm fine, Sergeant Pyke. Thanks for asking. Be right out."

"Don't forget to wash your hands. Remember ...."

"I know. I know. Infraction."

Debbie forwarded the story to the one person she had saved in her list of contacts. Retired Chief of Police Thomas Darrowby. She then whispered a message into her wristband, the words displaying on the interactive touch screen image projected onto the stall door.

I know you don't believe me when I say I did not kill any of those people. Especially my husband or my grandparents. I only ask that you think back to that night when Murcat Manor burned to the ground. You heard Emily speak inside your mind. I know you did. Your reaction revealed as much.

Take a look at this news clip and see for yourself the thirteen cats. They have the same names. Even Madelyn with the dark circles around her eyes that looked like nerdy glasses is there. You can't deny it. These are the same cats. And they will kill again at this resort as they did to Murcat Manor.

The reply came quickly as Darrowby's spoken response was displayed as text and visible on the interactive monitor. He used his own face for an avatar. Debbie hated that image and imagined wiping that stupid condescending trademark smirk off with a single, well placed punch to his jaw, much like Bob had done one night thirty-three years ago.

Mrs. Stevens, I see you're still up to your old tricks. But you can't fool me. I believe you still have your wits about you, as you always have. You got lucky with your attorney. You really should be with the murderers and serial killers in level 3.

Debbie spoke quick and quiet. She knew Rosie would burst through the door any moment.

You have to listen to me. Lives are at stake. We can't let this happen again.

Darrowby's words were stark, bordering on belligerent.

We? Surely you don't think you can pull me into your little world of madness. Now you're just pissing me off. My wife and I are preparing to entertain twenty family members for Thanksgiving, and you interrupt me with tales of your cats reemerging to do ... what? Kill more people? Do you think of me as some old goof with an advanced case of Alzheimers?

"Mrs. Stevens. Are you alright? What's going on in there?"

"Nothing," Debbie said as she hit the Mute key. "I'll be out in a minute."

Debbie touched Mute again and continued her conversation with Darrowby.

For the love of God, you have to listen to me. It's happening—starting all over—again. The cats. Emily. Just ... think back to that night at Murcat Manor. Emily talked to us. You heard her.

Darrowby again was quick to respond.

No. What I heard was the power of suggestion. Caused by you, Murcat Manor burning to the ground, and you killing my partner Kowalski. That's all. I didn't hear anything. Understand? I'm a smart man. So please don't interrupt my family holiday and insult my intelligence.

Debbie would have no more of Darrowby's denial. She had a few precious moments before Pyke would barge in.

No, you arrogant bastard. Emily spoke to us. To you. She called you Detective Dickhead. Remember? How else would I know that?

"Mrs. Stevens. Please come out. Or I'll have to haul you out of that stall myself."

"Coming." Good Lord, Pyke. Go dive your fat ass into that vat of mashed potatoes and gravy I made earlier. "I'll be right out."

Darrowby continued with a calm tone in his words. Debbie knew she had blown it, even after Bob's face and words reached out from the grave and spoke to her about respecting authority figures, treating them with the proper respect they deserved. She slapped herself on the forehead.

Detective Dickhead? How could I be so stupid?

Mrs. Stevens, even though I'm now retired, I'll be sure to have my friends at the Battle Creek Police Department send the request to a judge to have you once again re-evaluated and sent to trial for fifteen murders. Remember, there is no statute of limitations on murder. And they will only have to prove one.

"That's it," Pyke's voice echoed through the bathroom. "I warned you. Infraction. I have to write you up. C'mon. Let's go. And don't forget to wash your hands. Or that'll be another infraction."

Debbie was flabbergasted. Emily had beaten her. Again.

Now that hellcat was back with her twelve murderous cohorts. And there wasn't a damn thing she could do about it. Darrowby was her only hope to prevent another cycle of murder. And all the bastard would do was leer at her with that pompous expression on his mug.

Darrowby's face remained, ghosted on the screen. He still looked the same. Full head of silver hair and a mustache now, but still the same. Frozen. Smiling. Smirking at her.

Debbie stared back, nauseous to the point of vomiting, and typed one final word before ending the dialogue.

Bastard.

Other Books by Stephen Tremp:

The Adventures of Chase Manhattan Volume I: Breakthrough

"A scientific breakthrough of such magnitude it could radically alter the future of humanity—for better or worse—is in the wrong hands."

The Adventures of Chase Manhattan Volume II: Opening

"Then I saw three evil spirits that looked like frogs ... they are demonic spirits that perform signs, and they go out to the kings of the whole world, to gather them for the battle." Revelation 16: 13 – 14

The Adventures of Chase Manhattan Volume III: Escalation

"I know not with what weapons World War III will be fought, but World War IV will be fought with sticks and stones." - Albert Einstein

About The Author

Stephen Tremp writes Speculative Fiction and embraces science and the supernatural to help explain the universe, our place in it, and write one of a kind thrillers. His novels are enhanced by discoveries, breakthroughs, and current events in many fields of science. Understanding Albert Einstein's famous equation $E=MC2$ explains how the natural and the supernatural co-exist and complement each other.

Tremp has written *The Breakthrough Trilogy: The Adventures of Chase Manhattan*. His books have been in Barnes and Nobles and Borders Books across the country.

Stephen Tremp has a B.S. in information systems, an MBA in Global Management and a background in information systems, management, and finance. He lives in Orange County, CA with his family, a maltipoo dog, Meyer's parrot, and hamster.

You can visit Stephen Tremp at his Website www.stephentremp.com

Stephen Tremp

Proof

Made in the USA
Charleston, SC
13 November 2015